IT IS A BIT MESSED UP THAT I'VE BEEN DREAMING ABOUT LUKE TAYLOR FOR ALL THESE YEARS BUT NEVER ACTUALLY CONSIDERED WHAT HE IS REALLY LIKE.

NO WONDER I'VE NEVER BEEN IN LOVE.

I'M TOO BUSY DAYDREAMING ABOUT IT.

Also by Tom Ellen and Lucy Ivison

A Totally Awkward Love Story

Never Evers

freshmen

Tom Ellen & Lucy Ivison

EMBER

Text copyright © 2018 by Tom Ellen and Lucy Ivison
Cover art copyright © 2018 by Ray Shappell
Hand lettering by Erin Fitzsimmons

First line of "You're" by Sylvia Plath from *Collected Poems* (Faber, 1981) copyright © 1960, 1965, 1971, 1981 by the Estate of Sylvia Plath, used by permission of Faber & Faber Ltd.

Visit us on the Web! GetUnderlined.com

Educators and librarians, for a variety of teaching tools,
visit us at RHTeachersLibrarians.com

The Library of Congress has cataloged the hardcover edition of this work as follows:
Names: Ellen, Tom, author. | Ivison, Lucy, author.
Title: Freshmen / Tom Ellen and Lucy Ivison.
Other titles: Freshers.
Description: First American edition. | New York : Delacorte Press, [2018] | "Originally published as Freshers by Chicken House, London, in 2018." | Summary: Relates, in two voices, the experiences of Luke and Phoebe, who attended the same high school and are now experiencing the joys and angst of life as college freshmen in York, England.
Identifiers: LCCN 2017021751 | ISBN 978-1-5247-0178-9 (hc) |
ISBN 978-1-5247-0179-6 (el)
Subjects: CYAC: Universities and colleges—Fiction. | Friendship—Fiction. | Dating (Social customs)—Fiction. | Conduct of life—Fiction. | York (England)—Fiction. | England—Fiction.
Classification: LCC PZ7.1.E44 Fre 2018 | DDC [Fic]—dc23

ISBN 978-1-5247-0181-9 (trade pbk.)

Printed in the United States of America
10 9 8 7 6 5 4 3 2 1
First Ember Edition 2019

For Carolina —T.E.

For Cassie Cooper, Louise Geoghegan,
Nell Booker and Vicky Clarfelt—
I'll keep your secrets if you keep mine —L.I.

Part One

1

● ● ● ● ● ● ● **LUKE** ● ● ● ● ● ● ●

I was doing my best to focus on what Arthur was saying, but the buzzing in my pocket kept distracting me.

If I'd counted right—and I was pretty sure I had—this was the eleventh buzz since we'd arrived at the Jutland school's bar for the clothes swap party. The *eleventh*. A sudden rush of anger cut through me. Did she really expect me to spend the first night of freshman orientation standing outside talking to her? Wasn't the whole point of this week to talk to *new* people?

The buzzing stopped as Arthur pushed a luminous blue shot and a pint of lager along the bar to me. He was wearing a bright-red bathrobe over a sleeveless denim jacket, his sweaty black hair messily tucked into a yellow swimming cap. I had on my mum's 2007 Bon Jovi tour T-shirt under a massive multi-colored Mexican poncho. We both looked absolutely ridiculous.

But then, so did everybody else. Even the bartender was wearing a kimono.

The DJ yelled, "Jutland, make some noise!" and I realized Arthur's mouth was moving again, so I leaned in and tried to concentrate.

"I was supposed to live off-campus this year," he was shouting over the music. "Me and some friends had a house and everything. Even put the deposit down."

"So what happened?" I yelled back.

"It got fucking *condemned*. Like, literally, two weeks ago. Asbestos. So that's why I've ended up back in B Dorm next door to you." He did his shot and winced. "Still, could be worse. Most second years don't get to do Frosh Week twice, do they?"

I nodded and drank my shot. It tasted like vodka-flavored toothpaste. "What is asbestos?" I shouted.

Arthur downed half his pint in one go. "It's this sort of invisible presence that lives inside your house."

"Like Wi-Fi?"

"A bit, actually, yeah." He nodded. "But Wi-Fi that silently kills you in your sleep."

"Right. Shit."

The Klaxon horn went off, and he shrugged out of his bathrobe while I gave him my poncho. The bartender started lining up more blue shots on a tray as Beth came over with Barney. Or maybe it wasn't Barney. Was it Tom? Tom also had red hair. It might have been Tom.

"Beth! Barney!" Arthur yelled.

"Just seeing if you guys needed a hand," said Barney-Not-Tom cheerfully. He was short and skinny with a soft country accent and tons of orangey freckles. Beth was almost a foot taller

4

and had a sort of strict "valedictorian" vibe about her that was nicely accentuated by the Harry Potter robe she was wearing.

"One, two, three, four . . ." Arthur clamped the shots one by one between Barney's fingers.

"I'd rather have a gin and tonic than another of those shots, to be honest," Beth said sharply. "They're like drinking Listerine."

"No worries," said Arthur. "One G and T coming up. We'll bring it over with the rest of them."

"Thanks."

Arthur leaned in to me as they walked back to the table. "You wanna watch that Barney, by the way."

"Why?"

"He's a labeler. I saw him putting a Post-it note on his Nutella. We had a labeler in our hall last year. Total nutjob. Got kicked out in the second semester for shooting a squirrel with a BB gun. He was a chemistry major, too."

"Barney's studying geography, though, isn't he?" I'd only managed to remember that because me, him and Arthur were the only ones *not* doing chemistry in our hall.

Arthur finished his pint and slapped the plastic cup back down on the bar. "Yeah, well, it's all the same *Big Bang Theory* ballpark, isn't it? Except that geography is basically just coloring in. What are you doing, again?"

"English. You're philosophy, right?"

"Yeah." He ran a hand across his patchy black stubble. "I'm wrestling with the big-boy questions: What is the nature of truth? How can we find meaning in a Godless universe? *How* hot is that girl chatting with the DJ?" I looked at the girl in question, who was indeed hot. He picked up the tray, which was now dangerously overloaded with drinks. "Shall we get back?"

5

My pocket started buzzing again. Number twelve. I pulled my phone out. "I'll be there in one sec. Sorry, man, just need to quickly get this."

I slipped out the main door and the cold hit me hard. I pressed the phone to my ear. "Hey."

"Hey." Her voice sounded wrinkled and far away. The way it'd sounded pretty much all summer.

"Look, I'm sorry I didn't pick up, it's just—"

"I know," she said. "I know you're busy."

"I'm not *busy*, it's just . . . It's the first night. Obviously, everyone's out."

"I know."

Silence.

"So maybe I'd better go back in."

"OK. Have you met anyone nice?"

"The people in my suite in my dorm are all right. They've pretty much only talked about chemistry so far, because that's what they all want to major in, but they seem nice. And this one guy Arthur seems cool. He's a sophomore, though."

"That sounds good. Cool. I . . . I just wanted to check everything was OK. It felt like we didn't really sort stuff out properly this morning before you left. I didn't want you to leave when it was weird between us."

I sighed. "It's been weird between us all summer."

More silence. That was the first time either of us had actually admitted that out loud. For some reason it felt easier to say knowing she was two hundred miles away.

She still wasn't speaking, so I kept going; the booze and the pocket buzzing and the two hundred miles making me spill stuff that had been locked up firmly in my head until now. "And, I mean, the thing is, it's not gonna get any less weird now that I'm here, is it?"

"What do you mean?" she said quietly.

"I mean, I'm here and you're there. We won't see each other that much."

"Yeah, but you said, at Reece's party, remember, you said we could make it work?"

"I know, but . . . if this is us making it work, then maybe it won't work."

I heard her inhale sharply, but I carried on. "Like, I'm supposed to be working at other stuff, too, y'know? Meeting people. Making friends. But instead I'm standing out here talking to you. Do you really want me to spend the whole three years on the phone with you?"

"You're being a dick, Luke," she muttered.

I was, a little. But I was also *right*.

"Look, I'm sorry. It's stupid to talk now," I sighed. "I'm a little drunk. I'm wearing a bathrobe. I'll call you tomorrow." I wasn't quite sure why I'd added the bathrobe information.

"I don't want to talk about this tomorrow," she said, her voice getting lumpy with tears. "I want to talk about it now."

"Well, I don't."

"If you've got something to say, then just say it. Have you met someone else?"

This actually made me laugh out loud. "Of course I haven't fucking met someone else, Abbey! I'm out here talking to you! How *can* I meet someone else?"

"Do you *want* to meet someone else, though?"

"I *want* to go back inside."

I hung up before she could respond. But my pocket was buzzing again as soon as I stepped back in.

● ● ● ● ● ● ● **PHOEBE** ● ● ● ● ● ●

Luke Taylor was right there and I did not feel prepared.

I kept dancing, but the sight of him had kind of electrified my insides. The boy he was with passed him a pint of something green; Luke took a sip and grimaced. The horn went off and everyone started shrieking.

I needed to stop looking at him. I needed to call Flora. I turned in the opposite direction and came face to face with Negin, the girl in the room across from me. She was wearing a T-shirt with Princess Diana on it that said QUEEN OF HEARTS. I randomly decided to share the hysteria that was going on inside me. "A really weird thing just happened to me," I yelled. But she shook her head. "I just saw someone—"

She kept shaking her head. In a weird moment of madness, I grabbed her hand, which was a bit bonkers considering we'd only met five hours ago, and charged us to the edge of the dance floor. She looked a bit taken aback, and I saw her eyes wander, as if looking for an escape. But it was too late to turn back. I took a breath. I didn't know how to explain the last seven years of nothingness accurately. "This boy I have wanted for, like, my entire existence, is here." I realized I was still holding her hand. "Sorry." I let it go.

"Um." Clearly, Negin had no idea how to respond to my declaration. "Did you not know he was coming to York?"

8

"No, I *totally* did. I knew that—a lot." I nodded to try and communicate my back catalog of daydreams about me and Luke Taylor in York. "I've sort of been waiting for this moment . . . kind of." I was coming across mental.

"Right . . ."

"And now I don't know what to do." She looked at me for a beat and I rushed to babble over it. "I feel like if you saw him you would understand."

She glanced around the room. "Where is he?"

I physically jumped. "Don't *look* at him."

"I don't know who he is." Negin twitched, a hint of a smile on her face. She had a black bob with not a hair out of place, almost like a Lego person. Apart from the faded Princess Di T-shirt, she looked neat. Black jeans, Converse, no makeup. Like if a newscaster fronted an indie band. "Don't worry, it's fine. There aren't that many people in this room." She scanned it. "Three hundred, maybe. You'll bump into him naturally at some point."

Me and Flora usually went in for intensely rehearsed accidental bumpings, but Negin sounded confident, so I went with it. And anyway, when I looked back to where he had been, there was just a boy in a cow costume unrolling toilet paper and hurling it everywhere. We bought another drink and made our way back into the throng. There was a girl with rainbow-dyed hipster-bowl-cut hair up onstage, chatting with the DJ. I'd watched her from my dorm room earlier, moving in with the sea of other first years. Tonight, she was still wearing the same tracksuit pants and crop top from this morning, but now she also had a gold crown that was sort of hanging jauntily to one side, like she was in some kind of fashion shoot.

"How is that girl a first year?" I said. "Seems like she knows everyone."

"I saw her earlier and she was writing in marker on this boy's stomach." Negin didn't seem to have an opinion about this, just delivered the information matter-of-factly.

"What, like her phone number?"

"No, I think it was a line from a song or something." Negin rolled her eyes. "Deep."

"I saw her 'move in' this afternoon. But she didn't have any stuff at all. Nothing. She just walked into her dorm carrying a *colander*. She didn't even change clothes for tonight. Like, she's so cool, all she needs for the next three years is multicolored hair and a *colander*."

We kept staring at Bowl-Cut as the DJ gave her his headphones and she started waving her hands to the crowd.

We found the rest of our suite and all started dancing together. You could tell we were all from the same hall because of the luminous glitter this one girl from Liverpool, Liberty, had enthusiastically doused on us before we came out. Negin was dancing in her reserved way, and the really shy girl, Becky, was hardly dancing at all. Every time the Klaxon sounded she looked panicked. Liberty oscillated around the group, hugging us all and breaking out into random and unexpected stripper moves every so often.

The Klaxon sounded again, and Connor, the boy in the room next to me, jumped into the middle of the circle, and his mighty "First night of college" war cry reverberated around the room. None of us was in danger of forgetting his name, since he had KISS ME I'M CONNOR written right across his forehead. He took off his T-shirt and started swinging it around his head like a lasso, whacking my Yoda ears onto the floor. I bent down to get them, and when I stood up, I came face to face with Luke Taylor. He had appeared out of nowhere, just as I had forgotten about him for one second.

"Hey." I tried to smile demurely.

"Hey," he shouted over the music. The Klaxon went off and he handed me his bathrobe. "It's . . ."

There was this moment where I didn't know what he meant. And then I did, and it was like a stone had appeared in my stomach.

"Phoebe," I said.

"Yeah, of course." He smiled. "Phoebe. I'm Luke."

I could feel my face getting red and tight. "Hey."

Negin was trying not to seem obvious and was sort of half dancing next to me, her back slightly turned the other way. Her being there made it worse. I wanted to replay the night from the beginning and not have blabbed on about him like some desperate idiot.

I handed him the Yoda ears and he put them on.

"So random we're both here," I shouted brightly.

"Yeah, I kind of . . ." He felt in his pocket for his phone and then glanced down at it. "Sorry, I . . ." He didn't finish the sentence, just looked across the room and started to shuffle away. He didn't even say goodbye. I stared after him, sort of shocked. If I'd seen someone from school, even if I didn't really know them, I would have made an effort. We were two hundred miles away from home. We had known each other since we were eleven. It was like he actively didn't want to be associated with me. Like he didn't want anyone here to even know that we were connected. I took a deep breath and turned to Negin.

"So . . . that was him, then?" she said, cupping her fingers

11

around my ear so I could hear her over the music. I bit my lip and nodded.

She shrugged. "He's not all that."

"It was a big school," I said. "So not everyone knew each other." I felt ridiculous. Like some psychotic weirdo. We *had* only directly spoken, like, five times in seven years, but I thought he knew my name, at least. I felt like someone had taken all the air out of me. I made a conscious effort to pull myself together but I knew I had turned bright red. I looked at her and groaned. "Negin, I'm so embarrassed." I shook my head. "Honestly, what a fail." I tried to laugh. "I want to die."

She smiled really warmly and nodded. "Well, you might, actually. Apparently, there are about fifty freshmen deaths every year, on average, so, you know . . ." She shrugged.

"Mine could be the first one. *And* the first one to have been caused solely by dance floor humiliation."

Liberty beckoned us back into the throng, and I took a breath and decided not to let Luke Taylor's stupid blank ruin everything.

Josh, our second-year contact person, and his friends brought us all shots. Josh was tall and kind of stacked and had a shaved head, like he was in the marines. He had been so nice earlier: spent twenty minutes showing my mum where the outlet shopping center was on the map, and labeled each of our doors with stickers that had our name and a cute little picture.

"These are my roommates, Will and Pete," he shouted, and they waved. Liberty gave me a look to say *things are looking up.*

Will was classically good-looking. Tall, with boarding-school floppy hair and the kind of smile that only comes from knowing you're attractive. He leaned over and kissed me on the cheek to say hello. Pete was smaller and less chatty, and had somehow ended up wearing so many clothes he was almost drowning in them.

Some hip-hop song came on that they all liked and we started dancing. Me and Will started doing that thing where you look at each other and then look away. With every song that played, we moved a bit nearer. He was smiling at me, almost shyly, and I could sense Pete and Josh tactfully shift away as they realized me and Will were dancing closer and closer. I glanced around for Negin and the others but I couldn't see them anywhere. Will and me exchanged a smile one more time and then we were making out with each other. He was a good kisser, but I couldn't really get into it because I kept wondering if everyone was watching. Or if Luke Taylor was watching. Not that anyone, least of all him, would exactly care. The whole night had already descended into a bit of a meat market anyway. And even kissing a good kisser gets awkward when you don't really know the first thing about them and you're wearing a bathrobe.

"I'm just gonna go to the bathroom." I smiled and walked away, unsuccessfully scanning the room for people I recognized.

The whole night felt out of control. Like I needed to sort myself out and concentrate on making friends—not being rejected by Luke Taylor and kissing randoms. I couldn't see Negin anywhere, so I walked out the main doors and into a hall with vending machines. There was a darkened room labeled COMPUTER LAB that looked empty, but I could hear a weird noise coming from inside.

I creaked open the door. Gradually, my eyes got accustomed to the dark, and I matched the low, gentle sound with the shape in the corner. Facing the window and shuddering every so often. Someone crying.

Luke Taylor crying.

2

LUKE

I hadn't meant to say it. It just sort of . . . came out.

It was like she was pushing me, almost. Daring me to say it. "If you don't want to speak to me," Abbey'd hissed, "if you don't want to work at this, then maybe we should break up, Luke. Maybe we should just fucking break up."

And I'd said, "Yeah. OK. Maybe we should."

And then there was only the gentle hum of her crying in my ear, and this terrifying, exhilarating feeling, like I'd jumped off a cliff with no clue if there was water or concrete at the bottom.

I just sat there, listening to her cry, feeling the panic and the toothpaste-y vodka fighting for space in my chest, surging up into my throat and pressing against the backs of my eyeballs.

Then the phone went dead. And I thought: *Is that it?* Are we actually broken up? Can three years of your life really come to an end, just like that, in a dark computer room in the middle of the night? I covered my face but the tears wriggled out between my fingers. What the *fuck* was wrong with me? Half a day away from home and I was already falling apart.

I caught a glimpse of my reflection in one of the screens. This sweaty, moony, tearstained face with a pair of green Yoda ears on top of it. It was so ridiculous I actually started laughing. Which, if anything, made me look more insane. I took the ears off and dropped them on the table in front of me.

Suddenly, I heard a noise from outside, but when I looked up there was no one there. I wiped my face and checked the hall. Just that Phoebe girl from school, who was getting some chocolate out of one of the vending machines.

A little shiver of anxiety ran through me as I realized she might have seen what I was doing. Even if she hadn't seen it, she was probably still wondering what sort of maniac sits alone in a computer room at midnight.

"Hey," I said, trying to sound casual. She smiled and said "Hey" back. Her cheeks were flushed from the heat of the bar, and she had purply glitter smudged all across her forehead.

"You having a good night?" I asked, and she shrugged and smiled.

I suddenly panicked that my eyes might be red and watery, so I blurted, "I just took my contact lenses out." She nodded politely, and I realized that, if my eyes *weren't* red and watery, this might have seemed like *quite* a random statement.

She then said something I missed completely, because the bar doors burst open behind us and a blast of music and shouting filled the hall. A girl wearing bright-orange jeans and Pikachu earmuffs stepped out. She wobbled on the spot for a second and then sort of slumped down onto the steps in slow motion.

15

"Are you OK?" Phoebe asked her.

The girl blinked a few times and squinted at us, as if she was having trouble focusing. She smelled strongly of tequila and puke. We helped her up.

"Where are your friends?" I said.

"I don't know . . . ," she slurred. Then her face fell. "I mean, I've only just met them. . . . Do you think they *are* my friends? Do you think they *like* me?"

"Definitely," Phoebe said.

"Do *you* like me?" she asked, and I nodded. "Yeah, of course. We're both huge fans of your work."

Phoebe laughed, and the girl seemed satisfied by this, because she draped an arm around each of our shoulders. "OK, well, at least *we* made friends. We can be each other's friends, can't we? First Night First Year Friends."

"First Night Friends," Phoebe and I repeated, grinning at each other.

The girl took a deep breath and examined us more closely. It seemed like every change of facial expression required massive effort. "What're your names?" she whispered.

"Luke and Phoebe," I said.

She nodded. "Hi, Lucan Phoebe. I'm Stephanie Stevens."

"Nice to meet you, Stephanie Stevens. Are you going to be OK getting back to your dorm?"

Stephanie Stevens sighed and shook her head violently, like a grumpy six-year-old. "Noooooooo."

"Where do you live?"

She screwed her eyes up tight in concentration. "Seventeen Belmont Road, Sunderland, SR1 7AQ."

"No, I mean *here,* at the university—where in Jutland do you live? B Dorm? C Dorm?"

"Oh. I'm not in that school," she said. "I'm in Wulfstan."

Phoebe looked at the York Met University campus map that was pinned up next to the bar doors. Wulfstan was the next school down from Jutland on campus. "OK . . . Wulfstan College . . . This way."

We all linked arms, with Stephanie Stevens in the middle, and started trooping slowly down the covered walkway. A few ducks waddled up out of the darkness of the lake and started quacking along behind us.

It was crazy to think me and Abbey had done this exact same walk less than a year ago, on the campus tour. Trailing our guide from school to school around the huge, murky lake, we'd talked about whether people swam here in the summer and had taken photos on the grassy banks. We'd even had a winter picnic by the main bridge, with all the most random foods we could find in the "international" aisle of the supermarket. We'd sat there, chewing on South African biltong and weird German Haribos, and talking about all the things we were going to do here next year. The memory of it now seemed so detached from reality it was like it wasn't even mine. I shook it out of my head and turned to Phoebe.

"So how are your roommates?" I asked.

"They're pretty . . . nuts," she said. "We've got this one guy, Connor, who worked in Ibiza over the summer, so he's basically taken it upon himself to force us to have as crazy a time as possible."

I nodded. "There's nothing better than enforced fun."

"Yeah. Although I drew the line when it came to drinking tequila out of a bucket."

"Please don't mention tequila," muttered Stephanie Stevens darkly.

"What about your suite?" Phoebe asked me.

"Pretty much the exact opposite of yours, by the sound of it," I said. "No, they seem nice. Quiet, but nice. They're pretty much all majoring in chemistry, though, so they basically spent the whole evening before the party talking about polymers and matter. What are you studying?"

"English."

"Ah, nice. Me too. Maybe we'll be in some of the same classes together."

There was a pause, and Stephanie Stevens stopped and said, "I'm doing French and hotel management." Then she staggered away from us and threw up in a bush.

By the time we got to Wulfstan, the ducks had abandoned us. By some miracle, Stephanie Stevens managed to remember the code to get into her building, so we all staggered up the stairs, still arm in arm. In the hall, she fumbled for her key, opened the door, murmured "OK, then . . . night-night, First Night Friends" and collapsed face-first onto her bed. Her room looked exactly like mine: Same tobacco-yellow walls, same scratchy Brillo-pad carpet, same weird little brown cupboard that opened to reveal a sink and mirror inside it. She even had the same brand-new Ikea desk lamp.

"Do you think she's OK?" Phoebe whispered.

"Well, she's snoring," I replied. "That's got to be a good sign."

Phoebe winced. "Not if you're the person next door. Listen

18

to her. She sounds like a didgeridoo. And these walls are really thin."

I laughed. "We should probably put her in the recovery position, right? Just in case."

We gently rearranged her on the bed while she mumbled "I love my First Night Friends" over and over again.

"I'm a bit worried about leaving her like this," Phoebe whispered.

"Yeah. Let's have a cup of tea and then come back and check on her in a bit?"

"Um . . . yeah," she said. "Yeah, that sounds good."

We went into the suite's common kitchen, and Phoebe boiled the kettle and I found some of Stephanie Stevens' roommates' mugs and milk, then we walked downstairs, taking our teas with us. There was a little red bridge stretched across the lake, and we stood together in the middle, leaning against the edge, watching the steam rise from our cups.

It was freezing, and I could feel the cold and the tea starting to rub away at my drunkenness. I thought about Abbey and the phone call and all the utter, utter shittiness of the past few months. I'd spent the whole summer thinking that college would magically solve everything. I'd go to York Met, she'd go to Cardiff and we sort of wouldn't even need to have the maybe-we-should-break-up conversation. Ten hours into college and I was already learning important life lessons: don't be so fucking naive.

"Oh my god, *yes.*" Phoebe fished into the pocket of the bathrobe I'd given her back at the bar and pulled out a Twix. "Totally forgot I'd bought this." She opened it. "One finger each?"

"Nice." I took the chocolate off her. In spite of everything, I couldn't help wondering why I'd never noticed how pretty she was. Masses and masses of brown curly hair and an amazing smile.

I must have walked past her a million times at school. She couldn't have changed that much in ten weeks. Maybe I was just too hung up on Abbey to notice any other girls. But no, that wasn't it. I'd definitely noticed Isha Matthews. And Lauren Green. And Katie Reader.

But I'd never noticed Phoebe.

● ● ● ● ● ● **PHOEBE** ● ● ● ● ● ●

The whole thing was beginning to feel like an out-of-body experience.

This was exactly the kind of shit fourteen-year-old me was always daydreaming about. Well, maybe not Stephanie Stevens vomming everywhere and feeling like the pregame "Frosh punch" was kind of creeping ominously up my esophagus, but the Luke Taylor part. The part where I was now alone and kind of friendly with him. Like a weird *Doctor Who*–type thing where I had jumped back into my own eighth grade fantasies. I focused on looking unfazed and generally breezy and not babbling. Flora says when I'm drunk I over-touch people, so every time I got within ten inches of him I took a step back.

Luke took a sip of his tea, then sat down and let his legs dangle over the edge of the bridge. I followed suit, forgetting how my mug was much fuller than Luke's, and also that when it comes to smooth physical movement, I am a dud. For a split second I thought I just might tumble underneath the iron railing and into the lake. I made a kind of squawking sound and then landed on my bottom with a thump, like some sort of geriatric penguin.

I looked up and saw that Luke was shaking his hair out over the lake and tea was dripping out of it.

"Oh my god, are you OK? I'm so sorry." I *almost* reached out and touched him but managed to stop myself in time. "I prioritized the tea. I'm sorry."

"I prioritized the tea." He started full-on laughing, which made me laugh, too. "Good to know you value me less than some tea."

A part of me wanted to get out my phone and actually text that as a direct quote to Flora.

"Clumsiness is one of my defining features," I said. "My parents made me do Irish step dancing for three years to try to, like, train it out of me. But all it did was give me even more of a complex. There's a picture in my house where I'm wearing one of those ridiculous curly wigs. I mean, that is only going to give your kid more problems, not less." I pinched my thumb to try to physically stop myself babbling. At least I hadn't snorted. Snorting is probably the *least* sexy of all mannerisms.

Luke smiled. "My mum made me do flamenco dancing for a semester because my sister did it and she didn't want to pay for a babysitter."

"How old were you?"

"Old enough to know I was the only boy," he said. "They had to get me a special frilly shirt with red and black dots. I did an exam in it and everything."

"How did you do?"

He shrugged in mock modesty. "Oh, I can't remember. Passed with distinction. No big deal. Just a distinction."

I laughed. "I cannot imagine you flamenco dancing."

"I was all right at it, actually. Do you want some of my tea?"

"No, like I said, I prioritized the tea. I still have some left." I showed him my mug. "I feel a bit bad. These mugs have never been used. Look, they still have the label—£2:99, Home Goods."

"I'm sure whoever they belong to won't mind," Luke said. "And more to the point, they won't even know. Plus, we can always blame Stephanie Stevens."

"Yeah, we could leave them a note that says 'Stephanie Stevens did it.'"

We sat for a bit, just drinking our tea and staring at the lake. It made me realize how exhausted I was.

Luke sighed. "I really feel like today has been one of the longest days of my life. Waking up this morning feels like weeks ago."

I wondered if it felt longer for him because of what had happened to make him cry—whatever that was. Did it have something to do with Abbey Baker? Surely not. They were our year's golden couple. Out of nowhere, an image of them at the senior prom popped into my head. They looked like they belonged on the Oscars red carpet, not in the lobby of the Holiday Inn.

"Yeah, but we made it." I held my mug up. "Cheers. To making it through the first day."

He clinked his mug against mine and nodded. "Yup. Me, you and if Stephanie Stevens isn't dead, then her, too. We made it through the first day of college. And we both made a friend. *Two* friends, actually, if we count Stephanie Stevens. If she's dead we can definitely count her, 'cause she won't be able to argue with us."

I shook my head. "*Seriously,* why are people so obsessed with dying at college?"

"I don't know. Do you know Reece Morris?" Of course I knew Reece Morris. He was Luke's best friend.

"Maybe?"

"Anyway, he told me this story about this boy who fell in a dumpster on the first night of Frosh Week, got knocked out, and then got tipped into a landfill."

"What? That's crazy. See? It's not just dying. It's dying in weird ways. My friend from my hall, Negin, is obsessed with it, too."

"Oh, you've already *got* a friend, have you?" he said, raising an eyebrow. "That's awkward. I thought me and Stephanie Stevens were your First Night Crew. Anyway, if this Negin's your friend, then where is she?"

I actually had no idea where Negin was. Would she be angry that we had gotten separated? I pointed vaguely out across the lake toward Jutland. "Over there somewhere."

"That's a duck, Phoebe." It started swimming toward us.

"Look, it wants to be our friend." I threw a bit of Twix into the water.

"OK, fair enough." Luke smirked. "It's you, me, Stephanie Stevens, this girl Negin—whoever the hell she is—and that duck. That's it for First Night. Any more friends is overkill."

"It's weird, 'cause everyone says you don't ever speak to the people you make friends with during orientation ever again, but I actually do really like Negin."

He held his mug up. "Thanks. Me and Stephanie and the

duck haven't made the cut. Whatever. We've got each other, anyway."

Luke was actually funnier than I imagined. And less confident. He was quite soft-spoken, it turned out. He stared down blankly at the water. "I wonder what will have happened between now and, like, three years' time." He said it like he'd almost forgotten I was there.

"We'll be twenty-one," I said. "That feels so far away. What do you *want* to have happened?"

He didn't look up. "For everything to feel less complicated, I guess."

It was the first time he'd said something that wasn't just banter. It was like his real voice came through. I didn't know what to do. So I just stayed silent.

He swung his feet underneath the bridge like a kid. "Shall we go and check on our First Night Friend?" He got up and held out his hand to me. "Try not to fall in."

Even as it happened, I simultaneously imagined describing it to Flora. It was the first time I had ever touched him. I took his hand but didn't want to put my whole weight on him in case I ungracefully pulled him over and into the lake. We walked back into the dorm and up the stairs. In the kitchen, we washed our mugs carefully and put them back in the cupboard. Then we looked in on Stephanie Stevens like new parents checking on their baby in its crib. She was snoring so loudly her bookshelf was shaking.

We wandered back over the bridge and along the walkway. Music was still blaring from the Jutland Bar, but the overhead lights were on now.

We were walking side by side, and every so often our arms

brushed. I could feel my heartbeat upping its rhythm. Even though my eighth-grade phase of stalking the hell out of Luke Taylor was just an embarrassing memory now, I still really, really fancied him. More than even Max and Adam, the two people I'd *actually* slept with. A part of me didn't even have the guts to look at him, in case he could tell.

We stopped outside the Jutland Bar. We were facing each other, and not far apart. My tummy flipped over a few times. We were in a classic kiss position.

"See you tomorrow, then, yeah?" he said, and reached forward to give me a hug. It was just a quick, see-you-later, cursory one—the kind you would give someone you were going to see right after the next lesson. But it woke my whole body up.

I wandered back to D Dorm in a bit of a daze. I kept replaying the hug in my head. I texted Flora, saying, *LUKE TAYLOR BREAKING NEWS: EVERYTHING YOU CAN IMAGINE HAS ACTUALLY HAPPENED.*

Negin's door was closed but I could see her light was still on.

I knocked gently. "It's Phoebe," I said softly. "Just checking you're not dead."

"Not dead," I heard her say. Then she opened the door in her pajamas and smiled. "Sorry I lost you. I was waiting up to check you weren't dead, either."

●　●　●　●　●　●　● **LUKE** ●　●　●　●　●　●　●

The Jutland Bar looked like a bomb site. The lights had come up and people were staggering about, broken and sweaty and blinking at each other like ridiculously dressed moles. Five guys

25

in ripped bedsheet togas were on the dance floor, punching the air to "Build Me Up Buttercup." There was a girl wearing a full-length banana costume crying underneath the foosball table, while a girl in a Justin Bieber onesie comforted her. Two wasted guys were playing an aggressively competitive game above them, apparently unaware the girls were even there.

I felt empty. Not in a stupid, over-the-top, dramatic way. Just sort of . . . numb. And exhausted. I tried to let the phrase "We are broken up" sink in properly, but it was like entering the wrong password. It wouldn't compute. It felt unreal, somehow. The phone call and the computer room meltdown seemed like days ago. In a weird way, the whole thing with Phoebe and Stephanie Stevens had been the best part of the night. It had taken my mind off everything, at least. There was no way I should have been able to enjoy myself after what had happened, but Phoebe's sunniness was infectious. She was just so easy to talk to.

I couldn't see Arthur or anyone else from my hall, so I headed back to B Dorm. Even though it was nearly two a.m., I didn't feel like sleeping. I didn't want to give my brain the chance to properly process what had happened. I heard the soft thud of music coming from Arthur's room next door, so I tried knocking. His voice came through muffled: "Hang on. . . . Who's that?"

"It's Luke."

There was a pause. "All right . . . Come in, then. It's open."

For a second, I thought I must have heard wrong, as there didn't seem to be anyone inside. Over the music, I could hear a watery tinkling sound, like a burst pipe somewhere in the walls. But then, suddenly:

"Where'd *you* get to, then?"

From behind the open door of the sink cupboard, I spotted Arthur's sneakers.

"Oh, sorry," I said. "Didn't see you. You OK?"

"Yeah, man. Nearly finished."

Before I could ask him what he was nearly finished doing, I suddenly realized what the watery tinkling was.

"Sorry, are you . . . y'know? Peeing? In the sink?"

"Yeah. Obviously. What do you think the sink's for?"

"Well . . . not for peeing in, I wouldn't have thought."

"Look, mate, just 'cause we're not rich enough to get an en suite bathroom, like those posh fucks up in Gildas, doesn't mean we can't *improvise,* if you know what I mean."

I saw the sneakers bob up and down, and the tinkling stopped. Arthur stepped out from the behind the door, grinning. His face was red and shiny, and he was wearing the Superman cape I'd started the night with.

"All right! How—" He raised his forefinger, stopping himself midsentence. "Sorry, forgot to flush."

He reached back inside the cupboard and turned the taps on. My feelings about this must have been reflected pretty accurately in my facial expression, because he smirked and said, "Don't you worry, my friend, you'll be peeing in the sink in no time. I mean, the toilets in this dorm are literally *at the end of the hallway.*"

He switched on his Xbox and pulled a little bag of weed out of his pants pocket. "I'll have a cup of tea if you're making one," he said.

I laughed. "All right."

27

"See if there's any food in the kitchen as well," he whispered. "My mum bought me fuck-all this year. Just 'cause I'm not a first year anymore, she apparently thinks I don't need to eat."

"My mum got me *ingredients,* but no actual food," I said. "I've got, like, flour and salt and olive oil, but nothing I can actually *eat.*"

Arthur raised an eyebrow mischievously. "We could always break out Barney's Nutella. . . . I'm sure he won't mind if we have a *tiny* bit. . . ."

Three spliffs and ten slices of chocolaty toast later, we were lying nearly comatose on the floor. Arthur scooped out the last splotch of Nutella and examined the now-empty jar.

"They shouldn't make this stuff so fucking delicious," he groaned. "Having something *this* delicious is clearly going to cause problems within a communal living space. It's fucking *irresponsible* is what it is."

"What we gonna do?" I mumbled stickily.

He yanked open his bedside drawer and pulled out a Sharpie. "Fuck, I've only got a black one. If I had a brown one, we could just color the jar in, and he'd never know the difference."

"Until he decided to actually eat some," I said. "Which we've got to assume he will do at some point."

Arthur shrugged and chucked the jar back at me. "Just dispose of the evidence. He can't prove it was us, can he?"

I went out into the kitchen, but just then Beth's door opened and Barney stepped out, wearing what was presumably Beth's T-shirt, since it said LANCASTER GIRLS HOCKEY and stretched all the way down to his knees. Beth poked her slightly disheveled head out behind him, and the three of us just stood there, staring awkwardly at each other.

And then Barney said, "Is that my Nutella?"

After I'd apologized and promised to buy him a new jar in the morning, I went back to Arthur's to find him snoring loudly on the floor. I switched off the Xbox and headed back to my own room.

I lay down on the bed, surrounded by unopened suitcases and untouched Ikea bags, and stared at the dirty yellow ceiling. My phone had run out of batteries, and I decided, for once, to leave it that way.

3

I feel like how cool you are is in your DNA. Cool people naturally sleep until their sleep is interrupted—it's the mark of the
effortlessly rock 'n' roll. I wake up at seven most days. Maybe
earlier, if I've been drinking.

I forgot where I was for a second, and reached over to push
the thin brown curtain to the side and look out of the rickety
window. It felt weird. I wasn't on vacation. I actually *lived* in this
strange little room now, hundreds of miles away from home.
Across the road was a little village green and an old church with
some ducks waddling about, like a card you would buy for an
old person you don't know very well. A postcard of quiet English countryside life, but with a few thousand teenagers living
stage left.

I sat up in bed and scrolled through pictures of last night.
Flora had posted one that looked like some arty album cover.

She was sitting on the steps of some grand building in Leeds, wearing a ball gown, battered-up sneakers and a feather boa. Her bright bleach-blond bob lit up the black-and-white picture, all moody and messed up. On one side of her was a girl wearing a black dress with a slit and a *Breakfast at Tiffany's* tiara, and on the other, a boy in a disheveled tux. She had just captioned it "ball." She felt far away. With people I had never met, in a place I had never been, wearing a dress I had never seen before. It scared me a bit. Like she was slipping away from me. Even two weeks ago, if I had spent the evening with Luke Taylor, I would have literally banged her door down at 2 a.m. to tell her about it.

She still hadn't read my message from last night, so I started composing a long, rambling essay about what had gone on:

> Luke Taylor TOUCHED me 💀💀 He is so hot I wanna die . . . We drank tea, I think he actually is THE ONE. He used to FLAMENCO dance 💃 He is actually funny, oh my god, he cried . . . Luke Taylor CRIED 🐑

Then I realized the cry emoji made me a terrible person, so in the end I just deleted everything and wrote, "WAKE UP, CALL ME." *What* would make Luke Taylor cry? *Who* would make Luke Taylor cry? Luke Taylor *crying*. Luke Taylor crying had made him hotter. Sensitive, intense, troubled and achingly enigmatic.

Last night had kind of recast him as the lead in my day-dreams. In a non-weird-stalker way. With a bit of weird stalker thrown in. I wonder if boys ever lie back and daydream scenarios about girls. I wonder, if they were projected onto a screen, would they look the same as ours? It is a bit messed up that I've been dreaming about Luke Taylor for all these years but never actually considered what he is really like. Him crying and speaking and making tea and being a real person had given me a lot of material.

Not that I've *needed* material in the past, obviously. He just morphs into whatever I feel like him being at the time. In sixth grade, when I was on the soccer team, I always imagined us going to soccer camp together. Later it was seeing him at a gig, and then it was him joining Model UN and us both representing Swaziland or whatever. He's like the face of the life I want, whatever that is at the time.

No wonder I've never been in love—I'm too busy daydreaming about it.

I got dressed and wandered out into the unknown. I felt like a grown-up; in charge and independently up and off to buy food.

The whole campus was deserted. I couldn't see one single person and it was kind of scary, but turning back felt silly and defeatist. I walked along the path, following the signs, trying to work out the way to the store. It was zombie-movie freaky, being in this concrete jungle, totally alone, but knowing there were actually hundreds of people sleeping in buildings all around.

The store was closed, which felt anticlimactic. It was cold, even in my new duffle coat. And I was hungry. And then I couldn't remember which way I had walked. Or where Jutland was. I went back to the lake and tried to decide which way to go.

And then, out of one of the towering gray walls, a door swung open and a boy walked out.

So, it was me and this random boy in the postapocalyptic

York Met University. The boy looked back at the doors he had come out of as if he wasn't quite sure where he was or how he had gotten there. I realized I was staring at him. And then I realized I *recognized* him. He was wearing the Princess Diana T-shirt Negin had on last night, but it had various liquid stains and a footprint on it now.

"Phoebe!" Josh said, and hugged me. "You look lost."

"And you look cold. I am lost, actually. No one in my suite is awake and I thought I would go and buy some food." I sounded so square. *I* hadn't gotten shitfaced and woken up in a rando's bed. I purposely stopped myself looking behind him to the door he had come out of. "But the store is still closed and now I have absolutely no idea how I even got here."

"And just like that your RA appears, like a genie, to save the day." He looked like the hero in a Thomas Hardy novel. Tanned and solid and kind of open and honest looking. He had soft blue eyes that seemed out of place under his shaved head. He bowed ever so slightly. "You summoned me?"

"Yes. Clearly you are sneaking about campus in last night's clothes because *I* summoned you."

"I'm not sneaking," he said. "I don't sneak." He laughed like a kid who has done something naughty, then took a deep breath and closed his eyes and groaned. "I have to go to work."

"What? Now? It's eight-forty-five."

"Not till eleven, but still." He yawned and stretched his arms above his head. "I'm starving. Come on, I know where we can buy food."

We walked across the bridge I'd sat on with Luke. A duck quacked at Josh and he waddled after it, quacking back. A woman passed wearing a bright-red suit and matching heels. She smiled. "Josh, it's still late. Today is the last day. *Last day.*"

"Avril, that's why I'm up so early. I'm going to the library to do it right now."

"The library is over there." She pointed in the opposite direction.

"I've got to eat, Avril. Even boys with late essays have to eat." She shook her head but carried on walking, smiling to herself.

"She's the lady who works in the English office. She's, like, my best friend, Avril. She's who you have to talk to if you are gonna hand something in late."

"Sweet-talk, you mean?"

He shrugged. "I'm not even that subtle—I literally bring her cakes from my work and lay them out and am, like, 'Avril, here are some cakes, save me.'"

"Smooooth."

"Not the only one, am I?" He put his arm around my shoulder. "So you and Will looked friendly last night." His eyes twinkled.

"Yeah, he's really nice." And also really hot. I should have messaged Flora about that, too. The Luke Taylor interlude had knocked it to the back of my brain. Josh carried on smiling at me. "Stop. You're making me embarrassed. He's really nice." I had already said that. *Oh god.*

We came out into a little village square. We went into the store and Josh picked up a basket, his goosebumps calming as he hit the warm air. "Shall we make breakfast for everyone?" he said. "I feel like that's what a good RA would do."

I nodded. We got hot chocolate to warm Josh up, and milk and eggs, and then Josh put confectioners' sugar and sprinkles into the basket. "Are you gonna bake them a cake for breakfast?" I asked. "I thought you had to work. . . ."

"Trust me," he said. "I have four younger sisters. I know how to do a good breakfast picnic."

D Dorm was still quiet when we got back. Josh took out a bowl and started mixing the icing. "Do you think I can use this frying pan?"

"Yeah, it's mine. What are you making?"

Connor walked in as Josh cracked an egg. Connor was not concerned about appropriate dorm attire. He was wearing fleece shorts and a T-shirt that said LET'S GET MESSY. He walked straight into the wall before ricocheting down on a chair.

"Do you want a cup of tea?" I asked.

He laid his head on the table and groaned a kind-of yes, then Liberty walked in wearing a silk romper and fuzzy knee-high socks.

"Are you cooking?" she said.

Josh nodded. Connor laughed into the table. "The way you say 'cooking.' *Coooo*-king."

Liberty had the strongest Liverpudlian accent I had ever heard. "*Coooo*-king. *Coooo*-king." She said it loudly in Connor's ear and sat down next to him.

I started buttering a big pile of bread. Josh picked up the bowl of icing mixture.

"What are you doing?" I looked over his shoulder. "Are you gonna ice the egg sandwiches?"

"That looks disgusting," Liberty said.

"'Dis-gust-in,'" Connor mimicked, and she kicked him gently.

"When it comes to new experiences, you need to get over

35

what's in your head and just let your heart lead you." Josh shoveled an egg onto a piece of bread and sandwiched it.

"That's way too deep for me, mate," Connor said, and took a sip of tea. "Sounds like some Lord of the Rings shit."

I peered over the bread as Josh poured the icing on top of it and then covered it in sprinkles. "Fairy bread!" he declared proudly.

"Egg-fairy-bread, more like it." I ran over to my cupboard and took out the cookie cutters I had made my mum buy even though I have never baked a cookie before, ever.

I got a duck one and plunged it into the bread.

"Did you really bring cookie cutters to college?" Josh smirked.

"Do you *really* make egg-fairy-bread served with poetic life mantras?"

Negin and Becky wandered in. They had both gotten fully dressed.

"None of us died overnight," I said, smiling.

"I almost did," Negin said. "My room is freezing."

Becky lingered by the microwave. It was like she didn't know if she had permission to sit down.

"Becky"—Josh pulled a chair away from the table—"are you prepared to have your life changed?"

"Do you want a cup of tea?" I smiled as encouragingly as I could.

"Thanks," she almost whispered, and sat down next to Liberty.

Josh laid the duck-shaped iced egg sandwich in front of Connor.

Connor sat up and looked at it, then shoved the whole thing

in his mouth. He chewed, swallowed and then got up and put his arms around Josh, picked him up and walked him around the kitchen. "That is the most beautiful thing I have ever eaten. That is all I am gonna eat for the next three years. I love you."

"Negin, look, there's a rocket one. It matches the rocket on your door." I pushed the cookie cutter into the sandwich and presented it to her on a plate.

"I don't think we should use plates unless we *absolutely* have to. Or knives and forks," Connor said. "If you can eat it with your hands I think you absolutely should. D Dorm policy."

Negin didn't look convinced by the policy or the iced egg sandwich. She smelled it and then took a tiny bite.

Josh cut Becky a dinosaur and I took a picture to show my mum that the cookie cutters had actually been a good investment.

Then Josh downed the last of his tea and stood up. "OK, I have to go to work. And you guys have to go to Freshmen Orientation Fair."

"Do you wanna borrow my sweater so you don't freeze?" I said, and then looked down. It was white with a purply glitter outline of a rabbit's face. "Or . . . I can lend you another one."

"Don't worry." He smiled. "I reckon I can pull that off."

● ● ● ● ● ●   **LUKE**   ● ● ● ● ● ●

It looked like a cross between a garage sale and a circus. Hundreds of tables strewn messily across the huge hall, all surrounded by brightly colored, hand-drawn posters advertising every kind of sport, hobby or club you could think of, and presided over by wackily dressed, wide-grinning, way-too-hyperactive-for-this-time-of-the-morning people. Everywhere you turned, someone was yelling at you, or waving you over, or shoving a leaflet or a pen or a cookie in your hand.

Me and Arthur weaved our way through the madness, binge-eating cookies, both still heavy with last night's hangovers.

It had been beyond weird to plug in my phone this morning and see no new messages, no missed calls. All summer, I'd thought I'd feel relieved by that sight, but if anything, it made me more ill at ease. Like the guilt and the worry had suddenly been amplified.

I just wanted, so badly, for her to be OK. To be happy again. I'd sat on the edge of my bed, trying to actually, properly process what had happened, but then Arthur had pounded my door down, and the idea of missing Orientation Fair to sit alone in my room suddenly didn't seem like an acceptable option.

Arthur pocketed yet another novelty ballpoint pen offered by a psychotically jolly random person and glanced around the hall, anxiously. "I should be keeping my head down, really," he muttered. "After last year's fair."

"Why?"

"When I turned up, I was still drunk from the night before. I signed up for all sorts of random shit and I haven't been to a single meeting since."

Right on cue, a figure stepped into our path wearing baggy white overalls, with a black mesh mask totally covering its face. It was carrying a fistful of flyers that proclaimed: *YORK MET BEEKEEPING SOCIETY: A GREAT WAY TO MAKE FRIENDS . . . AND HONEY!*

"Hello, Arthur," said the figure in a stern northern accent.

"Haven't seen you at any of the meetings. You seemed so keen last year."

Arthur looked at his feet. "Yeah, sorry about that, man. I just, erm ... I prefer to beekeep by myself, to be honest. Just me and the bees. It's more of a private, personal thing for me, beekeeping."

The figure didn't move. "You've got your own hive, then?"

Arthur nodded. "Yep. Keep it in the bath."

The figure snapped. "You shouldn't keep hives in damp places, Arthur! Bees *cannot* cope with damp. That's the *first* thing we would have taught you at Beekeeping if you'd ever *bothered* to show up to a meeting."

Arthur flapped his hands apologetically. "Yeah, no, sorry. What I meant is I keep it in the oven. Or the microwave. I rotate it between the two." Then he added, "I don't know why you're so worked up about me, anyway, Martin. I'm sure you've got tons of recruits. Where's the rest of the Beekeeping Society?"

"He's over there," said the figure.

"Right, well, we should be off," Arthur replied, dragging me away by the arm. "I'm just showing Luke here around."

We moved away, and Arthur shook his head. "This is a fucking nightmare," he said darkly. "The bloke from the Fencing Club will probably stab me in the face if he spots me. Trust me, man, you should only sign up to shit that you're actually, *genuinely* interested in. Once they've got your email, they own your soul. They'll never let you go." He kicked at a bit of loose carpet. "I'll still be getting the minutes from those fucking beekeeping meetings on my deathbed."

Across the room, we noticed Rosie, Tom, Beth and Nishant from our hall signing up for Chemistry Club.

"They're already *majoring* in chemistry," groaned Arthur. "Why the hell do they have to sign up for Chemistry Club as well?"

A bloke on stilts wobbled by, yelling, "COME JOIN STILT WALKING CLUB!" and Arthur reached up to fist-bump him. "Yes, Danilo!" He turned to me. "That's Danilo. He's in my program. He's really into stilt walking."

And then, from a speaker somewhere in the hall, a girl's voice boomed out in a low monotone, like an airport announcement: "Arthur Watling, report to the karaoke stand immediately to perform 'Someday My Prince Will Come.' Once again, Arthur Watling, to the karaoke stand, please."

Arthur's face split into a grin, and he looked around wildly in search of the voice's owner.

"Arthur Watling, you should be wearing your glasses," the voice deadpanned. "Arthur Watling, I'm quite clearly in the corner, next to the Warhammer stand."

We walked over to the corner, past the shaggy-haired Vikings of Warhammer Club, where a good-looking girl in a red woolly sweater was sitting by herself at the Karaoke Club desk. She was waving a glitter-covered microphone at us, which was hooked up to a speaker on a rickety-looking stage.

"Yes, Reets!" Arthur said. "Since when are you heading the York Met karaoke squad?"

"I'm not," said the girl, undoing her topknot and letting her curly black hair explode out in all directions. "Never done karaoke in my life. I'm just minding the table for Liz while she gets some fries." She tied her hair back up again, then waved the mic at us. "I'm supposed to be trying to get people to sing."

"No chance," Arthur grimaced. "I know people in here."

"You sang last year," said the girl, arching an eyebrow.

"Shit. Did I?"

The girl laughed. "Yeah. 'Single Ladies,' if I remember rightly. Then you went and signed up for Warhammer."

"Fuck's sake. No wonder they all look so pissed off."

"No, I think that's just how they look generally." She turned to me and smiled. "I'm Rita, by the way. Me and Arthur were neighbors in our dorm last year."

"I'm his new neighbor, Luke. Nice to meet you."

She frowned. "Oh dear, poor you. Has he enlightened you on the virtues of sink-pissing yet?"

"He's outlined the basic argument for it, yeah."

"Yes, I got that spiel on the first day, too. Thing is, peeing in a sink's not quite as easy when you're a girl. Oh, thank god, here's Liz."

Liz—who was wearing a bright-green KARAOKE CLUB hoodie—reclaimed her microphone, and Arthur and Rita went off to get a coffee. They didn't ask if I wanted to come with them, which sucked a little, and I didn't ask if I could, so I ended up wandering around by myself for a bit, feeling my hangover start to dissolve slowly into a ravenous hunger and trying to put off thinking about Abbey.

I went and signed up for the soccer team, which was by far the busiest and noisiest booth in the hall. The guys at the table seemed to recognize me right away as one of their own; they all nodded and smiled, and one guy called Will shook my hand and said, "Nice to meet you, man. See you at tryouts, yeah?"

I suppose I *am* one of their own, really. Obviously, the whole point of college is to broaden your mind and try new things or whatever, but surely there's no harm in also sticking to what you know. And I *know* soccer. It's the one thing I really like that I'm actually, definitely good at. That's got to count for something.

I was starting to feel self-conscious about walking around on my own, so I went to join the line for free fries at the Nando's booth. But then I finally saw a face I recognized. Across the packed hall, Phoebe was standing at one of the tables, signing a form, while a pigtailed girl jabbered away excitedly at her.

Feeling lighter suddenly, I waved and walked over. "How you doing?"

"Hey! Luke. How's it going?" Her cheeks flushed a bit. She seemed genuinely pleased to see me. "I've been on the lookout for our old friend Stephanie Stevens, but no sign of her yet."

"I know, I feel quite protective of her now. Though she definitely won't remember us. What are you up to, anyway?"

"Just signing up for Feminist Club." She flicked the big bunch of purple balloons that was attached to the table. "They've got balloons and everything, so they must be legit. Have you put your name down for anything?"

"Erm . . . soccer, and that's about it so far."

"Ah yeah, of course, soccer." She snorted a laugh and then covered her mouth. "Sorry, that's my main memory of Monday assemblies—Mr. Weale's game reports." She adopted a surprisingly convincing Mr. Weale voice. "'. . . And Luke Taylor scored an exceptional hat trick on Saturday. Well done, Luke.'"

"I'm going to sign up for other stuff, too," I said, probably a bit too defensively. "I'm just not sure what yet."

"Yeah, me too." She nodded.

"So come on, then. What shall we do? We could sign up for something together."

She went quiet for a second. "Erm, yeah, OK . . . What?"

We both looked around us. "Maybe Caribbean Club?" she suggested, pointing at a table with a huge Jamaican flag behind it, where a small white guy with matted blond dreadlocks was nodding his head to a Bob Marley track.

"Do you think that guy is actually Caribbean?" I asked.

"I've spoken to him already," she said. "His name is Jeremy; he's from Guernsey. He told me that coming from a small island gives him a 'Caribbean mentality.'"

"Right," I said. "Well, I think we'll pass on Jeremy. What else is there?"

"I dunno. . . ."

I picked a balloon out of the Feminist Club bunch. "OK, tell you what: I'll flick this balloon and whichever table it lands nearest, that's what we'll sign up for."

She smiled. "OK."

I sent the balloon spiraling up into the air, way above the forest of heads and hands. We followed it and watched it descend slowly onto a table surrounded by broomsticks and cheerful-looking people wearing long, flowing black robes.

Phoebe raised her eyebrows. "Whoa. That looks quite . . . intense."

"No, come on!" I said, mock-sternly. "We said whichever one it landed on, we had to sign up for." It was weird. I suddenly felt this massive urge to prove to her that I wasn't just some boring, one-dimensional soccer player. That there was more to me than that. Even though, to be honest, I'm not entirely sure there is.

"Yeah, I know we said that." She nodded. "But . . . quidditch?"

"The balloon has spoken, Phoebe."

"Balloons can't speak, Luke. Not even in Harry Potter."

"The whole point of college is to try new things, you know."

"You sound like my mum," she scoffed.

"Well, your mum's clearly a legend. Let's do this."

We wandered over to the quidditch table and I scribbled our names down on the form. A guy with a Ron Weasley wig on told us there would be an "informal meet-and-greet" this afternoon.

"We've got to go," I told Phoebe. "We can't just sign up and then wuss out."

"Well, technically, we could do that . . . ," she whispered.

"No, we've put our names down now. We've *got* to go at least once." I stuck out my hand. "Shake on it?"

She grinned. "OK, OK. I'll be there."

We shook hands. Then we swapped numbers, but as I put my phone back in my pocket, I felt it buzzing again. I took it out and, with a little flutter of relief, saw that it wasn't Abbey. It was a landline.

I answered it. "Hello?" said a woman's voice. "Luke? Luke, this is Sally." There was a pause. "Abbey's mum."

4

● ● ● ● ● ● **PHOEBE** ● ● ● ● ● ● ●

It wasn't a date. That's what I kept telling myself. We were just randomly joining the Quidditch Club for a laugh.

But then it also sort of *was* a date. We had made an *arrangement* to see each other. And that led to lots of questions and mass internal hysteria. From "Should I wear my hair up?" right through to "If it came to it, would I actually screw over Abbey Baker and hook up with him?"

Obviously, yes. Although I *would* feel bad about it, because in ninth grade she let me join her group in dance when Flora was away and stuck up for me when Maud Evans tried to give me the role of a toothbrush in "Shake It Off." Plus, she cried when Mrs. Renchanova left. So I know she's nice, even though she is so good-looking that she really doesn't have to be.

In my head, she had made Luke cry by cheating on him with her hot hall mate at her college. Flora had kind of tossed that idea out when I spoke to her, and it had taken root in my mind and become the only logical chain of events.

The fact Luke had even suggested doing this whole quidditch thing had changed him in my eyes. In seven years of observing Luke Taylor, it never occurred to me or Flora that he might have a sense of humor. He cried *and* was funny. He actually might be my perfect man.

I readjusted my track pants. I had tried to channel cool as a cucumber Bowl-Cut Girl, but without the actual bowl cut it hadn't quite worked.

"It's here." Negin looked up. We were standing a few feet away from a very long, low shed-like building. There was a small clump of people standing near the door, all talking to each other. Luke wasn't there yet.

"OK," Negin said. "See you later." She put both hands on her backpack straps like a hiker and turned. I didn't want her to leave me alone, awkwardly waiting for someone in the quidditch clump to talk to me.

"Are you sure you don't want to come?"

She looked into the distance like she was having extreme contemplative thoughts. "Yes." She nodded slowly. "I'm one hundred percent sure I do not want to join the Quidditch Club."

"I'm not actually joining it, either." I lowered my voice midsentence. "And you really like Harry Potter."

"Yes, but I am Ravenclaw and I don't think anyone in Ravenclaw is actually into physical exercise." She rolled her eyes. "OK, I'll wait until he gets here."

"Are you guys waiting for Quidditch Club?" A really, really tall girl with a really, really posh voice was standing in front of us. "Can I walk in with you so I don't look like an *actual* weirdo?"

She didn't wait for us to say yes, just smiled really broadly. "Then again, that building is so small I probably won't even fit in it." She walked over to the shed building and stood with her back against it like she was being measured in elementary school. Her head almost reached the roof. "No, but literally, look."

She lolloped back over. "I'm Frankie."

"Phoebe."

"Negin. I'm not actually joining."

"Oh my god, *why not*?" Frankie said. "You literally have to come for, like, ten minutes because this is going to be *massively funny*." She reached her arms out as she said "massively" to physically show us how hilarious it was going to be. Without waiting for Negin to respond, she took her arm and started walking her to the shed door.

"Are you both in the same dorm?" she asked.

Negin and I nodded. Negin had kind of been swept up by Frankie against her will. I looked for Luke but I couldn't see him. "So, where're you from?"

Frankie made a really loud groaning noise and the other people waiting all looked at her. She spoke to them as well as to us. "No, don't. Genuinely. I actually might cry if I start talking about it." She didn't look like she was about to cry at all. "Basically, it's all my own fault." She laughed to herself. "Right now, I'm actually supposed to be in Costa Rica at a sloth sanctuary. But then when my exam results and acceptance letters came back, I just really wanted to go to college. Also, I found out that in Costa Rica they have spiders the size of schnauzers. Miniature, but still."

I laughed. "Had you already paid for your flights?"

"Yeah, so my dad hates me. They wouldn't buy me *any* new

clothes for school." She lifted up her leg. "That is why I am wearing these thick leggings. They can, like, stop a snake biting you in the jungle."

I stared at them. She nodded. "Honestly, these are like Bear Grylls–endorsed leggings. Try to bite these bitches, because you won't get through. I have no college clothes. Only jungle-survival gear. But if there is a zombie attack, I also have a mosquito net, a headlamp and a £300 nonreturnable monogrammed travel journal."

Negin still looked a bit shell-shocked by Frankie. "What's your major?" she ventured politely.

"Archaeology. They are massive babes for letting me in last minute. But because I'm not with the sloths, I got put in a suite with all these old people. And they are not interesting at all. I slept for a week straight before I came to prepare for all the partying of Frosh Week, and so far all they've done is eat some cheese together."

"Like mice," I said.

She laughed so loudly the whole clump stopped speaking to each other and just stared at her.

"They are *actually* mice," she sighed. And then she started doing jumping jacks on the spot. "Quick warm-up. So why are you guys here, then? Not at college, obviously, I mean here at Quidditch Club." She puffed. "I think I'm a natural chaser, TBH."

"I'm just here as a supportive friend," Negin said. "Phoebe is waiting to meet . . . someone."

Frankie jumping jacked forward, almost straight into Negin. "What, like a *date*?"

Negin nodded at the same time I shook my head. Frankie lit up.

48

"It's definitely not a date," I stuttered. "It's just this . . . boy."

"Please tell me," Frankie hissed. "*Please.* I live for stuff like this. Even more than animals or Harry Potter. This is my actual *life.* Don't freeze me out of the gossip." She put her face in between me and Negin's. "Tell me," she whispered again.

I scanned the whole campus as far as I could see, and there was no sign of anything Luke Taylor–shaped. "OK," I said. "There's this boy here that I kind of liked in high school. . . ."

"What's his name?" Frankie snapped.

"Luke Taylor."

"OK, go on."

"Well, I saw him at the fair and we both decided to join Quidditch Club."

"*We* decided, or he asked you?" Frankie's eyes narrowed.

"Well, he definitely wanted to join something . . . together."

"Done deal." Frankie clapped her hands. "Book the church, because you are in the *luuuuurve* business." She started jumping up and down again. "I would actually pay money to see how this plays out. Not loads but, like, maybe five pounds." She clenched her fists together and made an excited yelping sound. She looked at Negin. "Front row seats for us."

The door swung open and a redheaded girl dressed head to toe in pink, including her shoes, flung her arms above her head and squealed, "We're ready."

"When Luke Taylor comes in, do this signal." Frankie looked at the sky and let out a loud howl. The clump all turned around. "Just a subtle pack-howl, no big deal. Keep it caj."

The long, low-ceilinged room was totally empty. One entire wall was filled with pictures of extremely happy-looking people. Happy at *The Cursed Child,* happy on the Warner Brothers tour, and very, very happy playing quidditch. Above the photos were various ribbons and cups and house scarves. Along another there were some brooms lined up and, at the very end, one mop.

A boy was almost dancing around the room, offering people chocolate frogs from a plastic bowl.

"I don't think anyone here is Slytherin," Negin whispered.

"Oh my god. Chocolate frogs," Frankie yelled, and took three, handing me and Negin one.

I looked at my phone and then at the door. It was already ten past, and no sign of Luke. The longer he didn't come, the more nervous I got. I kept pulling my hair out of its elastic and retying it up. Like that would help.

A girl in army fatigues strode into the middle of the room and clapped her hands so forcefully it sounded like a shot. She had the stance of a bouncer and an expression to match. She looked like she could take down The Rock. Next to her was a small, incredibly thin boy wearing a Gryffindor sweater and pants that were so tight they were almost leggings.

"This is legit my fave club already," Frankie said in her stage whisper. "I mean, *come on.*" She unwrapped another chocolate frog and shoved it in her mouth, whole.

Negin saw me looking at the door again. "It's not even a quarter past," she said.

"It's not a big deal." I smiled, and she smiled back reassuringly.

"Welcome to Quidditch Club," said the incredibly thin boy. "I'm Brandon, I'm the cocaptain, and this is Misty, the other cocaptain. We decided not to have a vice because we are both equally important."

"Misty and Brandon," Negin mouthed.

I nodded. "Brandon sounds like someone who rides dirt bikes in California. And Misty, Misty sounds like . . ."

"A stripper." We all whispered it at exactly the same time, and in unison it became audible. Frankie coughed loudly to try to cover it up.

The door creaked and I heard a girl speak. So, not Luke. "Sorry, we didn't know whether to come in." Next to her was a stunningly attractive boy with glasses and masses of black curly hair. He was really tanned and was wearing a black polo.

Frankie made a quiet howling sound. "Luke Taylor is *insanely hot*. Well done, you."

"That's not him." I tried to sound casual but my voice came out flat.

"Well, would he do?" Frankie whispered. "Because oh my actual god."

We all looked at the curly-haired boy, and he smiled. "I'm gonna slouch to look smaller." Frankie bent her knees slightly. She shuffled closer to me with her knees still bent. "Are you OK?" she asked. Her face softened, and it was like for the first time she wasn't joking around. "Whoever this Luke Taylor is, he obviously doesn't appreciate the importance of quidditch."

"Or punctuality," Negin said darkly.

He wasn't coming. Whichever way you looked at it, it was a dick thing to do. I felt like such an idiot.

"It's fine," I said. "It's just weird because this whole thing was *his* idea. He seemed really into it."

Frankie put her extremely long arms around me. "I find boys in general *very* perplexing," she said matter-of-factly. "From now on, sisters before misters. But obviously, if Luke Taylor turns up late you can ditch us."

I laughed, and the skinny boy at the front started talking again.

"You are all now part of our quidditch family," he said. "We are the York Boggarts."

Negin couldn't suppress a smirk, but Frankie whooped loudly.

"Right," said Misty, and everyone went quiet. "Firstly, I can't emphasize enough that the real-life sport of quidditch differs vastly from the sport of quidditch you have encountered in the Harry Potter novels. We do not *actually* fly in this version of the sport. The York Boggarts are part of the Varsity league. Last year we finished at the bottom of the first division, which, I won't lie to you, was a blow. It is really encouraging to see so many new faces here this afternoon. The Leeds Obliviators are our main threat this season. But I am confident that with regular attendance at training we can turn into their worst fear, and *obliviate* them."

There was a beat where Misty almost smiled. It was like she was riling us all up to go over the top.

"This is extremely surreal," Negin murmured in her perfunctory way.

"Right," Brandon said, smiling. "Shall we do a quick warm-up game?"

We all got in a circle and introduced ourselves and told everyone what Hogwarts house we were in. I stopped looking at the door when we started playing catch with beanbags, accompanied by Harry and the Potters.

Quidditch was basically lots of running around with a broom between your legs and trying to dodge flat volleyballs. At one point, I was laughing so hysterically that I had to stand at the edge and compose myself. As we left, I realized I actually wanted to come back.

As soon as we were a few feet away from the hut, Frankie started shaking her head. "I'm sorry, but how funny was that whole thing? And also, LOLs that we actually tracked down the hottest boy at this whole university on the second day. I mean, maybe one of the hottest people in the whole *world*. And also, he is foreign, so he probably doesn't know anyone here. Vulnerable and in need of a tall woman to show him a good time."

"He really was unexpectedly good-looking," I agreed.

Negin nodded. "Even you must be able to see that he was hotter than Luke Taylor."

"I actually can't believe he didn't come," I said.

"Luke Taylor is dead to me," Frankie announced. "I mean, I know I've never met him but, still, he's dead to me." She stopped suddenly in her tracks. "Maybe he *is* dead. And that's why he didn't come. I mean, you know loads of people die during orientation week, right? Like, *millions*."

● ● ● ● ● ● **LUKE** ● ● ● ● ● ●

"We just think it's best if she doesn't go."

That's what she'd kept saying. And then she'd added, "Obviously, no one's blaming you."

But the thing is, if no one really *is* blaming you, they don't need to say it, do they? Not ten times in one phone call.

Obviously, everyone blamed me. Because obviously, it was my fault. I had stopped loving her. It was as simple, and ridiculously complicated, as that.

I don't know when it happened. It wasn't like a wake-up-one-morning epiphany. It had taken me all summer to realize it. After we got our acceptance and rejection letters back, the whole of August and September had merged into one long, tearful conversation about how it didn't matter that she didn't get into York Met, and we could still make it work long distance. And then, at some point, it had dawned on me that maybe I didn't *want* it to work anymore. Does that make me a massive prick? I don't know. Probably.

Actually, no. It *definitely* made me a massive prick. Because now she was missing out on college. Her whole life was broken in half. And it was all my fault.

"We just can't let her go to Cardiff like this, Luke," her mum had said. "She's had one bad knock already with her college-prep exam scores, and now, after what happened last night . . ." She sighed heavily. "I just don't want her getting any more knocks, you know? She was in such a state this morning, saying she didn't want to go next week. And I think for once that she's right. You've got to be in a certain . . . frame of mind to start university. And with everything that's gone on, she's just not ready right now. So we'll wait a year and . . . see what happens."

I hadn't really said much. I'd just let her talk. She'd said they were going away for a week or so, as a family, and that maybe it would be best if me and Abbey didn't speak for a bit.

I'd walked back to my dorm in a sort of numb daze. I thought about calling one of my friends. Reece or Harry or someone. But what would they say? It's not like I could talk to them about the endless missed calls or the constant nagging guilt or the crying in the fucking computer room. I wouldn't even know how to start that conversation.

I just wish I could understand what happened. What changed inside me. I mean, surely, if you don't feel the way you used to feel, isn't it better to be honest? To actually own up to it? Or should you spend the rest of your life pretending, just to keep everyone else happy?

I bought two Twix bars, went back to my room and fell into a lumpy, half-hungover sleep.

When I woke up again, it was dark. I stared at the empty walls, with the two unopened suitcases still sitting grumpily on the carpet. Outside, I could hear people bustling between the dorms, plastic bags clinking with pregame bottles.

To take my mind off the call, I unpacked and started putting some pictures up. I'd brought my tatty little red folder with me, where I keep everything of any emotional value—pictures, cards, letters, that sort of thing. But that hadn't really helped, because most of the stuff in it was Abbey-related. She was in pretty much every photo. All the letters and cards were from her. Who else would send me a letter? Her name was written right through my life. Who the hell was I without her?

There was a knock on the door and Arthur didn't even wait for a reply before kicking it open. He stood in the doorway, yawning stickily and blinking at me, the sickly sweet smell of weed wafting in with him.

"I will have a cup of tea, then," he said. "If you're making one."

I laughed despite myself. "I'm not making one. And we're out of milk anyway."

"There are two cartons in the fridge!"

"They're Barney's. They've got Post-its on them."

Arthur made a face. "Fuck's sake, milk is communal.

Everyone knows that. Certain things are beyond Post-its." He started holding up fingers. "Milk, butter, beer, chicken Kievs . . ."

"Did you eat his chicken Kievs? He was bitching about that earlier."

Arthur shrugged. "Like I say, they're communal. Clue's in the name: Kiev. Russia was the birthplace of communism."

He walked into my room and started picking through the stuff in my folder, snorting at random photos of me and Reece in ridiculous costumes. Then he held up a card that said LIFE BEGINS AT 40!

"Why the hell have you got this?" he laughed.

"Oh, it's just a stupid thing," I said. "Private joke."

Rita poked her head around the door. "Aw. Are you two decorating? I had to get a book from the library, so I thought I'd come and say hello. So weird being back at the old dorm."

"Reets, you're doing law," said Arthur. "Tell Luke that chicken Kievs are communal."

"We haven't covered chicken Kievs yet," Rita said. "That's not till junior year."

Arthur dropped the card on my bed and walked out. "Well, Rita will have a cup of tea with me. Rita's a real friend."

They left and I stared down at the card. It wasn't a stupid thing, really.

I pulled the others out of the folder. As well as LIFE BEGINS AT 40! there was GOOD LUCK IN YOUR NEW JOB!, HAPPY CHINESE NEW YEAR!, and TO THE WORLD'S BEST GRANDDAD!

It had started on Abbey's sixteenth birthday. We'd only been going out a couple of months, and I was coming back from vacation when I realized I hadn't gotten her a card. The card shop at the airport had a pretty shitty selection, and the only vaguely

56

birthday-related one said "You are 8 today!" and had a big color-ful button on the front. I gave it to her later that night, and she'd cracked up laughing.

After that, it snowballed: every Christmas, birthday and an-niversary, we competed to see which of us could give the most random, obscure, inappropriate card. I remember us both snort-ing tea out of our noses as she opened my personal masterpiece: "Congratulations on Becoming an Uncle!" last Valentine's.

That had only been, what . . . seven months ago? Back then, there was literally no part of me that could imagine life with-out Abbey. I was totally, completely convinced we would be to-gether forever. How the fuck can you just . . . lose that feeling? Why had I lost it and she hadn't?

I lay down on the bed again and tried to trace it back properly. It had definitely started around exam season. Our par-ents had both agreed we should spend less time together so we could concentrate on studying, and I remember noticing after a while that it was almost a relief to not have to see her every day. To have more time to myself. It was like this murky, guilty secret I carried around with me, and every time we were together, it got heavier.

And it was like the more I backed off, the more tightly she clung on. I started calling less and less; she started calling more and more. And slowly it was like all the fun was being strangled out of the relationship, and we were just spending time together because . . . that was what we did.

And then our test scores came back, and she opened that envelope, and as she crumpled down onto the bench in tears, it was like our whole future crumpled with her. We wouldn't be spending the next three years together at York Met. And that seemed big and scary, but deep down it also seemed exciting. Because for so long it was like me and Abbey were almost the same person. Or, maybe, just that we were completely defined by each other. To half the school I was just "Abbey's boyfriend," but now, for the next three years, I would be . . . me.

I should have told her, right there on that bench, how I felt. But I didn't. I just held her and kissed her and promised we would make it work.

I felt the tears start to prickle under my eyelids. It was ridiculous; this was supposed to be the most exciting week of my life, and I was wasting it, crying in my room. I could hear Arthur and Rita's muffled laughter through the wall. I sat up, took a deep breath and tried unsuccessfully to calm the frantic whirring guilty panic in my stomach. I washed my face, stuck a few photos up on the wall—all Abbey-less—then stuffed the cards back into the folder and pushed it under my bed.

I went and knocked on Arthur's door and he shouted, "It's open!" The room was thick with weed smoke. Arthur was slumped at the foot of his bed, playing Xbox, while Rita sat cross-legged on top of the comforter, drinking tea and reading a book the width of a house brick.

I took the spliff off Arthur, had a drag and offered it to Rita.

"Oh, no thanks," she said. "I don't smoke." She smiled down at Arthur, who was staring blankly at the TV. "I just come here for the sparkling conversation."

I took another drag.

"So how was Orientation Fair, then?" she asked, folding her page over and putting the book down. "Did you sign up for anything?"

"Yeah, soccer and . . ." It hit me. "Oh fuck!"

"What?" said Arthur. "Tell me you didn't sign up for the fucking Caribbean Club!"

Rita laughed. "Poor old Jeremy. He's always trying to get me to join that. I keep telling him: my *mum's* from Trinidad, I'm from Luton."

"No . . . ," I moaned. "It wasn't that. It was quidditch."

Arthur frowned at me. "What, the Harry Potter thing? Do people *really* play that?" He looked at Rita. "People can't *actually* fly, can they?"

"We don't cover flying till junior year, either," she said.

"I was supposed to go to this quidditch thing this afternoon," I muttered. "I completely forgot." Phoebe and the balloon and the handshake all suddenly swirled into my head.

"You dickhead," Arthur scoffed. "I told you not to sign up for anything you weren't genuinely interested in!"

"I *am* genuinely interested. Like, I was going to go, honestly. It's just . . . something came up."

Everywhere I turned I was fucking things up. I'd only just met Phoebe properly and already she probably thought I was a total prick. I suddenly felt I had to go and see her. To say sorry for not being there. Her dorm was only a minute's walk away. She'd be pregaming there right now. I stood up.

"I'm just going out for a bit."

Arthur paused the game. "Oh great; well, get some more booze while you're out, yeah?"

He dug into his pocket for a wrinkled £20 note. "There you go. Just get as much beer as that will buy. And maybe some chips. Lay's."

I headed out toward Phoebe's building, feeling the weed start to take effect in the form of a fuzzy warmth behind my forehead. I walked across the grass to D Dorm and looked up to see her through the first-floor kitchen window. She was talking to a tall blond girl and a guy with a shaved head. They were all drinking and laughing, throwing robot dance moves to some hip-hop track I could hear thumping through the glass.

I had a weird sort of moment of clarity. Why the hell did I think she cared whether I was at the quidditch thing or not? Who was I to her? No one. Someone she used to walk past in the hall at school.

I sat down on a bench and rubbed my eyes. Every window of every dorm was full of noise and people, and I suddenly felt tiny and invisible and completely alone.

I stood up to go, feeling the scrunched-up £20 note in my pocket and wondering how much cheap booze it would buy. I needed to try to get my head straight. To think a bit more clearly. And the best way to do that, I decided, would be to get really, really drunk.

Part Two

5

"None left," Frankie shouted from the other side of the costume shop. She groaned before disappearing. Me and Negin found her splayed out on the floor, wailing melodramatically. Her height meant she covered almost an entire aisle.

"Shame," the woman at the front of the shop said half-heartedly. "We've just been so busy this week."

Above the empty section where Frankie was lying was a label that said GHOST COSTUMES.

"This is *so hard*," Frankie whined, and closed her eyes as if she was going to fall asleep on the store floor. "I swear the last five nights have broken me."

I kicked her gently. "Come on. Last night of Frosh Week."

"All right, *Connor*, calm down." Negin shook her head and then peered at Frankie. "And what's happened to you? This morning you were so emoji-party obsessed you wanted to make a papier-mâché melon with a yoga ball."

"No, but *such* a good idea." Frankie opened her eyes. "If someone walks in papier-mâchéd-up as the melon, I'm gonna be *livid*. Same with the chick coming out of a cardboard-box egg."

Negin picked up a random scythe. "The ghost is so obvious."

"What about the moon?" I said. "We could all go as the moon at different stages of its development."

Frankie snorted from the floor. "You're supposed to pick an emoji and sex it up. It's the rule; everyone knows it. Like, sexy crocodile, sexy backpack, sexy loaf of bread." She flung her leg in the air and pouted. "Sexy the *moon* in different stages of development." She howled with laughter.

"Sexy bread," Negin repeated slowly. "Sexy. Bread."

Frankie held a finger up. "Girl, trust me, there will be at least one sexy loaf of bread there. Probably two or three."

"If you wanted to be sexy you would go as the bunny girls or the flamenco dancer or the . . . I dunno . . ." I got my phone out.

"Sexy bread," Frankie shouted.

The woman behind the counter glanced over at us. "I've got no Playboy bunnies left," she said. "And no sexy señoritas, either."

"See?" I said to Frankie. I looked at the woman. "How many bread costumes have you got left?"

"None. We've got a Heinz beans. . . ."

"I don't think there's a Heinz beans emoji." I looked down at Frankie. "We just need to find any old thing now. It's three o'clock. We just need to buy whatever."

"It's the last night of Frosh Week," Frankie said. "We'll remember it for*ever*."

Would we, though? It was impossible to know. There's *always* a chance that tonight is going to be the night you remember forever, but usually it never is. For some weird reason, I've never forgotten me and Flora sneaking out of our houses in the middle of the night in eighth grade and biking around the empty town square. Not the whole night, just this snippet, this moment of it, really. I don't know why my brain chooses to remember *that*, of all the nights that ever happened. Maybe tonight would be burned into my brain forever, too. Maybe tonight is one of those nights. Maybe.

Over the past five days, me, Negin and Frankie had started to feel like a little team. We messaged each other when we woke up and went shopping together and checked we were all not dead before we went to bed. It was a relief to have found people who were nice and who seemed to like me. They weren't Flora, but then how could they be? That's what's weird about the whole thing; how you're expected to be so insanely close to people you've only just met. I was still careful with Negin and Frankie; I tried to pick up on what kind of people they were and mirror it, to not do anything that would rock the boat of our five-day friendship. Maybe we were all doing that, though? Maybe we'd all talk about it one day.

I picked up some mouse ears. Maybe the mouse was a good middle ground between sexy and fun.

"Is there a nun emoji?" Frankie asked, clambering to her feet. She and Negin were still buried in their phones. "I swear there is."

"Who would need a nun emoji?" I picked up a plastic corn-cob and held it up to Negin.

"The pope?" said Negin. "The pope's on Instagram."

65

"Yeah, well, if there *is* a nun emoji, I'm going as that. I am *literally* the nun of the freshman class. I need to turn things around tonight."

"Nothing says *get with me* like corn on the cob." I held it in front of my mouth and smiled.

"There are *no* tall men," Frankie wailed. "I thought there'd be Dutch exchange students. I *hate* my height."

"Can you hate your height *later*?" asked Negin. "We've got, like, two hours. We need to focus." She went back to scrolling through her phone, and me and Frankie dutifully followed suit.

"Shut. Up." Frankie poked me in the arm and nodded toward the window.

It was Josh and Will, crossing the road. My whole face flooded with heat. They knew all about my first night make out session with Will now, and all about every one since.

"I can't see Will," I hissed. "Not now. Should I hide? I've never even seen him in daylight."

"Like a vampire!" Frankie yelled.

I had never seen him when we were not in a bar and either about to hook up or actually making out. I stared at the floor. We'd made out together for ages last night in the club. Only a few hours ago, really. But in the daytime, everything was different. I picked up a skirt labeled ROCK AND ROLL SWEETHEART and pretended to be examining it intensely. Frankie and Negin began "browsing with intent," too.

"I don't think this is subtle," Negin whispered as the door swung open and they walked in.

"Hey," I said, and waved. *Hard.* Almost to the level of flagging someone down in the street. I tried to tone it down by tucking my hair behind my ears and sort of shrugging. Which obviously looked ridiculous. Will smiled at me lazily. It was ludicrous how he still managed to look hot on three hours of sleep. I couldn't think of anything to say.

"There are no ghost costumes." Thank god Negin was there.

"And no bread. There was never actually any bread." And Frankie.

"If Connor was here, you know what he'd say." Josh smiled.

"Last night of Frosh Week!" we all chimed in a Connor-esque cheer.

"Exactly." Josh nodded. "How are you feeling?"

"We're all going to have a group nap to prepare," Frankie said. "And I've bought Crunchy Nut Cornflakes and two bags of giant chocolate buttons."

She offered them the open box of cereal we had been eating on our way around town and they both took a handful.

I was desperate to say something so the situation wasn't weird. "We don't know what to go as," I blurted out, slightly manically.

Will smiled at me. "Neither do we. You haven't got any huge cartoon eyes, have you?" The woman at the front of the shop shook her head. Will grimaced. "Stuff like this is not easy on a hangover." The fact he had even half referenced last night made me blush even more. We were facing each other and I felt like he was nervous, too. Negin and Frankie and Josh were talking to the woman. I shuffled my feet.

"They don't really give you much time to sort out what you're going to wear and . . . stuff." I sounded like a mum.

Will nodded. "Yeah, but no one really cares when you get there. Loads of people will just wear a hat or paint their face or something. Honestly, it's nothing to stress about."

67

Oh god, it was so awkward. We had made out for so long last night and it was just there, splotched between us, this giant mountain of unacknowledged physical contact. But weirdly, right now in the daylight, even accidentally brushing against his sleeve would feel like an invasion of personal space. I couldn't even look directly at him. Like he was the sun or something. This tiny moment of silence passed, and in it we both looked at each other. And it was like making eye contact kind of acknowledged the kissing all week on various dance floors. And then we both smiled at the same time and then it turned into a laugh. And we were both just laughing together, both knowing why but not saying anything.

Then he looked at his phone. "I've got to go to soccer try-outs in, like, an hour, so we better go."

The mention of soccer made Luke Taylor pop into my head. I hadn't forgotten about the whole first night. Although now I couldn't really remember what actually had or had not happened between him being *The One* on the bridge and *The One* who stood me up at quidditch. Frankie had taken to calling him "Luke Taylor, Quidditch Bailer," which, to be fair, was quite catchy.

I had seen him a few times over the week, but we basically just ignored each other. Which in any other situation would have been the major drama of my existence, but in this freshmen haze, with Will chucked in, it had just become a weird thing I blocked out of my mind. I think Luke Taylor is destined to be one of the enigmatic mysteries of my life. It's like we belong on different sides of a Venn diagram, and the first night of orientation week was a strange crossover that should never have happened.

"Ready?" Josh said, and Will nodded. "See you later," he said, smiling at me. "Hope you find something. I'm sure, you know . . . you'll look nice in whatever."

And then they left.

Frankie cackled so loudly the woman in the shop jumped. And then she was laughing so hard she could hardly breathe. She was doubled over. "'You'll look nice.'"

"Stop." I put my head in my hands. "Stop."

"You'll. Look. Nice."

Negin was laughing in a more genteel way. "I think it's sweet. And awkward. Awkwardly sweet."

"You'll look nice," they chanted while we bought mouse ears and cat ears and a plastic turtle and the corn. And after every time they said it, they burst into even more hysterics until it just started to feed on itself and none of us could really breathe.

"Why is everyone always having sex except me?" Frankie wiped away tears.

"I'm not having sex," Negin said.

"Yeah, and I haven't even slept with Will," I added.

"*Yet.*" Frankie handed me the box of Crunchy Nut Corn-flakes. "I think you need to carb load. You know . . . for later."

● ● ● ● ● ● ● **LUKE** ● ● ● ● ● ● ●

I was in the kitchen, nursing a hangover so horrendous I could literally feel it in my *bones.*

The past five days had basically snowballed into one long, hazy night out. It had been a weird drunken cycle of going out to whatever party was happening down at the bar, then coming

69

back up to Arthur's room, getting stoned, waking up on his floor, having breakfast, getting stoned again, playing Xbox, going out again, coming back, getting stoned ... And so it went, on and on and on.

I had been making a concerted effort to block out all thoughts of Abbey, and the best way to do that seemed to be to just keep going: keep drinking and smoking and partying so that my brain didn't have a chance to settle on her for longer than a few minutes. Occasionally, though, lying wasted on Arthur's floor at five in the morning, she'd float into my head, and a hot wave of guilt would sweep right through me.

I speed-ate a Nutella sandwich over the sink, keeping one eye on Beth's door, as I could hear her and Barney whispering and giggling inside. Then I went into Arthur's. He and Rita were playing what looked like a fairly intense game of Scrabble; she sat cross-legged on the comforter, hunched over the board, while he was kneeling on the floor, his elbows propped up on the edge of the bed.

"Yes, Luke," he croaked, not taking his eyes off the board. "Man, I'm fucking feeling it this morning. We should *not* have done those last Jägerbombs."

"'Gherkin,'" said Rita cheerfully, laying down some tiles. "Fourteen, plus a double-letter score on the 'K,' so that's ... nineteen. Quite pleased with that. Hey, Luke."

"Hey, Rita." I sat down on Arthur's wheelie chair. "'Gherkin.' Good work."

"Thanks. Your turn, Arth."

Arthur exhaled slowly and pinched the bridge of his nose. "Erm ... What words are there? I feel like I've forgotten all the words." He turned to me. "What are some words, Luke?"

Rita smiled at him like a nurse might smile at a patient. "You've got an 'S' there, Watling. Just do 'gherkins.'"

Arthur nodded and laid the "S" down. "'Gherkins.' Genius. This game is really fucking difficult when you're hungover."

"I'm quite enjoying it," Rita said. "It's like I'm playing against myself."

"You got your outfit for tonight?" Arthur asked me, shaking out a new tile from the bag.

"Yeah," I said. "Well, I just printed out a thumbs-up in the computer room. Gonna glue it to a white T-shirt."

"Classic." Arthur smirked. "You've really pulled out all the stops there."

"What are you going as, then?"

"Oh, you'll see, my friend. I've got this emoji thing locked down, trust me."

"What time are we pregaming, then?" I yawned.

Arthur snorted. "We can have our own pregame in here. The chemists are being boring as fuck, as usual. And I haven't seen Beth or Barney all day."

"I think Beth and Barney are shagging each other, actually," I said. "I forgot to tell you, I saw him coming out of her room on the first night."

Arthur spun around to look at me. "Fuck, you're kidding. I'm surprised he hasn't stuck a Post-it on her."

Rita threw a tile at his face. "Oi. You misogynist idiot."

Arthur took his cap off and ran a hand through his scraggly hair. "I definitely need a Twix after that bombshell. Who's going to the machine? I nominate Luke."

"You can't nominate me." I stood up, stretching my arms out painfully. "I've got to go to soccer tryouts."

"What, seriously?" Arthur looked appalled. "Can't they postpone that? It's Frosh Week. You can't make people exercise when they're hungover. It's a human rights violation."

"Yeah, well. It'll probably make me feel better in the long run."

"I highly doubt that," Arthur muttered.

Rita laid some tiles on the board, and he squinted down at them. "'Can't'? You can't have 'can't,' Reets! Even I know that. Where's your apostrophe? There's no apostrophe!"

"It's 'cant.'" Rita laughed. "It means, like, 'hypocritical bullshit.'"

"*This* is hypocritical bullshit," he huffed. "You can't just make words up."

Rita climbed off the bed and patted him on the shoulder. "All right, Watling. You Google 'cant' and I'll go and get us both a Twix, shall I?"

Arthur jumped up and hugged her tightly. "Maurita, I love you, man. You are literally the greatest person that's ever lived. Have I ever told you that?"

"Yes," Rita said. "Yes, you have. Now, give me some change for the machine."

Me and Rita stepped out of B Dorm into the mid-morning breeze. "How you finding Frosh Week, then, Luke?" she asked as we trooped along the covered walkway toward the vending machines.

"Yeah . . . It's good. I mean, it's pretty . . . crazy. But good. I dunno. How was your orientation?"

"Not great, to be honest," she said. "It's, like, there's so much pressure to have fun that you can't really . . . have fun. You know?" I nodded. "Plus, I was breaking up with my boyfriend," she added. "That was pretty grim."

Something I had learned about Rita over the past few days was that she didn't really do small talk. She came out with big, meaningful, surprisingly honest statements in the same way most people came out with comments about the weather. It made me really like her.

"Was he at York Met, too?" I asked. "Your boyfriend?"

"No, Jack's at Edinburgh. We both went off to college thinking it would be OK long distance, and then three days into Frosh Week he just called me and said it wasn't going to work."

"Shit, really?"

"Yeah." We got to the vending machine, and she started feeding a bill into the slot. "I mean, it's fine. And it's definitely for the best that it happened. He was actually a bit of a dick, to be honest. He used to wear a newsboy cap. And you can't really get away with that unless you're a farmer or a 1920s gangster."

"And he wasn't either?"

"Unfortunately not, no. So, yeah . . . I guess my memories of Frosh Week aren't that great on the whole. I mean, it's good that you're having fun and everything, but it does get better than this, trust me. Contrary to popular belief, this is *not* the best bit of college."

She smiled at me as the Twix bars spiraled off the shelf and clattered noisily into the machine's belly. For a split second, I considered telling her about Abbey. Just spilling everything that had happened from the day we received our exam results to right now, and asking her what she thought. I wanted to talk to someone about it so badly.

73

But if I couldn't get it straight in my own head, how was I supposed to explain it to anyone else? The truth was, I didn't know how to describe it without it sounding like I was the bad guy. Like I'd ruined Abbey's life. Which seemed to pretty much confirm that I *was* the bad guy. That I *had* ruined her life.

We said goodbye and I headed over to tryouts. The fields were all the way across campus, so I followed the covered walkway right around the edge of the lake, exchanging nods with people I vaguely recognized from drunken nights out. The grass was still shimmering with dew and the ducks were out in full force, quacking their heads off. It was bitterly cold, but the sun was glaring down in the bluish-white sky, making my hangover scratch angrily at my temples.

All the soccer bros greeted me enthusiastically, even when I told them I might genuinely throw up at any minute. "Don't worry, mate, we're all suffering," said one guy named Toby. "I haven't slept in four days."

The captain—a posh, floppy-haired guy named Will—gathered everyone together in the middle of the field. "All right, boys. Thanks for coming. I know it's not easy during Frosh Week. But we're just going to do a few drills and play a quick match—just take it easy and have a laugh, basically."

I'd seen Will before—most nights this week, actually—in various clubs, usually hooking up with Phoebe on the dance floor. I'd tried to go and chat with her a couple of times—mainly to apologize for bailing on quidditch—but she'd either been surrounded by people or attached at the lips to Will. It seemed weird to me that we hadn't even spoken since the Orientation Fair.

Will carried on: "Anyway, if you make the cut, we'll have initiations in the next couple of weeks, so be afraid. . . ."

A junior named Dempers, who was short, stocky and red-faced, added, "Be very, *very* fucking afraid."

An uneasy laugh rumbled around the first years, but Will just waved it away. "He's fucking with you, don't worry. We're not *that* bad."

In the end, tryouts were actually quite fun. My team lost the match—due largely to having Toby as the goalie—but I still scored twice, and I could tell I'd done OK by the way Will and a few of the others thumped me on the back as we left the field. For the first time all week, I actually felt happy and vaguely in control. Soccer's always had this weird effect of blocking everything else out; giving me something real and physical to focus on that means I literally can't focus on all the other shit swirling about in my head. At the end of a game, I feel battered and sore and tired, but I also feel *better*. Like I've been rebooted or something.

As we were all stumbling back to the changing rooms, I got caught behind Will and Dempers and a couple of the other guys who were huddled around Will's phone.

"Mate, have you seen the wall today?" Dempers was whispering excitedly.

"Classic Wicks," laughed Will.

"She was seriously fucking hot, actually," said another guy.

They suddenly realized I was behind them, and Will dipped the phone back into his pocket and grinned at me. "Good game, Luke, mate. See you tonight, yeah?"

6

● ● ● ● ● ● **PHOEBE** ● ● ● ● ● ●

"You look amazing." She really did; I couldn't stop staring at her. Liberty had really gone for it in the sexy cherub department. She was wearing Kawaii-type frilly white hot pants, white over-the-knee socks, a white tank top and giant white feathery wings. Unbelievably, she still seemed to have copious amounts of glitter left, and had lathered herself in it head to toe, which gave her a slightly oily, celestial sheen. She had brought her curling iron into my room and was doing her white-blond hair in ringlets. Negin was meticulously drawing whiskers onto Frankie's face and Becky was wrapping giant pieces of brown fur around her ankles.

"I don't think I look like a monkey." Becky jabbed a giant safety pin through some fur. "I look like a shire horse, if anything."

"No, but do the shy face," Frankie shouted. Becky put her brown furry hands over her monkey-painted eyes. Frankie burst out laughing. "Let me take another picture—honestly, it's amazing."

Negin had threaded her corn through some string and was wearing it around her neck. "I look like someone from the Depression."

"They would have eaten their corn, not fashioned it into a necklace," I said.

"I played Lennie in *Of Mice and Men* once!" Frankie screamed, putting her hand up like she was in a lesson. "Just saying." And she started shouting the word "alfalfa" again and again in a strange American accent.

"What *is* alfalfa?" Negin asked.

"No one knows; it's one of the great mysteries of the book," Frankie replied, still in character.

I looked at myself in the mirror. Negin had done a good job of my mousie whiskers—I just had to remember not to rub my face and smear them everywhere.

I was wearing jeans and a white tank top, and I had threaded a Babybel cheese through some of Negin's string and hung it round my neck. I adjusted my ears. I wasn't gonna stop traffic with a runway entrance like Liberty, but I felt good.

"My ears keep getting lost in my hair," I said.

"I like it. Your mouse is very Pre-Raphaelite." Frankie started making the plastic turtle walk along the floor.

"I was going to cut all my hair off before college," I told her. "But the hairdresser said cutting it would make it lighter and it would stick out sideways."

"I think that would look cool," Negin said. "I cut mine the week before I came." She got out her phone and showed us a picture of her with stick-straight, waist-length black hair.

"You look *so* different," we all chimed. She did.

"Do you think Bowl-Cut Girl did all the colors right before she came here?" I asked.

"I think she was born like that." Frankie shrugged. "I think she came out of her mum with a rainbow bowl cut. I *must* find out her name."

"I heard it was Persephone." Liberty had still only curled one tiny bit of hair.

"You said it was Ariel," Negin said to Frankie.

"Yeah, but I think that's just because she reminds me of a mermaid, and I got confused." Frankie was throwing the turtle in the air and catching it.

"Persephone is a cool name. It probably is that." I gave up trying to flatten my hair around the ears.

Becky's phone flashed, and she smiled at us apologetically. "Sorry, it's Aaron. Won't be a second."

She picked up her monkey tail and walked out.

"Becky and Aaron are one hundred percent goals," Frankie sighed. "You know he sent her flowers on the first day. They were literally at the check-in desk when she arrived."

"Ah, that's lovely." Liberty sighed. "The most romantic thing my ex ever did was piss my name in the snow."

Frankie shrieked with laughter, then added: "That's actually quite impressive, to be fair. You *have* got a long name."

We trooped out into the kitchen, where the boys were already assembled, drinking. All of them had painted their faces with thick yellow paint, and Negin had drawn various emoji expressions on each of them with black eyeliner.

Connor was wearing a top hat and a fake mustache and

seemed even more excited than usual. When Liberty started rinsing the mixing bowl to make the punch, he stopped her.

"Got a better idea!" he shouted. "To the bathroom!" He picked up a bag of bottles and a tub of Nesquik and charged off.

We all squeezed in to see Connor perched with one foot on either side of the bath, simultaneously pouring out a bottle of wine and a bottle of tequila. "We can turn this into a *giant* punch bowl!" he said.

I saw Negin wrinkle her nose slightly. The bath was absolutely *disgusting*. There was a dark-gray soap scum ring around the top and some long black hairs drooping off one of the taps. Even after Connor had poured in everyone else's contributions, plus two liters of Coke, a bottle of grape juice and the powdered Nesquik, the liquid inside barely covered the bottom of the tub. It looked like grainy, purple hand soap with a weird, shiny film across the top.

Connor scooped a glass into it and handed it to Negin.

"I don't drink," she reminded him politely.

"Oh, yeah, 'course," said Connor. "So is that, like, a religious thing, then?"

She shrugged. "In this case, it's more a not-wanting-to-get-gastroenteritis thing."

Connor chugged the glass himself. Then he leaped into the bath and lay down, knocking his frilly shower cap off in the process. "Come on, team!" he yelled. "Bath of booze!"

Josh came in wearing a donut pool floatie around his middle and his normal jeans and T-shirt. He looked at Connor. "That might not be totally cool with health and safety, but whatever. It's the last night of Frosh Week."

"Last night of Frosh Week!" Connor bellowed.

"Right," said Josh, "quick round of Never Have I Ever and then head to the bar."

We all went back into the kitchen and started arranging the chairs into a massive circle around the table, and I noticed Connor, still dripping with bath booze, position himself next to Liberty with one deft move.

"Guys, before we start, I just want to say thanks so much for adopting me," Frankie announced. "Honestly, I actually feel emosh. I love the old people because obviously, they share their prosciutto and cheese plates with me. But you guys *actually* saved me."

"You're an honorary D-Dormie," Josh said. "So you can start the game."

I looked around the table. I had been really lucky; everyone was so nice. Even people like Phillip and Nathan, who never got that involved, were here. We had formed a random but solid little group.

"I have never felt attracted to anyone in this circle," Frankie said proudly.

A murmur rippled around. Connor, Liberty and Josh all drank.

"Do you know by the time you leave college there is an eighty percent chance that the phone number of the person you are going to marry is in your phone?" Frankie nodded exaggeratedly as she said it.

"Have you got Will's number in your phone yet? That's the question!" As Liberty screamed it, everyone made cooing noises at me.

Will and me had somehow become a *thing*. I got nervous

when I saw him walk into a room, and giddy when he smiled at me. So far, in the realm of boys, college was definitely delivering.

"I read that, too, about the phone numbers," Negin said. "I'd like to see the evidence."

Frankie put her hand up again. "My parents met in college."

"It's just more stress," I said. "By junior year we'll all be scrolling through our phones hysterically."

"I have never puked in the shower," Connor bellowed, and then stared at Liberty.

"It wasn't *me*," she wailed, and pulled her angel wings around to cover her face.

"I have never had sex outside," Josh said, and took a big sip of beer.

You had to be so on your guard in these games, come across as grown-up and experienced and fun. I didn't really care, but for people who were really private—like Becky—it must feel like torture. I suddenly wondered if that was why she was still in her room.

Things progressed until there was no punch left in the bath, so Connor pulled a quarter-full bottle of vodka out of the cupboard.

"We need to go soon," Josh said. "Last round."

"I have never jerked off!" Connor shouted, and burst out laughing.

All the boys drank. Every single one. Even Nathan and Phillip. They all did. None of them looked the remotest bit shy, not like they had with some of the sex questions. I felt my face go ever-so-slightly red and I stared down at my glass. I glanced sideways to look at Frankie, but she was just talking to Negin as if neither of them had really heard. Liberty giggled to herself but kept her glass in her hand. I felt like between the girls it was suddenly awkward, even if between the boys everything had gotten more jovial. *Jerking off.* Even the phrase is a boy word. Boys *jerk off.* Maybe none of the girls drank because they didn't even associate the words with themselves.

For a second I thought about drinking, but I wasn't brave enough. Even Liberty the sexy cherub wasn't brave enough. It's weird how so many things in the world are unsaid.

Connor didn't notice. He turned the empty bottle upside down. "Let's go," he shouted.

●　●　●　●　●　●　　**LUKE**　●　●　●　●　●　●

Arthur opened his closet to pull out what appeared to be a large, puffy brown dress, held up by brown suspenders. Then he twirled it around and I saw the dress had two big googly eyes painted on it.

"It's the pile of poo!" he said cheerfully.

"Yeah, I can see that," I said. "Are you really wearing that?"

He downed the dregs of his lager and chucked the can at the trash, missing by a fair distance. "Yeah," he said. "I wore it last year, too."

"I thought you said you got off with three girls at the emoji party last year?"

"I did."

"What, dressed as a massive turd?"

"Yeah."

"Impressive."

82

"Thanks. Who knows? I might even beat that this year."

"What, really?" I said, genuinely surprised. "I thought you were . . . You know? You and Rita?"

Arthur laughed. "I wish." And then his grin dissolved for a second, and he blinked down at his shoes. "I mean, I *do* wish a bit." He caught himself and snapped straight back into joking mode. "But anyway . . . Come on, let's get going!"

We rounded up our suite mates from where they were pre-gaming in the kitchen and headed down to the bar. Beth had glued a hockey stick emoji to her sweatshirt, Barney was wearing a wink-smiley beanie and the chemists all had specially made T-shirts featuring the cry-laughing emoji in protective science goggles.

The bar looked easily the craziest it had all week. Everywhere you turned there were ballerinas doing shots, giant bunches of grapes dancing and tons of people wearing those big ball-shaped lightshades on their heads, sloppily painted yellow with random emoji faces.

Arthur spotted his sophomore friends Dan and Hassan at the bar, so we headed over. As I ordered some beers, I felt a damp plop on my right shoulder and looked down to see that a clump of stringy spaghetti had fallen on me.

"I'll have a pint and a shot, freshman," said Will, picking the pasta off my shoulder and putting it back into the plastic bowl he had strapped to the top of his head.

"Pasta emoji," I said. "Like it. Very niche."

"Thanks, mate. I thought so." He thumped my shoulder and leaned in. "Listen, we're not officially sending emails till next week, but I might as well tell you now. You made the team."

"I feel like they are having a heart-to-heart." Frankie took a sip of her drink. "Will keeps touching Luke Taylor meaningfully." We were all just standing in a row on the dance floor, watching them. Frankie grabbed my cheese necklace, pulled me toward her and stared into my eyes.

"Touching him meaningfully," Negin repeated, and shook her head.

"I know, when he's supposed to be doing that to Phoebe." Frankie burst out laughing at her own joke and sprayed me and Negin with Skyy Blue.

"Stop staring. Can we all go and dance or just do something else?" I pleaded.

Negin and Frankie ignored this and continued looking at them, so I did, too.

"Your greatest love sprung from your greatest hate." Frankie put her arm around me.

"Will hasn't sprung from him," I said. "And I don't hate Luke."

"Are you saying you *love* Will?" Frankie took another sip with her arm still around me, putting me in a kind of headlock.

"Will is obviously trying to pump Luke Taylor for information about you," she boomed.

"Luke Taylor doesn't *know* anything about me."

Frankie ignored this completely. She put her hand to her ear like she was reporting live. "Now Luke is saying, 'The biggest mistake I ever made in my life was bailing on quidditch. I just couldn't face Phoebe's beauty. I was intimidated. I was a pathetic excuse for a man. But now my heart burns for her. It yearns for her. I would literally die for her. She is my first, my last, my *everything*.' "

I stifled a giggle, but Negin frowned. "Bit creepy."

Frankie squeezed my shoulder hard. "Oh my god, and that hand movement Luke's doing now, see that? That means, 'I will fight you to the death for her, Will.' That basically means, 'Meet me by the vending machines at dawn, bring a pistol and the victor shall have Phoebe's heart.' "

"What, are they going to *eat* her?" Negin said.

I was laughing so hard I could barely hold my drink. "Stop!" I yelled. "They're gonna see us looking."

Frankie was still in full flow. "Now Luke Taylor is saying that Phoebe makes him insane with love. He is saying he would eat his own face just to be close to her."

This sobered me up a little. "Funny how he never indicated that all through school, and he probably still has a long-term girlfriend he is madly in love with."

Frankie unwrapped her arm from my shoulder and looked at me. "If you had to marry Will or Luke Taylor Quidditch Bailer right here, right now, or you'd be put to death, who would you marry?" She held her bottle up to my mouth like a microphone.

"Will," I said. "Obviously, Will. Because I really like him and he actually fancies me and he is actually really, really nice."

● ● ● ● ● ● ●   **LUKE**   ● ● ● ● ● ● ●

"Honestly, mate, fucking good effort today," Will said. "Not that many frosh get straight into first string."

He handed me a shot, and we clinked glasses and drank.

"Thanks," I gasped, just about managing to keep the minty vodka down.

I had to to concentrate fairly hard on not throwing up, and my right shoulder was totally heavy with spaghetti, but I still felt amazing. Even Reece hadn't managed to get straight onto the team at Nottingham.

"Oi, mate!" Will called to the bartender. "Two more, yeah?"

He passed me a beer, and I paid. "So, where are you from, then?" he asked, taking a sip.

"Kingston," I said. "What about you?"

"London, mate. Fulham. I swear we're pretty much the only Londoners in this whole university. It's fucking wall-to-wall northerners up here."

"Well, we are in the north, to be fair."

He shrugged, like the idea had just occurred to him. "So, what you studying?"

"English."

"Oh, mate!" He took a big swig of his beer, landing a massive dollop of spaghetti onto the bar behind him. "Fucking good ratio. So many girls do English. You'll be totally surrounded by girls in class, trust me."

"Oh, OK. Right. What are you doing?"

He frowned and wrinkled his brow. "Politics and Economics. My dad's choice. And he's paying for all this, so . . ." He swept his hands about grandly, as if "all this" literally meant the Jutland Bar. "Still," he carried on, "at least I'll get a decent job after school. Unlike you, who'll be stuck in a dumpster, writing poems."

"That's the dream," I sighed. "Although you don't walk straight into a gig like that. I'll probably have to intern in the dumpster for a few months."

He laughed and finished his beer just as Dempers came bustling over, looking even more sweaty and red-faced than usual. He was wearing a pretty horrendous gold T-shirt with a bright-green dollar sign scribbled on it; maybe the only person here who'd made less of an effort than me. A couple of the other juniors from tryouts were with him, and he introduced them as "The Ox" and "Geordie Al." They were both dressed in tiny black leotards, which was particularly distressing in the case of Geordie Al, whose thick, wiry body hair was poking out from every available corner.

He laid a furry hand on Will's shoulder. "Mate, when I said we need to find some first years tonight, this wasn't exactly who I had in mind."

Will laughed. "Chill out, I was just telling Taylor he made the team."

Al clinked his beer glass against mine. "Nice one, mate. Now if you'll excuse me, I'm off to locate some frosh of the *opposite* gender."

"As if you're getting anything tonight dressed like that," Dempers said, smirking. Al shrugged and smoothed his leotard down. "It's a conversation starter, innit?"

"You shouldn't need a conversation starter on the last night of Frosh Week," Will murmured, scanning the dance floor. "It's always mayhem."

Dempers nodded. "If you can't get some on the last night, you might as well chop it off."

"Oh, really?" Will pointed his chin toward the dance floor. "On you go, then, Dempsey . . ."

Dempers rolled his eyes. "All right, watch." He huffed off, and as we watched him go I spotted Phoebe and her mates by the speakers, all three of them staring straight at us. They saw me looking, and suddenly Phoebe's tall blond friend was doing a weird kind of robotic chicken move and the other two followed suit, dancing. I decided right then that at some point tonight, I'd finally go over and say sorry to Phoebe. End the awkwardness.

"What you doing this evening, then, Taylor?" Will asked. "Any hotties down your floor?"

"Erm . . . not really, no."

"Well, come on, then," he said, scanning the bar again. "Who d'you want introducing to?"

Geordie Al whacked him on the back, spilling more pasta everywhere. "Barnes has got himself paired off, so now he's trying to match up everyone else. What a fucking legend. What a gent."

Will shrugged modestly. "I'm not *definitely* taken. . . ."

"You've got with her pretty much every night this week," said The Ox, and I suddenly knew who they were talking about.

"She's hot." Geordie Al shrugged. "Hair's a bit crazy, but still. Hot." I wondered if I should tell them I knew her, too.

"Yeah, well, we'll see what happens," said Will. Then he turned back to me. "But come on, Taylor. You're a first year, for fuck's sake. You can't *not* get laid this week. That's, like, illegal."

"Ah yeah. Well, the thing is . . . I've sort of got a girlfriend."

It came out of nowhere, like a reflex. I wasn't even sure why I said it. But the thought of Abbey had the instant effect of sobering me up slightly.

Will nodded wisely. "'Sort of' being the operative phrase, there. Can't see that lasting long first semester, man, no offense. I had a girl when I started last year, too. That lasted all

88

of about four hours." He laughed loudly, then finished his beer and slammed it back down onto the bar. "Thanks for the drinks, anyway. We'll email about initiations and stuff next week."

Geordie Al leaned into me and started a long monologue about some drinking game he'd just played, as I watched Will walk right onto the dance floor, right over to Phoebe.

7

● ● ● ● ● ● ● **PHOEBE** ● ● ● ● ● ●

Will turned his key in the lock. He pushed open the door and felt for my hand as we walked in.

"OK, there's no bulb in the hall and a lot of crap, so go slowly."

I reached my other hand out and tried to feel for the wall but felt bike handlebars instead. The floor felt uneven underneath my feet and I kept stepping on random shoes.

"OK." He let go of my hand and patted the wall for the switch, and we both blinked as the living room lit up.

On one side it had a depressed-looking little red sofa that was missing one of its cushion covers. Opposite it was a wall with three bikes stacked up against each other. Various pieces of soccer equipment and some T-shirts randomly hung off them. Behind the bikes, the wall was covered in some sort of fantasy-soccer scoring system that had notes written in green marker with points next to names. Josh and Will were up there and then "Pete" and "Lolly." I think I had met Lolly—he had a strong Northern Irish accent and had started a conga line around the dance floor earlier. The apartment smelled strongly of rotting fruit.

There had obviously been some pretty heavy drinking going on, as the whole of the living room floor was covered in empty beer cans. There were also four Styrofoam boxes lined up by the sofa, some still with kebab and the remnants of fries. The carpet was covered in so much pasta that it was unbelievable there had been any left for him to wear on his head. He shrugged. "This house is disgusting. My mum won't even come in. She just waits in the car." He didn't seem embarrassed or anything.

"OK." He smiled at me. "Now I'm going to prove to you that I wasn't bullshitting about the midnight feast. Do you want a cup of tea?"

I nodded, and he disappeared into the kitchen. Usually, I go for intense, creative types. Well, I think the main reason I liked Adam was 'cause he was in a band for about seven minutes in tenth grade, and Max's final art piece was a painting of a girl with a tear on her cheek and I thought it meant he was deep and understood women. I suppose Luke Taylor doesn't really fit the troubled-thinker mold. But then, did I even actually like Luke Taylor, except to look at?

Will was just hot. No one could look at him and say he was unattractive. You could say you weren't into posh boys with floppy hair and perfect teeth and canvas shoes, but you couldn't say he wasn't hot.

The more I got to know him the hotter he was getting, too. Over the course of the week, Will had gone from random hookup to my kind of steady person. It would feel weird now to get with anyone else. We were in a weeklong exclusive thing. Well, in my head we were.

I pushed the various games controllers and some track pants out of the way and sat down on the sofa. The night had passed really quickly. As soon as Will had come over, pasta flying everywhere, everything had gotten more fun. He was one of those people who everyone seemed to know and everyone seemed to love. He didn't care about making a fool of himself. He danced to cheesy songs, and at the end got in a line with me and Liberty and Frankie and Negin and did the Macarena. And every so often we would make our way to the edge of the dance floor, and he would tuck my hair behind my ears and cup my face in his hands and start kissing me.

At one point, we were by the bar and they played "Jump Around." He grabbed me and started bouncing me around and then picked me up and kind of carried me to a space so we could keep dancing a weird kind of polka together. And I just couldn't stop laughing. Boys who make you laugh are everything.

I had made the decision then that I wanted to go home with him. Because why not? I was at college; it was the last night of freshman orientation. I'd never had a one-night stand. And it wouldn't even *be* a one-night stand. And who cares if it was anyway? Isn't the whole point that you're allowed to do what you want?

Will reappeared, holding a white box in one hand and two mugs in the other. "We've got no plates and no cutlery so we'll just have to eat it with our hands." He handed me a mug half filled with clear brown liquid. "We've got no milk, either—sorry."

"I actually dread to think what that kitchen looks like," I said, smiling.

"It's best that you never, ever go in there. We try to go in there as little as possible, to be honest."

He sat down next to me, on top of a heap of crap. He rested the box on his lap and started to open the sides gently.

"I feel like there's a kitten in there or something. You are being really careful."

He pushed the lid back to reveal four perfectly formed little cakes. There was a fox, a hedgehog, a mouse and a badger, all carved delicately out of marzipan.

"Wow. We can't eat them, they're works of art. They don't even belong in this house, no offense. Did you buy them?"

Will laughed. "Hell no. Josh works at Bettys in town. He gets, like, untold amounts of cake."

"If this is part of the job, I hope he really *can* get me in there, like he said he could."

"Is he actually doing that?"

"Well, he's landed me a training shift next week, so as long as I don't suck, hopefully I'll get it, yeah. Are you sure he won't mind us eating these?"

Will shook his head. "He's probably already eaten about twenty-five of them this week."

I carefully picked up the badger.

"I knew you'd go for the badger."

"How?"

"I don't know. Because it's the weirdest one."

"Oh right. Saying I'm weird, are you?" I leaned sideways and bumped him with my shoulder.

"No, I'm saying you're awesome." He smiled at me, and reached down and picked up the hedgehog.

"What does the hedgehog say about you?" I said.

"That I'm a pig. It's the biggest one."

"Oh my god, it's so nice inside—it's full of cream."

He nodded, and we both sat, just eating. And then the atmosphere changed that tiny bit. Like we both knew that we couldn't just sit there eating baked goods forever. They weren't really the main event; they were the reason we both latched onto so we could come here. Obviously, neither of us thought I was going to get up and leave after tea and cake. But it would feel random to just start kissing on the lumpy sofa. For the first time I felt nervous, because it was almost getting awkward; I just wanted it to be the next bit.

And then it was.

He leaned over and kissed me, and then we were kissing on the sofa for ages.

"OK," he whispered. "So my bedroom's through the kitchen. I don't want you to faint before we get there, so let's just run through with the lights off."

I started to laugh, and he jumped up and grabbed my hand and started to actually run, dragging me along with him through the dark kitchen and into his room. We fell with force in a heap on the bed and started kissing again, even though we were both still laughing. But we kissed our way out of the laughter.

I find moving from stage to stage really weird. He was on top of me but we were both still fully dressed. Which one of us was going to instigate getting undressed? I pushed him away gently and took my top off and then reached over and half helped him get his T-shirt off, too. Our skin was against each other. His chest felt kind of hard. More built than anyone I had ever been with, for sure. I knew he wouldn't be able to take my bra off, so I reached behind my back and unhooked it. We kept kissing and kissing, and then he reached down and tried to unbutton my jeans. I did it for him and wiggled out of them. I was naked except for my underwear. It was pitch-black, so he wouldn't even see the bright-blue lace set I had worn, just in case.

"Do you want to?" he whispered.

I kissed him and said yes, and he took his jeans off. And then my health teacher, Miss Hay, popped into my head.

I wonder how many people's heads Miss Hay has popped into just before they have sex. Miss Hay and her penis facts: "Any time you are naked near a penis, sperm can go astray and just get in you and impregnate you." Any time. It can go on his hands and then on your hands and then just end up in there. It can be on the bed and just swim up you. Miss Hay and her terrifying penis knowledge designed to ambush you just when you were supposed to be focusing on something else.

We started kissing again, and he reached down and put his hand inside my underwear, and then suddenly he just stopped and moved away. Neither of us spoke for about five seconds.

"I'm so sorry," he said through the darkness.

I wasn't sure what was going on. I was glad it was dark because it suddenly felt truly, horribly awkward. "Why?" I whispered.

"I shouldn't have drunk so much."

I had absolutely no idea what he was talking about, and the silence just permeated the darkness. Did he expect me to say something?

"We might have to wait," he murmured. "Until I'm a bit less drunk."

And then I felt awful for not realizing what he had been trying to say. I panicked. I wanted to make it better but I didn't know what to do. I crept across the bed and put my arms around his neck and kissed it.

"Honestly, it doesn't matter at all." I tried to make it sound really offhand, but in the silence it didn't feel like that.

We lay back on the bed next to each other and I wondered if it *was* because he had drunk too much. Maybe it was because he wasn't that hot for me? I pulled the covers up over me. I suddenly felt self-conscious about it. Like I might have caused it. I wanted to text Flora. Or Google it. My phone was in my bag in the living room. I hadn't even texted the girls to confirm I wasn't dead. The house still felt empty. We hadn't heard anyone come in.

I could tell from the way Will's body relaxed next to me that he had fallen asleep.

● ● ● ● ● ● **LUKE** ● ● ● ● ● ●

Arthur was either out, or passed out. He wasn't opening his door, anyway. I messaged him and he messaged straight back:

IN TOWN WITH REETS. MY ROOM'S OPEN IF U WANNA PLAY XBOX. HELP YOURSELF TO FRITOS ON THE BED.

I went into the kitchen, where the remains of last night's emoji pregame cans were still scattered across most surfaces. Rosie, Tom and Nishant were stirring a massive pot on the stove and having a lively conversation about something called "covalent bonding." They broke off when I came in and smiled at me.

"Hey, Luke," said Tom.

"Hey. You guys all right?"

"Yeah."

"What you making?"

"Well, it was supposed to be tuna mayo pasta," said Nishant. "But Tom forgot to buy the tuna . . ."

"And the mayonnaise . . . ," Rosie added.

"So, basically, it's my specialty . . . Extremely Dry Pasta," Tom said.

Rosie rolled her eyes and smiled at him. "That Jamie Oliver book your mum bought you is really coming in handy, isn't it?"

They all laughed. It was crazy to think they'd only known each other six days. They were already like a little family.

"Are you all starting labs tomorrow, then?" I asked them.

Tom nodded, and Rosie said, "Do your classes start tomorrow, too?"

"Yep. Should do some reading for them, really."

A silence descended, which Nishant burst by reigniting the covalent bonding conversation. It felt a bit awkward to shuffle around them, cooking my own dinner, so I just made some toast and took it back to my room. I found Barney out in the hall, knocking on Arthur's door.

"Just tried it," I said. "He's out."

"Oh right." Barney stiffened slightly. "It's just that I had some Fritos, but I can't seem to find them at the moment. I was wondering if Arthur . . . knew anything about that."

"I'll ask him when I see him."

"Thanks, Luke. I'll be in Beth's room." He cleared his throat. "Studying."

"OK, cool."

I sat on my bed and ate my toast and wondered if I was the

only person on campus currently all alone. Beth was with Barney, Arthur with Rita, the chemists with the chemists, everyone with someone else.

Orientation Week was basically over, and what did I have to show for it, except a series of increasingly bad hangovers? The only truly enjoyable bits had been playing soccer and making sure Stephanie Stevens didn't die. I hadn't really made any friends. Not real ones, anyway. Dad had met Ryan—my godfather—on his first night at Manchester. Reece was constantly posting crazy pictures of all his new friends at Nottingham. Was it bad luck or was it just . . . me?

I chewed my toast and tried to convince myself that it was just because soccer hadn't really started yet. Soccer was how I'd meet people. It was how I'd always met people. Or maybe I'd meet them in classes and lectures. But it was like the terror of not making friends was stopping me from actually making friends. Like, how can you relax and be yourself when you're constantly wondering if every conversation might be the beginning of a life-long friendship?

I finished my toast and started reading the first chapter of *Modern Romantic Poetry* for tomorrow's class. And then, after about three paragraphs, I gave up and watched *Rick and Morty* on Netflix.

When I went back into the kitchen an hour or so later, the chemists had relocated to Tom's room to eat their dinner, and Arthur was there instead, unwrapping something on the counter.

"Where d'you get to?" I sniffed the air. "And what the fuck is that smell?"

He turned around, his eyes sparkling with excitement. "I have found the bargain of the century here, man. I mean, literally, the supermarket Holy Grail. Only fifty quid . . . for this."

He stepped aside flamboyantly to reveal a massive wheel of Brie, about the size and thickness of a car tire. It was wrapped tightly in plastic wrap, but it still absolutely reeked.

"Didn't they have any edible stuff?" I said, pinching my nose.

He ignored this question and patted the cheese proudly. "Look at the fucking size of it! I'll literally be able to live off this beast all semester. I won't have to spend another penny on food."

"You can't just eat Brie for ten weeks, Arthur."

He raised an eyebrow. "That sounds like a challenge, Luke."

"It's not a challenge. You'd die. Probably. Plus, won't it go bad at some point?"

Arthur snorted. "Cheese can't go bad, Luke. It's already spoiled. That's the great thing about cheese. I could literally still be eating this in 2050. My kids could be eating this."

I opened all the windows as wide as they'd go while Arthur tried to jam the monstrous cheese into the fridge. But it was way too big. So he chopped it into six smaller, smellier chunks, then labeled each one with a Post-it. "Don't want Barney getting any ideas," he muttered. "This is definitely not communal."

He straightened up and dusted his hands off. "Right, that's that handled. I'll see you in a bit. Going out to meet Dan and Hassan and that."

"Oh, OK." I nodded. "Cool."

He stopped in the doorway. "Do you want to come?"

I shook my head. "Nah, thanks, though. I need to be up early for this safety presentation thing anyway."

"Oh yeah. I remember that from last year. Massively boring. Bring a book or something. Anyway, see you later, man."

I went and sat on my bed again and stared lamely at the wall as I listened to the muffled chatter wafting across the hall from Tom's room.

I thought about calling Reece but decided against it. When have I ever called Reece just "to talk"? Then, suddenly, without realizing it, my finger was hovering over Abbey's number. For some reason, I wanted to hear her voice so badly. To talk to someone who actually knew me, who actually cared about me.

Before I could make the decision, though, my phone exploded into life on its own.

I answered. "Hey, Will, what's up?"

"Hey, how are you?" he said. "You at home?"

"Yeah, just finished dinner. Why?"

"I had to come to campus to hand something in. Just wondered if you wanted a beer. They'll have *Match of the Day 2* on in the bar."

"Yeah. Sounds good."

A few minutes later I was down in the bar, which was by far the most deserted it had been all week. Will brought two bottles of beer over to our table, then flopped down dramatically into his chair.

"Fuck, man." He took a long swig from his bottle and wiped his lips. "Hungover essay-writing. Never, ever fun." He swept a hand through his hair. "I miss being a freshman. No pressure. Except to get fucked up every night."

I picked a sticky piece of spaghetti off the chair next to me. "They're going to be cleaning up after you all year in here."

He laughed. "I might make the pasta a regular thing. No matter how wasted I get, I'll still be able to tell where I've been."

"Did you have a good night last night, then?" I asked. I'd watched him leave around one a.m. with his arm draped around Phoebe's shoulders.

He raised his eyebrows and grinned. "Yeah. Good, mate. *Very* good." He picked carefully at the label on his beer bottle and left it at that.

"So how's your suite, then?" he said.

"Yeah, they're all right. I don't have that much in common with them, to be honest."

"Translation: they're boring geeks." He laughed, and I laughed along with him.

"No, no, they're nice," I said. "We're just not that similar, I guess. I dunno. I mean, it's just luck who you end up in a dorm with, isn't it? Some people get lucky, some people don't."

Which was about as close to "I'm fucking lonely here and I don't know what to do" as I could manage.

But it was almost like Will got what I meant. His smile dropped and he scratched harder at his beer label. "Yeah, well . . . You're on the team now, man," he said, not quite looking at me. "I mean, you've got us, haven't you?"

I nodded and smiled, as if that made me feel better. Then I realized it actually did.

Will's phone buzzed and he checked it, snorting a laugh at whatever had just come through. He dropped it back onto the table and stood up. "Just going for a piss."

I watched him walk off, then stared down at his phone, which was just lying there, unlocked on the table. In the split second before the screen went dark I caught a glimpse of a photo—what looked like a girl's face, asleep on a pillow.

I went to pick up the phone but it had already locked. So I just sat there, sipping my beer and watching the soccer flicker silently on the massive TV.

8

Frankie looked like a medieval king, her comforter dragging along the grass behind her.

"Too early," she was wailing. "I didn't even know it could *be* this early."

Me and Negin traipsed alongside her and onto the walkway. "What if Will's there?" I asked them. "Like, with Josh?"

"He won't be," Frankie yelled. "Who the hell would go to an eight a.m. safety presentation *by choice*?"

"Well, you," Negin said. "You're not even part of these dorms. You don't technically have to come to this."

"What?" Frankie stopped dead and stared at her. "Why are you telling me this *now*?" She turned and looked at D Dorm. "Just when I've come too far to turn back." She carried on trudging slowly behind us, wailing intermittently.

I really didn't want to see Will. I didn't think I could cope. It had been a full twenty-four hours now, and nothing. As Frankie had acknowledged, *no one* can be offended by a text of a guinea pig doing the Macarena.

Negin said Will probably didn't know he was supposed to respond to it, and that I should just chill. But I hadn't told them about the awkward sex thing. It was too embarrassing to admit to myself, never mind them, and even if I could face it, I didn't know them well enough for *that* level of humiliating awkwardness. I kept wondering if *the incident* was why he hadn't replied. I had told Negin and Frankie that I went back for a bit but that nothing had happened. Which was true. In terms of *stuff.*

Will's room didn't have any curtains and I had woken up at seven, like always. There wasn't even a fitted sheet on the bed. I felt like my mother, lying there, wondering how he could not mind sleeping on the bare mattress. I needed to pee really badly but I didn't even know where the bathroom was. I crept out and tiptoed about, but all the doors were shut and I didn't know which one it was. Will woke up as I was getting dressed and offered me a no-milk tea. We cuddled and kissed goodbye, and it had felt natural and couple-y. When I got back I had tucked in with Frankie—who'd crashed in my room—and sent him the picture of the guinea pig wearing a birthday hat doing the Macarena, and fallen asleep.

And he just hadn't messaged back.

We followed the walkway over a bridge toward Gildas College, and the Central Hall building came into view. It was huge and oval, and almost totally made of glass. It looked like a giant UFO. Frankie was still moaning on about the earliness.

"To be fair, Frankie," I said, "out of everyone at this university, you are probably the one most likely to fall in a river."

"Or start a fire." Negin nodded. "Maybe they heard you were coming and organized an emergency health and safety presentation. This whole thing is probably specifically tailored to you."

She ignored us and squinted at the crowds of people heading into the hall. "Is Josh holding a clipboard?" He was at the main door, ticking people off as they walked in. I wondered if he knew I had been in his house. It's weird that I went there and he was probably asleep in the next room not knowing I was downstairs. I wondered if Will had said anything to him about me.

Josh's jean pockets were filled with pens and he was trying to count people. He smiled at us, but he looked a bit overwhelmed. He was wearing a massive neon-yellow vest that said YORK MET. "You look like a teacher," I said.

"I look like a jerk." He laughed. "It's, like, the one important thing the RA has to do. Basically, if I check you off this list, and you die in a fire, no one cares. If you jump in the lake, that's fine. As long as you are checked off this list." He smiled at me. "Phoebe Bennet. Check."

We shuffled into the hall and sat down. Frankie's comforter was so massive it covered her and Negin entirely.

"This is immense," Frankie said. "It's like going to the aquarium. I love the aquarium. I even went there as my family thing for my eighteenth birthday and we all dressed up as manatees. *Look*, though. Literally *everyone* is here."

There was a kind of electric buzz being transmitted from person to person, getting more intense as it was passed along. There must have been a thousand people squeezed into the hall. Everyone from the past week was in the same room. *Everyone.*

Frankie held the comforter across her face, and me and

105

Negin leaned in. We all peered over the top. "I think this is drawing *more* attention to us, not less," Negin whispered.

A man got up on stage and started speaking, but no one paid any attention to him.

"There's the boy you hooked up with," Negin whispered triumphantly to Frankie, pointing with her forehead across the other side of the hall. "I *told* you you got with someone. He's even wearing the exact same red shirt. Red Shirt Boy. Look."

"This is the thing about you not drinking," I said to Negin. "You remember everything. You're like this abstinent elephant, keeping the doomsday book of freshmen regrets."

Frankie slumped down into the comforter until she disappeared. "*Don't* let Red Shirt Boy see me," she hissed. "My face is falling off."

Negin rolled her eyes. "Is not. You've only got a little dry skin round your nose."

"Literally all the greats are in here." I started pointing discreetly. "Beautiful Eyes Boy, Hot Quidditch Marco, Interesting Thought Boy, Afraid-of-Sex Phil. So many hot boys we might marry."

"None of whom we've actually spoken to," Negin added.

"*I've* spoken to Afraid-of-Sex Phil," Frankie said. "How do you think I know he's afraid of sex? I spoke to him at the quiz. I told him about my height, he told me about his fear of sex. We bonded."

"Interesting Thought Boy is so enigmatic," Negin whispered.

We all looked at Interesting Thought Boy. He was wearing a loose-knit sweater with holes in the sleeves, and scratching his chin while sort of gazing dreamily into the middle distance.

"Yeah, good old ITB." Frankie nodded. "He's probably philosophizing about what to have for breakfast."

The man on stage started demonstrating how to use a fire extinguisher, and then they played us a painfully bad *Crimewatch*-style reenactment of a girl wearing a trashy bandage dress, falling into a river. I just kept scanning the room, looking at all the people I had seen over the last week penned into the same space.

I somehow missed Luke Taylor on the first couple of sweeps, but then he came into focus. At school, he had always been surrounded by people, but he was on his own, politely paying attention to the video. He was so good-looking he seemed out of place. Like a Hollywood film star who had been plonked into *EastEnders*.

The man was pointing at the screen and telling us how you're only ever one Bacardi and Coke away from river death.

"Look"—Frankie jabbed her elbow into my ribs—"there is Quidditch Bailer himself."

"Already saw him," I whispered. "He looks amazing today. Like, *amazing*."

We all looked over at Luke. His white T-shirt and tan made him easy to find in his row. He ruffled his hair, leaned back and yawned.

"I feel like we're observing a lion in a documentary," Negin said.

"When I was little I had to go and see an educational psychologist because all I drew were lions." Frankie mimed drawing manically. "I had, like, a mania for drawing lions."

"Can we just all appreciate Luke Taylor for a second?" I said.

"I know he is a self-obsessed ass, but just push that to the back of your mind and you know . . . objectify him." I could feel Negin and Frankie rolling their eyes. "Come on, you can't deny it, he is insanely beautiful."

"I think he looks like a Ken doll," said Frankie. "He is very square. His face, I mean. And his hair."

"When did you stop drawing lions?" Negin whispered.

They showed us a final clip of a boy getting an STI test, and then we all filed out of the spaceship. "I'm going back to bed." Frankie yawned at me. "In your room. I'm also really hungry."

"Me too," said Negin. "Me and Becky are meeting early to get breakfast."

I left them and wandered toward the English department, where I had my first class and which looked like a dilapidated block of buildings covered in tattered old Drama Club posters. Everyone says making friends with people in your program is important, so you know more people than just the ones in your hall. I gave myself a mental pep talk about speaking to everyone but not seeming too eager-beaver. But then I got lost trying to find the classroom.

When I did get there, it was already almost full. The only person I recognized was Bowl-Cut Girl, who was wearing a low-cut, electric-blue vest dress thing and no bra. The dress was kind of draped over her and looked like it could just fall off at any time and leave her completely naked.

I did a jolly smile at everyone and said "Hi" as I walked in and took an empty chair. They all said an awkward "Hi" back.

Then Bowl-Cut leaned across and said, "You're in Jutland, right?"

I nodded.

"I've seen you around," she said, and smiled.

I felt sort of honored. Bowl-Cut knew who I was. I smiled back but didn't really know what to say, so I just said "Great!" and then felt a bit stupid.

I got out my pencil case and notebook and laid them out on the table in front of me. Bowl-Cut was directly across from me and I could not stop staring at her. She had a tattoo that went from just underneath one of her boobs right around her back. What did it say? I kept trying to make it out. She had scraped her rainbow hair back and was wearing no makeup but she still looked amazing. She didn't seem nervous at all. She was sitting cross-legged on her chair like a kid waiting for story time, like she had done this shit a million times before.

Another person came in and sat down. I'd been half wondering if Luke Taylor would be in my class, but clearly not. More awkward small talk about whether we had all read the books.

And then a guy walked in and sat down toward the front. He was wearing jeans that were covered in white paint and a faded red T-shirt that said THE VELVET UNDERGROUND. He had thick black hair that stuck up all over the place and was also splattered with globs of paint. He looked foreign, with that kind of tan that's hardened every summer and never goes away. Like the front man of a band that sings about being heartbroken in black-and-white.

"OK." He nodded and smiled at all of us. "The literature of memory. That is a kind of crazy thing, right?" He was French, maybe Spanish. Some incredibly hot kind of accented nationality. He was the . . . what is it even called? It's definitely not the "teacher." The class leader? The professor? He definitely couldn't be a professor. He was, like, twenty-five, max.

Bowl-Cut looked me dead in the eye and mouthed "Hot TA." *Teaching assistant,* that was it.

I smiled in agreement. It is a wonder that I have only slept with two people, because I fall for so many people at a time. If I was Bowl-Cut and wore artfully draped boob curtains, I would probably have slept with a hundred people already.

He took the cap off his dry-erase marker. "Just say anything, guys. When I say memory, what do you think about?"

"The past." Bowl-Cut didn't even put her hand up. Were you *supposed* to put your hand up?

Hot TA nodded and wrote it on the board. "What's your name?"

"Mary," she said.

I could not believe it. Mary. And I could not wait to tell the others. How is anyone even named Mary anymore? Mary, the most boring Bennet sister. Mary, the mother of God. Mary, the woman who used to babysit me after school when my mum went to Weight Watchers.

Hot TA tapped the board with his marker. "So what else do you think about when I say 'memory'?"

"Nostalgia," said a girl with French braids.

And then Luke Taylor walked into the room. Just like that. On cue.

"Sorry. I got lost." There was no chair for him to sit on. I had a wild thought about offering him mine, then realized just how insane that would be. Hot TA went and got him one from a stack at the side, and everyone shuffled up to make room for him. Bowl-Cut Mary smiled at me again as if to say, "Wow, all this hotness in one room," which made me instantly feel both terrified and certain that she was going to get with Luke Taylor, and also made me want to message Frankie and confirm that crushing on Luke Taylor was a universal thing, not just confined to me.

"What's your name?" Hot TA asked.

"Luke." He looked slightly flustered. Had I ever seen Luke Taylor flustered? Luke Taylor looked attractive flustered.

"What do you think of when I say the word 'memory,' Luke?"

Luke seemed slightly alarmed. "Erm, I don't know. Maybe extremes? Like things that are good enough or bad enough to stay in your head?"

Hot TA wrote it on the board and I copied it down, word for word, slowly. We wrote down our earliest memories and the colors we associated with them and then a memory of school and a memory of a vacation. We talked about whether you can manufacture memories and why so many of us remembered the same things.

Bowl-Cut Mary retied her hair and I saw that her tattoo said *I love, I have loved, I will love.* Bowl-Cut Mary had fucking *loved.* How had she had time to *have loved?* And how could she be so confident about the *will love* bit, too? I needed to get on with things.

I started to wonder whether Luke would talk to me at the end and whether he would mention the quidditch. And then Hot TA said we could take a five-minute bathroom break. Some people got up and left. I got my phone out. Luke was sitting across from me studiously copying things down from the board. I thought about speaking to him, saying some jaunty ice-breaking thing, but I couldn't think of anything. He had typical, scrawly boy handwriting.

I opened my camera and slowly shifted my phone up, trying

to look natural. And then I pressed the button and quickly put the phone down. I copied out the same sentence I had already copied out and then picked up my phone again.

"Up-close indisputable proof. Luke Taylor is the HOTTEST BOY ON EARTH." I made the O's with a pair of eyes for effect and sent the picture to Frankie.

Hot TA walked back in. Luke checked his phone and then put it away before copying one last thing off the board.

"You and someone else might both experience the same event," said Hot TA. "But the memories you form might be entirely different. Your memories are not about what actually happened, but about *you*. Who you are and how you experience the world."

I thought about Flora and the night with the bikes and whether she remembered it, too. I suddenly wanted to ask her. The conversation was getting quite deep, and people started talking about their earliest memories.

"Me and my sister had this teddy named Norvin," Bowl-Cut Mary said. "And it's weird because she swears he was orange but I know he was purple. And we are both one hundred percent sure."

Hot TA smiled. "What does that memory say about each of you?"

Bowl-Cut Mary shrugged. "That one of us is wrong?"

He nodded. "Let me tell you something. The night Ted Hughes met Sylvia Plath at a party at Cambridge, they both went straight back to their rooms and wrote about this amazing, intense, explosive connection. It was so important to both of them that they immediately documented it. The beginning of a love affair. Hughes writes about the blue velvet ribbon Plath was wearing in her hair, and she writes about the red velvet ribbon she was wearing."

"She must have known what color her ribbon was," Bowl-Cut said. "It was hers."

Hot TA nodded. "Maybe. You would think. You know, in all Plath's poetry she associates herself with the color red. And in all Hughes's poetry he associates her with the color blue."

"What does it mean?" another boy said.

"I don't know." Hot TA shrugged. "That he always saw her one way, but that she saw herself another. What do you think, Luke?"

Luke still looked a bit flustered. "I don't know. That sounds scary. Like no one is really seeing anyone else."

Hot TA nodded, and we read a Ted Hughes poem called "Red," and because I get emotional about everything I almost started to cry. When Hot TA turned to write something on the board, I sneaked a look at my phone.

And then I had the most intense physical reaction I have ever experienced. My whole body seized up and saliva flooded into my mouth. For a second I thought I might faint or be sick.

"Memory and writing cannot exist without each other," Hot TA was saying, but I could barely get a grip on what was happening.

I stared down at my notebook and curled my hands into fists to stop them from trembling. I looked at my phone again to make sure, and it was like a knife twisting in my chest.

The worst moment of my life had happened. And I was still living in it.

I had sent the message to Luke.

I had sent the picture of Luke . . . to Luke.

It was like everything suddenly tripped into slow motion. I almost felt like I'd floated up out of body, but then I realized my left leg was literally shaking under the table, and that brought me back down to Earth.

It took everything I had not to look at Luke. To see whether he was checking his phone. Maybe he'd already checked it. I felt simultaneously boiling hot and freezing cold. I needed to get out. Not just of the room, but out of York entirely.

I looked up at the clock. There were still thirty-seven minutes of class left.

I could hear a weird buzzing in my head, and my cheeks felt like they were on fire. If I said I was ill it would draw more attention to me. I tried to breathe evenly and keep copying stuff off the board, but my brain wasn't communicating properly with my hand.

And then I realized Hot TA was staring at me. Everyone was staring at me. *Luke* was staring at me.

"Phoebe?" Hot TA said, smiling. "What do you think makes a moment stay in your head forever?"

9

• • • • • •   **LUKE**   • • • • • •

Phoebe was up and out of the room faster than I had ever seen a human being move.

As soon as the TA said "See you all next week," she just snatched her bag off the table and bolted out the door. I'd barely even noticed him saying it. But then, I'd barely noticed *anything* he'd said once I'd looked at my phone and seen that message staring up at me. My first-ever college class and I learned practically nothing because I was obsessing over a twelve-word text.

As far as I could see, there were two possibilities. One: it was a joke. Quite a weird, inexplicably harsh joke but, still, a joke. She was winding me up. She wanted to embarrass me. Or maybe she thought I'd find it funny. Whatever, Possibility One meant that she was *clearly* crazy.

Then there was Possibility Two: that it was a *genuine* message, *genuinely* meant for someone else, *genuinely* saying that Phoebe Bennet thought I was "the hottest boy on Earth."

I much preferred Possibility Two.

I reread it over and over again as I walked back down the covered walkway to B Dorm. I dodged the ducks and nodded at randoms I recognized from Orientation Week, and slowly let the whole concept of Phoebe shift and transform in my mind.

It was weird. It was like the message had suddenly lit her differently in my brain. I wondered why I hadn't seen it before. She was definitely hot. She was really funny. That hour we'd spent together on the first night was one of the only times I'd felt relaxed and easy here. She had this openness and positivity about her that sort of drew you in, made you feel more open and positive, too. Even the occasional rush of Abbey-guilt couldn't stop me from smiling as I thought about her. By the time I was back at B Dorm, punching in the entry code and clambering up the echo-y staircase, I officially had a crush on Phoebe Bennet.

The hall was totally empty. The chemists were all in labs from nine to five and a knock on Arthur's door revealed he was out, too. I braved the socks-and-sewage brie stink and went into the kitchen to make a cup of tea. There were three sheets of printer paper propped up on the table, addressed to Arthur, with the heading: UNACCEPTABLE CHEESE SMELL. I started reading and had just gotten to the final paragraph about "missing Fritos" when Rita walked in. She immediately heaved and covered her nose.

"My god, that cheese is not messing around, is it?"

I waved Barney's essay at her. "He's already had a formal written complaint about it. Do you want a tea?"

"Yeah, that would be nice, thanks. Just sat through an incredibly boring class, so I need one. Is Arthur in?"

"Don't think so. I just knocked."

"Oh." She frowned and looked around the kitchen, which was spattered with cold, sticky pasta sauce, still holding her nose. "Well, we can't have a nice cup of tea in here, can we?" She unpinned the laminated fire safety sheet from the notice board, walked across the hall and inserted it carefully into the crack of Arthur's door.

"Erm . . . Rita. What are you doing?"

"It's fine," she said, biting her lip in concentration. "I used to do it all the time last year when Arthur wasn't in."

"Is that definitely legal?"

"I'm a *law student*, Luke," she said, as if that somehow answered my question. She gently jiggled the laminated sheet and tried the door handle at the same time. Suddenly, there was a soft click, and the door swung open. "Ta-da," she said, flopping onto Arthur's bed. I followed her in, and as we sat sipping our tea, I decided I had to tell someone about the text.

"Bloody hell," she murmured, reading it with raised eyebrows. "She's not very subtle, this girl, is she?"

"So do you think it's for real, then? Like, she actually means it?"

"Well, she clearly didn't mean to take a photo of you and then send it to you, but yeah. I think it's safe to assume that she wants your body."

I laughed and felt a little flickering glow inside me, like

someone had switched on the central heating in my stomach. "Do you think I should text her back?"

Rita rolled her eyes. "No, obviously don't text her back, Luke, you idiot. The poor girl's probably mortified. She's probably buried under three blankets, crying her eyes out as we speak. And what would you say, anyway?"

I thought about it. "Dunno. 'Thanks for the text' or something."

Her eyes rolled back the other way. "'Thanks for the message.' Brilliant. You might as well punch her in the face and be done with it." She took a sip of tea. "How do you know this girl in the first place?"

"Well, we went to school together, actually. But we didn't really know each other then. We met for real last week. I sort of said I'd go to that quidditch thing with her at Orientation Fair."

"Oh yeah. Why didn't you go, again?"

"I just . . . forgot."

She made a face. "Right, well . . . you should probably apologize. And make up a better excuse."

"Yeah. I guess."

"Do you actually even like her?"

"I mean . . . I hadn't really thought about it before. But now . . . yeah. I sort of think I do."

Rita groaned loudly. "So when she's just a random girl from school you don't give her a second look, but as soon as she accidentally informs you that she wants to jump your bones, you're suddenly in love with her. Men are such predictable jerks, honestly."

I didn't bother arguing with that, because, to be fair, she had a point.

She finished her tea and plonked the mug down on Arthur's bedside table. "Well, this has all worked out perfectly for you, hasn't it? You like her, she thinks you're the hottest boy on earth. . . . I mean, it's all good, by the sound of it. You don't have a girlfriend or anything, do you?"

I thought about Abbey, who I hadn't heard from in more than a week now; the longest silence between us for almost three years. "No," I said. "I don't."

Rita shrugged. "There you go, then. Say sorry for being a dick about the quidditch, and then, I dunno . . . ask her out or something."

Suddenly, we heard the tinkle of keys outside, and the door was kicked open. Arthur stood in the doorway, holding a massive cheese sandwich and frowning hard at us.

"You know I could report you to the police," he said, chucking his keys on the desk. "You have broken into my property. You are *literally* criminals."

"Oh, come on, Watling," said Rita. "Your room's like the living room. It's a communal space."

"It is *not* a fucking communal space!" Arthur yelled, jabbing his stinking sandwich at us. "This is my actual, private, personal room! What if I was in here doing something actually private and personal?"

"What, like peeing in the sink?" Rita said, smirking.

"*No.* Like seducing a girl or something."

Rita clicked her tongue against her teeth. "You won't be seducing anyone now that you constantly stink of Brie."

"Wrong, *actually*, Maurita. I'll be making out with sophisticated French women who appreciate once-in-a-lifetime supermarket deals."

They grinned at each other, and not for the first time I wondered why they weren't a couple. They seemed pretty much perfect together. But then, me and Abbey had seemed pretty much perfect, too. How the hell are you *ever* supposed to know if you're right for someone?

I stood up. "I'll leave you two to it."

"Are you going to soccer initiations?" Arthur asked eagerly. He'd become weirdly obsessed with them. He thought they'd be some kind of insane combination of Freemason ceremony and satanic ritual. Maybe he was right.

"No, they're next week. I'm going back to my room. Need to do some reading."

"Are they all right, then, the soccer kids?" Rita asked.

"Yeah, they seem cool," I said. "Why?"

"No, nothing. Just, we had that Will Barnes on the floor below us last year. Do you remember, Arth? He seemed like a bit of a . . ."

She trailed off and just let the sentence hang there, unfinished, in the air.

"He seems all right to me." I shrugged.

She smiled. "No, yeah. I'm sure he is. I don't know him, to be fair." Arthur flopped down in his swivel chair and she said, "By the way, Arth, you're not gonna believe what Luke just got."

Arthur turned to look at me but I headed for the door. "You can fill him in, Rita. I'd better do this reading." I clapped Arthur on the shoulder as I left. "You got a note about the cheese, by the way. First of many, I bet."

"That cheese is the best thing that's ever happened to me," he said stiffly.

I went back to my room and tried to read Ted Hughes's *Collected Poems*, but I couldn't stop my brain from flicking back to Phoebe. Rita was probably right: I probably was a predictable jerk. But knowing that Phoebe liked me had made me feel totally different about her. Maybe I'd even liked her all along, but I hadn't realized it. Maybe I'd forgotten what liking someone new actually felt like.

To be honest, it felt pretty good.

PHOEBE

"Honestly, this is the worst thing that's ever happened to me."

I genuinely couldn't think of anything more awful. I couldn't think of anything else period. I was trapped in it, like a hamster, running away as fast as I could but not realizing I was stuck in the plastic wheel.

Negin reached out and touched my arm gently. "Phoebs, do you know you're rocking?"

"It's probably PTSD setting in," Frankie said from the kitchen floor. She had crumpled into the fetal position when I'd showed her the message, and oscillated between sympathetic nods and helpless laughter ever since.

Negin reached over to my phone. "Don't touch it," I screamed, and snatched it off the table.

Frankie dissolved again. Her whole body was convulsing in hysterics. "You know Negin touching your phone isn't gonna make it worse, don't you? I mean, let's be honest, nothing could make—"

I let out a loud groan-wail hybrid. "It is the *second week* of college. How can I have done this? Oh *god*."

"You are pretty epic." Frankie threw her legs in the air above her. "Your love life is, like, fucking . . . dynamite."

"Will hasn't texted me back! Luke thinks I'm a freak! I don't have a love life!" I shouted.

"You do. Luke Taylor bailed on you. And then Guinea Pig–gate with Will and now . . ." Negin kicked her quite hard and she trailed off. "Sorry. I mean, better to have loved and lost than to have loved and then . . . accidentally confessed your love via text message."

Negin tried to fake-cough her way out of a laugh and kicked Frankie again.

"This is your fault anyway," I yelled at Frankie. "You were the one who said Luke Taylor wasn't hot."

Frankie sat up straight and screamed back at me: "Yes, but at no point did I make you send a photo of him . . . *to him*!"

I took a deep breath. "I still feel sick. My whole body is boiling and my face is really itchy."

Negin leaned in and squinted. "Yeah, I didn't want to mention it but you have got a kind of . . . rash."

"What?" I jumped over Frankie and looked at myself in the toaster. My face was covered in massive red blotches, and they were spreading down my neck.

"Accidental Text Rash!" Frankie bellowed through her fingers.

"You need to calm down," Negin said. "It's just stress."

"My face is burning!" I screamed, and started jumping up and down.

"OK, OK." Frankie sprang up, ran over to the sink and

started chucking the dirty pans out onto the floor one by one. The crashing reverberated around the kitchen. She turned the tap on.

"What should I do?" I turned to Negin.

"I don't know."

"Are you a doctor or not?" I screeched.

"As I have said a thousand times, I won't be a doctor for seven years."

Frankie was beckoning me to the sink. "OK, the plug is fucked, so just do it quickly."

"I feel like I'm on fire." I stared at the water.

"Just do it!" Frankie shrieked.

I put my face close to the sink, took a deep breath and closed my eyes. "I can't," I shouted, just before Frankie plunged my whole head into the freezing-cold water. The shock of it hit me hard, but it felt kind of calming. I couldn't really hear anything except my heartbeat and the water in my ears.

I gasped from the shock as I pulled my head out.

Frankie threw her arms around me. "I feel like I fucking baptized you."

"Erm . . . what are you guys doing?" Connor was standing at the door, looking very confused.

Negin handed me a dish towel with old bits of pasta stuck to it.

"We're just . . . daring each other to . . . dunk our heads in water," she coughed.

"Awesome." Connor ran over to the sink and plunged his face into it. Then he stood up and shook himself out like a dog. "Yes!" he roared.

"This is one of the strangest days of my life," Negin said,

and put the kettle on. Becky walked in. If she thought it was odd that there were two people drenched in water she was too polite to say.

"Tea?" Negin said to her, and she smiled.

"Do you want to get dunked in water, Becks?" Connor asked amicably.

Becky shook her head. "I've got loads of work to do, and I'm going out later."

"Fair play." Connor nodded.

"Can I tell them?" Frankie said. "D Dorm circle of trust."

"You're not even in D Dorm!" I screamed. I was starting to shiver uncontrollably from the cold, but I didn't feel like my face was burning quite as much.

"Phoebs took a picture of a guy and wrote underneath it that he is, and I quote"—Frankie made quotation marks with her fingers—"'the hottest boy on Earth.' Then she sent the picture to him by mistake."

Connor held his hand up to high-five me. "Phoebs. You are a comedy legend. I think that is fucking brilliant. If he doesn't like ya, who cares, move on, and if he does, he'll make a move now for sure."

"He has a girlfriend," I said.

"We don't *know* that," Negin pointed out.

"Anyway, whatever, I know he doesn't like me."

"How?" said Connor. "You're hot, Phoebs, and you're fun to talk to. Trust. I don't shit where I eat, but if I did, I'd definitely be up for it." He winked at me. Weirdly, it made me feel a bit better.

"When did you send the message?" Becky sounded genuinely concerned.

"Like, two hours ago," I said. "Honestly, this is the end for me and boys. And technology. No men, no technology. Period."

Becky took a sip of tea. "Well, he might text you back."

"Seriously," I wailed. "What am I actually going to do?"

"Isn't it obvious?" said Frankie. "Just avoid Luke Taylor *at all costs.*"

Part Three

10

Campus was so weird. It was like a really annoying alternate dimension. You were constantly bumping into all the people you *didn't* want to see, but the people you *did* want to see were never around.

I'd spent all week trying to "accidentally" run into Phoebe. We'd had two classes together, and both times she was sitting on the opposite side of the room.

I'd even tried skulking around the entrance to D Dorm, pretending to browse the vending machines for longer than was strictly necessary, on the off chance she happened to walk out. But no luck.

On the other hand, as I shuffled down the walkway that led off campus, I realized that this was the fourth time in as many days that I'd seen Caribbean Jeremy. He was sitting on the grass next to the lake, a big bag of Doritos at his feet, knocking out a fairly appalling rendition of "No Woman, No Cry" on an acoustic guitar. Because he had his eyes shut, he hadn't noticed there were two ducks with their heads in the bag, cheerfully stealing his chips.

I left campus and walked up the outer road, past the massive oak trees and the weird little bungalows where the PhD students lived. It had been a week of nothing-y limbo—just Netflix, microwaved lasagna and the occasional spliff with Arthur—but I felt like tonight would be the real start of college. This was when the next three years would actually begin. Soccer initiations.

They were happening in a slightly grubby-looking, flat-roofed pub just off campus, and when I arrived, there were about five other freshmen bumbling about nervously in the parking lot.

"They told us to wait outside," said one guy named Trev, who I'd spoken to a bit at tryouts.

He grinned sheepishly from under his floppy dreads. "You nervous?" He was quite short, with a sharp northern accent—Manchester, maybe.

"Not really," I lied. "You?"

"Probably the most I've ever been in my life, mate, yeah." He nodded. "I mean, second most, actually, now that I think about it. My brother was on *Jeopardy!* last year, and that was the most nervous I've ever been in my life. It sounds bad, but I wasn't even nervous for him, really. I was more nervous for me, like, that he'd say something stupid, and then people would make fun of him in school the next day. 'Oh, saw your brother on *Jeopardy!* last night—he made a total dick of himself.' That sort of thing. But in the end, he did quite well. He didn't win

130

or anything, but he got a Double Jeopardy. It was on flightless birds." He stopped talking and breathed out. "Sorry, man. When I get nervous, I ramble. It's a medical condition."

I laughed, and felt some of the tension in my stomach dissolve. "Yeah, well, I'm shitting myself, too, actually. When I get nervous, I lie and pretend I'm not."

A few other people arrived, including one guy who was easily a head taller than the rest of us. He had a stubbly beard and a huge, dirty-blond cloud of hair, and could definitely have passed for a *Game of Thrones* character if it wasn't for his bright-green raincoat.

Drunk Toby from tryouts arrived just behind him, clutching a half-empty bottle of schnapps. He started offering it around.

"Mate, you *do* know they're gonna be, like, drowning us with booze for the next five hours," Trev said.

Toby shrugged and took a swig. "Settles the nerves."

Trev gave me a look as a junior finally opened the doors to let us in. He led us into the back room of the pub, where there was one long, banquet-style table laid out in the center.

"Maybe they're just gonna cook us a really nice meal," Trev suggested.

We all took our seats, and I spotted Will milling about, as well as a few other sophomores and juniors I recognized. Dempers pulled a chair out at the head of the table and stood on it.

"Right, freshmen, shut up and listen," he barked in his fancy private-school accent. I could easily see him as a red-faced, sweaty politician in twenty years' time, shouting across the House of Commons. "If you do exactly as we say," he continued, "you will escape from this pub unscathed. However, if you disobey, you will be punished. . . ." He left what he probably assumed to be a dramatic pause, and then slammed his fist into his palm. "Severely punished!"

Trev leaned into me. "This dude," he whispered, "is a fucking tool."

Dempers reached down into a cardboard box and pulled out a bunch of metal handcuffs. There was a genuine gasp of either surprise or horror or both from the freshmen. All the older guys cracked up.

"Don't worry, this isn't some sick *Fifty Shades* shit," Dempers said, laughing. "You will all be handcuffed to one of your superiors"—he gestured at the sophomores and juniors—"and you will have to drink double whatever they drink. So, for example . . ."

He plonked himself down and clicked the handcuffs onto *Game of Thrones* and then himself.

"This is probably not a good time to tell you," Thrones said. "But I don't actually drink."

"Fuck off," Dempers snorted. Someone passed him a pint of Guinness, and he downed it, spilling most of it on his T-shirt. "Right," he gasped. "Now you. Two pints."

Thrones shook his massive curly head, sadly. "Like I said, pal. I don't drink." He had a deep, booming Yorkshire accent.

"Are you fucking kidding me?" Dempers spat. "Then you can fuck off, pussy."

I felt myself flinch inwardly, but Thrones didn't bat an eye. He shrugged, nodded, then stood up suddenly and walked off, yanking Dempers to the ground behind him. Dempers hit the floor with a loud smack, and a few people laughed.

"You fucking dick!" he bellowed.

Thrones took no notice; just carried on walking across the room, dragging the wriggling Dempers behind him.

"Oi! Fucking stop!" Dempers was screaming.

Thrones finally turned and looked down at him blankly, like he was a stone stuck in his shoe. "You might want to undo these handcuffs, pal, because I'm not dragging you all the way home."

Everyone was laughing now, even the older guys, and Dempers was almost purple with anger as he fumbled to undo the handcuffs. "Good fucking riddance," he shouted as Thrones walked out.

Will didn't look quite so convinced. Clearly, having someone Thrones's size on the team could only have been a good thing. He cleared his throat and waved his hands for quiet. "OK, OK, chill. You always get one walkout. Wouldn't be a real initiation without it."

Dempers chucked the handcuffs out, and everyone partnered up and started drinking. I was cuffed to Geordie Al, who for some reason insisted on calling me "Swift."

"That's four tequila shots you owe me now, Swift."

Between the third and fourth I asked: "Why Swift?"

"'Cause you drink like a fucking girl, man. Luke Taylor . . . Taylor Swift."

"Oh I see. That's a little bit tenuous."

He downed a gin and tonic. "That's two G and T's, Swift. Go."

After a while, Drunk Toby had puked so many times he was literally coughing up air, and Trev had just given up altogether. He sat groaning with his head in his hands while Dempers cackled and took photos of him. I was trying to stop the room from spinning, but my head and stomach were both pulsing mercilessly.

"Some of you are drinking slower than others," Dempers bellowed. "We need extra nominations."

I felt a hand clap me on the shoulder and looked round to see Will standing over me, smirking.

"I think Taylor could do with a more experimental drink order."

"Yeah," I slurred. "If you like."

Will reeled ingredients off the top of his head: "Whisky, instant noodles, mayonnaise, absinthe, mustard, Guinness."

Trev winced next to me. "Fuck's sake, man." Will grabbed a glass to prepare this lethal cocktail, but Dempers stopped him.

"No. He has to drink it . . . out of his shoe."

The upperclassmen all cracked up laughing. I looked at Dempers to see if he was serious, and his pinched, unsmiling face told me he was. The mood seemed darker suddenly, more violent. But being so completely wasted, I couldn't tell for sure.

"Get your shoe off, frosh," Dempers snapped.

"I'd rather not," I said.

He leaned down so his face was almost touching mine. He was so close I could smell his tangy, chicken pot pie breath. "Did you not hear me, frosh?" he spat. "I said . . . Get. Your. Fucking. Shoe. Off. Now."

A flash of anger momentarily sobered me up, and I felt like shoving his face away. The upperclassmen started chanting "Shoe off, shoe off," and the freshmen were just laughing nervously. I looked at Will, vaguely hoping he might step in and veto the whole thing, but he was chanting along with everyone else.

I took my shoe off slowly to a massive cheer, and watched as Dempers proceeded to fill it with the lumpy, greenish-black cocktail. He handed it back to me and I thought about the *Game of Thrones* bloke. How could he be that confident to just walk out? How could he be so sure he'd find other friends?

"Do it," Dempers barked. I could see blobs of mustard bobbing up ominously near the laces. I put it to my lips, feeling the noise in the room rise and rise around me, and hoped the drink would just knock me flat out and put an end to the whole evening.

But it didn't.

It just made me throw up, quite violently, on my other shoe.

The rest of the night happened in stop motion. One minute we were in a taxi into town, streetlights whizzing by in a blur, fresh air billowing through the window. The next, Toby was gabbling apologies and the taxi driver was shouting, "Fucking kids! Who the hell's going to clean this up?"

Then we were in some club somewhere, and I was trying to stay upright, as Will yelled in my ear over the music.

"Don't mind Dempers earlier," he was saying. "He gets a bit carried away."

"It's all right."

"Sure you've seen it all before anyway."

I nodded, but the truth was, drinking with the soccer team at school had always been much tamer than this. More of a laugh. Probably because me and Reece were in charge, and we weren't exactly going to force anyone to drink out of their own footwear.

Will got his phone out. "I'll add you to the group chat so you'll know about training times and that. Plus, y'know ...

some extra stuff." He handed me another Jägerbomb. "Some bonus material."

I've no clue how I got back to the dorm. I staggered into my room, opened the sink cupboard and tried to focus on my face in the mirror. But it kept dividing at the nose and swimming into two separate faces staring back at me.

I lay down on the bed and looked at my phone. The soccer group was already buzzing with pictures of me and Trev and Toby and everyone else throwing up. Most of them involved me and the shoe.

I scrolled up a bit and suddenly had to squint harder at the screen to make sure I wasn't seeing things.

In among all the puking photos there were three pictures, one after the other, of three different girls. Each was asleep in bed, their eyes closed, their hair messy on the pillow. Underneath the last one, Dempers had written: "Wall of Shame Top 3 from last year. Gauntlet laid, frosh . . ."

I felt my skin prickle. It was like putting your eye to a peephole, seeing something totally private that you knew you shouldn't have access to. I don't know why, but at that moment, for the first time since I'd got here, I really, really wanted to go home.

I closed my eyes to try to sleep, but the next thing I knew I was hearing voices.

"Hello?" someone was whispering. "Luke?" I looked down at my phone.

"Abbey?" I slurred.

"Luke . . . ," she mumbled. "Do you know what time it is?"

"No . . . What's going on? Are you OK?"

"You called me."

"Did I?"

She sighed. "You sound drunk." She sounded tired. She sounded like home.

"I'm not that drunk. How are you? I've been wanting to call you. All week." I watched the ceiling spin faster and faster above me.

"Why?" she whispered. It felt so good to hear her voice.

"Because . . . I don't know. Because I miss you, I guess. I was . . . Maybe I shouldn't have said what I said on the first night. I wasn't really thinking."

"You're not thinking now."

"No, I am . . . I just . . . York isn't how I thought it would be. I don't know if I'm fitting in here. I don't know if it's working out."

"So you thought you'd just call me and we'd get back together and everything would suddenly go back to how it was." She sounded tearful. "It's not that easy, Luke."

"No, I know. It's just . . . Maybe I'm not over you." The words seeped out of me before I could think about whether I really meant them.

"I'm not over you, either," I heard her say.

"Well," I said. "OK, then."

And then the ceiling stopped spinning, and I fell asleep.

11

I was irrationally nervous.

In the worst-case scenario, I wouldn't get a job at a café. It wasn't college entrance exams, losing your virginity or sky-diving, just another situation I had to walk into, not knowing what the hell I was doing, and hope for the best. I had tied my hair back into a tight ballet-dancer bun and it was making my ears ache, so I kept trying to wiggle them free.

I gently pushed at the door but it was locked. Josh was be-hind the counter, neatly laying out a row of giant scones. It was weird seeing him doing something so precise and un-boyish. The last time I had seen him he had been right in the middle of the dance floor of a club, really going for it. He was wearing a white button-down, and it made him look younger than he nor-mally did, like he was in a school uniform. I knocked gently and he looked up, beamed and came over to let me in. Josh hugs you properly. Not a formality hug, but one like he has been waiting for you at the airport for hours. You don't really get that kind of hug at college: a huge, tight, confidence-giving squeeze.

"Nice granny bun, Bennet. You OK?"

"Yeah, I'm fine, apart from the fact I'm exhausted 'cause Frankie has slept in my bed with me for three nights and she's a massive wriggler."

"That girl is an absolute nut. Last night she got behind the counter at the kebab shop and begged the guy to let her serve the fries." He shook his head. "Negin had to trick her to leave by saying there was a tall man giving out prosciutto in the street."

"I went home at midnight because I'm taking this trial shift seriously." I was—I needed the money, and working at Bettys Tea Rooms seemed slightly more romantic than Pizza Hut.

"Bettys are serious about people taking it seriously." He walked back over to the counter and handed me a box of scones and some gloves. I started to lay them out in a row next to his.

I wanted to say something about Will. I didn't want him to be this awkward thing in my friendship with Josh. I have enough awkward things with people at York Met to last me the next three years, and it's only been three weeks.

Even though I had now taken a solemn vow of chastity, including text message chastity, in front of Frankie, Becky and Negin, I was already notorious in the D Dorm love-life stakes. Since Guinea Pig–gate, Will just acted like he didn't know me when we were out. I'd seen him get with people in clubs, and I didn't really care. Well, I did care. I mean, I cared that I'd had this weird thing with him that included that first week of orientation and the bizarre night at his place and the guinea pig text. But apart from that I just wanted to be able to go out and not

139

have to *worry* about seeing him. Especially when I was already on high alert for Luke Taylor sightings. Twice, I've had to hide in the ladies' room waiting for the all clear.

"Are you wiggling your ears, Bennet?" Josh laid out his last scone.

"Yeah, I went a bit militant with the bun. It's giving me a headache."

"You look different with a bun. I can't believe all that hair can go so small." He leaned toward me. "Right, so Sandra will come up in a minute. When she does, just be super smiley. Like you're in a cult. Around here it's like, you've got to smile all the time. That's the main thing. You can be a murderer as long as you are smiling hard." He looked down. "Excellent cake-arranging."

"I'll be the judge of that." A stern-looking woman, actually wearing what looked like a *Downton Abbey* servant's uniform, came around the corner.

Sandra took me downstairs to the staff room and handed me a neat pile of clothes in a clear plastic bag and promptly left. I went into the staff restroom and pulled the shirt over my head and fixed the little brooch that came with it in the middle, where a bow tie would go.

"You OK?" Josh shouted from outside.

I opened the door.

"Yeah, I look ridiculous. And I don't know what this is." I held it to my waist. "Do you have to be really skinny to work here?"

"It's the hat thing," Josh said.

I looked in the mirror and put it on my forehead. "I don't get it. How does it go on?"

"I don't know. Guys don't have to wear them."

"That's the patriarchy for you."

"Hold on, turn around." He gently took a couple of pins out of my bun and my hair fell down. Then he gathered it into a ponytail and rewound the bun slowly, pinning it again, but more loosely. He held up each end of ribbon below the bun and tied them together with the hat thing on my head.

"I feel like you're getting me ready for school," I said.

"Four sisters. I can do fishtail braids, Dutch braids, French braids, those weird bun things on the side of your head, glitter partings." He patted my bun and we went back upstairs. There were lots more people there, and we had a team meeting where Sandra spoke a lot about specials and clearing tables and keeping the customers happy. I was still a bit nervous. She kept saying words I had never heard before and everyone was nodding knowingly.

"You'll be fine," Josh whispered.

I was on the counter for the morning and it wasn't that bad. I didn't have to work the register, just get the scones and cakes and biscuits and put them in boxes and hand them to a lady called Julie, who seemed to have an encyclopedic knowledge of every single thing Bettys had ever sold: "Do you have the Lady Betty peppermint creams?" "Only at Christmas, my love. Give it a few weeks."

Just when I felt like it was all going well, Sandra appeared behind the counter.

"That Laurel is ill again, so I'm afraid I'm going to have to put you on the floor, Phoebe."

My stomach churned. I had never waitressed before, and waitressing at Bettys seemed to be the Olympics of waitressing. Silver cake forks and tea strainers and lots of very white

141

tablecloths. I thought about the words "silver service waitressing" on my résumé, which referred to pouring champagne at my gran's seventieth.

I just kept getting hotter. People kept asking me questions I didn't know the answers to and everyone looked too busy to help. The quicker I took people's orders, the quicker more people seemed to sit down. I couldn't remember the table numbers and I couldn't remember all the teas and I couldn't seem to input the orders without taking so long that people started trying to wave at me to come over and see them.

I knocked over a tiny vase with a red tulip in it that was on one of the tables, and Sylvia Plath popped into my head. And that made Luke pop into my head, and I got a horror wave that I was getting my accidental text rash back, and then I couldn't remember what I was supposed to be doing. I had needed to pee for so long that the pain just began to feel normal. How can people get paid so little to do something so complicated? The panic was making my mind go completely blank. I couldn't remember what had happened three seconds ago.

Four women at one of my tables kept looking at me. I took a tray of sandwiches over to a group of Americans, and they shook their heads like I had done something wrong. I could feel sweat dripping down my back. I looked through the millions of little pieces of paper I had stuffed into my apron pocket. I found theirs. I had definitely taken their order.

"Sorry, honey," one of them said. "We've been here for a half hour and we haven't even been given our tea."

"I'm so sorry. Let me just go to the kitchen and check on your order."

"Just the pot of tea would be good," another said, and gave her friend a look as if to say I was a complete idiot.

Panic was rising inside me. I went downstairs and into the staff bathroom and looked over the slips again. I hadn't put their order through. And if I did it now it would go to the end of the orders and it would be another half hour until they got anything.

I couldn't think properly. I needed to just own up to it, find Sandra and tell her what had happened. I took a deep breath and walked out. Josh winked at me from across the room. I shook my head trying to indicate what had happened.

He smiled and said something that made the whole table laugh, and then he walked over to me.

"I think I've totally fucked it up," I whispered. "I forgot to put an order in."

"Don't worry," he said. "I can fix it."

But then Sandra appeared. "Are you all right, love?" she asked. "You're supposed to be upstairs." Her voice had an edge to it.

"Sandra." Josh wrinkled his nose. "I said to Phoebe I would put an order through for her, but I totally forgot. Don't blame her. I said I would do it, 'cause she had that many tables and we were quieter down here."

She shook her head. "Right, go and handle it." And then she walked away. I wanted to throw my arms around him, I was so relieved.

"Your hat's coming off," he said with a grin.

"Thank you so much." I was acting like he had pulled me out of the water after the *Titanic* sank. I needed to get some perspective on this trial waitressing shift.

143

"Well, I want you to get the job." He smiled. "So I have a mate here. I mean, I do like having twenty-odd mothers about but, you know . . . it would be a riot with you."

We got the tea and cakes for the table and served them together. Josh definitely had a way of talking to people that just made them like him, even before he had really said anything.

The lunch rush had passed and things were quieter. Josh and me re-laid all the tables and played Shoot/Snog/Marry in whispers between serving customers.

Four o'clock came around really quickly, and I got changed and tried to fold up the uniform into the same neat pile in which it had been handed to me.

"You keep it." Sandra smiled. "Welcome to Bettys."

Me and Josh walked out together, and when we got to the corner he gave me another one of his massive hugs. He hugged me so tight he lifted me up without even realizing.

"Thanks for getting me the job."

"I didn't," he said. "You got it for yourself."

It was getting dark. People were finishing their shopping and going back to their cars. We wandered along the cobbled street toward campus.

"Do you want to come to mine for a cuppa? It's on the way back."

I made a face. "Um . . . dunno."

"You mean 'cause of Will?" He sounded almost concerned. "Are you OK? About all that?"

I didn't really know what to say. I wondered what he knew about that night. What exactly Will had said about it, and what Josh thought.

We both looked in a toy shop window. "What would you go

for?" Josh pointed. "I reckon you would go for the Calico Critters rabbit family."

"I already have that one, obviously. It's a classic. I would go for the light-up Hula-Hoop. I mean, when did they invent those?" I peered through the window. "I reckon you are a Nerf gun kind of boy."

He crinkled his nose. "What? That's a massive insult. I would go for the teddy bear. I love a good teddy bear."

We kept walking in silence. "I am OK about it," I said. "The Will stuff, I mean. I just feel like . . . I just don't want it to be weird."

Josh nodded. "Yeah. Well, Will's . . . He's a bit . . ." He trailed off. "He's great in loads of ways, but . . . I dunno."

"I thought you two were really good mates," I said.

He dug his hands into his jacket pockets. "I mean, yeah. We were in the same hall last year and we both played soccer and it seemed really obvious from the start that we were gonna live together. And then his dad literally bought a house in York, so . . ."

We stopped outside a kitchenware store. "The living together thing freaks me out a bit," I said. "People are talking about it already. Like, getting houses together. Being roommates for all the years we're here."

"Honestly, Bennet, do not give in to the pressure. You don't have to decide straight away. I kind of . . . wish I hadn't."

"Do you still play soccer?" I wondered if he'd met Luke.

"No, I stopped at the end of last year. I played at school and everything, but up here, those guys are all quite . . . dunno. Can't describe it, really." He shook his head. "Like I said, I've got four sisters, so I guess I'm a bit more sensitive to all that locker room joking around."

145

I waited for him to say something more but he didn't. "Well, you can always join quidditch with me, Frankie and Negin. There's a social next week."

He smiled at me. "You never know, Bennet, might take you up on that, actually."

I peered through the store window. "Look, they have a whole wall of cookie cutters. I can spend all my wages stocking up for egg-fairy-bread sandwiches."

He nodded. "Yeah, we need to keep adding to our collection."

There were loads of them, in the shape of literally every object you could think of. I turned to Josh. "OK, which do you think's my fave?"

He narrowed his eyes. Then after a second, he said: "I'm going with the train one."

"Yes! That actually is my favorite."

"I know you so well, Bennet." He pointed. "Is that a phone-shaped one?"

I started walking again. "We are not buying that one. Phones are the root of every single problem in my life. Do you actually, really want to know what happened with Will?"

"Well, how graphic is it? I mean, will I see you in another light, Bennet?"

"I sent him a picture of a guinea pig doing the Macarena. And I never heard from him again."

Josh stopped still and then burst into laughter so loud that a woman crossed the street.

"Stop." I pulled my hat over my eyes. "Please. It's still raw."

He linked arms with me. "Don't worry. Trust me, guinea pig Macarena is amateur stuff. On Valentine's, when I was sixteen,

146

I wrote my girlfriend a cheesy love poem. And then accidentally texted it to my mum."

I pulled out my phone. "OK. That's bad, but this blows everything out of the water. If I show you this, we have to be friends for life." I found the message and handed it to him.

He squinted. "Luke Taylor is—"

I whacked him on the arm. "Don't read it out loud. It's horrific enough as it is."

"And you sent this to . . . ?"

I shut my eyes and nodded.

"Wow." Josh stopped and ran a hand over his shaved head. "I mean, yeah, there's no beating that. That's the Usain Bolt of embarrassing texts. That's made me feel a lot better, actually."

"Oh good. Great. Glad my shit-show of a life could be of service."

He sighed. "I feel like life is always manageable until you get girls involved."

"Or boys."

"People. Basically, you shouldn't get people involved."

"Or technology," I said. "Especially phones. You wouldn't catch Elizabeth Bennet sending a comedy guinea pig picture to Darcy. She'd have to paint it and then send it by horseman."

Josh shrugged. "Maybe she did do that—it just didn't make the final cut. It's probably in the bloopers."

"You know it's a book, too, right?"

"You know I'm studying English, too, right?" he shot back.

I sighed. "Maybe we should just throw our phones away and live like people from the olden days."

"Agreed; you stay away from phones and I'll keep living like a monk."

I scrunched my face up. "You don't live like a monk. What are you talking about?"

"An emotional monk. I have vowed to be an emotional monk. I'm not gonna fall in love with anyone again."

"Who were you in love with? Are they here?"

He shook his head. "Nah, she's at home. We broke up last year. She broke up. Broke up with me. Broke me." He sounded really serious.

I wanted to ask him more, but his face sort of told me not to. I feel like everyone has had some great love except me. Like, maybe it will never happen to me. Maybe I'm immune or something.

"I think we'll both be all right." He smiled at me. "And you're a Bennet, Bennet, so it is inevitable that one day, someone will tell you how ardently they admire and love you."

12

Will was muttering like a maniac and jabbing randomly at the quiz machine's buttons.

"Krypton . . . 1968 . . . The Diet of Worms . . ."

But he was getting every answer right. It was genuinely quite impressive.

"How the hell do you know all thi—"

"Shut up," he hissed. "We're one away from winning."

He squinted at the screen. "Who wrote the 1925 novel *The Trial*?" He spun around to face me. "Come on, English. This is all you."

I pressed the FRANZ KAFKA button, and a few pound coins clattered out of the machine. "Fucking yes, mate!" Will beamed, reaching down to collect the money. "Dream team."

He squeezed past the pool table and I followed him up to the bar. "Played that machine so many times last year that I still remember pretty much all the answers. I might be fucking my degree up, but I could definitely get first in pub trivia." He waved the bartender over. "What d'you want?"

"Nothing. I've got class. Got to go back to the dorm and get my stuff." Will shrugged and ordered a beer, and I wondered if I should maybe try to talk to him about Abbey. About what "I'm not over you" might actually mean.

Did it mean we were back together? It definitely didn't feel like we were. Mainly because I hadn't actually heard from her since the night we'd said it. It had been more than a week, and nothing. Not one single message. I'd been so wasted at the time that I was starting to doubt whether the conversation had even happened.

Will sipped his beer and asked, "Your suitemates're still boring as fuck, then?"

"I don't see them, really." I shrugged. "They're all doing chemistry, so they're usually in labs all day."

He nodded. "Cool. It's just ... I dunno what you've got worked out for houses next year, but we might have a spare room at my place."

"Oh, right. Really?"

It sort of knocked me for a loop. The chemists were already talking about getting a house together next year, and in my head I'd been working up to asking Arthur and Rita what their plans were. But then, they had their own friends and their own lives. They never actually texted me, or arranged to meet up with me, like Will did. Arthur had only ended up next door to me because of asbestos and random chance. It wasn't like we'd somehow bonded and found each other. The truth was, Will was probably the closest thing I had here to a real friend.

"Yeah, I'd be up for that," I told him. "Sounds good."

He started counting the quiz machine winnings out on the bar. "I mean, nothing's definite yet, mate. I need to see what Josh is doing."

"Of course, yeah."

I said goodbye and went back to B Dorm to get my bag, where I found Beth and Barney in the kitchen, furiously spraying air freshener to cover the stink of Arthur's cheese.

I headed up the walkway to my class, pulling my jacket collar tight against the bitter wind and thinking for the zillionth time about that Abbey conversation.

The hardest thing was that I had literally no one to talk to about stuff like this. Last night, I'd gotten so sick of all these doubts and fears nagging at me that I'd even called Reece. But all we'd ended up talking about was how shit Arsenal was this season. I couldn't get beyond the banter and pointless small talk. I couldn't ever find the space to say what I really wanted to say: that I was starting to freak out. About everything—friends and soccer and not fitting in. But mostly about the idea that I'd broken something in Abbey, something that couldn't ever be fixed.

It was like I was on edge all the time. Like I was slowly sinking, surrounded by people, and I couldn't shout for help.

My phone buzzed, and my heart did its usual mini drum roll, but it wasn't Abbey. It was someone on the soccer team, a freshman called Murf. I opened the message, which was another photo of a random sleeping girl—about the fourth this week.

You had to keep checking the group in case it was about practice or a game or something, but that meant you basically couldn't avoid these photos. Dempers called it "The Wall of Shame": whenever anyone on the team slept with a girl, they

151

put a picture up. But the thing was, the pictures weren't even the worst of it. It was the comments underneath that really gnawed at me. People rating the girls out of ten, saying horrible shit about the way they looked.

I checked my phone again. Dempers and Geordie Al had already commented: "3/10 . . . Rough as fuck m8" and "Any hole's a goal . ." I put it back in my pocket and kept walking.

When I got to the seminar, everyone was already sitting down. Phoebe was on the other side of the room, getting her books out of her backpack. She looked particularly pretty today; her mass of curly hair was pulled neatly into a bun at the back, so you could see the whole of her face.

I tried, and failed, to make eye contact with her as I walked in. We didn't even nod hello these days. As weirdly great as it had been to receive that text, I was starting to wish it had never happened. What was the point of liking someone if they were too embarrassed to ever speak to you?

The idea suddenly occurred to me that I could even things out by taking a picture of her right then and there and telling her how hot she looked. But I dismissed that pretty quickly as one of the worst ideas anyone's ever had.

Our TA, Yorgos, came in and dumped his bag on the desk.

"Right," he announced. "I'm afraid I've got some bad news for you all today. Presentations."

Someone groaned and Yorgos laughed. "I know, I know. Literature is supposed to be about sitting and writing, not standing and reading. But your essays will only make up seventy-five percent of your grade this semester. The other twenty-five percent will come from this presentation."

There was a louder groan this time, and Yorgos smiled again.

He looked a bit like a younger, skinnier, less terrifying Javier Bardem. "Don't worry," he said. "You won't have to go through this humiliating ordeal alone. You'll do it in groups of three."

He scanned the room. "And don't just grab hold of your two friends next to you. Let's mix things up a bit."

He flicked his fingers like an orchestra conductor, picking out groups of three at random. On the last flick, he took in me, Hot Mary with the ridiculous hair and Phoebe. "You three."

Hot Mary grinned at me, and I grinned at Phoebe, but Phoebe just stared down intensely at her notepad.

As soon as class was over, Phoebe bolted for the door, but Hot Mary blocked her off.

"I was thinking we could grab a coffee or something?" she said to both of us. "Chat about the presentation?"

A few minutes later, the three of us were seated in Wulfstan Bar, drinking grainy lukewarm cappuccinos, and Phoebe had *still* not made eye contact with me. In fact, neither of us had actually said more than about five words. Hot but Ridiculous Mary seemed quite happy to do all the talking.

"Like, I was thinking we should do the whole thing about memory, right?" she was gabbling. "We could put Ted and Sylvia at the heart of it, obviously, but we can also bring in shitloads of other memory stuff: Joyce, Nabokov, Proust . . ." She banged the table suddenly, causing half my coffee to bail out into the saucer. "Oh my god, we could make it a Proust-themed performance piece! Like, we could all sit at the front of the class, dunking bits of cake into cups of tea, talking about our earliest memories!"

She stopped speaking and stared at us, and I realized that she was finally expecting one of us to say something. She was wearing a green top with a sort of lightning-shaped split up one

153

side. I could see a gothic-lettering tattoo snaking down into her jeans, but I couldn't work out what it said.

I was focusing so intently on this that I momentarily forgot about the silence. Luckily, Phoebe didn't. "Well . . . I like the memory thing," she said. "We should definitely do that. I'm just not sure about the performance piece bit." She smiled softly. "I'm not that much of a performer."

"Oh, don't worry about that." Mary flapped her hands dramatically. "You can leave the performance stuff to me. I could maybe even read out some of my poems. I've got one called 'Winchester Casts No Shadows' that deals heavily with the theme of memory. . . ."

She reached down to get something out of her bag, and I saw that the tattoo said *I love, I have loved, I will love.* Out of nowhere, a memory hit me—a memory I didn't even know I had—and it was like stepping on a land mine.

I looked at Phoebe. "You *are* a performer," I said. "You were what's-her-name in *Grease.* Frenchie."

Mary stared at me. So did Phoebe. Mary was smiling a confused sort of smile, but Phoebe's face was impossible to read.

"I don't know why I just remembered that," I carried on, feeling a weird rush from looking into Phoebe's blue-green eyes for the first time since the Orientation Fair. "It was tenth grade, wasn't it? In the dining hall. You were great. I remember Annabel kicked her shoe off into the crowd and you ad-libbed a joke about it."

Phoebe smiled, then looked down at her coffee. "Yeah, tenth grade, you're right."

I'd only gone to see it because Abbey had been Sandy. She'd looked ridiculously hot in the end scene with the leather pants and blond wig. I'd actually thought about auditioning for one of

154

the boy parts, but Reece had laughed so hard when I told him that I'd chickened out.

"What the absolute fuck are you two on about?" Mary demanded.

"Me and Phoebe went to high school together," I explained, and her eyes widened.

"Oh shit, this is perfect. So, like, maybe we can weave that in? I could do my poems, and then you two can, like, reminisce about sitting next to each other in Physics or whatever."

This made me and Phoebe catch eyes again and smile.

Mary looked at her phone. "Oh fuckbags, I'm late for band practice." She stood up, artfully messing her multicolored hair with both hands. "You guys should totally come to our gig next week, by the way. We're called Fit Sister. We do Electro Tuesdays in Gildas Bar." She slurped the rest of her coffee and slammed the cup back down. "Anyway, chat later. Awesome brainstorm."

Then she bounded off. And just like that, I was alone with Phoebe.

● ● ● ● ● ● **PHOEBE** ● ● ● ● ● ●

The thing about Frenchie had totally freaked me out.

I'd basically been aiming to just keep my head down, not look at or speak to Luke, and then get out of the café as quickly as humanly possible. But him mentioning *Grease* had dredged up all this random stuff I'd completely forgotten about.

That play had been right around the same time Luke and Abbey Baker had started going out. Every night, I'd come out of rehearsals to see him kicking a soccer ball against the wall, waiting for her. And then I'd go home and daydream pointlessly about what it'd be like if he was waiting for me instead.

Now that Bowl-Cut had disappeared, being alone with Luke definitely felt like too much to handle. It was like the text was flashing in front of me every time I looked at him. It was all just way too humiliating. I grabbed my bag, and was about to make an excuse and leave, when he spoke.

"So, Mary's quite . . ." He raised his eyebrows. "Isn't she."

That made me laugh, in spite of everything. "Yeah," I said. "She is."

He mopped up some of his spilled coffee with a napkin. "I mean, there's no way I'm sitting at the front of the class, dunking cookies in tea and talking about my earliest memories."

"Yeah, I'm not really into that, either." I still had one hand on my bag, ready to jump up and leave whenever the conversation stuttered or broke down. But it didn't. It kept going.

"Have you seen her tattoo?" Luke asked.

I nodded. "'I love, I have loved, I will love.' *Pret*-ty deep."

"Yeah," he said. "Although it also sounds a bit like exam verb conjugation."

"True. Can you imagine what her poems are like?"

He raised his eyebrows again. He looked so hot. I tried not to think about it, as thinking about how hot Luke is tends to be what gets me into trouble. "I know," he said. "It might actually be worth sacrificing twenty-five percent of our first semester grade just to hear them."

We both laughed, and I thought, *Is this what being a grown-up is? Can proper adults accidentally text someone confessing their undying love, and then just have a friendly coffee with them afterward? Is that really how the real world works?*

156

"I don't want to be mean about Mary," I said. "I actually really like her. To be honest, me and my friends are kind of obsessed with her."

He nodded. "I'm kind of obsessed with her, too. I'm sort of attracted to her, but she also sort of terrifies me."

Hearing him say he was into Mary was definitely too much. I grabbed my bag handle a bit tighter, and Luke must have spotted it because he reached for his bag, too.

"Well," he said, "we're both agreed that we're mildly obsessed with Mary, so that's good. You heading back to Jutland?"

We finished our coffees and started wandering slowly back together. It felt like we were walking on ice. Feeling our way carefully back into normality. Every time it started to feel natural and easy between us, I remembered the text and imagined him reading it and wanted to dissolve into the ground again. I prayed we didn't bump into Frankie and Negin, as that really would send the awkwardness levels off the chart.

"So," Luke said, "what's all this Ted Hughes and Sylvia Plath stuff about memory? I sort of missed all that in the first class."

He didn't add: "I missed it because I was laughing my arse off at a text you'd just sent me calling me the hottest boy on Earth." But he must have been thinking it. It was the first time either of us had mentioned that day, and I felt my neck getting red. The text rash was following me. I pushed my scarf up to hide it.

"Well, basically," I said, "what happened was, Ted Hughes and Sylvia Plath met at this party, and it's, like, one of the most epic and intense meetings in literary history. She bit his cheek and it bled."

"What? That's a bit harsh."

"No, I think she just liked him. Or it was like some kind of expression of . . . something. I don't actually know. But she definitely bit him, and from that moment they both knew that for better or worse they were tied together. Like they were meant to meet. And they both absolutely believed in that kind of fatalistic moment."

"Right."

"But it's just weird because they both wrote about it in their diaries, but one of them got this insignificant detail wrong. The blue or red ribbon thing. So Yorgos was saying it means a lot because they are poets, and color and imagery is significant, I suppose."

Luke nodded slowly. "So it's like either the ribbon was blue, and he saw her clearly, for the person she was . . . or it was red, and he never really saw her. He just projected onto her what he wanted to see?"

"Yeah, exactly," I said. "I agree with Mary, to be honest. It was her ribbon. She must have known. So it was like he misread her from the very start."

I could feel Luke looking straight at me. "OK, right," he said. "I get it."

● ● ● ● ● ● **LUKE** ● ● ● ● ● ●

I didn't get it.

Was that what had happened with me and Abbey? Had I misread her from the start? Or had she misread me? Maybe she'd thought I was calm, steady blue, when really I was fiery, ruin-your-life red.

Thinking about Abbey made me suddenly feel guilty about liking Phoebe and even finding Mary hot yet terrifying. And then I felt guilty for thinking about Abbey and Mary when I should have been focusing on what Phoebe was saying. And then I got so frustrated with it all that I kicked an acorn off the walkway, scattering a bunch of squirrels.

"Poetry's too complicated," I muttered.

Phoebe laughed. "What do you like, then? Like, who's your favorite writer?"

"I dunno. I like John Fante and Ken Kesey. I like Hemingway a lot."

"Luke!" She looked at me in what seemed like mock horror but could just as easily have been actual horror. "Hemingway was a violent drunk."

"I don't mean I like *him*," I said. "I'm sure he was an absolute dick. But I do like his writing. I like how you can feel he's really burning to find some sort of meaning from life. All these obsessions with shark fishing and bullfighting and big-game hunting—like, doing crazy, dangerous stuff to feel more alive."

"So, basically, loads of innocent animals had to die just for one drunk guy to 'feel more alive'? I think I'll stick to Jane Austen."

We strolled past Jutland Bar and the computer room and the vending machines. It was weird; it was like we were slowly finding a rhythm again. Nowhere near back to the easy banter of the Stephanie Stevens night, but not a million miles from it.

"I've got a good book on Ted and Sylvia, actually," Phoebe said. "It was my mum's—she was really into them. I can always lend you that if you want. Especially if we're gonna be doing this whole presentation on them."

159

"Yeah, that'd be great, actually. Thanks."

We were now right at the end of the walkway, where the path split, with D Dorm to the left and B Dorm to the right. We both stood there for a second, fidgeting with our bags and not looking at each other.

"Well . . ." Phoebe let the word hang in the air between us. I really didn't want her to go. I wanted to keep hanging out with her.

"Maybe . . . I could get it now?" I tried. "The book, I mean?"

She fiddled with her massive scarf and looked up at her window. Then she said: "Yeah. OK. Cool."

D Dorm looked exactly the same as B Dorm, but the absence of Arthur's headachey cheese smell made it seem more welcoming somehow.

Their kitchen was in a much worse state than ours usually is, but Phoebe's room was way tidier and nicer than mine. She'd actually bothered to decorate properly, for a start. There were pictures Blu-Tacked up all over the walls, and little multicolored fairy lights strung over the sink cupboard. She reached up to get the Ted and Sylvia book from her shelf, and I squinted at some of the photos.

"No way," I said. "Is that . . . Book Day?"

Among all the shots of Phoebe and her mates, there was a group picture of our whole school in ninth grade, with everyone dressed as different characters.

"Yup." She knelt next to me on the bed and smiled as she looked at the picture. I peered harder at it, rocking forward on my knees. "Found you," I said.

"The hair's a giveaway," she sighed, taking a fistful of it and smoothing it out along her shoulder.

"Are you . . . what?" I looked closer, but I still had no idea. "A cloud?"

She laughed. "I'm the mouse."

"Oh, right, I get you: the mouse." I nodded. "The mouse. The generic mouse of literature. Which mouse?"

She rolled her eyes. "The Gruffalo mouse. Look." She pointed at the girl next to her, who appeared to be dressed as the devil. "Flora is the Gruffalo. Do you remember Flora?"

I did remember Flora, but I didn't know she was called Flora. "Yeah, I remember her," I said. "Gruffalo and Gruffalo Mouse. That's a bit . . . niche isn't it?"

She shrugged and handed me the Ted and Sylvia book. "The niche stuff is the best stuff. Are you even in this picture or were you too cool for Book Day?"

"Of course I'm in it." I pointed at tiny, spiky-haired, fourteen-year-old me, squashed between Reece and Harry in the back row. "I'm the greatest literary character of all time. Boy in an Arsenal jersey."

Phoebe made a face. "You wore a soccer jersey to Book Day?"

"Yeah, someone, somewhere, in the vast expanse of world literature has definitely worn an Arsenal jersey. The guy out of that Nick Hornby novel, for a start."

"The guy out of *Fever Pitch*?" Phoebe scoffed. "Classic."

"It *is* a classic, thank you very much."

"Whatever. You're just crap at dressing up. Admit it. What did you wear to the emoji party? A smiley face or something, wasn't it?"

"Thumbs-up, actually."

"Well, you could've made more of an effort," she said,

laughing. And even though I knew she didn't mean anything by it, it still made me think of the quidditch bail. And Abbey. And all the other fuck-ups I was leaving in a long trail behind me.

Could've made more of an effort. That would probably be written on my fucking gravestone.

I sighed and slumped from kneeling to sitting on the bed. "Yeah, it's true. The thing is, Phoebe, I guess I'm just, y'know . . . a bit of a prick, really."

I smiled at her, but she didn't smile back. She just stared at me hard. Which was quite disconcerting, as we'd only really been making nervous, fluttering, two-second eye contact since we got into the room.

"You're not a prick, Luke," she said slowly. Then she scooched away from me slightly and started looking at the other photos. "Do you remember Zoe Kenney's seventeenth?" she asked. "In her dad's massive house?"

"Erm . . . yeah," I said, although I had no recollection of Phoebe being at that party at all.

"Well, you remember when Chris Isaacs and Alex Paine and those guys showed up? They were really drunk and they started giving Justin all that shit? Going on about how his long hair made him look like a girl?"

The memory started to defrost in my head. It was a horrible moment. They'd pushed Justin Hader on the floor and Chris had grabbed a pair of scissors, telling him they were going to give him a proper haircut. A boy's haircut.

"Yeah," I said. "I remember."

"You were the one that stopped that," Phoebe said quietly. "You pulled Chris off him. You got them to leave him alone."

162

"Chris Isaacs and Alex Paine were the biggest assholes in the whole school."

"Yeah, but they listened to you."

"Only 'cause I was on the soccer team with them."

"Yeah, well, either way . . ." She looked at me again, right in the eyes. "That awful thing didn't happen because of you. And I remember thinking, at that moment . . ." She trailed off and then shook her head gently, like she was embarrassed or something. She smoothed out another fistful of her long, curly hair. "Well, I remember thinking Luke Taylor's not a prick, anyway."

I tried to laugh, but it got stuck in my throat. It was like she'd shaken me awake suddenly; reminded me there was more to me than what had happened with Abbey. I sat there in silence on the bed next to her, pretending to look at the photos, and for the first time in forever, I actually felt OK.

13

• • • • • • • **PHOEBE** • • • • • • •

"I can't believe how *long* your hair is," Liberty said. Every time she clamped the straighteners near my head I jumped a bit, internally.

"Yeah, but does it look *good*?" I asked.

"I have never in my life seen anything like it." She said it totally sincerely.

"Liberty, that is not a reassuring answer. 'I have never in my life seen anything like it.' That's what people say about nuclear explosions or those people who have plastic surgery to make themselves look like cats."

"No, it's just, you look *so* differe—"

Frankie crashed in and did a sort of exaggerated double take. "What the *what*? Mate, *what* is happening?"

She bent over next to me so her face was right in front of

164

mine. "Mate, I *literally* didn't recognize you. As in, this is freaking me the fuck out." She was shaking her head. She leaned back out into the hall and shouted: "Negin! Negin!"

I jumped up and looked in the mirror. Straightened, my hair reached all the way to my butt. I actually did look like a completely different person. Frankie held her phone up and took a picture. Then she banged on my wall. Liberty had dissolved into laughter. "Connor! Connor! Where *is* everyone?" Frankie stood in the middle of the room and just started shouting. "Becky! Nathan!" She walked over to my bed and opened the window. "Anyone, please? I can't experience this alone—"

I cut her off. "OK, let's focus. I have to see Luke in an hour."

Frankie made a face. "You've seen him, like, every day this week."

"I know, but today is the actual presentation." I looked at Liberty. "Should I wash it out?"

Frankie picked out a piece of my hair and peered at it. "No way; I mean, firstly, it could create a whole new beginning for you and Luke. As in, you could literally pretend to be another human being. Like, 'Phoebe had to leave, but I am—Horatia, the new person in your presentation group. I will never send a photo of you to you because I am Ho—'"

I ignored her and turned back to Liberty. "Seriously, I know this represents an hour and a half of our lives, but should I wash it out?"

Liberty shook her head. "No way. It's like red lipstick, you just have to get used to it."

"What should I wear?"

Frankie opened my wardrobe. "What would Horatia wear? That is the question."

Liberty jumped up and down. "I'll lend you some of my clothes."

"Liberty, me and you have very different styles." Liberty's style was unashamedly sexy. More "Ibiza VIP lounge" than "romantic poetry seminar." "I think the hair and then me turning up looking so glamorous might make people think I was—"

"Horatia!" Frankie shouted. "She's, like, Sasha Fierce. Like, Horatia wouldn't pretend the Luke Taylor text never happened. She'd just be all, like, 'Yeah, that is how I test my men. Do you wanna stroke my long, straight hair or not?'"

"Can we stop talking about the text?" I pleaded.

"I will *never* stop talking about the text," Frankie said, crossing her arms. "It's literally the most hilarious thing that's ever happened to me. And it didn't even happen to me."

I laughed. "Yeah, well, I can only cope with seeing Luke if I do this weird mental exercise where I convince myself I never sent him that photo."

It was true. Me, Luke and Mary had met up in the library every day for the past three days, and I'd only managed to get through it by burying the text somewhere deep inside me. Just literally pretending it had never happened. But the truth was, the more we hung out, the less weird and awkward it was starting to feel.

"I bet Luke probably keeps that message as his screen saver," Liberty said. "Has he honestly never mentioned it?"

I shook my head.

"So weird," she sighed. Then she turned to Frankie. "Can I have a Sasha Fierce name, too?"

Frankie shrugged. "You don't need one, girl, but yeah, OK. What about Hercules?"

"Ooh, Hercules, I like tha—"

She was cut off by Connor's boom from the kitchen. "Waffles!" I knew he was beating his chest as he said it. "Waaaaaaaaffles."

The kitchen door opened and Connor poked his head through. "We have made waaaaaaaffles."

We walked into the kitchen, where he and Nathan were standing over a machine.

"You bought a waffle maker?" I said.

"Whoa, you look totally different." Nathan seemed genuinely shocked.

Frankie held up her phone. There was a picture of me spliced next to Cousin Itt. Underneath she had written "Freaky Friday."

"We've melted M&M's, Twix and Honey Nut Cheerios together," Connor said proudly. "Although the Honey Nut Cheerios aren't really melting."

"Connor, do you think I look ridiculous?" I said.

"She means do you think Luke Taylor will think she looks ridiculous?" Frankie corrected.

Connor shook his head. "I would like to say he won't notice the hair, but you do look like a child from a Japanese horror film, so he probably will." The waffle maker started smoking and he flapped at it with a dish towel. "But then, y'know, that's the beauty of liking girls, isn't it? Never knowing what crazy shit they're gonna do next. Like, wearing those wedge shoes, or having nails like Wolverine or making you take the same picture millions of times. I, personally, love it."

167

Frankie had her arm around me, so we shuffled over and added Connor to the huddle. "Strangely, you've actually made me feel better."

I went and got changed into the most boring outfit I could think of: jeans and a white T-shirt. The hair was enough of a statement without Liberty's over-the-knee boots.

I tucked my hair into my duffle coat and packed my bag. Even aside from all the Luke stuff, I was actually a bit nervous about the presentation. It was the first thing that really counted. As I walked to class, I tried to retract tortoise-like into my hood to take attention away from my hair.

I thought Luke was late at first, but then I saw him on the grass outside the English building on his hands and knees.

"What are you doing?" I stood on the path looking at him.

He smiled up at me. "I forgot the leaves."

"Mary will kill you." I laughed. "The leaves are, like . . . the whole thing."

"Yeah, but the thing is, now that I actually need some leaves, there are none. The whole place has been covered in them, and now the wind has blown them all away or something." He looked genuinely quite stressed.

"It's because you are looking at a patch of grass where there are no trees. Why would there be leaves when there aren't any trees?"

He stood up. "Oh yeah, right. That makes sense." I swear he went a tiny bit red.

I pointed at the trees on the other side of the lake. "Hurry up, we've got time."

We rushed across the bridge, and I realized it was the same

bridge we'd sat on back on the first night. When I looked at Luke, he was staring right up at Stephanie Stevens's dorm, but neither of us said anything.

We paced about, picking up random leaves. "They're a bit damp," he said.

"OK, well, you find them and I'll dry them with my coat."

He handed me a leaf and I started wiping it dry.

"I mean, this whole thing is ridiculous," he moaned. "Why did we let Mary lead us down this damp-leaf-ridden path of madness?"

"'Cause neither of us had any ideas whatsoever."

He handed me the last leaf and I smoothed it out. "They look a little raggedy, but they'll have to do."

We met Mary outside the seminar room. She was wearing tons of mascara and had a silver star stenciled just underneath one of her eyes. Plus, her usual baggy track pants and crop top. Was she so hot she was actually immune to the cold?

She hugged us both. "Luke, did you remember the leaves?"

He nodded. "Yeah, of course. Got them yesterday." I shook my head and mouthed "idiot" at him. Then Mary did a kind of overly dramatic double take as she properly took in my hair.

"Shit, Phoebs. So much hair. Such good hair. Phoebe with the good hair."

Luke nodded. "Yeah, I meant to say, earlier. It looks really different. Like, good different. I mean, it looks nice curly, too. But, like, this—it also looks really . . ." He sort of puttered to a stop as he saw Mary biting her lip. "Nice," he finished.

Mary whistled. "Smooooooth. Save that silver tongue for the presentation, Taylor."

I should've said something about the hair earlier.

Obviously, I'd noticed it right away. With Phoebe, the hair is always the first thing you notice. And it did look really good. But I never know what to say in those kinds of situations. Like, if you mention it, it's like you're making a big thing of it. But if you don't mention it, you're a jerk. You literally can't win.

We all sat down in the classroom. Yorgos arrived and started telling us how excited he was for our presentations. He picked Martha and Liverpool Paul and Katie first. They got up and opened their PowerPoint. They had a PowerPoint; we had a bag of damp leaves. I was starting to get very nervous.

Mary looked like she didn't have a care in the world. She even looked slightly bored. I nudged my notebook toward Phoebe and wrote "Are we fucked?" on it. She wrote "POSSIBLY YES" underneath in block capitals.

Liverpool Paul finished his monologue about Chaucer and everyone clapped. Then Yorgos started talking about how vital good research is. I had the sudden feeling that I was about to fail my first real piece of university work.

"OK," Yorgos said. "Mary, Phoebe and Luke. Let's see what you've got."

Mary was straight out of her chair, handing out the leaves with a kind of smug look on her face. "Our piece is experiential," she announced, and I saw Phoebe wince slightly.

She handed Yorgos a leaf and then walked over to the door and turned off the lights. "Everyone close your eyes," she said in this heavy, Acting 101 voice.

Me and Phoebe stood on either side of her at the front of the room. "We want to take you on a hypnotic journey . . . through memory," she continued. "Through your own memory, but also into the connective memory of everyone who has come before you."

The corner of Phoebe's mouth twitched. Even though it was our presentation, and I was standing at the front, it was like I couldn't concentrate on it. I just looked across the not-that-dark room at everyone with their eyes closed, holding a moldy old leaf.

"Feel the veins," Mary was whispering. She had a way of whispering that was actually louder than her normal speaking voice. "Think of how they reach out to one another. Think of your mother's hand reaching out for yours on your first day of school. And think of the hand reaching out behind her, and the one behind that. And all the hands that came before you, reaching out into the darkness. Reaching back and back and back."

People were actually feeling their leaves. "Think about the love you have felt," Mary said. "Think about single moments of time that have changed your—or someone else's—life forever."

I tried very hard not to think about Abbey.

"Think about the secrets you keep inside you," Mary continued. "Feel the veins connect and think about the secrets other people hold in their veins, too." She was holding her hands out like Gandalf and speaking in a slow, kind of dreamlike voice. Me and Phoebe both looked down at our sheets.

"'You were blue,'" I recited.

"'Clown-like, happiest on your hands,'" Phoebe said.

"Think of your ancestor, walking in the snow to find food," Mary whispered.

"'When you can no more hold me by the hand,'" Phoebe read.

"'Nor I half turn to go, yet turning stay.'" I tried to match Mary's somber tone, but didn't quite get it.

Mary shuffled to the back. She shouted, "Speak, memory!" then switched on the light.

No one said anything for a few seconds. They just sat there, blinking and holding their leaves. There was just this long, awkward silence. Then Phoebe cleared her throat and launched into her short, non-leaf-based analysis of "Ariel" by Sylvia Plath, which was scarily impressive and eloquent, and I bumbled through my bit about Ted Hughes's "Last Letter," most of which I'd nicked from the book Phoebe had lent me.

And then Mary beamed around the whole class and said: "Yeah, so . . . that's it, basically. Keep the leaves. Remember us every time you look at them."

Everyone clapped, and Yorgos shot us a big smile and got the next three up. And I had absolutely no idea whether it had gone well or not.

Mary definitely seemed to think it had. She literally danced out of the room when it was all over.

"I totally respect everyone else's approach, but ours was obviously the best. I mean, the fact that Yorgos actually took his leaf with him when he left . . . Like, I actually think it made him see stuff differently. I hope so."

She linked arms with us both and we wandered down the hall.

"I feel like I might sleep with Yorgos at some point, y'know," Mary said, as if she was mulling over what to have for dinner. "Like, I know it's a cliché to sleep with your TA, but when they're that hot . . ."

"Yeah, seconded," Phoebe said. "I think his hotness makes him impervious to clichés."

"Thirded," I said, and they both laughed.

Mary stopped. "You guys are coming to Fit Sister later, right?" She said it like it wasn't actually a question, more a statement. And in the third person, like she wasn't even in Fit Sister.

"Definitely, yeah," I said.

"Cool. I'll see you there. Just need to go pick up the smoke machine. . . ."

● ● ● ● ● ● ● **PHOEBE** ● ● ● ● ● ● ●

I spent two hours pulling every single item of clothing out of my wardrobe, before deciding I didn't own anything cool enough to wear to a Fit Sister gig. I settled on classic wallflower jeans and a plain T-shirt and vowed to buy an electric-blue vest dress just in case this ever happened again.

I met Luke outside Gildas Bar, and as soon as we walked in I felt self-conscious.

The whole place was full of people who looked like they were one hundred percent part of the Bowl-Cut tribe. People with bright-aqua hair tied in buns on top of their heads. A girl wearing a Run DMC tank top and a sequined skirt, and another one wearing baggy combat boots but also a wedding veil. She was just randomly wearing a full-length wedding veil. The boys

173

were all good-looking in a cool, alternative way, dancing wildly with their shirts tied round their waists and nodding every time the music changed.

Me and Luke, sitting at the side with our drinks, looked like a mum and dad who had accidentally walked into the wrong tent at a festival.

"I do not feel cool enough to be here," he whispered.

I wanted to say, "You are, but I'm definitely not." But I just said: "Me neither."

The lights went down and a few people cheered, and suddenly Bowl-Cut was up on stage, standing behind a massive keyboard and a microphone. Under the black light you could see she had UV stars painted all over her stomach.

Next to her was a hot guy with shaggy hair and a moth-eaten sweater. He was also standing behind a keyboard and mic stand. It took a couple of seconds for me to place him, but as soon as I did I whipped out my phone.

"Such a groupie." Luke shook his head as I pressed "record."

I covered the clip in hearts and sent it to Frankie and Negin: "Interesting Thought Boy is performing LIVE before my eyes."

"We are Fit Sister," Bowl-Cut yelled into the mic. "You guys aren't ready for us yet . . . but your kids are gonna love us."

She and ITB both started whacking their keyboards, making a kind of music I have literally no idea how to describe. It sounded a bit like a computer game playing underwater, with Mary's distorted singing over the top. She actually had a really good voice.

People at the front started dancing. Or, not really *dancing* dancing, but sort of swaying and bobbing their heads and jerking about wildly.

"D'you think that guy's all right?" Luke nodded at a guy in a Sherlock hat who was flailing his arms around a tower of speakers. "He looks like he's having a seizure."

"Everyone here is nuts, but in the coolest possible way. Like, treading the line between headlining-at-Glastonbury and being-committed-to-an-insane-asylum." I took a sip of my drink. "I'm definitely the geekiest person here."

"Geek power." Luke raised his fist in salute.

"You are so not a geek. You're one hundred percent pure jock."

Luke actually looked offended. "I hate that word. It's like you're just a dick who's not interested in anything except soccer."

Negin and Frankie had sent a photo back; they were both in their pj's, drinking hot chocolate. Frankie had written:

Can't BELIEVE you wouldn't let us come. As if we really
would have embarrassed you in front of Quidditch Bailer.
Tell ITB that Negin is his ONE TRUE LOVE.

Negin had just written:

Do NOT tell ITB that. How's the date going . . . ?

On stage, ITB was now holding a small bell up to his microphone and ringing it gently in time to the drumbeat. I took another picture.

"I'm sure you're interested in other stuff," I said to Luke. Then, because it was dark, and I was half drunk and feeling brave, I added: "Just not quidditch, obviously."

He turned to look at me and shook his head. "Honestly,

175

Phoebe . . . I have wanted to talk to you about that for ages. Something just . . . came up, and I felt so, so bad about it and I actually really wanted to go and—"

"It's fine. Actually, it's really fun." We both glanced at a couple exaggeratedly waltzing next to us.

The song ended, and Bowl-Cut jabbed her finger at me and Luke: "Yes! Big up my leaf memory class bredrins!"

A few people whooped around to us, and we both grinned at them. Then the music started bubbling and squelching again, with Bowl-Cut wailing all over it, and Luke said: "Come on, we've got to at least try to dance after she basically dedicated the gig to us. . . ."

We made our way down to the front and started copying the Sherlock guy. It went from awkward to really, really fun in the space of about five seconds. After three songs, we were both laughing and sweating so much we had to go back to the bar.

"Honestly, can I come to the next thing?" Luke shouted into my ear as we ordered more drinks. "Quidditch, I mean. I really, genuinely want to."

He stuck his hand out.

"We've shaken before, Luke Taylor," I said. "You are not a man of your word."

He pulled a leaf out of his pocket. "I swear on the rotten leaf of memory."

"OK." I shook his hand.

Then the lights came up, and Mary was bouncing down into the crowd, hugging people. She came over to us, with a few other girls in tow—including Sequined Skirt and Wedding Veil, who had now taken her wedding veil off.

"You guys came!" Mary howled, hugging us both.

"Of course." Luke smiled.

She thumped the bar. "I demand to have some booze." The bartender appeared and she started ordering.

I pointed at the FEMINIST CLUB badge on Wedding Veil girl's lapel. "I feel bad, I still haven't been to any meetings," I said. "I signed up at Orientation Fair."

"You should totally come." Wedding Veil smiled at me and then at Luke. "You too."

"Yeah, I'd definitely be up for it," Luke said.

Bowl-Cut handed him a shot. "Luke's on the soccer team, so he's more into oppressing women than emancipating them, aren't you, Luke?" She clearly meant it as a joke, but the girl with the sequined skirt bristled a bit, and stared at him hard. "Are you really on the soccer team?"

Luke nodded.

"So is all that Wall of Shame stuff true, then?" she asked, and suddenly everyone was looking at Luke.

"What's the Wall of Shame stuff?" I said.

"They take photos of girls they sleep with and then rate them out of ten and shit," said Sequined Skirt. "It's fucking Donald Trump–level dickishness."

"Yeah, and it's only a rumor, Jen," frowned Wedding Veil. Then she turned to Luke. "Right?"

I felt myself getting hot. What if it was true? Had Will taken a picture of me when I was asleep? He might not have texted me back, but he wasn't *that* much of a bastard, surely? Panic started to rise up in my stomach. I hadn't even slept with Will. I had just slept *with* him.

177

Luke downed his shot and winced. "Yeah, it's not true," he said, wiping his lips.

Bowl-Cut punched him on the shoulder. "See? If my man Taylor says it's bullshit, then that's good enough for me."

Luke smiled at me, and I felt relief cooling my whole body as I thought, *Me too.*

14

● ● ● ● ● ● ● **LUKE** ● ● ● ● ● ● ●

It freaked me out how quickly it was happening.

How quickly I'd gone from crushing on Phoebe in this vague, daydreamy, nothingy way, to liking her in solid, this-might-actually-happen concrete.

When I was around her, I was constantly on edge. I felt that weird, unexplainable electricity you get when you like someone new. I hadn't felt that since Abbey sat down next to me at the start of tenth-grade French, and it made me scared and guilty and excited all at the same time.

Just thinking about seeing her made me pick up my pace as I left the field. It was a weirdly warm morning for late October, and me and Will were strolling back through Jutland after an early five-a-side. We'd played our first real game last week—against Chester University—and lost 4–2, so Will was insisting we all practice at every available opportunity.

I hadn't really been able to focus on today's game, because I was so caught up in Phoebe thoughts. We'd arranged to meet at our poetry class and then head straight over to the quidditch thing afterward.

"You coming for a beer, then?" Will asked, looking at his phone.

"It's not even half past ten."

"Is that a yes?"

"I've got class." I considered telling him about quidditch but instantly decided against it. Firstly because I was fairly certain he'd tease me, but also because I still wasn't sure what had actually happened between him and Phoebe. I'd seen him get with tons of girls over the past few weeks, so he couldn't have been that into her. But I still wondered what he'd think if he knew I liked her. And I wondered what she thought about him.

His phone beeped and he flashed it under my nose. "Fuck, man. She's hot. Well played, Geordie Al."

I looked at the photo and figured this was as good a time as any to try to say something about the Wall of Shame. About how off I thought it was.

I tried to sound casual: "By the way, I never told you. I was out a few nights back and this girl said something about the Wall of Shame stuff. Like, how she'd heard rumors about it."

Will's face tightened. "You didn't say anything, did you?"

"No . . ."

His face relaxed back into a smile, which made me feel sort of dirty and complicit somehow. As if I'd told that lie out of team loyalty rather than just panicking under the pressure and shame and blurting it out.

"Some girls are so fucking uptight, honestly." Will shook his head. "I mean, people take pictures of people all the time. It's just a joke."

I nodded. But it really didn't feel funny.

"I'd better go," I said.

I sprinted all the way across campus, hoping I'd get to the lecture early enough to get a seat next to Phoebe. But in the end, I was still five minutes late. I took a deep breath and pushed the doors as gently as possible, but they squeaked ridiculously loudly, and about a hundred heads turned to look at me.

"Ah . . . There's always one, isn't there?" said the professor, peering up over his glasses. "In you come, quick as possible."

There was only one free seat—in the middle of a packed row near the back. I squeezed my way through, apologizing to the muttering people who had to stand up. Finally, I sat down, massively relieved not to be the center of attention anymore.

And then my phone went off.

And a hundred heads turned. Again.

"There's always one, isn't there?" said the professor again. "Although it's not usually the same one." The muttering had now blossomed into full-blown laughter.

"Right . . . ," said the professor sternly as I put my phone on silent and took out my copy of *Modern Romantic Poetry*. "Let's get back to it. Now then, by 1542, Henry VIII's alliance with the Holy Roman emperor Charles V causes him to intervene in the Italian War . . ."

I stopped unpacking my bag and looked around the hall. I couldn't see Phoebe. In fact, I couldn't see a single person I recognized, apart from the massive *Game of Thrones* guy who'd walked out of the soccer initiation. And he'd definitely not been in any of my other classes. He was sitting two seats down, scribbling notes and scratching his stubbly rust-colored beard. He looked across at my poetry book and wrote something on his phone. He slid it over to me: "WRONG ROOM PAL."

I slumped forward onto the desk as he tried to stifle his laughter.

An hour later, I had a decent—if ultimately useless—grasp of Henry VIII's foreign policy, and me and the giant shuffled out of the hall and introduced ourselves properly. His name was Ed, and since he was in Gildas College—where the quidditch thing was happening—we ended up walking in the same direction. He was so tall that his dirty-blond Afro nearly brushed the top of the covered walkway.

"How was the rest of that initiation, then?" he asked.

"Your walkout was probably the highlight."

He smiled. "That Dempers seemed like a right dick."

"Yeah. He is a bit. But the rest of them are cool. Mostly."

Ed just shrugged.

"Do you really not drink, then?" I asked him.

"Nah, never," he said. "Tried it once. Had five pints of lager. It had no effect whatsoever. Must be my size, I suppose. So I don't bother with it now. Just stick to the pineapple juice. Much tastier."

"But didn't you think about drinking just for that night? So you could get on the team?"

"Not really. I mean, I like soccer and that, but if being on the team means putting up with all that bro bullshit, then I'm best off out of it, I feel. Plenty of other stuff to do here."

We crossed the Stephanie Stevens bridge, and something stopped me in my tracks.

"Fuck. I know that smell. . . ."

Rita and Arthur were lying on the grass, both leafing through massive books while Arthur ate a wedge of Brie like a pizza slice. He almost choked on it when he spotted Ed. "Jesus, look at the size of him," he sputtered.

Ed sniffed deeply. "That's good-quality Brie, is that. Very nice."

"Exactly." Arthur snapped his book shut. "I wish you were in our hall. I'm surrounded by fucking savages. No offense, Luke."

"None taken," I said. "Ed, this is Arthur and Rita. Arthur and Rita, Ed."

"Where are you guys off to?" Rita asked.

"I'm going to this quidditch thing. You guys should come if you want."

Rita's lips twitched. "Ah . . . Accidental Text Girl?"

"Who's Accidental Text Girl?" Ed asked.

"No one. It's too long to explain. Look, are you guys coming or not?" I checked my phone. "I'm late as it is. And it could be quite fun. It's just a friendly game, I think. There'll probably be free food. And free pineapple juice."

"I've got class," Rita said, but Arthur stood up and dusted his coat off. "Yeah, fuck it, I'm in."

Ed shrugged. "Me too. Though if anyone tries to handcuff me, I'm straight out the door."

● ● ● ● ● ● **PHOEBE** ● ● ● ● ● ●

"Sorry, but if he bails this time, none of us are speaking to him again. Ever. The end." Frankie didn't look angry, she looked upset.

Negin nodded and sipped her cream soda–and–syrup butterbeer. "Me and you haven't even spoken to him anyway.

183

But yeah, to do this twice he'd have to be either mentally unhinged or genuinely evil."

"Or dead," I said hopefully. "I mean, why did he miss class? This is so upsetting it's tragic. I kept telling people I was saving his seat, and then I had to sit with an empty space next to me for the whole hour." I really, really thought he'd come. "He's such a *dick*," I added.

"Scrap that, no he's not." Frankie squeezed my arm. "And, sorry, but who the *hell* is that with him?"

We all looked over at the entrance to the hall. Luke was walking toward us, smiling, with two other boys next to him. I didn't even realize I was smiling back until Negin whispered: "Look how cute you are. It's disgusting."

Frankie still had a tight grip on my arm. "Sorry, but I think I might actually die. *Look. How. Tall. He. Is.*"

She squeezed harder with each syllable.

"Sorry I'm late," Luke said. "Went to the wrong room."

"I can vouch for that—he did." The tall boy nodded.

"Nothing's started yet." I tried to sound offhand, but seeing Luke in the flesh was weird; because I spent so much time intensely thinking about him when he wasn't there, it was like dreams and real life muddling together.

"I'm Luke." He smiled at Frankie and Negin.

"Arthur," the boy next to him added. "First-time quidditcher. Or is it quiditchee?"

"Quidditcher, I think," said the ridiculously tall boy, who had a strong northern accent. "If you're doing the quidditch, you'd be a quidditcher. Like, if you're doing a murder, you're a murderer." Then he smiled at us. "I'm Ed, by the way."

"So it's Ed and Arthur," I repeated.

184

"And you're . . . Luke, was it?" Frankie said "Luke" as if it was a strange foreign name that she was hearing for the first time. "Yes, I think Phoebe's mentioned you."

I made a mental note to kick her later in her sleep.

"You have to go and sign up." Negin nodded over to the table where Brandon and Misty were sitting, and the boys wandered off to join the line.

Frankie slipped her arms around us as she watched them go: "He's tall and fit and he knows about grammar and quidditch and murder. He's literally the perfect man. He—" She broke off as Luke came back. When she'd turned to Negin, I whispered, "Does Ed have a girlfriend?"

Luke smirked at me. "I don't know—why, are you interested?" Our eyes met for a second.

"No . . . ," I said slowly. He was still smiling his fit smile at me, and I willed myself not to go red. "I was asking for Frankie. She's been looking for a tall man since the first night of Frosh Week."

"Noted. Let's make it happen." He looked around the hall at people warming up and comparing broomsticks. "So what goes on at this thing, then?"

"Right, well"—I pointed at Brandon, who was bobbing up and down excitedly—"that's Brandon. He's the jolly one. And that"—I pointed at Misty, who was wearing a dark-red camouflage hoodie and looking pissed off—"that's Misty. She's the not-jolly one."

He looked at me. "Misty?"

I nodded. "I know, I know. Me and Negin and Frankie have already discussed it." We both laughed, and then Brandon gathered us all together in a little circle.

185

"Right, thanks for coming, gang," he said. "I'm seeing some new faces here this afternoon, which is super exciting, isn't it, Mist?"

Misty was looking at us like she wanted to kill us, but she still agreed that it was super exciting.

Brandon carried on: "Competitive matches start next week, so today will just be a bit of fun. We'll play a few friendlies among ourselves. Right, grab some brooms, people," he shouted. "Let's do this!"

I realized I was going to have to actually do physical exercise in front of Luke Taylor. I tried to sneak a look at him in a non-bait way. And when I did, he was looking right back at me.

● ● ● ● ● ● ●   **LUKE**   ● ● ● ● ● ● ●

The Brandon guy was the most excitable person I'd ever seen. He was like someone had trapped a rabbit in a human body, then wrapped it in a Gryffindor robe.

"OK, so for the friendlies, we usually divide up into houses," he yelled. "So let's just see if we have anything even resembling equal numbers...." He looked around the circle, and his gaze rested on Arthur. "How about you, mate? Didn't see you at our first meeting. What's your name?"

"Arthur."

"Great. And what house are you in?"

Arthur shrugged. "No idea. I don't really care about Harry Potter, to be honest."

Brandon smiled, completely unoffended. "OK, cool; well, let's put you in Hufflepuff, then."

Arthur snorted. "Fuck off. No way am I Hufflepuff."

Frankie let out a yelp of laughter so loud it echoed around the hall.

Misty stepped forward and clapped Arthur on the shoulder proudly. "Yeah, you're right. Hotheaded, fiery, passionate . . . You're Gryffindor through and through, aren't you?"

Arthur sniffed and tried to regain some of his composure. "Yeah, I guess. Maybe. Whatever. I mean, it's not like I care either way."

"Oh, well, in that case," said Brandon, "if you don't mind being Hufflepuff . . ."

"No, we've said I'm Gryffindor now, haven't we," Arthur snapped. "So I might as well definitely be Gryffindor. Definitely."

We split up into two groups. I got put in Ravenclaw with Ed and Negin. We were playing Hufflepuff, who had Phoebe and Frankie on their team.

"I've been given a fucking mop!" I heard Arthur yell from across the hall, where Gryffindor was getting ready to take on Slytherin. "I'm supposed to be a wizard, not a caretaker!"

Somebody blew a whistle, and even though half of us had no clue what to do, we started playing.

One of the freshmen chucked the ball at me immediately, and I saw Phoebe sprinting toward me. For half a second I had the ridiculous idea to just keep hold of it, and see if she would crash right into me.

But I didn't. I chucked it to Ed, and Phoebe pulled up an inch from my chest.

She hitched an eyebrow and smiled. "So close." Then she sprinted off again, and I suddenly wondered whether I was the first person in history to feel horny on a quidditch field.

Ed was legging it down the wing, the ball clamped under his arm. He stopped short in front of the goal hoop things. Frankie went galloping madly toward him, but he chucked the ball right past her into the top hoop.

Our team all went crazy, and even Frankie started clapping, until one of the Hufflepuffs shouted: "You're not on their team!"

The Hufflepuff keeper immediately started scanning for a decent pass. I drifted over to Phoebe and stood right behind her.

"Right, I'm marking you, Bennet," I said. "There's no way you're getting past me."

She stepped backward into me gently, scraping the inside of my leg with her broomstick. "This isn't soccer, Luke Taylor." She turned to look at me, her cheeks flushed. "This is a real sport, yeah? You're out of your depth."

I was finding it pretty hard to concentrate on anything except Phoebe, but I tried to get my head back in the game as the Hufflepuffs were jogging out of their area.

Someone shouted, "Mark up!" and I yelled, "Got Phoebe!"

"No one's marking me," Frankie bellowed, looking directly at Ed. "I mean, someone should be marking me, shouldn't they?" Ed was totally oblivious to this; he was just watching the ball.

One of the Hufflepuffs tried a long pass, but Ed plucked it out of the air with his tree-trunk arm. He chucked it to Negin, who stared at it blankly for a second and then burst off down the wing.

It stopped everyone dead. "Negin," hissed Frankie. "Are you joking?"

Negin was unbelievably quick. The Hufflepuff beaters launched three "bludgers" (flat volleyballs) at her, but she dodged them all. Without slowing down, she sent the ball straight through the top hoop, and our team went crazy again.

Misty stood up and shouted from the sidelines at Ed and Negin: "You and you—what are your names?"

They told her, and she started scribbling furiously on her notepad.

It was weird: that same edge that comes out in me on the soccer field suddenly came out here, too. I really wanted to win.

Hufflepuff got a goal back, but me and Ed passed the ball around neatly, then I sent Negin off on another blazing run. Again, she slammed the ball through the hoop, and the three of us high-fived.

Brandon jostled about among the chaos, slapping people on the back and randomly shouting encouragement. He'd grin at you if you did something right, and he'd grin more brightly if you did something wrong. When Frankie nearly decapitated him by swinging her broom at the ball, he just fell about laughing and started calling her Belinda Broomswing.

Eventually, when we were 14–10 up, another whistle blew, and the Ravenclaws all cheered and collapsed to the floor. I felt sweaty and tired and the happiest I had been in ages.

Misty asked me and Phoebe if we'd mind putting the goal hoops away, and I could feel Frankie's and Negin's eyes on us as we wheeled them out into the hall. We found the storeroom and propped the hoops up against an old Ping-Pong table. And then we just stood there, still red-faced and a bit out of breath, looking at each other. Realizing that we were completely alone in a dusty back room. Just smiling and breathing and not saying anything. We both knew it was gonna happen, and it was sort of exciting and excruciating at the same time.

Phoebe mumbled, "OK, then . . ." and we both laughed awkwardly. I felt my heartbeat up its pace, and just as thoughts of Abbey were starting to tumble into my head, she leaned forward, and then I leaned forward, and then she closed her eyes.

And then it was like I stopped thinking altogether.

I put my arms around her, and we were suddenly right up against each other, sticky with sweat, and kissing harder and harder.

15

● ● ● ● ● ● ● **PHOEBE** ● ● ● ● ● ● ●

Frankie took her full-to-the-brim bowl of Wheaties and hot milk out of the microwave and tiptoed to the table so it wouldn't spill. Negin and me were eating honey on toast.

"I'm gonna leave it to dry for a bit," Frankie said. "I only like it when it's turned into a kind of paste." She picked up a bag of sugar and started shaking it out over the top of the gloopy brown mixture. Negin wrinkled her nose slightly.

"So would you say Luke Taylor is your official boyfriend now?" Frankie took an un-offered bite of Negin's toast.

I shook my head. "As if. Would you say random-freshman-kiss is *your* boyfriend? We've kissed. Once."

Negin shook her head. "Come on, it's different. You've had this *really* long buildup."

Since it had happened I'd been permanently giddy. I had never had this feeling, about anything, ever. The closest was when I was so bored in study hall that I entered an online competition and won a luxury trip to Disney World for my whole family. It was the same kind of initial quake and then tremors of fuzzy, giggly aftershock that made me feel like some kind of epic hero.

"Did you tell Flora?" Negin asked.

"Yup. She literally started hyperventilating. She acted as if we had achieved it together. Like a joint Oscar win." She had just kept saying, "You've fucking *kissed* Luke Taylor. You *did* it," over and over again. Which was pretty much what was going through my head, even in real time as it was actually happening. Like my subconscious was yelling, *What the hell? This is cracked out. Is this even real?*

Frankie started to eat the congealed sugar crust on her Wheaties. "He obviously likes you. I mean, he texted you *'good night.'* 'Good night' is the most meaningful message you can send someone. It's more than 'I love you.' 'Good night' actually incorporates 'I love you.' Because you only text people you *love* 'good night.' No one has ever texted me 'good night.' Literally, no one."

"I just really want to know what happened with him and Abbey," I said. "But it's impossible to find out."

"Is there any way you could, like ... bring it up casually?" Negin suggested.

"No, because that will instantly make me seem like a crazy person who wants to marry him."

"Fair. Both ways. I mean, you do." Frankie poured another layer of sugar into her bowl. "I was telling my mum about it last night. Do you know the woman from Abba married her stalker?"

I snorted into my tea. "OK, stop saying stuff like that out loud. Although, you know, I only have about four memories before I saw Luke Taylor. I know because I counted them recently."

Negin looked up from her toast. "You specifically counted the number of memories you have before you first saw him? That's really weird. No offense, but that is a bit stalkerish."

"I think it's romantic," said Frankie. "But I have a really bad memory, so I don't have a lot of memories before the first time I met Ed yesterday."

"I didn't specifically count them in relation to him. We're doing memory in one of my courses. Like how memory is what makes literature. How you can't have the written word without memory."

"I have no clue what we do in archaeology." Frankie yawned. "They keep talking about science. No one ever told me it had anything to do with science. I'm absolutely crap at science." She took another mouthful of Wheaties paste. "So what *is* the deal with this Abbey, then?"

"I can't find anything out about her," I said. "As in she used to be social media obsessed and she has, like . . . disappeared."

"Oh my god, do you think Luke Taylor killed her?" Frankie said.

"He does play sports." Negin nodded. "More testosterone."

"*You* play sports," I said.

"Negin's killed mad amounts of people," Frankie shouted. "With her resting bitch face alone."

I got up and put more bread in the toaster. "Seriously, though, Abbey has vanished. Literally vanished. And now I have absolutely no way at all of finding out what happened between her and Luke."

"Except asking Luke . . ." Negin shrugged. "Which would be fairly straightforward."

"Obviously, I'm not gonna do that."

Becky walked in wrapped in a massive coat, carrying a pile of packages.

"Beckster!" Frankie shouted, even though she was about a few feet away from her. She held up her hand and Becky put the boxes on the table and very gently high-fived her. "How come you're back?"

Becky tucked her hair behind her ears. "Me and Aaron had a fight, so I got an earlier train." I looked at her more closely. Her eyes were ever so slightly red.

I jumped up and pulled out a chair for her. "Are you OK?"

She nodded. "Yeah, I just . . . It'll be fine. I'm gonna call him in—" She stopped before her voice cracked. Her face tightened and she stared hard at the table. I wanted to say she could go back to her room if she wanted to. That she didn't have to cry in front of us. It was weird how little we all knew each other in some ways. Did Becky have a Flora to call and cry on the phone to? Frankie and me exchanged a look, and Frankie sat down next to her and put her hand slightly awkwardly on her shoulder. Becky gulped and shook her head, and I could tell she was trying her hardest to stop it but she couldn't. She cried gently for a bit while we watched hopelessly. After a while her sniffs became more widely spaced, and Negin went and got a roll of toilet paper and handed it to her.

She wiped her eyes and then scrunched the toilet paper up in her hands and finally just said, "It's not how I thought it was gonna be."

It was almost too big a statement to respond to.

"The 'best days of your life' thing is made up by old people with mortgages and stuff," Negin said. "It's obviously weird to just uproot your life."

Becky nodded. "I really miss him. We used to see each other every single day. We used to meet up to walk to school together. I told him I would stay exactly the same, and I *am* exactly the same, I think. . . ."

"No one can stay exactly the same," I said. And I thought about Flora and her new friends and how strange it made me feel.

Frankie leaned her head on Becky's shoulder. "Sometimes I think about how weird it is that if you look in a mirror from one second to the next, then you look exactly the same. But, like, if you stayed in front of a mirror for five years, would you *see* yourself change?"

Negin shot her a look that indicated she would have had something cutting to say if Frankie had made this statement in another situation.

"I don't want to change," Becky said. "I really just wish I could have frozen time this summer. I feel like everything was okay then, and I just want it to be then again." She nodded. "I really love Aaron."

"Becky, he obviously loves you. You just had a fight. People fight all the time," I said. "Just call him in a bit."

She nodded. "I might go home on Tuesday."

Frankie shook her head. "Tuesday is Halloween. You have to come to the nine-nine-nine thing. Pregame's here first. I'm making cocktails inspired by everyone's personalities." She squeezed

Becky's hand. "I mean, you say vodka and Fanta to me, with a dash of green syrup." She picked her bowl up and tipped the last of the milk into her mouth.

"All we have currently is vodka, Fanta and some green syrup," Negin said. And then Becky did smile a watery smile. I thought she might get up and go to her room, but she didn't, so she must have wanted to stay with us, jabbering on about shit.

Frankie picked up one of the parcels and started unwrapping it. "Speaking of the nine-nine-nine party . . ." She tore open the plastic packaging with force and emptied the contents onto the table.

A weird white plasticky dress with a red cross on it fell out. We all looked at the cardboard insert with a stripper-type woman on it that said SEXY NURSE COSTUME. Frankie sniffed it. "It smells really weird. Like markers. Shall we try them on?"

We traipsed back to my room, and she immediately started flinging her clothes off. Becky zipped her up in the costume, and she turned around and threw her arms in the air like she was opening a show in Vegas.

"It weirdly makes you look even taller," I said. "I think it's because the dress is so tiny. Your legs look insanely long. Like they are three-quarters of your body."

"Like a daddy longlegs? Bitch." Frankie scowled and changed to another model pose. "What am I supposed to do? Go to the giant's costume emporium?"

"If someone spills their drink on you, at least you can just wipe it off." Negin squinted at her. "Is it made of pencil-case material?"

"No, Negin, I just look like an actual pencil." She tried to pull the thigh-high things up but they only reached a bit over her knees. "I thought the only people who actually wore garters were Victoria's Secret models, so why are they so short?"

"I'll have the opposite problem," I said. "I bet mine are too long and go right up to my ass."

"And there is this gap for my boobs, but I have no boobs to put in it." Frankie swung around to Becky, who was sitting on my bed. "Becky, you aren't a bitch like these two. Be honest, if you were Ed, would you find me in any way sexual in this outfit?"

Becky looked a bit overwhelmed by the question. "Um . . ."

Me and Negin burst out laughing. "Sorry, you are sexual," I said. "It was just Becky's face . . . and the way you said 'sexual.'"

"Fuck you all," Frankie said, and one of the stockings fell around her ankles. She plonked down next to Becky. "Do you know my mum is actually a nurse? And they don't even wear this shit. They wear tunics like women at drug stores. Maybe I should have got the £23:99 one. Did you get the £23:99 one? Come on, I want to see yours."

Usually, I would have felt a bit self-conscious showing people my body, but Frankie seemed so at home in hers that it kind of made me want to feel at home in mine. Even if I didn't.

I think, in my whole life, Frankie was the only girl apart from Mum I had seen completely naked. In PE at school, everyone was so careful, wriggling around inside their Aertex tops. Even when I had been away with Flora, we had put our bikinis on in the bathroom. But the first night Frankie had stayed in my room, she had just stripped off, and it had kind of mesmerized me. Partly just seeing another person's naked body and partly because she didn't think it was weird. Like she had never gotten the memo about squirming around in your T-shirt to take your bra off at a sleepover.

I opened the plastic packet and started to get changed, trying to affect Frankie's no-fucks-given vibe.

"You look way more like an actual nurse than Frankie does," Negin said. "I think the green color helps."

"I feel like one of the fairies from Cinderella. It really poofs out at the waist."

I sat on the bed and tried to work out how to put the stockings and garters on. In the end, we had to watch a YouTube video to figure it out. I stood up and looked at myself. "The thigh highs kind of funnel all my fat upward and then it spills over the top of them. Like I'm a cupcake and my fat is buttercream icing."

"Why are boys so into them?" Frankie said. "Can you ask Luke? Let's get a picture. Do a nurse face."

I stood up straight and did a sort of stern-but-kind face. Negin shook her head as she took the picture.

"I think the garter thing is because of olden-day prostitutes." Frankie undid her other stocking. "And maybe they lust after nurses because they're . . . kind?"

"I find boys really weird sometimes." I looked at myself in the mirror. "I will definitely sweat shitloads in this fabric. Fuck it. I'm not gonna wear it. It's a joke. Who am I?"

Frankie flopped down on the bed. "Well, if you're not gonna wear it, then I'll feel even more ridiculous. Do you think we can get the £12:99 back?"

"Let's just both not wear it. In fact, let's just agree to never wear garters, ever. I'm not a prostitute from the olden days. Or any kind of health worker. So it would be false advertising."

"Agreed," said Frankie. "Let's shake on it."

"Just wear scrubs like me and Becky." Negin shrugged. "We're gonna steal them from the medical building tomorrow. We'll steal you some, too."

My phone started flashing on the bed. I looked at the screen, then looked up. "Fuck."

"Who is it?" Negin frowned. "Why do you look so scared?"

"Oh my god, is it ISIS?" Frankie yelled.

"Yes, it's ISIS!" Negin yelled back. "They always phone Phoebe before they strike."

Becky laughed, a really loud proper laugh, and looked like herself again. The phone was still flashing and I didn't know what to do. "It's Luke," I said.

"Shut. Up." Before I could stop her, Frankie snatched it out of my hand.

"Don't be a twat, Frankie!" I screamed. "This is my life."

"'This is my life,'" Negin repeated, and she and Becky cracked up again. Frankie shushed them and hit "answer." "Hi, Luke Taylor." She jumped up onto the bed and held the phone so high I couldn't reach it.

"Oh my god," I whisper-groaned, and jumped onto the bed next to her, elbowing her in the stomach to try to get the phone back.

"Yes, it's Frankie. It was delightful to meet you yesterday. Top, top quidditching on your part . . . What . . . Oh, right . . . Oh, really?"

199

I mouthed, "What's he saying?" Her face changed, and she nodded frantically at the window.

Standing on the grass outside, looking up at us with a slightly bemused expression, was Luke.

●　●　●　●　●　●　　**LUKE**　●　●　●　●　●　●

"Is that how you always dress for breakfast, then?"

Her mouth twitched, like she was trying to pin back a smile. "Yeah. Obviously. It's D Dorm tradition. We wake up, put on our latex nurse outfits, have some Wheaties . . ."

I looked back at D Dorm as we headed up the walkway to our class. Frankie was still wearing the costume and dancing at us through the kitchen window.

"So were they for the nine-nine-nine thing?" I asked.

She tilted her head at me. "No, Luke, I just randomly prance about the place dressed like a sexy nurse."

I tilted back. "Well, you might." I was slightly disappointed she hadn't come downstairs still wearing it. I wondered how long I should wait before trying to kiss her again. It was pretty much all I'd thought about since yesterday.

"What are you going as?" she asked.

I shrugged. "I'll probably just borrow a lab coat off one of the chemists. Go as a doctor."

She buttoned her jacket up against the wind. "It's weird how people consider doctors and nurses inherently sexy. Like, why?"

"Well . . . they do spend a lot of time around naked people."

"Yeah, but naked people who are either sick or dead."

"True. And no one finds undertakers sexy. To be honest, I

200

reckon guys just like any outfit that shows a lot of bare flesh." I put my hands up. "I apologize for my gender."

She nodded. "Apology accepted. I should warn you that me and Frankie have decided to fuck the whole sexy nurse thing off anyway. We're just gonna wear scrubs with Negin and Becky."

"Good plan."

"Is Ed gonna come? Frankie's obsessed with him." She stopped and slapped her hand across her mouth. "Don't tell Ed that, obviously. Unless he's obsessed with her, too. Is he obsessed with her, too?"

We kept walking. "No idea. I'll pump him for info next time I see him."

"No, Luke. You have to be subtle."

I looked at her, mock-offended. "I am subtle, Phoebe. I'm super subtle. Don't worry about that."

She half glanced at me, her mouth twitching again.

We got to the lecture and found seats near the back of the hall. It was so packed that everyone was bunched right up together, like sardines on ridiculously uncomfortable folding seats. Because me and Phoebe were sitting so close, our legs kept brushing under the desk, and after a while it became a sort of game. One of us would nudge the other, the other would nudge back harder, with both of us trying—not very successfully—to keep a straight face.

Because of all this, by the time class finished, I had learned literally nothing. I wondered as we walked out if I was ever going to take in *any* new knowledge during my three years here. If my parents knew my loan was being spent on nudging legs and obsessing over text messages, they'd be fucking furious.

We traipsed up the hill to the library and got the books we

needed for the next seminar. When we were back outside, I suddenly realized that we had no more legitimate, scheduled reasons to keep hanging out.

"Do you fancy a cup of tea or something?" I asked hopefully.

"Yeah, that'd be nice."

We went into the vaguely litigious library café, Starcups—which was halfheartedly decked out with rubber skeletons and pumpkins—and got teas and M&M cookies. Then we went and sat underneath the massive tree by the edge of the lake. It was jacket-and-gloves cold, but the air was fresh and the sky was clear blue. The ground was covered in acorns, and Phoebe picked one up. "I used to love playing with acorns with my brother."

A memory bumped me out of nowhere. "Hey, do you remember when Tom Gale got suspended for whacking Dhiraj on the head with one of these? When was that? Seventh grade?"

"Oh yeah. We had a whole assembly on 'acorn safety' the day after. But I thought it was Dhiraj who conked Tom after Tom shot him with a BB gun. Tom Gale was definitely a bit of a psycho."

"I still find it so weird that we have all these memories in common, but we didn't even know each other until the start of this month." I handed her the biggest, glossiest acorn I could see. "Here, this will definitely win any clash you'll ever enter. You'd be able to knock Tom Gale out cold with this one."

She smiled and put it in her jacket pocket, and I suddenly couldn't wait any longer. I leaned over and we were kissing again.

It felt even better than yesterday, but we definitely weren't at that point yet where we could go straight back into post-kiss normal conversation. As soon as we broke apart, a slightly awkward silence settled.

I glanced across the lake and noticed a big group of people milling about on the other side. One of them broke away, and it seemed like he was looking at us, but he was too far away to tell. Suddenly, he stuck up a hand and waved, and I realized it was Will. We both waved back. It was impossible to read his expression. The silence felt heavier suddenly.

"I might live with Will next year, actually," I said, without really knowing why. Just to break the silence, I guess. "I mean, it's not definite or anything. . . ."

"Oh right." Phoebe nodded. "Cool." She picked up another acorn.

I wondered again what she thought about Will. How serious their Frosh Week thing had actually been. I didn't care that they'd probably hooked up, but I did care that he might have taken a photo of her. That she might be up there somewhere, on the Wall of Shame, with Dempers and everyone posting comments about her. Since I could only see the group from the day I'd been added, there was literally no way of knowing.

"I'm freaking out about the whole house thing, to be honest," Phoebe said.

"Surely, you'll live with Frankie and Negin?"

She shrugged and stared down at the acorn. "We haven't talked about it yet. Negin's got loads of mates in her major, and Frankie knows literally everyone on campus. So I dunno."

"Yeah, the whole thing's really stressful."

I looked across the lake and watched Will a second longer as he walked away.

Part Four

16

Turned out I did *not* look sexy in scrubs.

They were enormous on me and smelled like toilet cleaner. But it was kind of awesome. Like being in a club, wearing an invisibility cloak. Usually, I spend all night checking in the mirrors how much the humidity is making my hair frizz, but I just didn't care this time. And, collectively, it made us all go insane.

At one point, I took a running jump and launched myself into Josh. He was dressed as a fireman and had literally not left the dance floor since we'd arrived. He managed to catch me, but the force sent us both crashing into the speaker.

"Bennet, you are crazy tonight," he shouted at me.

"It's always inside," I yelled. "It just pops out into the world every so often."

The song changed, and he closed his eyes and started to do

such exaggerated rave-y hand moves that people had to step back to give him space.

I felt someone's arms around my waist and a kiss on my cheek. "Ed is here," Frankie yelled in my ear. "Like, here. Not here. But near. Near here. In the club. I feel sick."

"Do you need to go to the bathroom?"

"No, sick with *love*. I just need to dance. Dance it out." She kissed me again. Even Negin and Becky were off the rails tonight. Becky had let a boy dressed as a policeman carry her to the DJ booth to request a song, and Negin was introducing some of her premed friends to the quidditch team.

Luke waved his stethoscope at me from across the room, where he was talking to Ed and Arthur. I'd become sort of addicted to him. I liked being alone so I could think about him uninterrupted. I liked rereading his texts and smiling to myself and thinking again and again about things he had said or moments that had passed between us. I had become one of *those* people. I had become obsessed with memory and had started collecting stuff. Napkins from cafés we had been to and notes he had written me in the library after we had been told to shut up. It had been less than a week, but I was in it so deep. I missed him as soon as he left. I wanted him to text me straight away. But in the club it was perfect. Like we both knew the other one was there, and that we would go home together, so we could just relax and have fun until then. Every so often we would catch eyes across the dance floor and it felt amazing. Like he was addicted to me, too.

Negin squeezed through the crowd and mouthed: "Do you want a drink?"

We walked over to the bar. "Is it weird being sober when everyone else is wasted?" I asked her.

She smiled. "The most annoying thing is that everyone constantly repeats themselves."

I nodded. "Is it weird being sober when everyone else is wasted?"

She rolled her eyes and waved the bartender over. "Phoebs, I just heard something. . . . A girl in my program told me this thing about the soccer team." She looked down like she was debating how to say whatever it was she wanted to say. "She said they do this gross thing. They take pictures of girls they've . . ." She made a face. "Anyway, they take pictures of them asleep and then rate them on the group chat."

I shook my head. "It's totally fine—I've heard this whole thing already. Honestly, it's totally not true. You can tell her she doesn't have to worry. It's just a stupid rumor someone made up."

Negin smiled weakly. "Are you sure? She sounded really upset about it."

"Honestly, Negin, one hundred percent. Someone asked Luke about it at Bowl-Cut's gig. He said it's bullshit. And he is, like, their star player, so he would know, right?"

Negin picked up her bottle of water and handed me my gin and tonic. She took a breath and almost said something else.

"Thank you for worrying, though," I shouted. I almost added that I had been worried about Will when I'd heard about it. But I didn't.

At just past midnight, I said goodbye to the girls, and me and Luke left.

We bought french fries and walked home slowly and then snuck back into my dorm and made tea.

In my room, we lay next to each other, staring at the ceiling.

"I wonder who has slept in this room before," I said. "These halls were built sixty years ago. So at least sixty people have laid in this exact same place, staring at the ceiling."

I pulled a bit of the comforter back and climbed underneath. He did the same. I reached over and switched the lamp off. And then wondered if he realized it was a sign that I knew he was staying.

He lifted his arm up so I could nestle into his shoulder. "Tuck in."

Neither of us had talked about when we were going to have sex. He had slept in my bed for the past few nights, and we had done stuff but not gone all the way. But this didn't feel like the past few nights.

We just lay there, talking about random things until we both fell asleep. When I woke up we were detangled. It was still dark outside, and condensation was trickling down the window. Luke put an arm over me and pulled me closer to him. I wriggled around. We were facing each other. He leaned a tiny bit farther in and opened his eyes and then closed them again, and we were kissing. We kissed for ages, and then, bit by bit, we were both undressed.

I kissed him on the stomach and then wondered if I should go down on him. I get so nervous about blow jobs. It's like this thing that you can be bad at. You can't really be bad at someone putting their penis inside you. Unless it won't go in. But as long as that happens, it's sort of deemed a success. Flora gave a blow job to a boy in Majorca, and he fell asleep while she was doing it, so she was obviously messing it up somehow.

I kissed him again and then did it. Just for a few seconds. Long enough to say I had done it but not long enough to mess it up in any way. Unless only doing it for a few seconds *was* messing it up. He made a noise as if he liked it. And then he threw the comforter back and cold air hit me and I shivered a bit.

"Do you have a condom?" I whispered. And then it hit me: the complete, total, bonkers surrealness of me, naked, asking Luke Taylor, naked, if he had a condom. I had to physically strain to keep from laughing. Or grabbing my phone to text Flora.

I tried to look at the ceiling politely while he put it on and then wondered if I should pat him on the back or something to keep some kind of connection going.

He turned around and kissed me. And then he pulled back a bit. In movies people just put it in easily. Like it's not complicated to get it in the right place. Like it will just happen automatically without some kind of map. I held it and put it in me a tiny bit.

And then he was inside me. And it actually felt good. Really good. The surrealness resurfaced and I giggled by accident.

"Are you laughing at me?" he said, smiling. "This is not the moment you really want a girl to start laughing uncontrollably."

None of it felt awkward. I wouldn't say I totally lost myself in the moment. I still wondered about what I looked like and if I should be doing some porn star thing I have no idea how to do. But it was the closest I had ever felt to being myself while having sex.

211

Afterward, I needed to pee, but the toilets felt so far away.

"Erm, Phoebe?" Luke sat up suddenly. I was too tired to open my eyes and look at him.

"Hmmmm?"

He paused. "Where's the condom?"

17

"Shit! Fuck! No! What?!"

Phoebe was hopping around the room in circles, pulling her pajama bottoms on and hissing random swear words.

I rubbed my eyes. I couldn't quite get my head around it. This seemed like way too much to handle at three o'clock in the morning. Though, to be fair, it probably would've been too much to handle at any time of the day. The cold, clammy feeling that something very, very bad was happening started to unfurl in my stomach.

"Fuck . . . Phoebe . . . I'm so sorry. What can we do? What happens now?"

"I don't know, Luke," she snapped. "Funnily enough, this has never happened to me before. I don't usually just walk around the place with condoms stuck inside me."

"OK. Well . . . I'm sure we can figure this out."

She yanked open the door. "OK, great. That's very reassuring. I'm going to the bathroom." She checked to see if the hall was empty, and then she was gone. I heard her socks padding quickly along the floor.

I pulled on my boxers, edged my way out and knocked gently on the bathroom door. "Phoebe? Is everything OK?"

"Not really," she hissed through the door. I could hear her breathing heavily.

"What . . . should I do?"

"Can you go get Frankie and Negin?"

"Erm . . . OK. Will they be up?"

"I don't know! Just get them!"

I went to the door I was fairly sure was Negin's and paused outside it. My phone said it was 3:07 a.m.

I knocked softly, and I heard Negin murmur what sounded like "Not dead." I thought she might be talking in her sleep, until Frankie's much louder murmur added: "Not dead, Phoebs, both not dead. Go away, Phoebs."

I knocked again and heard them both groan simultaneously. Then there was lots of shuffling, and Frankie's voice getting progressively louder as she approached the door. "I don't know what the fuck you are doing knocking us up at three in the morning. You should be letting Luke Taylor knock you up. 'Ooh, Luke, knock me up, you're so good, Luke, oooh—'"

She opened the door and blinked at me. She was wearing a comforter like a toga, and her hair was sticking up all over the place. "Luke Taylor. I was literally just talking about you."

"Erm, yeah, sorry to wake you, Frankie. It's just that Phoebe . . . She needs you. She's in the bathroom."

She made a face. "Is she puking? Can't you deal with the puke? You *are* her boyfriend."

"Well . . . not technically . . ."

Frankie narrowed her eyes. "Not technically puking or not technically boyfriend?"

"Frankie, can this wait? Phoebe actually, genuinely needs you. Like, now."

She sighed and swung the door fully open to reveal Negin under another blanket in the bed. "Fine. Negin, let's go. The sisterhood calls." Then she turned back to me: "So what's actually wrong with her?"

⦁ ⦁ ⦁ ⦁ ⦁ ⦁ ⦁ **PHOEBE** ⦁ ⦁ ⦁ ⦁ ⦁ ⦁ ⦁

I could hear people talking in the kitchen.

I could smell the toasties they were eating. I couldn't think at all knowing they were so close. I should have brought my phone. I couldn't really go back and get it now. I just had to get this over with.

I started speaking to myself in my head, like before a test. Everything is going to be OK. You can do this. I rolled my shoulders back like I was about to start an Olympic sprint. Fuck. The longer you wait the more freaked out you're going to get.

I took a deep breath and pushed my fingers inside myself. I tried to move them around, but I couldn't feel anything. I sat back down on the toilet seat and then pulled my underwear fully off. I put my leg up on the toilet, the same way Flora taught me when I put a tampon in for the first time. I pushed my fingers

215

inside again and for a second I thought I felt it. Every time I tried I felt a bit more nauseous. It was definitely there, I just couldn't get hold of it. Oh god.

I tried to breathe deeply and then I realized I was rocking back and forth like a lunatic. My face was so boiling. I put my cheek against the cold wall and a hot tear squeezed out. Maybe I should call Mum? Or Flora? Or the National Health Service hotline?

There was a soft knock on the door. "Phoebe." Negin sounded totally calm. "Are you OK?"

"Phoebs," Frankie hissed. "Luke told us what happened. Don't panic. Negin is a doctor."

"Negin is not yet a doctor," Negin corrected her.

"I am freaking out," I whispered. I sounded crazy. It came out like a wail.

I heard the kitchen door open and people tumble out. I shut my eyes.

There was a wallop on the door, and I heard Negin say: "Phoebe's in there." Then Connor bellowed: "Phoebs, you vomit legend! I had a tactical puke earlier and carried on."

I heard him and the others bundling off down the hall and then slamming their doors. As I opened the bathroom door, I realized I was actually crying. "I don't want to go to the hospital."

Frankie was holding a toastie and Negin was wearing her fleece pajamas. They hugged me, and we walked quickly across the hall to Negin's room.

"Where's Luke?" I whispered.

"In your room," Negin said. "I told him we would get him when you wanted him."

"When you no longer had his condom womping around up

216

your cavities." Frankie took a bite of toastie and Negin gave her a look. "Sorry." She reached over and held my hand. "It's gonna be OK."

"Have you tried to get it out?" Negin said gently.

"Yes, I've been trying for, like, ten minutes."

Frankie yanked her hand out of mine. "You've just put your vag juice on me."

"I've washed my hands, obviously."

"There will still be vag juice traces. I don't even want to eat this toastie now. Cheese and Marmite and crotch." She took a bite of the toastie and then threw it in the trash. "I suppose people eat vag juice all the time, but still . . ."

"What am I going to do?" I put my hands over my face.

"Have you Googled it?" Negin pulled her phone out of its charger. "You Google it, too," she barked at Frankie.

"My phone is in the kitchen," she said, and walked out.

"It will be fine, I promise." Negin's voice was really calm and comforting. "It's in Google predict. So it obviously, you know . . . happens."

Frankie came back in holding a jam sandwich and her phone. We all sat on the bed in silence while they Googled.

"Phoebs, have you really, like . . . got in there and tried?" Frankie said. "'Cause people on here seem to think you can definitely get in there."

"People on where?"

"The Internet. *Cosmopolitan.*"

"I don't know if that is . . . reputable." Negin was scrolling down her phone. "But I can't find it on this health website."

"There are loads of Yahoo! answers." Frankie shook her head. "Man, some of these people . . . I get why people ask the

217

questions, but who goes around answering them? Smileyturtle underscore happydayz, with a 'z,' says: 'Dude, sex before marriage is against God.' He's written it in capitals: 'AGAINST GOD.'"

"Why do you think it's not on the site?" I looked at Negin.

"Because maybe it's too . . . impolite."

"I actually love Luke Taylor." Frankie flopped back onto the comforter. "His little face was so confused. He looked like a newborn otter. What is going on with you and Luke Taylor anyway?"

"Frankie, there is a condom lodged in her vagina," Negin said. "This is not the time for relationship analysis."

Frankie sighed melodramatically: "'Luke Taylor's so dreamy he got a condom lodged in my vagina.'"

"Is that supposed to be my voice?" I said. "I'm not Welsh."

"What kind of moves was LT pulling, then, eh?" Frankie took a bite of her jam sandwich and thrust her crotch forward.

I started laughing, and then I literally couldn't stop. I really hoped Luke couldn't hear across the hall.

"Just a friendly reminder that you still have a condom stuck in you." Negin flicked my cheek with her finger. "Are you still drunk?"

"No," I gasped. "I think I'm in medical shock and now it's making me hysterical."

Frankie leaped up. "Have you tried jumping up and down to make it fall out?"

She started jumping and the whole room began to shake. I stood up and jumped in the air a couple of times.

"Anything going on down there?" Frankie asked as she came to a stop.

"No. What am I going to do? I literally have no idea what to do."

"I know what to do." Frankie grabbed her phone.

"Are you calling an ambulance?" Negin wrinkled her brow. "Because this is not an emergency situation."

"It fucking is," Frankie said.

"I don't need an ambulance!" I shouted.

"Mummy," Frankie barked into the phone. "Mummy, wake up, I need you. It's an emergency."

There was no sound at all on the other end. "Mummy?" Frankie said again. She put her phone on speaker.

"Sorry, darling," the voice crackled. "I had to go into the sitting room and shut the door. Are you OK, Francesca?" Frankie's mum sounded like a radio announcer from the war.

"Basically, Mummy, in a nutshell, you know Phoebs, well, basically she had sex with this boy Luke Taylor—"

"Oh, well done, Phoebe," her mum interrupted cheerfully. "Yummy Luke from school."

"Are you joking?" I mouthed at Frankie, but she held up a hand to stop me.

"Anyway, Mummy, they had sex, and now the condom is stuck up her vag."

"Oh Christ." Frankie's mum sighed. "Is she there with you?"

I nodded.

"She is, Mummy, but she's too embarrassed to speak. She's just nodding."

"It's not embarrassing at all, Phoebe, darling," Frankie's mum's voice boomed. "I have seen all sorts of things up there in my time. Even a bottle of Wite-Out."

"Mummy is a nurse, remember." Frankie frowned. "She doesn't just look up people's vaginal passages for fun."

"Do we need to go to the ER?" Negin mouthed at her.

"Do we need to go to hospital, Mummy?"

"I don't think so," the voice crackled. "If you keep calm I can tell you what to do. Wash your hands, Frankie, darling. You're going to have to try to get it out."

Frankie recoiled. "Mummy, that is absolutely gross. I am not putting my hand up there." She looked at Negin. "Can't you do it? You want to be a doctor."

"Darling, it's going to be absolutely fine. Phoebe, lie down and put a cushion underneath your bottom. Frankie, try to find a light and go and wash your hands."

There was a frantic little silence while I moved Negin's toy elephant off the pillow and lay on the bed, staring at the ceiling. Just as I was plucking up the courage to speak to Frankie's mum, Frankie came back into view above me, wearing some sort of miner's light on her head.

"See, I'm using my gap-year stuff, Mummy. I've got the headlamp on."

"Oh, darling, well done," the impossibly posh voice chimed. "You just need to approach this rationally. It's probably gotten stuck on the side, near the top, OK?"

I couldn't see Negin's or Frankie's faces, and they'd gone completely quiet.

"Erm, you're going to have to crack out your chacha," Frankie told me. "We can't do it through your Minnie Mouse pajamas."

I wriggled out of my pj's. Frankie whistled. "Very neat. Perfectly trimmed lawn you've got there. You clearly knew Mr. Taylor was going to be—"

"Frankie." Frankie's mum and Negin said it at the exact same time.

"This is the worst thing that's ever happened to me," I groaned.

"Don't be ridiculous, Phoebe," the posh voice tutted. "There are people in camps in Syria."

"Oh god . . ."

"Phoebe, just relax—she won't be able to do it unless you are relaxed."

"Just imagine I'm Luke," Frankie cooed.

"Shut up."

"Mummy, I can't see anything, even with the flashlight," she whined.

"You need to get closer and really look. Then just slide your finger in and do a sweep."

"What the fuck are you talking about, Mummy? Phoebs, I can't do this. We'll have to go to the hospital."

"Let me look." Negin sounded almost angry. "Don't speak for a second, Frankie."

I flinched as her fingers went inside me and I felt it being pulled out.

"Negin, you fucking legend!" Frankie shouted it so loudly it must have woken the entire building.

I stood up and we all stared at the shriveled condom lying on Negin's navy blue sheet.

"It's a boy!" Frankie shouted. And Negin laughed harder than I had literally ever seen her laugh. Even Frankie's mum was laughing on the phone.

"Mission accomplished." Frankie grinned, and then threw her arms around me.

18

"So . . . ," I said. "This is not how my nights out usually end."

"Or begin, I hope," Phoebe added.

"No, exactly. At no point in the beginning, middle *or* end of my average night out do I normally end up in the family planning clinic. I swear."

We both laughed awkwardly and shuffled on the hard, uncomfortable, bright-orange chairs. It had been a pretty restless night's sleep, and now, at the rarely experienced hour of 8 a.m., we were sitting in the waiting area of the campus sexual health center, which was all the way across campus.

"Seriously, Phoebe. I'm really sorry. This is obviously quite, *quite* shit." I reached down to squeeze her hand: "Hope you're OK?"

She squeezed back: "Yeah, course—it'll be all right. It's not like we didn't use protection. It's just that the protection didn't end up being as . . . protective as we'd have liked. I might get, y'know, tested, though. Just to be sure."

"What, for . . . if you're pregnant?"

"No, they give you the morning after pill for that. I mean for, y'know . . ." She lowered her voice. "STIs."

"Oh, right. Yeah, definitely. But I mean, that should be OK, shouldn't it? I've only slept with one other person. And we were both each other's first."

What with all the condom terror, I hadn't really had time to process what had actually happened last night. I had slept with someone else. Someone who wasn't Abbey. It's not like I didn't know it was going to happen eventually, but now that it had, it still felt massive. Like things had changed permanently, and there was no going back.

There was a pause while Phoebe studied—or pretended to study—a brochure called "Ten Things You Didn't Know About Chlamydia." Finally, she said: "Oh right, so really? Abbey Baker's the only girl you ever . . . ?"

"Well, yeah." I shrugged. "We went out more than three years. Started going out when I was fifteen."

Phoebe nodded. It felt weird talking to her about Abbey. It felt weird even thinking about Abbey, to be fair. I'd been trying not to think about her at all over the past week. Which had actually been surprisingly easy. Worryingly easy. Every time she popped into my head, it was like my brain automatically chucked her straight back out again.

I knew I should tell her what was going on. Especially now that me and Phoebe had actually slept together. But telling Abbey the truth hadn't exactly worked out over the past few weeks. Telling Abbey the truth had done nothing but cause us both fuckloads of misery. So telling Abbey the truth didn't really seem like a viable option.

Phoebe was flicking absently through the chlamydia brochure. Or not "brochure." Leaflet, I guess. "Brochure" makes it sound like chlamydia is a holiday resort.

"How about you, then?" I asked. "Y'know, since we're being honest."

She dropped the leaflet and held up two fingers. Then she said, "Well, actually, now it's . . ." She added another finger.

"Oh yeah? Who are the other lucky guys, then, eh?"

She blushed, smiling. "Do you remember Adam Kramer? And Max Fulda?"

"Erm . . ." For a second I could only focus on the fact she hadn't said Will's name. I had to make a conscious effort to actually respond. "Don't remember Adam, but I had Art with Max in tenth grade. He was seriously good."

"Yeah." She nodded. "He's at Goldsmith's now. We sort of went out for a couple of months just before school ended."

"You didn't think about trying to make it work long distance?"

"Not really. I guess we both thought it would be better to meet some new people."

"Well, you've done a great job there," I said, and we both laughed, drawing irritated glances from the other people in the waiting room.

A lady with a clipboard bounded in and called, "Phoebe Bennet?" I gave Phoebe another hand-squeeze, and she got up and followed her out. I sat there reading about chlamydia and wondering whether I should try to call Abbey at some point.

Or at least message her. Just to make sure she was OK. The thought suddenly occurred to me that if I didn't, we might never speak to each other again. Would I be all right with that? It's, like, you go through all this stuff with somebody—grow up together, basically—and then one day they're out of your life forever. There's nothing else that goes from a hundred to zero that quickly. With friends, you just drift apart slowly or whatever: you never actually say "We're not friends anymore" or "Our friendship's over." But with girlfriends it's like it's everything and then, suddenly, it's nothing. Is that how it always happens? In three years' time would Phoebe just be another person I never spoke to anymore?

Finally, Phoebe came back into the waiting area. "She gave me the morning after pill, and I took the test," she said. "So, hopefully, all good."

We walked out into the sharp, cold, morning sunlight to see Will heading straight toward us. I felt a little spasm of panic, but it was way too late to try to avoid him. He was with his roommate, that Josh guy who worked at Bettys with Phoebe.

Josh was smiling. Will wasn't.

"All right, you two," Josh said brightly. "Top night last night. I thought we did the emergency services proud." I noticed him and Will were both staring down at my hands, which I thought was a bit weird until I realized I was still holding the chlamydia leaflet. I stuffed it into my pocket, and Josh hitched an eyebrow. "Having an eventful morning?"

Phoebe shuffled her feet and laughed. I stayed silent and so did Will, so Josh filled the awkwardness by murmuring: "Ooookay, then."

I could feel Will's eyes on me, but he didn't say anything.

"Where are you guys off to, then?" I asked, trying to sound casual.

"Library." Josh grimaced. "Got essays in for tomorrow, and we can't work at ours because the boiler's fucked and it's freezing." He half smiled at Will. "And the landlord here won't sort it, so . . ."

Will shot him a half smile back, but the annoyance in it was obvious. I realized I hadn't actually chatted with Will about the house stuff since he'd first mentioned it. I needed to get that sorted out. The chemists in my hall had literally already found their place for next year and signed the contract.

Another chasm of awkwardness opened up, and Josh scratched his head and chucked one more "Oooookay, then" into it. I'd only met him a couple of times, when we were out and drinking, but he seemed like a really good guy. I was massively glad he was here right now, anyway. Just me, Will and Phoebe would have been genuinely unbearable. Josh grinned at Phoebe: "You working Friday, Bennet?"

"Ten to four." She nodded.

"Cool. Well, see you both later, then."

"See you at three, right?" I said to Will. He nodded without making eye contact, and they both walked off.

"You've got a game this afternoon, then?" Phoebe asked as we headed back toward Jutland.

"Yeah. Leeds. Apparently, they're pretty good."

"Right . . ."

I wondered if we were ever actually going to talk about Will directly. But then, maybe there was nothing to talk about. Maybe there was no awkwardness. Maybe I was just being paranoid.

Coming off the field later, after Leeds had effortlessly battered us 6–1, I tried to catch up to Will, but he marched straight off into the changing rooms.

Trev fell into step alongside me. "He's not exactly a good loser, is he?"

"Guess not."

"Their third goal was his fault, to be fair."

That was definitely true, but I wasn't convinced that was what was bothering him.

"Dunno why we even turned up today, to be honest," Trev sighed, wiping his forehead with his sleeve. "It was pretty demoralizing."

"I dunno. I still enjoy it, actually, even when we get beaten."

"You're weird, Taylor."

"Thanks, mate. Your goal was good, at least."

He ruffled his sweaty hair. "Yeah, thanks. When you're five foot six you get an added buzz off scoring a header. You coming tonight, then?"

"Probably, yeah," I said, shrugging.

He grinned at me. "Try not to sound too excited, mate."

Wednesday night was Sports Night, which basically meant the whole team went into town together, got shit-faced and ended up in some kebab place, where Dempers would invariably get us chucked out by performing a lewd act with the condiments.

I'd usually arrive at every game with some bulletproof excuse about why I wouldn't be able to come out afterward, but when it came down to it, I never had the guts to bail out. I always secretly suspected that Trev knew how I felt. Because I secretly suspected he felt it, too.

Back in the changing room, Will was already stuffing his jersey into his backpack while Dempers banged on about some photo on the group chat.

"Wicks should be banned for life for that one," he yelled, hurling his water bottle across the room.

"It's true, she was a fucking dog, Wicks," said Geordie Al. "I'm surprised your camera didn't break."

Wicks—a tall, blond, extremely self-satisfied sophomore—held his hands up and said, "Her face was ropey, but trust me, boys, the tits were amazing."

"Well, next time, let's have a shot of her tits, then," said Dempers.

Will zipped his bag up and his eyes fell on me. "Have you checked the Wall today, Taylor?"

"No, haven't seen it," I said.

Geordie Al leaned across and showed me the photo on his phone. Another girl lying asleep in a messy bedroom. Not knowing she was having her picture taken. Not knowing she was being passed around a changing room.

I nodded and said, "Huh," which I'm pretty sure wasn't the desired reaction but was the only thing I could think of.

Geordie Al cocked an eyebrow at me. "Swifty obviously doesn't think she's that bad."

"He's a freshman," bellowed Dempers. "He'll fuck anything that moves!"

Everyone laughed again, but Will was still looking at me with a weird, cold smile on his face. When the laughter died down, he said: "No, seriously, though, Taylor. Now that you and Phoebe Bennet are a thing, you've got to get a photo up on the

Wall. Bit unacceptable to still be on zero pictures six weeks into first semester."

I felt my face heating up as everyone turned to look at me.

"Told you that girlfriend-from-home thing wouldn't last, didn't I?" Will smirked.

"No, no, it's not like that," I said. "Honestly, me and Phoebe are just . . . friends."

"Oh, really," Will scoffed. "'Cause obviously, I go to the sex clinic with all my friends."

"Nice one, man," Dempers cackled at me. "Pregnant or herpes? Or both?"

Will ignored this and turned back to me. "Seriously, though, Luke, mate. When's the Phoebe photo going up?"

Trev caught my eye and then looked away. Me and him were pretty much the only ones who didn't comment on the photos.

"Honestly, man, it isn't like that," I stuttered. "I'm still with Abbey. From home."

"Stick up a photo of Abbey from Home, then," said Geordie Al, and everyone cracked up. I laughed along with them, hating them, but hating myself slightly more.

Will shrugged, like he was bored by the whole conversation now. He pulled his backpack over his shoulder. "Oh well, whatever. I'm sure Phoebe Bennet will find her way onto the Wall somehow."

And before I could process that properly, he yelled, "Hurry up, then, you fucking girls. Taxis into town!"

19

"How are you dancing? I can't even walk." I squeezed the mop in the bucket.

"You are shit at mopping," Josh laughed. "You do weird show-mopping. Did you just mop the shape of a star?"

"It's a snowflake."

"Have you just chucked all the water on the floor? Do you ever wanna leave here? It's like you want to spend the night in Bettys's kitchen."

"Well, at least I wouldn't have to walk anywhere."

Josh picked up the mop and started systematically working it around the floor. "Phoebe Bennet: too posh to mop. Too tired to dance. Too full to eat another vanilla slice."

"I've had two. I'm sorry. My back aches."

"I thought it was your feet, you shirker. Go and start taking inventory in the freezer."

I was about to tell him how the freezer reminded me of *The Shining*, and every time I went in there I freaked out, but I thought that might be a step too far. I pulled the incredibly heavy door open and walked in. It was completely silent. I took my shoes off and put my feet onto the freezing floor and padded about, letting the cold soothe them.

I took the clipboard off its hook. I was completely alone. I tried to remember the last time I had actually been by myself and I couldn't. Apart from being in the bathroom, every second of my day was spent with other people. Even at night, I shared a single bed with either Frankie or Luke. I sat down on the floor and leaned against the wall at the back of the freezer. The cold crept through my bun and right to my head. The buzzing ache in my feet spread through my body.

I took my phone out of my pocket. My mum had messaged me a picture of Fat Cat asleep on my Turtles pillowcase. Seeing it made me feel lost and kind of disconnected. I tried to call Mum but there was no reception. I hadn't been home at all since coming to York. Becky went home every weekend. Maybe I should go back for my birthday, just do a family thing. For no reason at all I started crying.

It was ridiculous. Nothing had happened. I shut my eyes and let it wash over me for a second.

"Bennet?" Josh was standing at the door. "Are you OK?"

I nodded. "Yeah, I am, just . . ." I didn't know what to say. I didn't really know what was going on. "Just leave me for a minute, honestly. I'm embarrassed. I'm a shambles of a person." Trying to speak was making me more tearful. I sniffed in a disgusting attempt to try to pull myself together and wiped my eyes. "Honestly, just give me a second."

He nodded and walked out. But as soon as he did I wished he hadn't. I scanned the clipboard and told myself I would get up and start counting in exactly three minutes. I felt like I could fall asleep. It was like the tears had drained me, left me totally exhausted.

The door creaked again, and Josh was peeking back into the empty kitchen. "OK, coast is clear." He pulled the door shut. He was holding two steaming cups in one hand.

He crouched down next to me. "Do you want the tea or the hot chocolate?"

I reached out and took the tea.

"Scoot over." He sat down.

"Imagine if we got trapped in here. This is how they killed people in the Cold War." I leaned my head against his shoulder.

"Bennet, you do know that's not why it's called the Cold War?"

"It's in a Bond film. They kill the man in a freezer. Or it might be a sauna, actually."

I closed my eyes and neither of us said anything. The silence just rolled over us.

"Are you OK?" he said softly after a while. "I've never seen you upset. It's horrible. You're such a smiley person usually."

I nodded against his shoulder. He smelled like chocolate and fabric softener. "Yeah. I really do think I'm just tired. I miss my mum today. It's the first time I have, like, for real. I'm nineteen soon. It'll be the first birthday I won't be with my family."

"Well, you could go home for it."

I shook my head. "Nah, I don't want to, and the girls are organizing something, I think."

"What do you want to do in your twentieth year, then,

232

Bennet? If me and you are sitting on the floor in this freezer one year from today, what one thing do you want to have done?"

The steam off the tea was dissolving the ice on the shelf and making it drip. "I dunno."

"Come on, it can be anything. So you can say 'The year I was nineteen, I . . . '" He scooped his finger around the edge of his mug to get all the foam.

"I feel really boring. Can I get back to you?"

He tilted his head on top of mine. "Yup. This freezer is actually warmer than my house."

"Has Will still not fixed the boiler? Are you definitely moving out next year?"

"I think so. It'll just be . . . easier."

He took two Bettys cookies out of his pocket and gave one to me. "So how's your ever-eventful love life, then?"

I elbowed him. "I told you I don't have chlamydia."

He laughed softly. "You get in some scrapes, Bennet, I swear."

"All right. We don't need to list them." If he knew about the condom, he'd probably die laughing right here in the freezer.

"But you and Luke are solid, right?" he asked. "It's not him making you sad?"

"No. He is one of the really, really good things. Well, I think he is. I just wish I knew what was actually going on between us. As in, I am in it, living it and I don't really know. Like, we see each other every day. We spend most nights together. We text each other. We cook together. Don't those things, added up, mean that we are a couple?"

"Well, it sounds pretty couple-y."

"But I don't exactly know what happened with his ex and he

never talks about it. And he was a bit off about Frankie taking a picture of me and him together at the nine-nine-nine thing. I dunno . . . I hate this stuff. Like, how you never know what the status is. What the status of your own life is. I mean, is there an amount of time that passes, and then you just kind of are a couple, whether you've said it out loud or not?"

Josh shrugged. "If you're worried about it, just ask him. What are you scared of?"

● ● ● ● ● ● ● ● **LUKE** ● ● ● ● ● ● ● ●

For a moment, I thought she was Abbey.

It was just a few seconds, in that weird, fuzzy state between sleep and waking, but still, I could have sworn it was Abbey's head resting softly on my chest. Then my phone buzzed on the bedside table, and reality came sliding back into focus.

It was the morning after yet another night before; another night where we'd both gone out separately, gotten drunk, then ended up back in bed together.

I woke up the same way I always seemed to wake up these days—with a throbbing head and a tongue that felt like the top of a pool table. I tried to swallow, but my mouth didn't have enough moisture, so I ended up making a weird sort of clicking noise at the back of my throat, like a radiator coming on.

Through the door, I could hear the chemists having an un-necessarily loud conversation while smashing saucepans about. Eventually, they headed off to their labs and I lay there, listening to the soft flutter of Phoebe's breathing and thinking about Abbey. I thought about how *I'd* feel if *she* slept with someone else. Like, I *really* thought about it. Hard. I tried to imagine her telling me, and exactly how I would react. I decided that, honestly, I'd be happy. I just wanted her to be OK. I wanted us both to get on with our lives.

But then, was I really getting on with *my* life? I still wasn't totally sure if I was ready to start something new. Something *official*. I liked Phoebe—a lot—but the idea of getting into something serious seemed so much riskier now. What if things ended with her the same way they had with Abbey? What if I was destined to go through life just screwing stuff up and hurting people? What if I was *never* brave enough to start another relationship because I was so sure it'd all turn to shit?

Truth was, I'd spent all this time worrying that I'd fucked Abbey up, but I never really considered that maybe she'd fucked me up a bit, too.

My phone buzzed three times in quick succession, and Phoebe snuffled and shifted under the comforter. I couldn't reach the phone without lifting her head off my arm. She scratched her nose, blinked a couple of times, then grabbed my phone and passed it to me.

"Was that your alarm?" she mumbled.

Four new messages from the soccer group flickered open. A photo of a girl I vaguely recognized from somewhere, with Will's and Dempers's and Wicks's increasingly grim comments underneath.

I switched the phone to silent and locked it. "It's just the soccer team."

Phoebe rolled over, still half asleep. "Mm. What're they saying?"

"Just about practice later."

I pushed the comforter back and then suddenly remembered I was completely naked. Being naked with Phoebe when we were drunk in the middle of the night felt like the most natural thing in the world, but I still wasn't quite ready for it in daylight.

I wriggled my foot out of the bed and used it to blindly sweep the floor for my boxers. I connected with something and reached down to grab it, only to find that it was just my T-shirt. My boxers were, for some reason I couldn't quite remember, all the way across the room.

"I just need to grab my, erm . . ." Instead of finishing the sentence, I put my shirt on and stood up, tugging it as far down my arse as it would go and waddling to the door like a penguin in a cocktail dress.

I put my boxers on, and when I came back from the bathroom, Phoebe was sitting up in bed, putting her bra on.

"Do you want some breakfast?" I asked.

She frowned. "Well, yeah. But your kitchen smells so, *so* bad."

"It's all right, I've got a system now. I just open all the windows."

"But it's *November*. It's freezing."

"Yeah, so then I turn the oven on full and leave the door open."

She wrinkled her nose. "Still not sure."

"All right. One sec."

I went and knocked at Arthur's and a muffled zombie-moan told me he was still in bed.

"I'm putting your cheese in the bath," I shouted through the door. "Just for half an hour."

There was another moan, which I took to mean, "Please, go right ahead."

When I'd moved the cheese and aired the kitchen, Phoebe ventured in, wearing my pajama bottoms and a T-shirt, and we sat munching toast.

"Hey, who's that girl Ed's always with?" she asked, putting two more slices in the toaster.

"Which one?"

"You know. The blond girl who looks like she's in a Wes Anderson film."

"Oh right. Sarah, or Sophie, or something. From his floor."

"Are they together?"

I shrugged. "Dunno. Don't think so." I got the jam out of the fridge. "I have tried to pump him for information, honestly. But Ed doesn't exactly talk much about his feelings."

She rolled her eyes. "Well, can you try harder? Frankie's eternal happiness basically depends on you."

Arthur's door swung open and he emerged, scruffy-haired, wearing his comforter like a huge coat.

"Here they are." He yawned. "The lovebirds."

We both forced a laugh.

"What we saying, then?" He peered at my plate and scratched his chin. "Toast?"

"Yes, Arthur. That's what this is."

He picked up one of my pieces, which I'd just coated with jam, and walked back to his room.

"Right, I'm back to bed for a spliff and some Schopenhauer. If you need me, you know where I am."

He slammed his door. Phoebe smiled at me. "I remember

you saying on that first night how the people in your hall weren't that great. But Arthur is really nice."

I nodded. "Yeah, he is. I do feel a bit better here now. It's just that I'm not that similar to most of them, and I guess that freaked me out at first."

She took a sip of tea. "Are you still gonna live with Will next year?"

"Erm . . . maybe." The atmosphere tightened slightly. I'd barely even spoken to Will in the past few days. He hadn't texted me all week. "I need to talk to him about it."

We finished breakfast and she headed off back to her dorm. Even saying goodbye was weird nowadays. Full on lip-kissing always felt way too couple-y in the mornings, so I just went for a kind of half-arsed cheek kiss that morphed uncomfortably into a semi-hug.

"See you later," she said.

Back in my room, I found my phone humming with Wall of Shame comments, but I didn't even look at them. Instead, without thinking too much about it, I wrote Abbey a message:

Hey. Long time . . . How are you? Really hope you're ok.

I didn't hesitate, just pressed "send." Then I lay back on my bed and tried to wrap my head around the impossible-to-understand medieval literature we were supposed to read for next week's seminar.

A few minutes later, she replied:

Hey. I'm good. Much better anyway. I miss you.

20

The library was the most distracting place I'd ever tried to work. We'd been there for two hours but all I had done was wander around the English section twice and watch who was going up and down the stairs. My phone was already in my hand when Frankie texted us. I looked up at her. She was sitting on the other side of the huge room, accidentally-on-purpose right next to the Renaissance History section, with her hair arranged into a just-got-out-of-bed messy bun to complement her casually chic gray cashmere sweater and matching slate eyeliner.

Her text said:

The OTHER woman is here—wearing a fishing coat— her face looks like one of those toys babies push shapes through.

Ed's possible love interest, Sophie or Sarah, was walking across the floor to the Sociology section. She was wearing a yellow rain coat and had a perfectly normal face. I gently nudged Negin. We both looked at her and she smiled slightly awkwardly, like she wasn't sure if she was supposed to know us. My phone flashed again:

OK this is horrendous, we now have to leave.

We wandered out into the cold and trudged down the hill.

"I don't know why I bother, honestly." Frankie's bottom lip jutted out as she unpinned her hair and kicked a can off the path huffily. "Ed never comes in the library anyway. I think he's so intelligent he doesn't need to."

Negin nodded. "Yup, that makes perfect sense."

Frankie squealed and jabbed her finger at the Starcups window display. "Oh my god, free hat with every gingerbread par-*tay* la-*tte.*" She broke out into a sort of canter. "Holidays are coming," she chanted as she tumbled down the hill and into the café.

We followed her inside. "Look! The mice are here." She waved enthusiastically at a group in the corner. "Roomies!" she yelled, and threw a clenched fist in the air.

"When was the last time you actually went back to your suite?" Negin asked.

"When Fiona helped me with my first essay and made macaroni and cheese. I go back there for archaeology talk and food. They are the greatest. I hope to be exactly like them when I am old."

"What are they? Like, twenty-two?" Negin whispered.

"Fiona's twenty-*three*." Frankie pouted.

We sat down with our red cups. "I actually feel Christmassy now," I said. "The semester is going really quickly—I can't keep up."

Frankie pulled on her free, synthetic, red pom-pom hat and sniffed her drink. "My mum actually won't let me come home before Christmas. In case I change my mind and won't leave."

"My mum is the opposite," Negin said. "Every day she texts me and is, like, 'It's your brother's birthday, come home,' or 'We're having chicken, come home,' or 'Your father can't get Netflix to work, come home.'"

"This tastes like a warmed-up almond croissant," I said, sipping my latte.

"Guys." Frankie readjusted her bobble hat. "Deep and meaningful. The reason I bought your drinks is because I'm trying to bribe you. I've actually been super uptight about this." She took an exaggerated deep breath. For a split second I wondered if it was about Luke. "I don't know how to say this." She pulled the hat down fully over her entire face and let out a warbled groan. I whacked the table and she jumped.

"Doyouguyswannalivewithme?" She yelped it so quickly it sounded like one word.

Everyone in Starcups turned and looked at us. It made me laugh involuntarily with sheer joy and relief.

Me and Negin both nodded.

"Awkward." Frankie pulled the hat up to reveal one eye. "Why aren't you guys saying anything?"

"We both nodded," Negin said, laughing. "Assertively nodded."

"OK, well, I couldn't see that so I felt really sad. But now I'm super happy. I was also thinking we should ask Becky." Frankie took a massive gulp of par-tay la-tte and I could see Negin was relieved.

"Definitely," I said. I couldn't stop smiling. "We'll need two doctors with the amount of disasters we have."

"*You* have." They said it at exactly the same time. Then Frankie downed her latte. "Let's go home and celebrate."

We linked arms as we walked home and showed each other Pinterest boards with cushions and photo walls and brightly colored kettles.

"Let's go and ask Becky," Frankie said as we pushed open the doors of D Dorm.

We walked past our own rooms and stood outside Becky's door. Frankie looked at us both and then knocked. But as she did, it swung open. We all stood looking in.

It was totally empty. Nothing on the walls. The bed stripped. The curtains still closed. It looked exactly the same as the day we had moved in.

"Do you think we can go in?" I asked.

"Well, she's not here." Negin stepped inside and me and Frankie followed her. With us three in the room it felt full, but still completely empty.

Frankie sat on the bed. "I don't understand. We saw her yesterday."

"Maybe she's just moved rooms," Negin said. "Let's text her before we jump to conclusions."

Frankie opened the desk drawers and the sink cupboard. "It's all just . . . empty."

All the jolliness of the last hour had disappeared. We walked silently back down the hall and pushed the kitchen door open.

Everyone was in there. It was completely packed and boiling hot. They were all standing at the table, gathered around something.

"Oooo . . . that one is bad." I could hear Liberty in the center but I couldn't see her. I watched Frankie's face change. She could see something I couldn't over the top of the crowd.

"I've got that pillowcase," Liberty shouted. "Exact same one. It's from Dunelm. Can't believe it."

I pushed past Nathan and Phillip and the others. Connor was sitting in the middle of them all, at a laptop. On the screen there was a picture of a girl. Well, half a girl's face, slumped on a pillow. She had brown hair and freckles.

"I know that girl," Connor said. It was the quietest and most serious he'd ever sounded. It was actually scary. "I swear she's in my program."

"She looks like she's having a dream. She's kind of smiling in her sleep." Liberty said it like she was cooing over a baby.

Connor scrolled up and another girl's face appeared, her red hair pressed against the pillow and her mouth gaping slightly open. My hands started to feel tingly and all the blood rushed to my ears. I felt like I was going to vomit.

"Fuck, is this actually real?" Frankie said.

"Where did you get these?" Negin asked, and Connor turned to her:

"Someone leaked them to The Tab. They're everywhere."

Liberty squinted at the screen and read out one of the comments underneath. "Ginny Weasley's rank sister." She laughed and then covered her mouth straight away. "Sorry, that's horrible."

"This is just grim, man," Connor muttered.

I felt dazed. I wasn't sure if anyone else had noticed it, but the comment underneath it was from "Luke Taylor." I peered closer at the screen. It wasn't about the girl; it was just him asking what time everyone was meeting for practice. But it *was* from Luke Taylor.

I thought about the Fit Sister gig; the way he had sounded when he said it wasn't true. I didn't want to look at Negin or Frankie. I let Liberty and Nathan crowd me out as they huddled closer toward the screen. I shut my eyes for a second and took a deep breath.

And then Connor flicked to another screenshot and the whole room went silent. I couldn't see the screen very well, but I knew what was on it. Deep down, I must have known Will had done it. I didn't want to cry in front of them all. I would have to try to pretend like I didn't give a shit. Liberty took a step back and looked at me. I tried to arrange my face to look normal and pushed in front of Nathan.

But the girl in the photo wasn't me. It was Becky.

● ● ● ● ● ● **LUKE** ● ● ● ● ● ● ●

"Man, you guys fucking suck," said Arthur, high-fiving Rita triumphantly. "One more game?"

Ed shook his head and finished his pineapple juice. "Got an essay to write. Plus, y'know, getting battered six games in a row isn't exactly doing wonders for my self-esteem."

We were in Wulfstan Bar, killing time between lectures, seminars and essays by playing table soccer. Which had been fun at first until me and Ed had realized that Arthur and Rita were basically an unstoppable dream team; she was rock-like in defense, he was insanely quick-flicking in attack.

"Me and Reets *are* a bit good, there's no denying it," Arthur admitted, digging into his pocket for more change.

Rita shook her head. "The amount of time we wasted at this table last year."

Arthur waggled the coin at Ed. "Come on, Edward, don't be a dick. You can write your essay later."

"I'm not being a dick," said Ed. "And it's Mund."

"You what?"

"It's Ed*mund*, not Edward."

Arthur nearly spat his beer out. "Are you fucking *kidding* me? Your name's *Edmund*? Are you literally from the Middle Ages? Is that why you're doing Renaissance History? Because it's *when* you were born?"

"The Middle Ages and the Renaissance are different periods," Ed said drily. "And I'm Edmund 'cause of Edmund Hillary. My dad's into mountain climbing and all that. Anyway, I'll see you guys later."

"Later, Ed," I said.

"I bid you farewell, good Edmund!" Arthur shouted after him.

I watched him go, slightly annoyed he hadn't stayed longer. Over the past few days, as I'd seen less and less of Will, I'd started to form this stupid, probably overoptimistic idea that me, Ed, Arthur and Rita could live together next year. I wanted to sound Ed out on it first, but for all I knew, the three of them already had houses figured out.

The idea of being the one person on campus without anyone to live with was too fucking terrifying to think about.

Arthur turned back to me: "Come on, Luke, one more game. Cheeky little one-on-one. I'll even play left-handed."

"You *are* left-handed." I grabbed my bag. "And I've got a class in, like, ten minutes, which I've done literally no reading for."

"What's it on?" Rita asked.

"Medieval literature. This book called *Sir Gawain and the Green Knight.*"

"Should've asked Edmund about it," muttered Arthur. "He probably wrote the fucking thing."

"I am genuinely quite worried. Like, if I get asked anything I will be totally screwed."

Arthur leaned in, conspiratorially. "OK, look, if you promise to play one more game, I'll let you in on my foolproof, works-every-time, haven't-done-the-reading trick."

Rita frowned. "What trick?"

"You know—Arthur's Law. I discovered it, that's why it's named after me. It's a simple yet effective rule to be employed whenever you haven't done the reading for a class."

"Sounds ideal," I said.

"Sounds like bullshit," Rita said.

Arthur ignored her. "Basically, Arthur's Law states that the first person to speak in class will not get asked to speak again. If you step up straight away, the TA forgets you're there—they try to get everyone involved *except* you."

"OK . . . But what do I say?"

Arthur shrugged. "Doesn't matter. It can be the most mean-ingless, obvious, pointless thing in the world. Any old shit off Wikipedia. Just say it first and you're in the clear for the rest of the day. Trust me. Get on Wikipedia now, then let's play."

"Can't. My phone's dead."

"Fuck's sake. Use mine."

I quickly memorized an appropriate comment off the *Gawain* Wikipedia page, and then we played one more game, which Arthur won, 8–2.

When I got to the seminar, Phoebe was already there. But she hadn't saved the seat next to her, like she normally did. Katie and Liverpool Paul were seated on either side of her.

I said "Hey" but she didn't even look up from her book. A couple of people giggled awkwardly, and Paul saved me from total humiliation by saying "Hey" back, which was pretty nice of him considering we'd only spoken twice.

Feeling a bit flushed and confused, I went and sat on the other side of the room, next to Mary. Our TA—a short, curly-haired man called Hugh—came in and started speaking straight away, which left me trying desperately to make eye contact with Phoebe and wondering what the hell was up with her.

"So what did everyone think of Gawain?" Hugh was saying. "And don't say that he's basically a medieval James Bond. Even though, to some extent, that's true."

There was a split-second pause, so I dived right in: "I thought it was interesting how the pentangle on Gawain's shield came to represent the five virtues of medieval knights: chastity, generosity, courtesy, piety and friendship."

A suitably awestruck silence followed this, and Hugh smiled. "Yes, that's a good point, Luke."

Mary gave me a shit-that-was-impressive grin, but Phoebe still wasn't looking up from the desk. I wondered if something had happened between her and Negin or Frankie. But then, why would she be taking it out on me?

"What did everyone else think?" Hugh asked, looking

around the room as people shuffled in their seats. "Picking up on what Luke said, some critics see the book as a satire on chivalry. What do you make of that?"

No one piped up, and I sat there smugly, wondering who he would pick on. He swiveled his chair back to me. "How about you, Luke? You seem to have really gotten to grips with this text. Did you see it as a satire?"

All eyes were back on me. Except Phoebe's.

"Erm . . . yeah," I mumbled. "I mean, sort of. I guess."

Another silence followed this. It was noticeably less awestruck than the first one. Mary was biting her lip and staring up at the ceiling.

"Right," said Hugh, dragging the word out to last about five seconds. He swiveled back to the group. "I mean, what was everyone's take on the meaning of the Green Girdle?"

No one seemed to have any particularly strong thoughts on the Green Girdle, so he turned back to me again. "Luke—the Green Girdle?"

I felt myself starting to go red. "Erm, well, I was more . . . I actually thought the pentangle was more interesting, actually, as it represented—"

"The five virtues, yes, you said." Hugh nodded. "Right. Maybe we should all read the first part of the text together, as a group, and see what we can get out of it. Mary, can you kick us off?"

Mary started reading, and I sat there next to her, feeling my cheeks burn and trying to figure out the most painful way to murder Arthur.

When class finally ended, Phoebe was out of the room quicker than the accidental-text day. I ran and caught up with her in the hall, trying my best to be casual. "Hey. So if Arthur ever tries to give you advice about homework, trust me—"

She didn't stop, just kept walking.

"Phoebe!"

"Fuck off, Luke." She didn't even turn around to say it. I caught up with her again.

"Phoebe, what's up? Are you OK? What's wrong?"

She finally spun around and looked at me. Her face was hard, and her blue-green eyes were shining with anger.

"Did you take any of me?" she said. I noticed the strap of her backpack was trembling, and then realized it was because *she* was trembling.

"Did I . . . What are you on about?"

"Come on. Let me see your phone. Did you take any of me?"

"My phone's dead. Seriously, what is going on?"

She shook her head bitterly: "Oh, that's a coincidence." Then all the hardness went out of her face suddenly and she just looked . . . tired. "You're such a prick, Luke. You lied, right to my face."

My first thought was Abbey. But while I was turning to ice on the inside, I kept up the performance on the outside: "Lied about what? Phoebe, what's going on?"

"For fuck's sake, Luke! You can stop pretending now." People were streaming out of another room, slowing down to watch us.

"Pretending about what?"

Phoebe looked close to tears. "The . . . 'Wall of Shame'? Isn't that what you all call it? And don't fucking *lie* again, Luke. I *saw* you on it. And now Becky's gone. She's left college. Not that any of you give a shit. So don't fucking speak to me anymore. I don't want to know you."

The streams of people had passed now, and in the silence I could hear the soft hum of the vending machines.

Phoebe turned to go. "I don't know why I thought . . . Fuck it. You're exactly what you were at school. A dumb fucking jock."

I stood there numbly for a few seconds, watching her walk off, not knowing what to do or what to think. Then I felt a tap on my shoulder and turned to see Mary strolling past.

"Cheer up, Pentangle." She smiled. "It's not the end of the world."

21

● ● ● ● ● ● **PHOEBE** ● ● ● ● ● ●

To everyone else I acted like I was furious with Luke. Like I hated him. And in part that was true.

But other things were true, too. That I was lonely. That I felt paranoid that no one liked me anymore. That maybe people were suspicious that I had known. That I was guilty by association.

I went to bed earlier than everyone else and imagined them talking about me in the kitchen: saying that maybe things could have been different with Becky if I hadn't been some lovesick moron. I felt like some vital part of me had suddenly become unsteady. My foundations had cracked. I hadn't seen Luke as he really was. I had been having sex with—falling in love with, even—a person who wasn't really there and I couldn't even figure out if it was my fault or not.

And like a clichéd, pathetic dick, I missed him. He had kind of seeped in and distorted everything on the inside of me, and everything on the outside of me, too.

I slipped off to the library alone to do my reading. It crossed my mind that I might see Luke. I had a random fantasy where he explained how it was all a terrible mistake and we kissed in front of everyone, and another concurrent one where I punched him in the face.

I had crossed my arms on the desk, and was almost asleep on them, when Frankie and Negin found me.

"Phoebs," Frankie whispered, her face right next to mine. She laid something wrapped in a piece of printer paper in front me. The paper unfurled to reveal a quite-squashed cloud-shaped fairy sandwich.

"Josh popped in to see you," Frankie said. "And you weren't there, so we made these and kept you one."

"Don't know how the fried egg will taste cold," Negin added. "But it's the thought that counts."

They sat down opposite me and I bit into the cold congealed egg and icing. It still tasted quite good.

"Do you wanna get a coffee?" Negin asked. I nodded, and started to collect up my things.

"I need to photocopy stuff first." We wandered down the stairs and into the weird little room filled with whirring photo-copiers. We waited in the line and watched a boy copy page after page of a book called *Why Do Buses Come in Threes?*

I noticed a group of girls swing through the security gates and walk past us. And then one of them turned on her heel and started back toward the photocopy room. Two of her friends broke away and followed her. I realized the first girl was

Sequined Skirt from the Fit Sister gig. And Bowl-Cut Mary and Wedding Veil were behind her.

"So." Sequined Skirt girl chucked her bag on the floor and looked right at me. "Your boyfriend is a fucking lying *arsehole*." She shouted it into the silence of the library and the quiet whirring of the photocopying. The boy stared straight ahead like he hadn't heard, but he tensed. My whole body shook with adrenaline. I didn't know what to say.

"Are you still with him? 'Cause fucking hell—"

"Jen, you're acting like a *psycho*." Mary put a hand on the girl's shoulder and shot me an apologetic look. "Phoebe is my mate, and it's not her fault she shagged a guy who turned out to be a jerk." She shrugged. "I mean, we've all done it."

Jen's face softened slightly and she half glanced at me. "OK, sorry. This whole thing's just utterly rancid. You're not still with him, are you?"

I shook my head and looked at the floor like I was being scolded.

"This is *so* not Phoebe's fault," Frankie snapped. "Like, come on, how *can* it be? Luke lied to her, too."

"And Becky, the girl who left, is our friend," Negin said gently.

Mary's eyes widened. "Is she OK?"

"We don't know," I said. "She won't reply to any of our texts or calls. She's just disappeared."

The boy at the photocopier collected up his pages quickly and snuck out. Jen stood in front of the door. "OK, so what the fuck are we gonna do about this? The pictures are literally *all* over campus. This is the time to annihilate those bastards."

A middle-aged man carrying a pile of books tried to walk into the room but Jen held her hand out. "We're having a meeting in here, sorry."

"We need to do something to humiliate them," Mary said. "To make them get how cruel and disgusting they are. To make them understand that it's not a joke."

"That Becky is a real person," Negin said, and Jen nodded. "Exactly."

Becky had become sort of famous. The girl who left school because she was so ashamed. It was awful. We had talked about it nonstop: when she might have slept with that soccer bloke, whether her boyfriend knew, why she hadn't told us at the time. Why she hadn't told us she was leaving. Even Connor felt bad about it. He said if he saw the boy who posted the picture he would knock him out.

"It's their last game of the semester next week," Jen said.

"Yeah, that is the moment." Mary nodded.

"Laxatives?" Wedding Veil suggested. "In their water bottles?"

"I think we should graffiti the field," Frankie said.

"Yeah, but how would we actually do that without someone seeing before and getting rid of it?" Jen shook her head.

"I've got an idea," I said. They all looked at me, and I felt scared and excited at the same time.

● ● ● ● ● ●　**LUKE**　● ● ● ● ● ● ●

The only sound was the echoey *clack-clack-clack* of Will's studs on the tiles.

It was ten minutes before kickoff, but no one seemed

254

particularly pumped. They were all either checking their phones or lacing their shoes or just staring down at the changing-room floor.

One of the freshmen, Murf, suddenly piped up. "The girls in my dorm have literally stopped speaking to me," he said. "Like, I'll go in the kitchen and they just literally pretend I'm not there." He laughed. "It's like . . . fuck's sake. Chill out."

"People are so fucking touchy, honestly," Geordie Al said. "It's not even *that* bad."

Will stopped pacing and looked at him. "It was obviously Louise who took those screenshots," he told him. "She must've known you were fucking around on her. She was probably trying to get you back."

Geordie Al scratched at his stubble. "Maybe . . ."

"It could have been a lot of people, to be fair," Wicks said.

"Whoever did it, did it anonymously," snapped Dempers. "So we aren't gonna find out, are we?"

"Yeah, well . . ." Will started pacing again.

Over the past few days, all anyone had talked about was who might have leaked the screenshots. To be quite honest, I didn't give a shit. It was literally the last thing on my mind.

Phoebe had basically cut me out of her life. She wasn't returning my calls or texts. Rita and Arthur had barely spoken to me, too. Worst of all, though, a girl had left York. Her whole life had been ripped down the middle, and it was all our fault. My fault. I could have stopped it. First Abbey, now Becky. It was like everything I touched turned to shit.

I glanced over at Trev, who was just staring down blankly at his unlaced boots. I wondered if he was thinking what I'd been thinking all week: that it wasn't worth it. That being friendless

255

and houseless and alone for the next three years was still much, much better than being part of all this.

There was this Sylvia Plath poem we'd done that I couldn't get out of my head lately. It was about her keeping this box of bees in her house, and being half terrified, half fascinated by it. By the chaos that would come if she opened it. The last few nights, lying awake, I kept thinking: That's me. It's me and the Wall of Shame. Until last week, it had been something I'd just done my best to try to ignore. But now it was like the bees had busted out and they were swarming through the house, stinging people, and I couldn't just sit there, pretending they didn't exist anymore. I had to actually *do* something.

"What's gonna happen, you think?" asked Wicks nervously. "Like, do you think we'll all get in trouble for this?"

Will exhaled, bored. "How can we get in trouble for it? It was just fucking around. The girls weren't naked or anything, were they?"

"That Becky girl did drop out, though," said another second year quietly. "I mean, that's pretty . . . serious, isn't it?"

Dempers finished lacing his shoes and glared at Geordie Al. "If you hadn't nailed that Becky in the first place . . ."

"I don't even know why you did," Will muttered. "She's rank."

"Yeah, well, why d'you think it's called the Wall of *Shame*?" said Geordie Al, trying to lighten the mood and failing quite spectacularly.

Will looked up at the clock. "Anyway, come on," he murmured.

We all trooped out onto the field. The Manchester team was already out there, and it slightly freaked me out to see that we had the biggest crowd we'd had all semester. Not that they looked particularly supportive. There was no cheering or applause as we came out; just odd little pockets of nervous chatter. I had the sudden feeling people had turned up to see more than just a game of soccer.

The whistle blew and we kicked off. I tried to focus on the game, but I kept noticing commotion in the crowd—ripples of movement that stopped as soon as I turned to look at them.

I'd just fed Will the ball, and he was tearing off down the field, when the commotion suddenly exploded into something else.

About thirty girls streamed onto the grass around us, shouting and screaming. At first, I thought they were all wearing brightly colored clown suits or something, but after a second I realized it was pajamas. They were all dressed in pajamas.

Our team and the Manchester lot just stood there, frozen, as the pajama-clad girls stormed the field around us. I spotted Phoebe, Frankie, Negin, Mary and some of the girls from the Fit Sister night.

The crowd was going even crazier than the girls themselves; they were laughing, clapping, cheering, whooping, shouting. I stayed there, glued to the spot, with absolutely zero clue what was going on.

Suddenly, as quickly as it had started, it was over. The girls dropped in unison down onto the muddy grass and lay there, totally still, like a load of weirdly dressed dead bodies.

The Manchester team and the ref looked even more confused than we did. The bloke who'd been marking me leaned in and whispered: "Does this normally happen, mate?"

Will had been frozen like the rest of us, watching all this with his mouth hanging open, but now he finally managed to get himself together. He strode across to Mary and Frankie, who were both lying on their backs in front of him. The crowd was so loud he had to yell down.

"OK . . . ," he shouted. "What the fuck?"

"What d'you mean?" Frankie shot back. "I thought you liked looking at sleeping girls."

Then Mary sat up and glared around at me and the rest of the team. "Yeah, come on! What's wrong with you? Get your fucking phones out!"

Will sighed and bent down toward her, his hands on his knees like he was talking to a naughty little kid.

"Yeah, OK, you've made your point. Can you fuck off now, please? We are actually trying to play a game here."

My eyes found Phoebe among all the madness. She was lying on the center circle in her blue pajamas with whales, but I couldn't see her face. Like everyone else, she was watching Mary and Will.

Will stood up: "You guys are so fucking lame." Then he chipped the ball over to me. "Taylor." He nodded. "Let's just keep playing."

I looked at him, then at the crowd. I couldn't see a single face in there—it was just a sea of phones pointed straight at me. I thought about Becky again, and the idea suddenly occurred to me that if this was a cheesy American film, I'd probably pick the ball up, walk over to Will and punch him in the face.

But it wasn't, and I didn't. Instead, I just kicked the ball gently back to him and started walking off.

"Where you going, Taylor?" he shouted. "I said keep playing."

I turned back around to look at him. "You can keep playing," I said. "I'm done."

For some reason, he smiled at this and then nodded. "Yeah. I fucking *knew* it was you, wasn't it, Taylor?" he said.

Before I could say anything back, Frankie shouted something at him—something I didn't hear, because of the wind and the noise of the crowd. Will looked down, and his whole face crinkled with scorn.

And then, suddenly, he booted the ball at her.

For a split second, the whole crowd went silent. It was like all the air had been sucked out of them. There was just the dull thud of the ball hitting Frankie's chest, and then her strangled sort of half-gasp-half-scream.

I didn't think; I just reacted. I was suddenly sprinting toward Will, with no plan for what I'd do when I got to him. Out of the corner of my eye, I saw Trev had had the exact same idea—he was streaking out ahead of me, aiming straight for Will.

But somehow, Ed got there first.

He bolted out of the crowd, threw himself at Will and just *flattened* him. I expected him to start hitting him or something, but he didn't. He just shifted his weight and sat there calmly on top of him.

"Frankie," he said. "Are you all right?"

Frankie stood up and dusted herself off. "Yeah, I'm fine." She stared down at Will with her hands on her hips. "What is *wrong* with you?"

"Get the fuck off me, you fat fuck!" Will was screaming at Ed.

"It's not fat, mate," I heard Ed say. "It's muscle, thank you very much."

Dempers stomped over, but Ed just smiled up at him and he shrank backward, and suddenly Frankie was dancing about

259

madly in her *Adventure Time* pajamas, and the crowd was roaring with laughter, and Mary and Negin and the others were cheering and taking photos of Will as he wriggled out from under Ed and stormed back to the changing rooms.

And I just stood there, on the edge of the field, wishing I could celebrate with them.

22

None of us took our pajamas off.

We did a sort of victory lap of Jutland. For Frankie, it was an *actual* victory lap. She ran in a circle around each college, clapping her hands at the bemused-looking people in the windows, like she had just won the Olympic 100 meter.

Bowl-Cut Mary did a backflip. She just casually did it, as if before she came to college she had been a professional gymnast, as well as a singer in an electro band and a tattooed, pastel-haired siren.

"I *love* Bowl-Cut," said Frankie, flopping down on the grass outside the dorm.

"She's *so* hot," I sighed. "But still, she's just a person. An unobtainably cool one, obviously, but still, a person."

We watched her dancing by the lake with Jen and Wedding Veil and the rest of them. Her oversized nightie said

MY MARXIST FEMINIST DIALECTIC BRINGS ALL THE BOYS TO THE YARD on it, and she was wearing leggings with cartoon David Bowies riding unicorns.

"I kind of just want to admire her from a distance," Frankie said. "I'm worried if we get *too* close to her, the illusion will be shattered. It's like, my mum used to be obsessed with Colin Firth—like, *obsessed*—and then she saw him in Macy's buying scales—kitchen ones, not weight ones—and she spoke to him, and he was polite and everything, but he clearly just wanted her to fuck off. And I just feel like if I *really* get to know Bowl-Cut Mary she might not be everything I hoped and dreamed, you know?"

The sky cracked and it started to rain—big, heavy droplets—so all of us piled up into the dorm, our pajamas and hair dripping like crazy as we ran up the stairs.

Connor, Liberty, Nathan and Phillip were pregaming in the kitchen, and Connor marched straight up to me, Frankie and Negin and bundled us into a group hug.

"Were you at the game?" Negin laughed.

"'Course I was." He broke out of the hug, grinning broadly. "Never been so proud to be a D Dormer. You guys were fucking amazing." He held up his vodka and Coke. "For the Beckster."

"The Beckster!" Frankie shouted.

Liberty leaned into me. "God, I hope she's OK."

I nodded. "Me too. I just wish she'd reply to our texts."

"I've got an appointment to see her TA this week," Negin said. "And I'm saving all her lecture notes."

Connor put on some incredibly loud hip-hop and started pouring drinks for Bowl-Cut and the rest of the girls. The kitchen was already heaving, and the noise was so loud we were soon attracting people from all over Jutland. It was like a celebration. Within half an hour, it seemed like everyone on campus was stuffed into our hall—every room was packed with people I'd never seen before. There were even randoms sitting in the shower, drinking.

Connor waved his phone at us. "You know you're famous? Everyone's Story is just videos of you guys storming the field."

It was raining so hard that you could hear it above the music, but it was so hot inside that the windows had steamed up. Liberty had made a kind of dance floor in the middle of the kitchen and was madly showing off routines she had invented to various Justin Bieber songs. Everyone seemed like they had been wound up and set off.

I went to the bathroom and saw I had a message from Flora:

What are your b-day plans BEST ONE?

I wrote back straight away:

I haven't seen you in forever. Can you come up for it next week? It's the day before our Christmas Ball, but we can still GET ON IT.

She sent back:

YES YES YES!

I came out to see Connor hauling his mattress off his bed and shoving Nathan's and Phillip's skateboards underneath it.

"Right, clear the hall," he shouted. "D Dorm chariot coming through."

Negin grabbed Liberty, Nathan and Frankie, and all of us ran as fast as we could and jumped onto the mattress, whooping like mad as it sped down the hall, faster and faster and faster. People came out of their rooms and showered us with beer as we flew by.

The mattress crashed into the kitchen door, and we all fell off, screaming with laughter. "Again, again," Frankie was yelling. Then she looked up and suddenly went pale.

"We call dibs next." Ed was there, scratching his damp curly hair and grinning down at us. And Luke Taylor was standing right beside him.

Ed hugged all of us, but Luke just nodded and leaned awkwardly against the kitchen counter.

"We could hear you guys from B Dorm," Ed said. "Although, to be fair, they can probably hear you in Scotland."

I snuck a look at Luke, his hair still wet from the rain, and wondered if I would *ever* stop feeling stuff for him. Like, when I am fifty, will I still look at him and feel scared and excited and on edge? I feel like it will never go away. It got written into my DNA so long ago that my body doesn't know how to undo it. If Luke Taylor murdered someone I'd probably end up marrying him in prison.

If Connor sensed any awkwardness, he didn't show it. He just thumped beers into Ed's and Luke's hands, and then started dragging the mattress back up the hall.

"So, Luke Taylor . . . ," Negin said. "What are you actually doing here?"

Frankie nearly choked on her cocktail, and even Ed winced and clenched his teeth.

Luke shuffled against the counter and took a swig of his beer. "I just wanted to say sorry, I guess. Because I really *am* sorry. I've felt so shit about it all semester. So guilty. It's not an excuse or anything, I know. But it's the truth."

Everyone was looking at him, but he was looking at me. "I've been such a dickhead. I don't know what else to say. I don't know why I didn't do anything earlier, but then when Becky left, it was just . . ." He took another sip of his beer and looked around at everyone this time—Negin and Frankie and Ed, and then back to me. "I'm so, so sorry," he said again, and I could feel how much he meant it.

Connor came smashing into the door again, with a whole new mattress-load of randoms falling off behind him. He stood up, dusted himself off and shouted: "Right . . . Never Have I Ever."

Suddenly, there was only the scream of chairs scraping and glasses clinking and people cramming themselves frantically around the table.

"Sorry, Luke Taylor," Frankie shouted, pouring herself another drink. "We'll have to return to your soul-searching later. Never Have I Ever takes priority."

Luke looked quite relieved. He unwrinkled his brow and ran a hand through his hair. I saw Ed punch him on the arm and grin.

"I have never been in love," Liberty shouted. And I looked at Luke. I didn't mean to; it was an insane, drunk, instantaneous reaction. He looked at me. And then we both looked away.

"I have never vomited blue puke," Connor shouted, and he and Frankie both drank.

"I have never sleepwalked," Liberty squealed.

Frankie held her glass up and looked around the table. "I have never lied about jerking off." Then she drank. Everyone burst out laughing. "I literally don't know why I lied about it before," she said.

And then, one by one, all the girls drank. And everyone was thumping the table and cheering.

Connor stood up on his chair. "To everyone jerking off," he boomed. "We are *all* wankers. Everyone in D Dorm is a wanker!"

Ed frowned. "I'm not *in* D Dorm."

"It's all right, mate." Connor smiled. "You're still a wanker to me."

Ed squeezed his shoulder. "Thanks, man. That means a lot."

"Let's play Sardines," Liberty squealed, and suddenly everyone was charging down the stairs, out into the driving rain. It was pitch-black and freezing, but it felt amazing to be out in the cold after how boiling hot the kitchen had been.

We ran to the clearing behind the buildings, which was flanked by massive, manicured trees. It was *so* muddy. Loads of us had fallen on the way and looked like we had just swum through a bog. There was a trail of shoes that people had discarded in favor of going barefoot.

"Phoebs is *it*!" Liberty shouted, so I ran off, and they all started counting. I kept falling over, and by the time I'd found a decent hiding place, inside a bush, my entire face was caked in mud. I sat there quietly, thinking how I wanted and really *didn't* want Luke to be the first one to find me. But then Negin's face poked through the leaves.

"Fuck, you're good at Sardines," I whispered. "Sardines and quidditch. Your two major life skills."

She settled down beside me. "It's *so* cold."

"I think my alcohol blanket's wearing off," I moaned.

"I don't even *have* one of those," she said, wiping the wet mud off her forehead.

"I'm so excited about our house," I said. "I'm so, so glad we all met." And because I was drunk I just threw my arms around her. "Sorry," I whispered. "I know you're not a hugger."

"I think I've become *more* of a hugger." She smiled. "What can I say? College has changed me. I still don't like puke, though."

Then Connor, Frankie and Liberty emerged through the leaves. "We could hear you guys laughing from three trees down," Connor hissed. "You might be good at feminism, but you're shit at hiding."

"'Good at feminism,'" Negin repeated. "I might get a T-shirt with that."

"You could put 'Shit at hiding' on the back," Connor suggested.

"Can you guys shut up? I don't want Ed to find us," Frankie whispered.

"Why not?" I said. "He's your knight in shining armor."

"I know. But I'm too nervous to speak to him."

"You need to get over it, Frankie. He's not gonna Colin Firth you, I promise."

"What's Colin Firthing?" whispered Connor. "Is that, like, a sex thing?"

267

Frankie shrieked, and suddenly Ed was clambering into the bush, too. "All right, who's screaming in here?" He was so big that his knees stuck out through the leaves. "I'm guessing that was you, Connor?"

Everybody got hysterical, and then suddenly Luke was peering into the bush, too.

"Luke Taylor," said Frankie. "I'm not sure there's room in this shrub for the likes of you."

"I'm not sure there's room in this shrub for the likes of *anyone*," said Negin.

Luke looked uncomfortable. Almost shy, like we were at elementary school and he was trying to join in our game but not sure if we would let him. He took a step backward and nodded, accepting that he wasn't welcome. I scooched closer to Negin and gestured at the little patch of mud beside me. Neither of us said anything as he smiled and sat down.

Part Five

23

● ● ● ● ● ● ● **LUKE** ● ● ● ● ● ● ●

Rita looked down at the book. "I feel like it's too precious to actually touch. How much was it?"

"Fifty-five quid," I said, and she whistled: "*Luke.* Going all out."

We were drinking Oreo milk shakes on the bus back from town, where I'd spent a good half hour riffling through various dusty bookshops until I'd finally found it. An early edition of *Ariel.*

"I hope she likes it," I said.

Rita handed it back. "She will."

The present had been her idea. Well, not the book itself, but the idea of getting Phoebe something special for her birthday.

But the extra thing—the surprise—had been all me. It had come to me on that mad night in D Dorm, right after I'd made

271

my garbled apology to everyone. I suddenly knew what I needed to do. I hadn't even told Rita about it yet. I hadn't told anyone.

A week had gone by since the Sardines craziness, and it had quietly, inexplicably, turned into the best week of the semester so far. Not because everything was suddenly perfect: it wasn't. Random girls still gave me evils as I walked through campus, and the D Dormers were as frosty as ever, but at least it was all out in the open now and not some shadowy, guilt-ridden secret that I had to carry around on my own.

Me and Phoebe definitely weren't back to whatever we had been before Becky left, but we were edging closer. We'd spent most days together in the library, whispering and laughing and people-watching, when we should have been working on our essays. We hadn't even kissed again yet, but in a weird way it felt like we were closer than before. Like, now that everything had been knocked down, we could actually start to build something new.

Will had gone home the day after the game. No one even knew if he was coming back. All soccer stuff was on a sort of hiatus. The morning after Sardines I'd gone and spoken to Arthur and Rita about it all. The Wall of Shame, everything. Just laid it all out and told them how awful I felt. And how I knew saying sorry didn't make it better, but I was still really, really sorry.

Rita had told me: "You know, Luke, for someone who's not a dick, you can be *such* a dick." But then Arthur had thumped me gently on the arm, and they'd both told me how much they'd hated the first semester, too.

A buzz in my pocket shook me out of the memory, but before I could check it, Rita said: "So are you and Phoebe actually a thing again now?"

"I don't know, really. I feel like tomorrow, at her birthday thing, maybe . . ." I took a sip of my drink and stared out of the bus window. "I don't know. It's still kind of awkward. I want us to be a thing again, but I'm not sure whether she wants it. I don't really feel like she's really forgiven me—"

"Which, let's be honest, is fair enough," Rita cut in sharply, and I could tell she was only half joking.

I nodded. "I know, I know. I really fucked up. Shit, man. Why do things have to be so messy?"

"They don't." She shrugged. "I mean, we're not sixteen anymore, Luke. It is possible to sleep with someone a few times and for things not to be awkward afterward."

"Not sure about that."

"Well . . . me and Arthur."

I nearly choked on my milk shake. "What? Seriously?"

She smiled. "Yeah, seriously. We had a little thing in the first semester. I was still rebounding pretty hard from Jack. And me and Arth just got on so well. We were spending loads of time together, and . . . it just happened."

"Shit. Then what?"

"Well . . . I think he wanted it to turn into something more serious, but I wasn't sure. I mean, I'd literally just split up with Jack. So I suggested that maybe we should just be friends for a bit and see what happened. And a year later, we still are friends. Really good friends." She pushed the bell for the next stop and stood up. "And who knows what'll happen in the future? In spite of my good taste, and his many, many shortcomings, there is still something about that boy. . . ."

I lifted my knees to let her pass. "I can't believe it. You and Arthur. I've always thought you'd make an amazing couple."

"Ha! Maybe. Who knows? I'll probably end up marrying him." This idea made her snort into her milk shake for a good five seconds.

She got off the bus outside her house, and I stayed on till campus: the end of the line. I walked the long way back, around the lake, toward Jutland. It was bitterly cold, and I could feel the book bumping against my back through my backpack. I thought about giving it to Phoebe at her birthday dinner tomorrow, and how she might react. And then I thought about how she would react to the surprise.

As I passed the library, I remembered that buzz in my pocket. The message was from Reece. It said: *Shit man, you OK? You seen Abbey's Instagram?*

A little quiver of shock ran through me—mostly at the fact that Abbey literally hadn't even crossed my mind in the past week. I checked her Instagram and saw that she'd posted a new photo just a few hours ago. She was smiling brightly in it, and weirdly my first thought was to wonder how long it had been since I saw her smile like that.

My second thought was: Who the fuck is the guy kissing her?

By the time I got back to my dorm, I'd tried to call her five times. No answer. I unlocked my room and kept trying. Nothing. Just the first two seconds of her voice mail, over and over again: "Hi, it's Abb—" Hang up. Redial.

The guy in the picture had glasses, black hair and a full beard, like a real adult, even though he couldn't have been more than a couple of years older than us. They were standing on a beach somewhere, wrapped up in scarves and sweaters, Abbey's hair billowing out sideways in the wind. He had his eyes closed, and was kissing the side of her mouth, while she half kissed him back and half grinned at the camera. At me.

I tried her again. No answer. I felt panicked suddenly. On edge. What the fuck was wrong with me? Why was I reacting like this? I thought back to that morning in bed with Phoebe a few weeks ago, when I'd wondered how I'd feel if Abbey met someone else. I'd really thought I'd be OK with it. Relieved, even. Happy.

But clearly, Hypothetical Me was much more stable and mature than Actual Me. Actual Me, as it turned out, was a fucking pathetic dick. Actual Me was suddenly wondering if breaking up with Abbey had been a huge mistake.

But then, were we *really* broken up? That night after the initiation, I'd said "I'm not over you," and she'd said "I'm not over you, either." What the *fuck* did that actually *mean*?

After an hour or so, sick of feeling this cold, gathering panic, I gave up and went for a walk across campus. I purposely left my phone in the room, picturing it swollen with texts and missed calls by the time I got back. In the end, I was out of the dorm for all of about six minutes—I basically jogged to the vending machines and back—and the phone was just as Abbey-less as it was when I left.

I picked it up and tried her again. No answer. Arthur knocked on my door and poked his head around: "Yo, what you up to?"

"Nothing."

"Who were you calling?"

"No one."

"Want a spliff?"

"No, I'm all right."

"Bit of cheese?"

"No."

He shrugged. "Suit yourself."

As soon as he'd closed the door, my phone buzzed. I leaped on it, but it was just a text from Phoebe, asking if I wanted to have coffee with her and Flora before the dinner tomorrow.

I chucked the phone back onto the bed, but it burst straight back into life again. It was ringing now, and Abbey's name was flashing across the screen. I felt my heart kick into double-time.

"Abbey?"

There was silence, and for a horrible second I thought she'd hung up. Then she spoke, really softly.

"Hey, Luke . . . Are you OK?"

A weird sense of calm came over me. Like, now that I'd finally gotten through to her, everything was going to be all right.

"I just needed to speak to you. Where've you been? I've been calling for ages."

"We've been driving back from Sussex. I've been down there quite a bit lately, staying with my gran."

"Cool. How was it?"

Another pause. "Yeah, it was good."

I couldn't dance around the subject of the photo any longer. "So . . . what's his name?"

She sighed heavily. "Luke . . ."

"Oh, his name's Luke, too? That's a coincidence." I was being an ass, and I knew it. But then, as we've established, Actual Me is—and probably always will be—an utter ass.

She sighed again. "His name's Marcus."

"Marcus?"

"You don't need to say it like that."

276

"Who the fuck is named *Marcus*?"

"He is."

"Right. So is he . . . ?" I ran out of words. "Who is he?"

I listened as she explained how they'd met. How his family had rented a cottage next to her gran's. How they'd spent most of the past few weeks hanging out together, going for walks by the sea. How he'd just finished college—he was twenty-two, he'd majored in classics at Oxford—and was now trying to figure out what to do with his life. How they'd bonded over both being in what Marcus referred to as "a transitory stage" of their lives.

If I'd disliked the bloke after seeing that photo, I absolutely *hated* him now.

"Are you together, then?" I asked when she'd finally finished talking about Marcus and all his incredible achievements. "Like, is he your boyfriend?"

"No, Luke. Of course not."

"Well, you look pretty cozy in that picture." I was reaching new, previously unexplored levels of brattiness.

She half-sighed-half-tutted. "Look, I'm sorry if I embarrassed you or whatever, by putting that photo up, but—"

"I'm not embarrassed, Abbey," I snapped. "I don't care what other people think—I never did. I just care about what *I* think and what *you* think."

"Well, what do you think?"

"I think . . ." What *did* I think? "I think it's really weird seeing you with someone else. Not just weird. Horrible."

There was silence again. Then she said: "Luke, you need to figure out what you want."

"I don't know what I want," I said lamely.

"Well, you said you didn't want me anymore," she said. "*You* broke up with *me*, remember?"

"I said I wasn't over you."

She groaned. "You only said that when you were drunk and lonely and . . . confused or whatever."

"Well, I didn't know you were going to run off straight into the arms of some fancy dickhead named *Marcus*."

"He's not fancy."

"So you're not disputing the dickhead part?"

She ignored this. "Look, I didn't *know* I was going to run straight off to Marcus. I *didn't* run straight off to Marcus. I didn't plan any of this. I'm sorry. But isn't this what you wanted? I'm *OK* now, Luke. At least, I think I'm on the way to OK. Aren't you happy about that?"

"Yeah. Of course."

"Luke . . ." Her voice wavered and sounded heavier suddenly. "Trying to get over you has been the hardest, most awful thing I've ever had to do."

I didn't know what to say to this. I felt like the conversation was snowballing out of control. I was saying things I wasn't sure I meant. I felt tired.

"What are you saying, then?" she asked finally. "Are you saying you want to get back together?"

"No. Or . . . maybe. I don't know."

"Great," she snapped. "Well, your decisiveness is really reassuring."

"Sorry."

I heard her click her tongue irritably. "Shit, we can't talk like this. I hate not being able to see you. It's crazy talking about this stuff over the phone."

"I know. It feels like years since I last saw you."

"Yeah. I know." She exhaled heavily. "Shall we just talk tomorrow? I'm tired; we've been driving for ages."

"Yeah, OK. Speak to you tomorrow."

I knew I should try to think hard about what I really wanted. Try to get everything straight in my head. I texted Phoebe back and told her I couldn't meet tomorrow in the daytime, as I had to do schoolwork.

Then I looked down at the *Ariel* book poking out the top of my backpack and wondered what the fuck I was going to do.

24

Seeing Flora tumble out of the train and onto the platform made me unexpectedly tearful. I sprinted over to her like she was my long-lost love. In a way she kind of is, I suppose. She is the memory stick that carries anything that has ever happened to me that meant something. The sight of her is like a jolt connecting me to every version of myself I have ever been, all at once.

She was wearing the old red duffle coat that was her dad's in the eighties. It was sort of falling off her shoulders because she was carrying so many random bags. Underneath, she was wearing a knitted sweater and the lime-green flares she had bought from an Etsy shop that were too small so we hacked the waistband off.

"Best one." She cuddled me hard. "Happy birthday. I thought you would look different but you look exactly the same. Are you *crying*? I *joked* to my mum you would cry, but now you actually *are*."

"You know what I'm like. Why do you have so many small bags? You look like a crazy bag lady."

"Because I didn't bring a small suitcase to college, only one massive one."

I slung three of them over my shoulder and then linked arms with her.

It was a weirdly warm day for the first of December, and the sun made York look quaint and picturesque. We wandered through the cobbled streets and took a photo by the wall. Flora reached out and ran her fingers across a brick. "It's weird that an actual medieval person stood right here. . . ."

"I find stuff like that totally crazy. Do you remember when Mr. Gillcrest told us that if you stood on a star and looked at the world you would be looking at it in Tudor times? And I still don't get that thing about the human race fitting in a sugar cube." I reached out and put both my palms on one stone.

"You remember the weirdest things." She put her hands next to mine. "I am so excited to see you with Luke Taylor. Like, *beyond*."

"OK, well. Just know that it isn't going to happen until I have laid down some ground rules."

Flora started tiptoeing her way along a crack in the pavement and held her arms out like she was on a tightrope. She looked at me and winked. "What's it worth? 'Cause I have *material*."

I jumped in front of her. "I mean it. However drunk you get, whatever happens, you cannot say . . . anything. I mean, I feel like it's best if you don't ever speak to him."

"What, so you'll be married and I'll be godmother to your kids but I'll never have spoken to him?"

"Yup."

She put her arms down. "OK, I'm obviously going to play it perfectly. I'll be, like, 'Oh yeah, Luke, I couldn't picture you when Phoebe mentioned you, but actually, yeah, now I recognize you.'"

"You're overacting. It's not a pantomime."

"I'm not—you're paranoid. Who won the drama cup?" She took a bow at a random man walking past.

"Look. I just . . . I'm nervous. This week has been really weird."

It was weird because suddenly the gap between who I was on the inside and who I was on the outside had become like a crater. Outside there was the casual, confident me who agreed with Negin and Frankie that maybe Luke didn't deserve to be forgiven, and that I could do better. And inside was the real me, who was spending way more time with him than I was letting on, and was getting deeper into it than ever. And now Flora was dive-bombing right into the middle of it all and I was going to have to negotiate it.

"We have been together every day," I told her, "but we haven't even kissed yet."

"Romantic. Like a weird Amish dating trial."

"No. I just think he wants us to get it right this time. He said he wants tonight to be amazing."

"Maybe he'll flamenco dance in the middle of the restaurant." Flora snorted. "Anyway, is this real? Like, actually *real*? Like, *Luke Taylor*. Marauder's Map Luke Taylor? Love potion Luke Taylor—"

I jumped on her back and she screamed. "This is exactly what I am talking about. You have to *shut up*."

She nodded. "OK, OK. Promise."

"Do you actually?"

She held my hand. "Obviously." She squeezed it. "I'm messing with you. I would rather die than fuck it up. I feel like this is happening to me, too. It's happening to us."

We walked into the main bit of town, to the huge glass windows of Bettys.

"Oh my god." Flora walked right up to the window where an elderly couple were eating strawberry meringues and cupped her hands and peered in. "Bettys is *fan*-cy. It looks like the kind of place Daisy Buchanan goes for tea." She started to Charleston.

The couple stared disapprovingly at her, and she smiled at them and backed away. "There is a full-on line to get in. Like a club. Is this real?"

She walked into the main door for people who only want to buy things over the counter. I followed her in and scanned the room but Josh wasn't there. I felt a bit disappointed.

Sandra appeared. "Josh isn't here, love. He's on his break. Do you want something to take home with you? Is this your friend?"

Flora bowed slightly. "Yup. Friend-from-home. Best friend, in fact."

We picked a cake each and Sandra put them in a box and tied it with ribbon.

"He's probably at the pastry shop," she said as she handed it to me. "And he's already had four slices of cake."

Him not being there made me realize how much I wanted Flora to meet him.

And then, as we wandered back down the street, something pushed between us and linked both our arms. "Now then, Birthday Girl." Josh was still holding half a meat pie in his hand, which he took a chomp out of. "Do you want one? I've got two more. It's not your *real* present, obviously."

"Two more?" Flora said disapprovingly. "And you've already had four slices of cake."

"Spying on me when you don't even know me?" Josh shook his head. "I'm Josh." He held out his paper bakery bag in greeting.

Flora shook the bag. "Flora."

Josh and Flora are the type of people who have that easy confidence that means they can make friends with anyone in about thirty-five seconds.

"Are you coming out tonight?" she asked.

Josh shook his head. "I'm working."

"He's actually working my shift, so I don't have to work my birthday."

"I'm gonna come out afterward, though. Would never let Miss Bennet's birthday go uncelebrated." He held out his arms and gave me a massive hug. "Happy birthday." He picked me up as he said it and then waved us goodbye while shoving the rest of his pastry in his mouth.

"Well, he is attractive," Flora said. "Apparently, York Met is full of eligible bachelors."

We walked back to campus, and I started to feel weird about Flora being there. Like she was an anachronism who didn't belong in Jutland D Dorm, but in my bedroom or the high school common room or Finnegan's on a Friday night.

When we got back to the hall, it felt like a bit of an anti-climax, because no one was there. I showed Flora my birthday present from Frankie and Negin—a set of big wooden letters to decoupage for our house next year. They were all of our initials, including Becky's. Then we went into the kitchen, made instant Quaker oats and crumbled a Crunchie bar over the top.

"Shall we have a nap?" Flora ran her finger around the bowl and ate the last bits of Crunchie-flavored oatmeal.

We got into our pajamas and climbed into opposite ends of the bed.

"Luke Taylor has slept in this bed," Flora mumbled. "That's fucking weird." I checked my phone. Luke still hadn't texted since telling me "Happy Birthday" at ten a.m. It was making me nervous. Of all the days to not be in touch. But maybe he was busy buying my present or something. I wondered if he was working on a surprise party in our hall, or decorating the restaurant or something?

And then Flora fell asleep and I lay there imagining how the night would be. I thought about Luke hugging Flora and then, when I wasn't there, telling her how much he liked me. How they would get on and Flora would ask us both to go and see her in Leeds. I wanted to look really good, because tonight did feel like something I would remember forever.

I woke up to faint knocking on the door. "You in, Phoebe?" It was Negin.

"Yeah, we were just napping," I called gently. Flora wriggled around. I opened the curtain up a bit. Negin pushed the door and craned her head in.

"Hey, I'm Negin. Do you guys want a cup of tea?"

"That would be amazing." Negin wanting to be nice to Flora made a wave of happiness wash over me.

Flora wriggled around to face Negin. "That would be *legit* amazing."

By the time Frankie came over, all we had achieved was making room for Negin on the bed and drinking another cup of tea and eating the other two Crunchies in the pack. Frankie had brought a seaside bucket and spade with donkeys on them to use as a punch vessel and stirrer.

"Erm, we're not leaving for another three hours," I said.

"It's your birthday, Phoebster. That means we're drinking tonight, and we're going *hard*."

She sat down on my floor and started filling the bucket with brightly colored juice and then vodka. She opened a bottle of Coke and poured it in and started mixing it with the spade. "I feel like a witch making a brew." She peered into the bowl. "Make Ed want to kiss me," she muttered in a slow zombie voice as she stirred.

We started getting ready, but the longer Luke didn't text me, the more anxious I got. I tried to be as breezy as possible and only allowed myself to check my phone every four songs.

"Have you seen Luke today?" I tried to sound casual. Frankie and Negin shook their heads. They didn't look like they were acting.

"Haven't you?" Frankie asked.

"No, no, I mean, he knows I'm with Flora so . . ."

They all nodded.

"So what do you think of Luke Taylor?" Flora said conspiratorially. "I mean, I don't *know* him, you guys do."

Neither Frankie nor Negin said anything immediately, and then they both nodded exaggeratedly. "Yeah, he's really nice. Really, really nice." The way Negin said it made me nervous. I didn't want to get into all the Wall of Shame stuff. To be honest, I'd given Flora a slightly abbreviated version of it all, playing up Luke's walk-off at the game and almost making him out to be the hero of the whole thing. I turned the music up but Flora kept talking.

"I mean, you must understand how crazy this is for me. Like, I spent seven years of my life investing in Phoebe's Luke Taylor obsession, and it's, like, now her and Luke Taylor are an *actual thing.*"

Negin and Frankie nodded again.

"You guys know about the Marauder's Map, right?" Flora asked.

"Flora, shut up." I hit her on the knee. "This is exactly what I was talking about earlier."

"Oh, come on, I can tell Frankie and Negin."

I rolled my eyes. "OK . . ."

Flora shuffled up onto her knees and leaned forward, swishing the spade like a wand. "Basically, in eighth grade we found a copy of Luke's schedule in the library and hand-drew a Luke Taylor Marauder's Map so we knew exactly where he was at all times."

Frankie whistled, and Negin said: "We could do with that now, to be honest." I laughed along with them, but my stomach was tenser than ever.

Connor and Liberty and the others met us in the kitchen and we took pictures and played Ring of Fire. I kept going to the bathroom to look at my phone, but nothing. He said he would come. He *knew* Flora was coming. When I came back into the kitchen, Flora, Negin and Frankie all exchanged a look.

"Have you heard from Luke?" Flora asked casually. "Why don't you text him?"

"Yeah, I'll see where's he's at." I shrugged like it was no big deal as I got my phone out and wrote:

Are you coming for the pregame? If not, see you at browns at 8?

I put my phone in my pocket and made myself not look at it for the rest of the game. I pretended to have forgotten my lip gloss and ran back to my room just so I could check my phone without them seeing. He had *seen* the message. I took a deep breath. I only sent it half an hour ago. He might be doing anything, really. But what?

As I walked back to the kitchen I could hear them all talking through the door, but when I opened it, they went quiet suddenly.

"What did Luke say?" Negin asked.

"Oh, nothing yet. I think he's finishing his essay."

She smiled, and Frankie said, "Luke Taylor . . . what an enigma."

I laughed. "What do you mean?"

"No, nothing. Just . . ." She trailed off and looked at Negin, like she was tagging her into the conversation.

"I just wonder if he has . . . issues," Negin said quietly, and Flora handed me a massive drink.

I was leaving the library when I got Phoebe's text. I checked my phone and saw she was getting ready to go to Brown's with Flora and everyone.

I wandered around campus aimlessly, and thought about calling her, or even heading over to her dorm, but I didn't. Eventually, I just sent her a message that said: *Sorry, been so hectic today, see you at dinner later x.* Which basically translated as, *Sorry, I'm a massive jerk,* but at that moment I couldn't think of anything better.

I hadn't even had time to sort the surprise out. It was supposed to be the big thing for tonight—bigger than the *Ariel* book, even—but I'd been so weighed down with Abbey thoughts all day, I'd forgotten all about it.

I got back to my dorm, fully intending to flop down onto my bed and try to get my head straight before I headed out to the dinner. But when I opened the kitchen door, I thought I was hallucinating. Like, maybe the half spliff I'd had earlier with Arthur was making me see things. But there was no way Arthur's rubbish weed could cause such a heart-stoppingly realistic apparition.

"Hey," Abbey said.

"Hey," I heard myself say back.

She stood up, and I thought she was coming over to give me a hug or something, but she just stayed on the other side of the table, scratching her elbow awkwardly.

"This girl let me in," she said. "Hope that's OK."

"What the hell are you doing here?" I meant to say. But instead I said: "Yeah, of course."

She wrinkled her nose. "It smells quite bad in here."

"That's the cheese," I said, flicking Barney's latest note on the fridge.

I was having serious trouble coming to terms with the fact that she was *actually* here. Here in York. Here in my hall. She looked healthy and happy—or maybe just healthier and happier than the last time I'd seen her. She was wearing her long, dark-blue coat, and she must have just gotten here, because her cheeks were still pink from the cold. It felt like so long since I'd last seen her.

In the end, she answered the question without me even asking it.

"I know this is a bit out of the blue, but after yesterday, I just thought it would be better to talk for real," she said. "Face to face."

"Yeah, definitely." I nodded. "It's good to see you." And it really was. I felt the sudden urge to go and hug her, to hold her tight and feel her pressed right up against me, with her head tucked neatly under my chin. She used to say that's how she knew we were meant to be together—because we clicked into each other perfectly, like a jigsaw puzzle.

"Can we go somewhere the smell can't get us?" she asked, frowning. I unlocked my room and she followed me inside.

"So . . . this is where it all happens?"

"Yeah, I guess. If by 'where it all happens,' you mean 'where I try to understand what the fuck Ted Hughes is going on about.'"

She sat down on the bed and cracked a smile. "I bet you haven't changed your sheets once yet, have you?"

I smiled back. "Good guess."

"And I bet your mum put these on for you."

"Yeah, yeah. You know me so well."

It was meant as an off-the-cuff comment, but I felt the air tighten around it. She really *did* know me well. We were together nearly three and a half years. That had to mean something, right?

I sat down on the bed next to her. "So . . . what's going on, then?" I asked.

She smoothed a crease in the comforter. "I don't know. I just . . . after we spoke yesterday, I wanted to see you. To talk about stuff properly. About what's happening. Or what's going to happen."

"OK." I had no idea what was going to happen, but even more worryingly, I had no idea what I really *wanted* to happen.

Earlier, getting stoned with Arthur, I'd tried to think about what I'd do if Abbey told me she wanted us to get back together. I eventually concluded that my head would say no, but my gut—or was it my heart?—would say yes. Why can't bodies think as a *whole*? Or was it just *my* body?

There was a knock on the door. The handle swiveled, and Arthur's head appeared.

"I will have a cup of tea, then, if you're mak—" He saw Abbey and stopped. "Oh. Hi."

"Hey." Abbey smiled.

"Abbey, this is Arthur. Arthur, Abbey."

"All right? Just seeing if you fancied some Scrabble action, Luke, but no worries. I'll see you later. Nice to meet you, Abbey."

"You too."

When he'd left, she looked around the room: "It's so cool, this. It's like living in a big apartment building with all your friends."

"I'm so sorry about you not going to Cardiff," I said. "I can't believe I haven't even told you that yet."

"It's OK." She nodded. "I really think it was for the best. I think if I'd gone this year, I would have ended up dropping out in, like, two weeks. I just know I wasn't in the right place for it."

"But you're going next year?"

"Yeah. My mum and Miss Sawyer sorted it out."

She stood up and started flicking distractedly through the books on my desk. She picked up the *Ariel* book—Phoebe's present—and murmured, "This is pretty," and I thought about how my life was starting to become so messy I might never untangle it.

She put the book back on the desk. "Sorry, Luke. I don't know what's up with me at the moment. It's quite random to just get on a train and come up to see you."

"No, it's not random. I mean, it is a *bit* random. But good random."

"I just thought it would be better if we actually *saw* each other. That it might help us both figure out what we wanted."

"Yeah. Definitely." There was a pause while she stared down idly at my *Modern Romantic Poetry* anthology. Then I said: "Do you fancy a cup of tea?"

I went back out into the kitchen and checked my phone. I had two missed calls from Phoebe. I checked her Story: they were on the bus into town. In the picture, she was smiling brightly, wearing an IT'S MY BIRTHDAY, BITCH badge that I assumed was Frankie's doing. Using every bit of mental strength, I forced out all traces of guilt and concentrated on boiling the kettle.

We drank our teas, and then I cooked us some gloopy,

slightly burnt tuna mayonnaise pasta, which Abbey actually seemed quite impressed with, mainly because it was the first meal I'd ever made her that didn't involve a microwave or my mum. We ate it at my tiny desk, sat so close that our plates overlapped at the edges, and laughed about stupid stuff: what people from school were doing on their gap years, how her fancy friend Veronica had converted to Buddhism within forty-eight hours of arriving in Thailand. It almost felt like the beginning again; the early days of ninth grade, when we were just getting together, realizing how much we liked each other, how well we seemed to fit.

But there was also this weird, nagging sense of unreality about it all. Like we both knew deep down that this was an odd sort of flashback that couldn't possibly sustain itself in the long run. At some point, we had to talk about the future.

When we'd finished eating, I went and washed up, and checked the pictures of Phoebe and the rest of them in Brown's. I told myself I could think about all that later. I just had to get through whatever was going to happen with Abbey, and then I could make the world's biggest apology to Phoebe tomorrow. I went back into the room and said: "So what do you want to do?"

She shrugged. "Well, I was sitting on a train for three hours, so it'd be nice to go out for a bit. You could show me York."

"There's not much to show."

"Erm, excuse me. I'm sure your mum told us York was the UK's second most popular tourist destination?"

"Yes, I think she only mentioned that seven hundred times over the summer."

She laughed. "Well, then."

We walked off campus and followed the little leafy back

streets into town. Even though I was purposely aiming us in the exact opposite side of the city to where Brown's was, I still felt a constant thrum of terror as I imagined Phoebe or Frankie or Negin stepping around every corner.

We'd just turned onto the main road, which was lined with identical red-brick terraced houses, when I heard a sudden burst of music and shouting.

"Oi! Taylor!" I looked up to see Trev leaning casually out of a top-floor window, waving a can of lager at me. The room behind him was packed with people, dancing and shouting and drinking.

"Trev!" I shouted up at him. "Is this where you live?"

He shook his head. "No idea whose house this is. But I'm sure everyone's welcome. You coming in?"

I looked at Abbey. "Erm, no, I don't think so."

Abbey shrugged. "I wouldn't mind. It'd be nice to meet some of your friends."

"No, I really think—"

"Luke Taylor! Get the fuck inside!" Drunk Toby had materialized next to Trev at the window, brandishing a half-empty bottle of vodka.

"We could just say hello." Abbey smiled.

"I'll let you in!" Trev yelled, disappearing back into the room.

Feeling the panic in my chest step up a few gears, I pushed the broken gate open. Trev ushered us into the living room and I realized I recognized nearly every single person inside it. Misty and Brandon and the quidditch team were all here. Hot Mary was chatting with Liverpool Paul on the sofa. Even Caribbean Jeremy was sitting on the carpet, inexpertly rolling a stupidly big spliff.

Drunk Toby came galloping down the stairs and whacked me on the back. He handed me a can of Stella and then started introducing himself to Abbey. Trev turned to me: "What's going on with Will, then? Do you think he's actually gone for good?"

"Dunno," I said. "I haven't heard anything."

"I heard he had to see the provost. They might disband the team."

"Shit, really?"

He took a swig of beer. "I was thinking, you know, if they do, we should just start our own thing next semester. No initiations, no dickheads, no Dempers. Just playing soccer and having fun."

"That's actually a really good idea," I said.

"I've already told Toby," Trev said proudly. "He's on board."

"I reckon Ed would be into it, too."

We clinked cans and he staggered off toward Jeremy, who was now attempting to light his precarious spliff. I looked past them, over at the doorway, to see that Negin and Frankie had appeared, and their eyes were shooting daggers at me.

And next to them, Abbey was talking to Phoebe.

25

Abbey Baker looked as neat and perfectly groomed as she always had.

She has that Kate Middleton–type hair that no one really has in real life, long and bouncy and perfectly blow-dried. She was wearing an impossibly white cotton tank top with little purple strawberries embroidered on it tucked into her jeans. Her white Converse didn't have a single mark on them. Her nails were painted pale lilac to match the strawberries. She had hugged me like we had been friends at school. Not a cold, I-don't-really-give-a-shit hug but a warm, genuine one.

"Phoebe, I want to know *everything*," she said. "It's so shitty being on a gap year. I keep seeing photos of people going out every night and I'm just sitting with my mum and dad watching *Countryfile*." She laughed gently. Everything she did was sort of reserved.

I was trying so hard to keep smiling that it was difficult to concentrate on what she was saying. I felt like if I pretended it was just me and her in the room I might be able to get through.

I couldn't look at Flora next to me, or over at Frankie and Negin. Flora was deliberately not looking at one corner of the room, so I knew that's where Luke was. The nerves in my tummy were mostly because of Flora. Because she is an unknown quantity. She could say anything at any moment.

"I love your trousers. We match." Abbey took a sip of her drink and smiled at Flora. "I want to be able to wear vintage stuff but I just don't know where to start. You always look amazing. You need to give me some tips."

Abbey was *nice*. I had never heard a bad word about her. She had always been in the popular group but she was one of the ones who everyone knew was actually OK. She was sweet to everyone. She ran the homework club with the seventh graders when she was in tenth grade. She was the full package, really. *Girlfriend* material.

Flora looked down at her seventies flares, which were covered in psychedelic pineapples and strawberries. It wasn't Abbey's fault. I looked at Flora. She must feel it. That Abbey didn't deserve to be hurt. That she hadn't done anything. I willed her to be nice.

"Strawberries are clearly the thing. Phoebs, here . . ." Flora unpinned her strawberry brooch and leaned over and jabbed it into my tank top. It dug into me.

"Ouch."

"Oops, sorry." She fastened it. "Strawberry crew."

Abbey got out her phone. I smiled as she took the picture. She showed it to us. I didn't look like myself. Or maybe I did but I just felt so weird that nothing seemed normal. Flora was half smiling. A kind of noncommittal smile. Like she didn't want to give anything away one way or another. Abbey was doing a perfect off-duty model smile. Warm and accessible and polished.

I looked across the room by accident and saw Frankie and Negin. Frankie's face looked different, too. She was usually so animated that I had never really stopped and realized that she was actually quite beautiful in a statuesque, almost old-fashioned way. When she wasn't scoffing she looked like a woman from a Victorian painting. The kind of face people used to call handsome. She was expressionless almost. She looked grown-up.

"I need the bathroom," I said, and didn't look at Flora but just crossed the room. In my peripheral view, I thought I saw Luke's shape but I made myself keep moving forward.

There was someone in the bathroom. I could hear footsteps behind me. Neither Frankie nor Negin spoke. We just stood outside the bathroom, all waiting together. Hot Quidditch Marco walked out carrying a cup of blue liquid. None of us said anything.

He smiled. "You look serious." The way his Italian accent said the word "serious" would usually have made Frankie burst into an impression. But she didn't. He held the blue drink out. We all shook our heads in a way that said "not now."

We crammed in and locked the door. You could tell boys lived here. It was functional with a grimy edge. I sat on the toilet and Frankie and Negin sat on the edge of the bathtub. None of us spoke. And the longer none of us said anything the harder it got to break the silence. I felt like it should be me. Like they were waiting for my cue. To see whether I was angry or sad or confused. They didn't want to jump in any direction until I had.

"I just . . . I don't know . . . I hope Flora is OK." It was empty. Of course it was. Flora would be OK on Mars, psychedelic flares and all.

"She'll be fine. She knows her . . . kind of." Frankie was serious.

"I don't want her to feel like I've left her."

Negin shook her head. "She won't."

"I don't want her to make anything . . . weird." This was closer to the truth. I couldn't bear for her to make me endure some public scene.

"I don't think she'll say anything to Abbey," Negin said gently. "If she was going to she would have done it by now."

I nodded. I wasn't going to cry. I wasn't angry. I just wanted to evaporate. To not have to live through what was coming. There was a knock on the door. My stomach lurched intensely. It must be Luke.

"You all right, ladies?" It was Josh's voice.

"Phoebe isn't very well," Frankie said to the door.

"I'll get you some water," he called back, and we heard his feet thud down the stairs.

The silence continued until he knocked on the door again. Negin opened it and he handed her a cup of water. "Classic Bennet, peaking too early." None of us responded, and he seemed to catch that something was going on. "Hope you're OK." He leaned over and touched me really gently on the shoulder and then left, shutting the door behind him.

"Shall we just go?" Frankie said. "There's no point sitting in here for hours."

"I'll go. Flora will come with me. You two should definitely stay. I mean, Ed might be coming . . . I don't want you guys to—"

"To be honest, I think this evening is a bit cursed," Frankie said. "I don't think I want tonight to be me and Ed's night anyway. I think tomorrow will be a better day for . . . everything."

I just needed to get from the bathroom to the front door. It was, like, fifteen steps. As soon as I was out I would be OK.

"I don't want to say goodbye to anyone," I said.

"We'll just say you are really ill." Negin put her arm around my shoulder. It was so unlike her that for a split second I felt tears prick. "Ten seconds and we'll be out of here."

"I'll go and tell Flora," Frankie said.

Negin held my hand as she unlocked the door. She squeezed it. We walked out. I could hear everyone in the living room and in the kitchen. A couple I had never seen before was making out in the hall.

"My coat's in the living room," I whispered to Negin.

She nodded. "OK, wait here, I'll get it." She walked in just as Flora walked out. She was shaking her head like she was slightly pissed off. She looked up and saw me. She threw her arms around me. "Let's get the fuck out of here."

Negin came out holding my coat. I put it on and shuffled toward the front door. As we passed the living room I heard my name.

"Phoebe?" I looked up. It was Abbey. "Are you leaving?" She looked so earnest.

I nodded. "I don't feel very well."

"Luke!" Abbey shouted. "Phoebe Bennet is leaving."

Flora shook her head. "Fuck's sake." She said it under her breath and Abbey's face flickered momentarily.

Luke appeared beside Abbey. I made myself not look at him.

"I don't have my bag," I said to no one in particular.

"I'll get it." Abbey turned and went back into the living room.

"Hope you feel better." Luke's voice sounded tiny.

"You're a fucking asshole." Flora said it plainly and clearly but low enough that only we could hear it.

"Flora, please." I reached down for her hand but she shook it away from me.

"No, Phoebs. Don't try to make it better for him."

"Stop. I don't want—"

"Fine." She looked at Luke. "Go and enjoy the party, Luke. It's Phoebe's birthday, after all, so it's important we all really have a good time." She handed him her glass of punch and smiled a huge fake smile. "Enjoy."

Abbey was standing behind Luke, holding my bag. She reached over and handed it to me. I knew she had heard. And I knew that she knew. She looked the same as she had twenty minutes ago, perfectly coiffed, but her face couldn't hide it. She was broken. She looked at me and something in her eyes triggered something in me. I knew I was going to cry and that there was nothing I could do to stop it.

"Thank you," I said, and put the bag over my shoulder.

"Fuck. My stuff is in the bedroom." Flora turned and bounded upstairs. And I ran out the door.

The cold felt so good. I ran to the end of the street and turned the corner. I was right in front of the bricks that me and Flora had touched only a few hours ago. It felt so weird. So much had changed. How could it all have changed so quickly?

I let myself start crying.

"Phoebe." I turned around. Josh was there. I let him hold me. And then I was physically shaking.

It was weirdly violent. Like my whole body was part of it, these long convulsions that I couldn't stop. I couldn't breathe and I couldn't control myself. It was so loud. Not tears, but huge gasping wails. Every time I tried to stop they sounded more strangled and desperate.

The force of his hold steadied me. I let him hold me so tight that all the sounds were buried in him. It went on and on until the gulps slowed to every ten seconds or so. He just held me and held me. Rocked me gently in a kind of rhythm that matched how I was crying until it was soothing and I didn't want him to let me go. I couldn't speak and he didn't speak. I stepped away and the cold air hit me and I gulped an aftershock of a cry. Josh didn't seem to need to say anything. It was like he would have stood next to me endlessly, not needing any kind of explanation or movement. I opened my mouth to speak and breathed in, but I didn't know what I wanted to come out. I wiped my nose with my sleeve.

Finally, I said: "I feel sick." I didn't know if I did. I didn't even feel like I was connected to myself, like I was in my own body. I just said it because I felt like maybe it could be true.

He nodded. "Do you have a hair tie?"

I took mine off my wrist and he took it from me and tied my hair into a ponytail. "You'll be fine now. Nothing worse than sick in hair. Just feel free to really puke your guts out now if you need to."

A rasped laugh came out of me. "OK. Thanks." I stared at the pavement. "What a *shit* birthday."

"Well . . ." He took his backpack off. "OK, Bennet, it hasn't been ideal, I get that. I mean, I'm sure other birthdays have been better. But you haven't had *my* birthday present on other birthdays."

He pulled out an extremely crumpled package with Thomas the Tank Engine wrapping paper.

I smiled weakly as he handed it to me and unwrapped it slowly. They were cookie cutters. A cupcake, a ladybird, a cactus and a train. I cupped them all in my hands. "Thank you. I love them. Especially the train."

He nodded. "I told you, I knew you were a train person."

"It's really weird." I held it up and looked at him through the middle of the train outline. "I told Flora today, and I was going to tell you."

"Tell me what?"

"I decided what I want to do with my twentieth year."

"Indeed, Miss Bennet?" He picked the cactus up and looked at me through it. "Well, what is it, then?"

"I want to go traveling. Like around Europe. Inter-*railing*. You know"—I held up the train—"on trains."

We looked at each other through our cookie cutters.

"Well," he said, casually looking to the side. "Are you going on your own, you know, just training it about on your own or—"

"Well, I might ask some people, you know, I don't know. I'll have to see, if anyone . . . wants to come."

He looped his arm through mine and pulled me in toward him. "Let's get you home."

But I didn't want to go home. I wanted to be close to him. I pulled back and looked at him and took a step forward. And then I kissed him on the cheek, gently, near his mouth, and then moved across and kissed him again, closer this time. He cupped my face in his hands and made a sort of quiet, frustrated moan.

"Phoebe . . ." He took a step away and put his hands in his pockets. "Let's get you home." He sounded upset. Almost angry. I had never seen him even vaguely angry before.

I could feel myself going red. I got my phone out and ordered a cab. He walked away a bit and stood with his back to me.

"Phoebe—"

"Don't say anything. Like, please. I just can't face anymore tonight."

"Phoebe, I just . . . Listen. You know what I want in my twenty-first year?"

"What?" I almost shouted it.

"To know that I will know you for the rest of my life. For forever."

"Yup." I shook my head as I said it and turned and started to walk up the road. "Whatever." I could hear his paces behind me. "Will you at least leave me to feel humiliated alone?"

His paces stopped. We had only walked about five feet. The cab slowed down and I got into it, keeping my eyes fixed on the floor.

"Are you getting in?" the driver asked, and Josh must have shaken his head because the driver shrugged and wound the window up.

He glanced in the mirror and it made me do the same. He had clearly assessed the situation in one bored flick of the eye: *drunk student.* My mascara had run all down my face, and my eyes were still red and swollen. Neither of us spoke. I looked at my phone just in time to see I had seventeen messages before it died. So I just peered into the darkness and tried to block everything out.

Finally, we slowed to a stop. "Mind how you go, love. They're never worth it."

It made me smile. "That's what my mum says. She says you shouldn't trust anyone with a Y chromosome between the ages of fourteen and thirty-seven."

He nodded. "Sounds about right."

I slammed the door shut and looked up at D Dorm. The kitchen was lit up but all the rooms were dark. I was glad no one was there to have to explain it all to. Music was still playing in the bar and I could see some people playing foosball. It was sort of comforting to see life going on as normal.

And then I saw him.

He was standing alone at the bar, swaying ever so slightly from side to side, drinking a beer. It was the first time I had actually seen him since the soccer game. I didn't want him to see me so I started to walk quickly, but I heard the doors swing open as I passed.

"Phoebe!" Will shouted.

I kept walking.

"*Phoebe.*"

I stopped and turned to look at him. That confident swagger had completely disappeared. He just looked lost and a bit desperate.

"Can I talk to you?" he said. "There is something I just really, really need to say. . . ."

By the time I caught up to Abbey, she was almost halfway into town. But she wouldn't even stop to look at me.

"Abbey, please . . ."

She just carried on storming forward into the freezing night. "Please let me explain," I said. "I'm so sorry. I'm a fucking idiot."

"Fuck. You. Luke."

"Where are you going?"

"Train station."

"Abbey, don't be crazy. There won't be another train back now."

She spun around and looked me straight in the eyes. "Oh, OK, fine. So what? Shall we just go back to the party, then?"

"Well, no, obviously not, but—"

"Why the *fuck* did you even take me in there?" she hissed.

"Because you wanted to go," I said pathetically.

"Yeah. That was before I knew the girl you've been secretly fucking would be there, too."

I looked down at the pavement.

"So you have?" she said.

I looked back up at her but didn't speak. She closed her eyes and nodded.

"Right," she said with her eyes still closed. "Did you know she would be there?"

"Of course not," I muttered.

"So how long were you thinking you could keep this up?"

I almost laughed. "How long . . . Abbey, you're talking like I'm some fucking criminal mastermind, or, like, serial playboy. It should be pretty obvious that I *wasn't* thinking. About anything.

It's like I haven't been thinking all semester. I've just been . . . blindly moving forward, smashing into stuff as I go."

Abbey was shaking her head, staring down at her feet. I kept going, feeling a strange lightness at finally telling the truth. "I've been trying to fit in and make friends, but everything keeps falling apart. It's, like, school was so . . . easy. With you and Reece and soccer and everything, it all just slotted into place. But here, it's different. It's like nothing fits properly." I exhaled and watched my smoky breath mushroom out like a speech bubble above our heads. "This thing with Phoebe," I said quietly. "It was the first thing here that seemed to fit."

Abbey looked up at me, tears glinting in her eyes. "Why didn't you tell me about her, Luke?" she shouted. Like, *literally* shouted. I saw a light go on in the window nearest us.

I shrugged. "Same reason you didn't tell me about Marcus?"

She turned around again and started walking.

"Abbey, I'm sorry."

"Fuck off."

"Seriously, please. There won't be any trains now."

"I don't care."

"And even if there are, it'll be ridiculously expensive at the last minute."

She stopped suddenly and spun around furiously to face me. "I'VE GOT A YOUNG PERSON'S FUCKING RAILCARD, LUKE!" she screamed.

It was so loud that two guys in the restaurant across the road popped their heads out.

I couldn't help it. It was like something just snapped inside me.

"Are you actually fucking *laughing*?" Abbey whispered.

307

"I'm sorry . . ."

"You're such a . . ." But then she was laughing, too. Laughing and crying at the same time. Big gulping laughs sloshing into big groaning sobs.

We stood there for a few seconds like that; barking like mad seals, while the guys in the restaurant just stared at us.

Then she wiped her eyes with her sleeve and sat down on the wall of the house we were outside. "Oh, fucking hell, Luke." She took a deep breath and blew it back out. She sniffed and stared down at the pavement. "Phoebe Bennet," she said blankly. "From school."

I shook my head. "No . . . well, yeah, but we're not *together*, or anything. . . . We sort of were, though. I don't know what we are, really." I paused. "I'm so sorry, Abbs."

She looked up at me, eyes glistening. "No, it's all right, I suppose. I mean . . . we were broken up. We *are* broken up."

"Yeah, but still. I should have told you."

She shrugged. "I should have told you about Marcus."

"Well, yeah. Fucking *Reece* told me about Marcus. Or, at least, he told me to check Instagram."

"Yeah. Sorry. I shouldn't have put that picture up."

"Why did you?"

She opened her mouth to answer and then stopped. Then she suddenly burst out laughing again. "I wanted you to see it," she said, shaking her head. "I don't know what's wrong with me."

"It's all right. I don't know what's wrong with me either. At least we're confused together."

She dried her eyes on her sleeve again and took a couple more wobbly deep breaths.

"Why did you come up, Abbey?" I asked. "I mean, do you want us to get back together?"

"No, I don't think so," she sighed. "I don't know what I want, really. I just wanted to see you. I've missed you."

"Yeah, I've missed you, too. Still, you've got old Marcus now, haven't you. . . ."

She snickered. "Marcus is a *dick*, Luke. His Instagram is, like, ninety percent Latin proverbs."

This made me lose it again: "I *suspected* he was a dick, but I didn't want to say anything."

When we'd both stopped laughing, she said, "But I guess he did make me feel better."

"Well, maybe he's not a *total* dick, then."

She looked at me. "Does Phoebe Bennet make you feel like that?"

"Like what?"

"Better?"

I didn't really know the answer to that. To be honest, the idea that Phoebe would ever even want to be in the same room with me again seemed pretty unlikely, so it was hard to assess my feelings for her. But still, I gave it a go.

"I really like her, yeah. I like being with her." Abbey smiled sadly and nodded. I shifted closer to her along the wall. "I really want you to be OK, Abbs."

"I think I am now," she said softly. "But it's weird, you know? Like, half my bedroom wall is pictures of me and you. And now . . . what am I supposed to do with them? Put them up in the attic and forget about them? Or just throw them away? I don't want that. I don't want to forget that we ever happened."

"Me neither. But why do we have to? I wouldn't ever change

309

what we had. I was so happy with you. Maybe it's the right thing that it's over, but that doesn't mean it shouldn't have happened. I'm glad it did."

"I'm glad, too," she said, smiling. "But maybe we shouldn't see each other for a bit, though. After tomorrow, I mean. It might be a good thing. It might mean that we *can* see each other in the long run."

"Yeah. I really, really want that."

She reached into her bag and handed me an envelope. "Here. I forgot to give you this. Early Christmas card."

I opened it. It had a picture of some golf clubs and a pint of beer on the front, and it said: TO A WONDERFUL STEPDAD ON FATHER'S DAY.

"Shit," I said. "That's good. That's really good."

Inside the card she'd written: *Luke—whatever happens, you made me the happiest I've ever been.*

We walked back to Jutland arm in arm. Back in my room, I made tea and gave her the bed, even though she insisted it wouldn't be weird if we both slept in it. But it really felt like we'd gotten past something tonight—something we'd never really gotten past in the summer—and it seemed stupid to risk going back a step.

I laid out three pairs of jeans and a jacket on the floor beside her, and tried unsuccessfully to get comfy. I thought about Phoebe. About how our relationship—or whatever the hell it was—really had been the one thing here that had actually made me happy.

"You sure you're all right down there?" Abbey murmured in the darkness.

"Yeah, I'm all right. 'Night, Abbs."

"'Night, Luke."

And I really *was* all right.

At least, I was all right until about four-thirty a.m., when a piercing electronic scream burst down the hall and zapped me awake.

"Mmmph . . ." Abbey sat up suddenly, her hair over her eyes. "Whassat?"

"It's the fire alarm," I groaned over the noise. "Come on, we'd better go down. It won't be a drill at this time of night."

I shrugged on my jacket and handed Abbey my old parka, and we wandered downstairs, where half of Jutland was already shivering outside in their coats and pajama bottoms.

Arthur bumbled over, barefoot and wrapped in two zip-up hoodies, looking extremely worried. "Fuck, man, I think this was me, you know," he whispered. "I had a dream that I was making cheese on toast. Maybe I actually *did* make cheese on toast. Maybe I was sleep-toasting."

"You can't sleep-toast, Arthur. It's impossible. Also, for someone who smokes as much weed as you do, your dreams are surprisingly boring."

He wasn't listening. "If this turns out to be my fault, I'll be out on my ear, man. I set the alarm off last year, too. Trying to light a spliff off Rita's hair straighteners."

I nodded across to D Dorm, which was also leaking pissed-off, half-asleep people. "I wouldn't worry about it. They're evacuating the other dorms, too. It was probably someone in there."

Negin, Frankie and Flora were already outside the entrance, shivering together, wrapped in a comforter. They all turned at the same time to look at the main staircase, where Phoebe was shuffling down the steps, sheepishly.

With Will right behind her.

26

I didn't look up, but I knew everyone was staring at us.

Will had already started to walk away, but as he did he shook his head and almost laughed to himself. "Whatever," he muttered, pushing past me. "You're a fucking bitch."

Before I was even sure I'd heard him right, he disappeared down the walkway, back toward the bar. I looked around for someone to acknowledge what had happened but there was no one. I scanned the crowd but the only person who met my gaze was Abbey. Luke was next to her, his eyes on his feet. I smiled at her, and she smiled back. A watery acknowledgment of something that I couldn't decipher.

Negin, Frankie and Flora were outside the other entrance. The staff was counting us and holding clipboards and yelling for people to keep still and be quiet. I tried to walk over but one of them told me in no uncertain terms that was not allowed. The girls just stood, huddled together, not speaking. It was like they genuinely had no idea I was there, but I knew that couldn't be true.

People had comforters and blankets wrapped round them. Some were starting to make loud jokes and a few were even singing. But this vacuum surrounded random little circles of people scattered across the grass. One where Luke and Abbey stood completely still, not looking at each other; one where Frankie, Negin and Flora were avoiding even glancing in my direction.

Finally, we were allowed back in. I trudged slowly back up the stairs. Not even Connor really acknowledged me as he shuffled to his room.

Negin's door was already shut. I knew I should be brave: knock and explain everything to them, so that bit of my life, at least, was OK again. But I was too scared I would mess that up, too, and end the night with less than nothing. So I didn't.

I pushed my door open and looked at my phone. I stared at the picture of a cake Mum had sent earlier. It had my name on it. In the message she'd written *Celebrating in your honor xx*.

As I climbed into bed, my whole body felt heavy, but my brain was whirring like mad. I curled myself up into a ball under the comforter and stared out through the window at the silent little church outside. I closed my eyes and tried to rock myself shut like a seashell, to block out every single thought. How could every part of my life have unraveled within three hours? I thought I would never sleep, but I went from being awake to completely unconscious in one single beat. I didn't wake up to do that weird alcohol pee you do in the night when you've been drinking. I didn't dream. I didn't even move.

I woke up to Flora picking her stuff up around me.

"My train is in an hour." She didn't look at me as she said it, just kept gathering her makeup off the floor and chucking it randomly into her array of canvas bags. She seemed calm, but underneath I knew her heart was beating really fast. The classic girl freeze-out. I'm angry at you, but there is no way I'm going to come right out and say it.

She sighed as she scrunched up her pajamas and shoved them in.

"I slept in Negin's room." She said it like I had asked the question first.

"Sorry . . . You could have—"

She rolled her eyes. "Yup."

"I'm sorry I left you at the party."

She didn't look at me. "It's totally fine. Honestly, I actually had a really good night after you left." I couldn't tell if she was mocking me or not. Her voice was so even.

"I was just really upset and I wanted to get out of there."

She nodded but still didn't look up. "Yup . . . last night was certainly full of drama." It was belittling, like she was making out I had loved every minute. Like I was some attention-seeking drain.

I laughed to try to defuse it. "Just so you know, nothing happened with me and Will. It was actually really weird. As he left, he called me a bitch."

She picked up her little pot with the confetti stars that she sometimes stuck underneath her eyes, but she did it so forcefully they all scattered across the room. Tiny gold and silver stars wafted to the floor.

"He called you a bitch, did he?" she snapped as she started

trying to pick up the stars. "*Poor you*, Phoebs. Do you want a cuddle? Do you want everyone to stick up for you? Do you want a special party just for you? Like, what is it you want?"

"I'm sorry. I really . . . I know it looks weird he was in my room. He's the boy who—"

"I know who he is." It was almost scornful. "I just don't know who *you* are." She turned and actually, properly looked at me for the first time. "Like, Phoebe, I came to see you. I paid money and spent a week making you a photo scrapbook. I was excited yesterday. I have *missed* you. And you just spend the whole time talking about, or being treated like shit by, Luke fucking Taylor. I mean, I don't give a shit what happened with Luke, or this Will person. I care about the fact you are my friend. You are my *best* friend, Phoebe. But who are you? I was worried about you. Really, *really* worried. I called you a million times, but you just ignored me. You just left that party, left me on my own."

She gave up on the stars and carried on packing her bags. "I don't know. D'you remember in summer how we talked and talked about going to college? Like, how we couldn't wait for our lives to actually start? *You* were the one who saw school as this whole new beginning, but all you've done is come here and act like it's still eighth grade, and the only thing in your life is fantasizing about Luke Taylor. Who, by the way, in real life, is a dick. You're confusing *our* Luke Taylor with the real one."

She picked up her phone and looked at it. "My taxi's here."

And she walked out. Just like that. I hadn't even gotten out of bed.

I could hear Frankie and Negin in the kitchen with the others. Drinking tea and laughing as if life was normal. I went to my door three times and couldn't get up the courage to open it. I got dressed really slowly and meticulously and brushed my hair section by section.

When I finally managed to walk to the kitchen and push the door open it was almost midday. Frankie, Negin and Liberty were all sitting at the kitchen table. "Morning, Phoebs." Liberty smiled and then walked out, clearly feeling the tension.

Neither of them spoke.

"Hey," I said, and shuffled over. I didn't even feel like I had permission to sit down. Connor appeared at the door and then quickly disappeared again. Frankie took a sip of her tea.

"How are you both feeling?" I tried to keep my voice even.

"I just . . ." Frankie stared at her empty cup. "The thing with Will. I just found that really strange."

"After what happened with Becky . . . ," Negin added. I felt like it was a line she had rehearsed, something she had wanted to get out before I even came in.

It was like this tangled spaghetti mess. Everything in my life was twisted together so tightly that it was impossible to separate. If one bit of it went wrong, everything else did, too. I almost didn't have the energy to try to explain it all. "OK . . . ," I started. "Look. *Nothing* happened with Will. When I got back, he was in the bar."

They both looked down at their cups. What if they didn't believe me?

"He saw me, and he came out and just kept repeating himself again and again and saying he was in so much trouble. That he was already failing his course and now he was gonna get kicked out of York, and that he was a good person and that people had to realize that he was a good person. He told me his dad hates him, which was fucking strange, and I just didn't know what to say. He was just so drunk. So I made him a cup of tea and—"

Negin put a hand up to stop me. "You made *Will* a cup of tea?" She sounded disgusted.

"I know, it sounds weird. It *is* weird. But he seemed so desperate. He was in such a state. And then he told me that he had been called to see the provost and that he needed to sort things out or the soccer team would get disbanded and he would get expelled."

"Good, he should get chucked out." Frankie shrugged. "That was the whole point of the protest."

I nodded. "I know, I know."

"Did you tell him that?"

"I just said that it was a mess. He asked me to come and see the provost with him today. As, like, a character witness. Someone who was in the protest but didn't want him to get chucked out. Who could vouch for him and say he was a decent guy." Frankie laughed sharply at that. "I told him no, obviously," I continued. "But he kept asking and he got more and more upset that I wouldn't do it. Like, he was almost crying. And then the fire alarm went off."

Frankie and Negin looked at each other. "Right."

"Do you want a cup of tea?" Negin said quietly. I nodded.

"Honestly . . . I really, really know that last night was a fucked-up mess and that I acted—"

"Yeah, it was," Frankie said. "But not really because of you." She smiled at me softly. "The Abbey thing was awful, Phoebs."

"Yeah. It feels like this domino effect of fucking awfulness piling up around me. Like I'm drowning in it. The last thing I need is to go to a *ball*. I need to go to a mental institution."

"There's no milk," Negin groaned.

We trudged downstairs to buy some. Frankie hadn't bothered to change out of her pajamas and still had her comforter wrapped around her. We walked into the shop and some people looked at us and exchanged glances. We bought the milk in a slightly tense, exhausted silence. As we walked back we noticed a group of people staring at the notice board outside the bar. We slowed down and it took me a second to compute what I was seeing.

It was right in the middle, pinned on top of loads of other sheets. In grainy but all too clear black-and-white. Asleep, head tilted back on the pillow, hair frizzing in all directions, mouth lolling wide open: a photo of me.

●　●　●　●　●　●　●　　**LUKE**　　●　●　●　●　●　●　●

I watched Abbey's train shrink until it was a tiny speck on the horizon. Then I found a bench and just sat there pointlessly for a bit, looking up at the display board and listening to the announcer's dreary voice echoing around the walls.

It was weird to think that this time tomorrow, I'd be heading home. Seeing mum and dad again. Seeing Reece and everyone. Spending the whole Christmas holiday summing up first semester to various relatives in short, socially acceptable sound bites. "Yeah, it was good. Tiring, but really good." That's probably what I'd go with. I mean, how can you *actually* describe the first semester to anyone? How can you possibly express the confusion and awkwardness and freedom and fun and terror and just general batshit insanity of it all? You can't. You just have to live through it.

I got up and started trudging slowly back down the platform. For some reason, something Arthur had said last week kept circling around and around in my head. It had been about three in the morning, when we were stoned watching Netflix, and he'd started going on about this philosophy book he was reading. He said the person who wrote it, some Russian-sounding guy, had this theory about how human beings aren't just one single, unified "I"—they are actually billions of separate, tiny "I's", all pulling in different directions to try to get what they want.

At the time, I'd just told him to shut up so I could concentrate on *Iron Man 3*. But now, after Abbey and Marcus, and Phoebe and Will, and everything else that had happened this semester, the whole concept suddenly made sense to me. Walking through this freezing station, I didn't feel like a real, unified person; I felt like a swarm of stupid, confused, jealous "I's," all stuffed into the same body.

At least things with Abbey finally felt OK. Or on their way to being OK in the long run. But things with Phoebe . . . Seeing her come down those stairs last night with Will had been grim. *Really* grim. I hated the idea of them together, but did it actually change the way I felt about her? It was weird; the more I thought about it, the only thing that all my "I's" seemed to agree on was Phoebe.

That was when it hit me. Maybe it wasn't too late for the surprise.

A lot had changed in the last twenty-four hours—Abbey

had come to my room, Will had come out of Phoebe's—but it didn't really make any difference. The truth was, I'd been acting all week like this whole thing was just about me and Phoebe, when really that was obviously bullshit. It was way more important than that.

I looked up at the display board again and dithered for a few seconds, wondering whether this actually was or was not a good idea. Standing there, in what was quite literally the cold light of day, it could very easily be considered a *bad* idea.

But no. It had seemed like a good idea last week, when Ed had told me about Jamila. And it had seemed like a good idea every day since, as I sat in the library with Phoebe and thought about what it would mean to her.

So it still felt like a good idea now. Or, at least, I had to *make* it a good idea.

● ● ● ● ● ● **PHOEBE** ● ● ● ● ● ●

The door was bright red with an over-the-top eagle knocker in the center.

It didn't match the front garden, which was full of dead plants and a few black trash bags. There wasn't a doorbell. I lifted the eagle's wings and knocked. The knocks sounded much clearer and more sure of themselves than I did. I could hear footsteps thudding toward the door and felt a shudder of nerves.

"Wait a second, I can't find the keys." It was Will's voice. I looked at the gate. I could still run away.

A key turned in the lock and it opened. Will was wearing brushed cotton pajama bottoms and a T-shirt with Michelangelo eating pizza that had a speech bubble saying I'M A PARTY DUDE. And he was wearing glasses. He just stood there.

"I didn't know you wore glasses." I don't know how I thought I would start it. But not like that. Not in a small talk, I've-just-bumped-into-you-at-the-optician's sort of way.

"Yeah, only for watching TV and . . . stuff."

There was a silence. I looked down at the floor, which was still covered in restaurant leaflets and unopened letters.

"Josh isn't . . ." He ruffled his hair. For a second I thought he was trying to suppress a yawn.

"I wanted to talk to you, actually." My voice didn't shake. I was impressed by how level it sounded.

He looked behind him. Hoping for someone to come and save him, maybe.

"Come in." He extended his arm, welcoming me. "Would you like a cup of tea?"

"Yeah. OK. Thanks." Accepting tea felt like I was coming in peace. I was supposed to be confronting him, and he was ruining it with his boarding school manners.

He shut the front door behind me, and our mutual uneasiness made the seconds slow down.

I cleared a patch on the sofa and thought about the last time I'd sat here. I listened to him put the kettle on. He popped his head around the door. "We haven't got any milk. Or tea bags. Do you want hot Tang? Or Josh has got some Fanta?"

"Fanta would be great, thanks."

I had to say something as soon as he came back in or I would just end up having a polite glass of Fanta and leaving, like a surreal interlude to this whole fucked-up thing.

He handed me a dirty-looking glass and I took a sip. It was

completely flat, like drinking sugared water. I wondered what Will's family home looked like. Some massive country estate with boot scrapers and a chrome convection oven and a dog named after a Greek philosopher. I wondered if his dad really did hate him, and if he even remembered telling me that.

He had left the kitchen door open. I could see right through to his bedroom. To the bed with its burgundy comforter and still-bare mattress. I almost made a joke about him still not having put a sheet on. How sick am I?

If I let any more small talk happen, I wouldn't do it. I stared into the Fanta, took a deep breath and then looked straight at him. "Why did you put that picture up on the notice board?" My voice was louder and angrier than I had expected.

His face tightened for a second, then relaxed. "Phoebe, I didn't," he said slowly. "The boys on the team think it was Taylor. I mean, you did . . ."

He left it there. But I didn't. It was so ridiculous I actually laughed. He was like a little kid.

"Will, I *know* it was you. You were angry when you left. You called me a bitch."

He shook his head. "No, I didn't."

"At least admit it. This is a joke. What's the point when we were both *there*? Luke Taylor might be a complete jerk in many, many respects, but I know for a fact that he wouldn't . . ."

I couldn't think of the words to make him understand. *Were* there even words that could describe all this?

"He wouldn't do something to deliberately make someone . . . to humiliate someone on purpose."

He ruffled his hair again and laughed awkwardly, shifting his weight from leg to leg. "OK, I hold my hands up." And then he actually, literally, held his hands up, like he was saying he'd eaten the last chocolate at Christmas. "I am a *massive* dick. And I was really wrecked. I just thought you could maybe do me that *one* little favor, which would basically mean I wouldn't get kicked out of college. But, obviously, that was too much of a hassle. . . ."

"Are you being serious? Will, the whole thing is completely disgusting. It's sick. Becky *left* school. A girl *left* because she felt so bad about it." I didn't shout. I just let the words fall plainly between us.

He sighed. "Yeah, but come on, Phoebe. Like, she probably had issues anyway. If *that* is gonna make you leave college, then . . . Come on. That is just ridiculous." He snorted slightly. "I mean, the photos thing . . . It was just supposed to be a laugh between the team. And now, honestly, people are acting like it was some gross, creepy, terrible thing."

"Yeah," I said. "Because it is."

He took his glasses off and started cleaning them on his T-shirt. "Just so you know, I didn't start that stuff. Like, god, that was actually nothing to do with me. Just cause I'm the captain, people are making out like I invented the whole thing."

"You still took *my* picture. And then you printed it out and put it on the notice board. . . ." He didn't say anything. He looked out the window. I wondered if he was thinking about that night. The night we *didn't* have sex.

He picked up his phone and looked at it. Like he was bored. "Look, I'm probably gonna get kicked out for it anyway. Like I say, I admit it. I am a bad person."

But I knew from the way he said it that he didn't really believe it. That he thought saying sorry made everything better.

That he actually thought he was a great person underneath it all.

"I don't know why Josh was ever friends with you," I said quietly. "I don't know why anyone is friends with you."

He laughed again, nervously. "Me neither, what a douche. Phoebs, I hope things are OK between us now, anyway, like, thanks for coming to clear the air."

"It's not clear." I thought about telling him about my own appointment with the provost, but I didn't. I got up. "I just wanted to see what you would say."

Neither of us knew how we were supposed to say goodbye. I should have marched out and slammed the door behind me but I just picked up my bag and then fumbled about checking if I had everything. Then I made a kind of awkward face and walked to the door. He politely followed me, his autopilot charm kicking in. The unopened mail scrunched underneath my boots. I put my hand on the lock to open it.

"See you later," he said quite brightly, really.

I half turned back to him. "Honestly, you just don't get it. And even being chucked out of York won't make you get it. I'm going to tell the provost that you actually spent time finding that picture, and printing it out, and taking it to the board, and finding pins so you could put it there so that people would wake up and laugh at me. But nobody did. Everybody just thought you were gross and said, 'I hope he gets chucked out.' Honestly, I really hope you *do*."

I didn't walk out feeling any kind of triumph. I didn't feel any better about any of it. Just a tiny bit better about myself.

Later, as we all wandered over to Central Hall, I sort of wished I hadn't worn Flora's dress. She had lent it to me before

324

everything had happened, when everything we owned was still shared. As we were getting ready, I'd sent her a picture of me wearing it and written that I missed her. She still hadn't texted back.

The dress wasn't even a *dress*, really. It was a nightie from the 1930s. It was ivory silk and had initials embroidered on the front that said *EWR*. We had spent ages wondering what names they stood for.

"I can't even talk to you normally," Frankie said to Negin as we headed up the walkway. "You're *so* different in evening wear."

Negin looked like Audrey Hepburn in *Breakfast at Tiffany's*. She was wearing a plain black dress with a high neckline. With the dress and her bob and her small diamond earrings, she made everyone else look like they had tried too hard.

Frankie was in plain red silk, and Liberty was wearing a white floor-length dress with a slit. She had stepped up her usual glitter game to include a single hand-painted-by-Negin silver glitter snowflake on her shoulder.

The spaceship building looked amazing. Totally different from the safety presentation day. All the chairs had been folded down into the floor to make a giant wooden dance floor, and the walls were covered in tinsel and fairy lights and holly. A massive Christmas tree loomed right at the back of the hall, throwing its shadow over the DJ stage. I tried to pick out Luke among the swarms of tux-wearing boys, but I couldn't see him.

We waited patiently in the line to have our photo taken. An arch of silver and white balloons had been put up specially for the occasion.

"I want to take my shoes off already," Frankie groaned. "And eat. I wish I had brought those Mini Cheddars with me."

"Come on, then," the photographer shouted, and we all crammed in under the arch. I adjusted the fake fur shrug thing Liberty had lent me, and smiled as brightly as I could into the lens.

"Any couples come into the middle," the photographer said.

"No couples here, mate," Connor bellowed. "Single and ready to mingle: D Dorm middle floor."

"Have you seen Ed?" Negin whispered to Frankie.

She shook her head. "Do you think if I had seen him I would have just kept that information to myself?"

The photographer walked along the line manually adjusting our poses before saying: "OK, best Christmas smiles."

"Last day of semes—" Connor's yell was cut short suddenly. He burst out of the formation and sprinted across the hall. Our eyes all followed him and found Becky at the entrance.

She was standing in a long blue dress, smiling. And standing next to her was Luke.

27

Connor was charging madly toward us and my first thought was: He's going to punch me. He is literally going to punch me in the face.

But he didn't. He just picked Becky up and carried her victoriously back to her screaming hall mates, who swallowed her in an onslaught of hugs and kisses and war whoops.

I just stood there, by myself, watching it all happen and feeling simultaneously really pleased and slightly awkward. All week I'd had this picture in my head of me turning up at Phoebe's birthday dinner with Becky in tow, and the two of us being given this hero's welcome. Obviously, that plan had completely gone to shit over the past twenty-four hours, but still . . . at least something good had come out of it.

Phoebe broke away from the Becky huddle and looked over at me. She was wearing this long white dress, and it brushed the

327

hall floor gently as she crossed to me. I couldn't read the look on her face. But then, I never really can.

All she said was: "How did you find her?"

"This girl in Ed's hall, Jamila, used to go to school with her," I said. "She gave me her address."

Her eyes widened a little bit. "What, you actually went and physically *got* her?"

I nodded. "She only lives, like, an hour away."

"That . . ." She fiddled with the weird fur scarf thing she was wearing. It was like she was trying to find the right words hidden somewhere inside it. "That was an amazing thing to do," she said finally. "You have a weird ability, Luke Taylor, to be the hero and the villain at the same time. Like, concurrently."

"Right . . ." I shoved my hands into the pockets of my dad's too-big tuxedo jacket. "Is that a compliment, or . . . ?"

She rolled her eyes, but she was smiling. "No, it's definitely *not* a compliment. But it's still impressive. It's, like, just when we are all going to sentence you to death for doing something terrible and unforgivable, you go and do some miraculous thing that saves you at the eleventh hour. I mean . . . how did you convince her to come back?"

I shrugged. "To be honest, I think she was already convinced. She said she'd told her boyfriend about the photos and everything, but they'd made up and they were back together now. So I think she would've come back next semester anyway. All I did was convince her to come back for *tonight*."

"What did you say?"

"Just that I was so sorry about everything that happened, and that no one, literally *no one*, had fucked up this first semester more than me. But *I* was still coming back. I told her we should both look at it like first semester didn't happen. Like, next semester we were starting again from scratch."

We looked over at Becky, who was still being joyously manhandled by Frankie, Negin and the rest of them. She caught my eye for a second—or maybe it was Phoebe's eye—but whosever it was, she looked happy. Definitely the happiest I had ever seen her.

I turned back to Phoebe. "This is gonna sound weird, but can we go outside for one second? I've got to give you something."

"That sounds ominous. . . ."

"Please, just one sec."

I grabbed my bag and she grabbed her coat and we walked out of the hall and started following the edge of the lake around to Wulfstan.

"So look . . . ," I started. "I know it's awkward to mention your birthday—"

She cut me off with a humorless snort-laugh. "Last night was pretty much a disaster from start to finish."

"Because of me." I nodded.

She didn't look at me. "Well . . . at least eighty percent because of you, yeah."

We got to the First Night Bridge and both automatically sat down on it, with our legs dangling out over the edge. The hum of music and laughter from the hall carried across the lake toward us. Earlier, on the train back with Becky, I'd tried to rehearse this whole big speech in my head, but, like everything else this semester, I ended up just bumbling straight into it without thinking.

"Phoebe, listen," I said. "I know that everything that

happened with Abbey yesterday makes me out to be a complete asshole. And obviously, the reason for that is because I *am* a complete asshole. But you have to know: I barely spoke to her all semester. Yesterday she came up here out of the blue. And I know it was awful, and I'm so sorry, but it was also good because we finally sorted everything out. We just needed to see each other and say the last things we had to say, and say goodbye properly. And we've done that. And the truth is . . . I told her how much I like you. Because I really, *really* like you. And I want us to be a couple. Like, an *actual* couple. You have been the best thing about college. The *only* good thing."

I stopped to catch my breath, but Phoebe didn't say anything. She was just watching the water lapping softly at the bank below her. I reached into my backpack.

"I should have given you this yesterday. And it's not wrapped because I am a jerk. And, y'know, also because I was busy heroically bringing Becky back. . . ."

She gave me a pretty hefty eye roll for that, which, to be fair, I deserved.

"But anyway . . . happy birthday."

I handed her the *Ariel* book, and she just stared down at it blankly, like I'd given her a bus ticket or something. Finally, she said: "It's beautiful."

"Do you really like it?"

She turned to look at me. "Of course. Thank you. It will be on my shelf forever." She touched the yellowy, frayed corner of the cover, gently. "I love things like this. Like, when you look at them it reminds you suddenly of some really specific memory. Something you thought was buried, but then you touch this kind of emotional portkey and it all comes back to you."

"Yeah." I nodded, even though I wasn't entirely sure what she was on about. I was mainly wondering if and when she was going to respond to my declaration of . . . not *love*, exactly, but pretty serious *like*.

Suddenly, she said, "Why were you crying on that first night?" and I must have flinched or something because she added, "I saw you in the computer room."

I exhaled. "Well . . . me and Abbey had had this awful summer and I just couldn't take it anymore. We broke up that night. Or . . . started breaking up. I don't know. It feels so long ago. But I felt like there was all this pressure welling up inside me, and it just got to be too much . . . I can't really describe it." I shook my head. "I can't really describe *anything*. I think about that a lot. I feel like the words that can explain what is actually happening inside me don't exist."

She looked at me and almost laughed. "Listen . . . this is awkward but I really don't care anymore." She took a deep breath. "I had the biggest crush on you at school. I feel like I'm on a TV show doing some big reveal, but whatever, there it is. Secret's out."

I didn't really know how to respond to that. I was more interested in whether she liked me *now*. So I just said: "Well, that's nice . . . thanks," which for some reason made her laugh so hard that her fur thing fell off and nearly dropped in the water.

I grabbed it before it could tumble over the edge. "Hang on, do you mean even in tenth grade when I had that ridiculous, shaved-at-the-sides haircut?"

She laughed again. "Well, it lessened then, obviously. That was when I turned my attention to Max Fulda."

"Thank god. I would have lost all respect for you."

331

She wrapped the fur back around her neck, and I wondered if maybe I should try to kiss her.

She stretched her legs out over the water and sighed, and then looked me dead in the eye. "To be honest, Luke, and obviously I may live to regret this, but . . . I just don't think I want to be with you."

● ● ● ● ● ● **PHOEBE** ● ● ● ● ● ●

He opened his mouth to respond, but I kept talking.

"I want us to be friends," I said. "Proper, *real* friends who would be there for each other whether we were getting with each other or not."

He closed his mouth and then nodded. He looked out across the lake.

"And right now," I said, "don't you need a *proper* friend more than you need a girlfriend?"

He smiled sadly. "Well, yeah. I haven't got too many real friends at the moment."

"That's not true."

He straightened his back and reached over to hold my hand. "Phoebe, seriously, I know things have been really messy, honestly, I know that, but—"

I shook my head to cut him off. "*Things* haven't been really messy, Luke. *You've* been really messy. And your mess has started to mess me up, too. So if you really do like me, then be a good friend and don't let that happen."

He breathed out slowly, like he'd just been deflated. But he kept holding my hand. Finally, he said, "If friends is your final offer, Phoebe, I guess I'll have to take it."

I wriggled my fingers around his, into a handshake position: "To friendship." He laughed and we shook on it. He was really handsome in a tux. Clean-cut and broad and grown-up. He looked like he was born to wear it, and walk down a red carpet having his picture taken.

We clambered to our feet and started to walk back around the lake. When we got to the hall I said, "I'm just going to put the book back in my room. Don't think Sylvia would forgive me if I got Jägerbomb all over it."

He nodded. "See you in there."

I watched him walk off into the madness of the ball, where Ed and Arthur and a few others were cheering and waving him over. And that was it. I had rejected Luke Taylor. Eighth-grade me would have died from shock at that sentence. It actually made me laugh out loud, to myself, like a lunatic. And then I wanted to tell Flora. I got out my phone and saw she had texted back:

You look awesome, best one. If you ruin that dress I will kill you xxx

I went back to my room and squeezed the *Ariel* book on the little bookshelf. Who knows, maybe Luke Taylor *would* turn out to be the love of my life, but in order to ascertain that, I would have to actually get to know him first, and pay real attention this time.

I wandered back down the deserted Jutland walkway, and as

I crossed the parking lot I could see Josh was near the entrance to the hall. As I came in, he turned and smiled and I felt a bit nervous. He started walking toward me, and I wondered what we would say.

"What time you heading home tomorrow?" he asked. There was a tension in his voice I had never heard before.

"Think my mum's coming at midday."

Neither of us knew what to say next. In my head, I replayed the moment I had tried to kiss him. It was almost unbearable.

Just as I was about to make an excuse and walk off, he threw his arms around me. And I hugged him back. And we both just stayed there in the hug. The words we'd said had felt all strange and wrong and not what we meant, but the hug felt right and not weird and how things really were.

We broke away and looked at each other and I didn't understand what was happening between us. What he felt and what I felt and what everything meant. But there was loads of time to figure that out.

"I'll see you later, Bennet." He smiled.

I found Frankie and Negin at the edge of the dance floor, watching Becky get frantically waltzed about by Connor. Luke was on the other side of the hall, dancing with Arthur and Rita and everyone. There was still no sign of Will, or any of the other soccer boys.

"So . . ." Frankie took a sip of her drink. "Glad you and Luke Taylor are love's young dream, because my life as the nun of York Met is continuing without my consent."

Negin gave me a look that said: *Things are not good.*

"Shape-Face Girl and Ed are over there," she whispered. I

followed her glance to where Ed and Sophie-or-Sarah were kissing, right in the middle of the dance floor.

"Oh shit," I groaned.

Frankie huffed. "Maybe if *I* had a banana mouth and perfectly circular eyes *I* could bag an attractive tall man, too."

"Well, I'm not with Luke Taylor, either," I said. "So you can also sign me up to the York Met nunnery."

"Me too," Negin sighed. "Interesting Thought Boy is getting with some random girl."

"What?" We followed her gaze. I didn't recognize ITB at first without his holey sweater. He looked less philosophical in a tux. But there he was, his tongue down the throat of some rand—

"That's not a random!" I yelled. "That's *Stephanie Stevens.*"

"Who?" Negin and Frankie said in unison.

I shook my head. "I should never have saved her life. I should have let her choke on her own vomit."

We stood in a row, my head leaning on Frankie, and Negin's head leaning on me. We just watched Stephanie Stevens and ITB, and Ed and Sophie-or-Sarah like we were watching late-night QVC.

"Oh well . . ." Frankie sighed. "I think we should just get Becky, dance our asses off, then go back and decoupage our letters and competitively eat cheese toasties until one of us dies from a cheddar overdose."

"Sounds good." I looped an arm around each of them. "I mean, you know loads of people die in freshman year right? Like, *millions.*"

ACKNOWLEDGMENTS

We owe *at least* one round of Jägerbombs to all the following people:

Everyone at Chicken House for being amazing as always. Our fantastic editor Rachel Leyshon, who suggested so many of the best twists and turns and various other things in this novel: we bloody love you, Rachel. Huge, huge thank-yous also to Barry, Rachel H, Elinor, Jazz, Esther, Kesia and Laura for being brilliant and for doing so much for us. We really appreciate it.

Our incredible agent, Kirsty McLachlan, for being a constant source of advice, support and highly reassuring phone chats throughout the entire writing process.

All our mates who either experienced the stuff in this book alongside us, or generously donated their stories, or just sat in various pubs with us over the past two years, reminiscing about all aspects of uni life. Most notably: Laura Allsop, James Amos, Kate Baker, Max Baldwin, Jonathan Bray, Chris Carroll, Alexie Cottam, Jonathan Driscoll, Louise Gaskell, Yasmina Green, Christina Heaps, Harvey Horner, Ryan Kohn, Tim Lee, Michael Lindall, Robin Pasricha, Jodie Peake, Neil Redford, Matthew

Sharkey, Ed Shirley, Jeremy Stubbings, Ella Sunyer, Peter Todd and Alex Trotter.

Shauna Kavanagh for WAY too much to mention, really, but here goes: reading countless drafts, offering phenomenal (and vitally useful) feedback, explaining to us what the hell Snapchat is (even though we still don't really get it) and providing us with high-quality tea and biscuits on our recce in York. You were a massive part of this book, Shauna, and we owe you big-time. You are a truly amazing and inspirational person. THANK YOU.

Vanessa Long for very kindly having us to stay and buying us Bettys treats when we went back to York to illegally break into Derwent halls and relive our youth.

Holly Bourne and Anna McCleery for reading early drafts and giving us invaluable feedback. You are both proper legends.

Families Ellen and Ivison for being a great bunch of lads and giving us so much love and support.

Diana, Rosey and Jessyka Battle for cups of tea and teen angst.

Everybody in the ridiculously supportive and amazing UKYA and UKMG communities, most notably: Emma Shevah, Non Pratt, Lisa Williamson, Juno Dawson, Liz Hyder, Maura Brickell, Nina Douglas, bloggers extraordinaire Jim & Debbie, Peter Bunzl, Honor & Perdita Cargill and Abi Elphinstone.

Kate Sullivan, Allison Hellegers and Myrthe Spiteri for their fantastic support from the US and the Netherlands, and generally just for being awesome.

Tom would also like to thank Anna Hards and Laura Yogasundram for their friendship and general greatness over the past fifteen years, and also for kindly donating Interesting Thought Boy (and so, so much more . . .).

And Lucy would like to thank Richard for sacking off

Cambridge to come to York and sit on bridges with me. As well as reminding me of a million ways we were in the Autumn of 2001.

Plus, Frankie Colborne-Malpas for being Frankie. I am writing this just as you are (supposed to be) revising for your A-levels and have all of the freshers' experience to come. I can't wait to hear about how the real Frankie lollops through it all. You are an extremely special, talented and hilarious person and I will always, always want to know what you are up to, so don't forget who your librarian is when you make it to the big time. . . .

And to Negin Tellaie for being inspirationally brave and brilliantly witty. Thank you for letting me borrow you as my inspiration for Negin. I hope you like her.

The Francis Holland class of 2017 for telling me their university hopes and dreams. Most notably: Lily Carr-Gomm for being a first-draft reader, Bella, Alice, Issy, Renata, Marina, Lydia, Phoebe, Andrea and, of course, the best library prefects a gal could wish for, Alix Sharp and Lily Sayre.

The staff at Francis Holland who are the most supportive and lovely people anyone could wish to work with. I am so lucky to be a person who never wakes up and doesn't want to go to work, even when I've been writing all weekend. Your constant support and cake provision keeps me going. Tally, Cat, Pip, Jo, Dorian, Tash and my 11+ sisters Raff and Caroline all made writing this book a little bit more fun. I would also like to formally acknowledge my head teacher, Lucy Elphinstone, who has always supported me as a writer as well as a librarian. I wouldn't be able to pursue both of my passions without her help and understanding.

And, lastly, from both of us, to all our Derwent College friends from 2001 to 2005. This one is for you. . . .

**Continue reading for a preview
of Tom and Lucy's riotously funny first novel!**

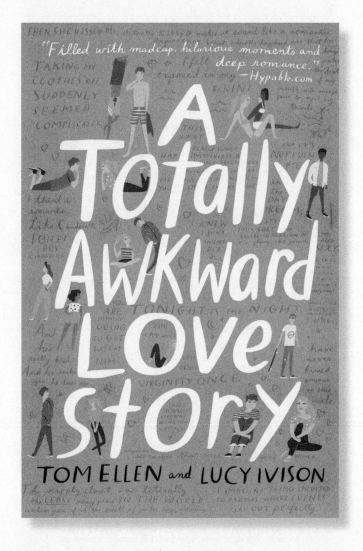

HANNAH

Grace burst into my bedroom with such force that she nearly fell over.

"Freddie isn't in France!" she announced triumphantly as Tilly came crashing in behind her.

I sat up in bed, where all morning I had been watching videos of baby sloths and tutorials on how to do cat-eye eyeliner flicks.

"Are you *sure*?" I asked.

"Yes!" Tilly yelled, and started doing a little victory dance on the spot.

"But I stalked him this morning," I said, "and there's a picture of him actually standing in front of the Eiffel Tower, holding up a baguette and pretending it's a mustache. He literally couldn't be more in France if he tried."

"Yeah, he *was* there," Tilly squealed, "but then the most amazing thing happened: his house got robbed and they had to come home early!"

"Obviously, it's really bad about his house and everything," Grace cut in dutifully.

"Yeah, yeah." Tilly nodded. "Obviously . . . but the point is . . . he's coming to Stella's tonight. Fact."

"Fact," Grace repeated. "And you are totally going to get with him. Tonight is the night. . . ." She crinkled her nose and smiled.

I kicked off the comforter and swung my legs out of bed. "What? No . . . I'm not ready."

"You *are* ready," Grace soothed. "You are totally in the right place. He's so the right person."

"No, I don't mean *emotionally* ready. Obviously, I'm *emotionally* ready. I mean I'm *literally* not ready. I haven't gotten out of bed for three days. I look like an absolute mess."

"You look like you always do," Tilly said.

"Thanks, Tills."

"Seriously, Hannah," said Grace. "You've always said Freddie was the one you'd lose it to. The only reason it hasn't happened yet is because you've been on exams lockdown for, like, the last four months."

"Fate was keeping you apart," said Tilly grandly.

"And now fate's brought you back together," said Grace. "Have you got any food?"

"Excuse me, I thought we were talking about the role of fate in my life?"

"Yeah, but I'm hungry—I can't contemplate fate on an empty stomach."

I slumped back into bed. "Go downstairs and have a look, then. My mum hides the snacks above the microwave."

They clomped down to the kitchen. Grace was right.

I'd put losing my virginity on the back burner until after my College Board exams. Although "losing" is such a random word for it. It's not like you're gonna find it under your study guide, is it?

I used to dream about losing it to someone fragile and kind. Someone who understood me and was really cool but didn't care what other people thought of him. Someone with dark, curly hair who tanned really well and spoke Italian. Or maybe *was* Italian.

Freddie Clemence is not fragile, kind *or* Italian. He's not the love of my life. At least, I *hope* he's not, or I won't have much of a life to look forward to. But surely, if everybody held on to their virginity until they found the love of their life, there'd be a lot more virgins roaming around.

Half the problem is that I do the same thing with boys that I do with clothes: I imagine an outfit before I go shopping rather than just waiting to see what's in the stores when I get there. I daydream scenarios that will never happen. I think about boys falling in love with me who in real life wouldn't look at me. And it's not even me in the daydream; it's this sort of celebrity version of me, all glossy and poised and sexy. I imagine being invited to parties where events play out perfectly. How I'll meet the love of my life and he'll be inexplicably drawn to me and say things like, "I would die for you, Hannah." And then we'll have sex in a car like in *Titanic*.

In reality I'm either making out with Freddie in a corner or cleaning up someone else's puke because I feel bad for the person whose party it is.

But maybe Stella's party will be different. Everyone's

finished their exams now, so it's going to be massive. Ninety people have accepted the invite on Facebook. And now that Freddie is back early from France, maybe it *is* a sign. Maybe now *is* the right time. It's not love, but I just need to get sex over with so I can get on with living my life.

Tilly and Grace stomped back up the stairs and flopped onto my bed, clutching two packets of Ritz crackers and a jar of peanut butter.

"I hope you never take Zac down," Tilly said, staring up at my ceiling. "He's been there as long as I've known you."

She was looking at the sticker of Zac Efron I'd put there when I was twelve so he would be the first thing I saw every morning.

"It's *never* coming down," I said. "Zac is my first love. I may have moved on—"

"To Freddie," Grace interrupted.

"—but he will always have a place in my heart."

"And your wardrobe," Tilly said. "Do you still have that T-shirt with his face on? That was crazy."

"Says you in the Aztec-print harem pants."

Tilly swung her legs in the air to show them off. "I have nothing else to wear. My mum isn't doing any laundry because she's on strike. She wants me to learn how to do stuff before college."

"Well, you'd better learn quickly," I said. "You're never going to meet a boy and get out of no-man's-land dressed like Aladdin."

Tilly is in hymen limbo. She's the walking undead. A sex zombie. Max Lawrence *did* go inside her, but not all the way and only for a few seconds. She said it hurt too much, so he stopped. And then he got off with Amber Mason at a party, so Tilly dumped him. She couldn't have known at the time that it was her last-chance saloon. She might have given it a better go if she had known. But Tilly's a wimp when it comes to that kind of thing—she almost fainted when she got her HPV shot.

How can we live in a world where they can identify serial killers from their DNA but we can't figure out if Tilly's a virgin or not? We've Googled it a hundred times, but the more you try to research it, the more philosophical the whole thing gets.

Like, what *is* losing your virginity, anyway? When your hymen breaks? But that can happen horseback riding or doing gymnastics, or even *swimming*, apparently. I could have lost my virginity to Acton Municipal Pool, for all I know. If it's just the hymen thing, then what about gay people? It must be the act of someone else being inside you; after all, boys lose their virginity even though nothing breaks. So maybe it's a mystical, intangible thing? Like the Holy Spirit.

Out of all of us, Grace is the only one who has lost her virginity. She fell in love with Ollie last year and they've been inseparable ever since. I don't know how they're going to cope when they go to college. Grace hasn't told us what having sex actually feels like, though. It's like once you've done it you become unable to speak about it. Can anything be *that* amazing? Maybe nothing feels epic when you're actually living it.

We sprawled out across the bed and started rambling on about other things: what we'd wear to the party and what color we would dye our hair if we had to pick one color for the rest of our lives (me: chestnut; Tilly: platinum; Grace: stay the same). And then conversation inevitably turned to the missing member of the group.

"Do you *really* think she's at his house?"

Tilly was sitting on my bed with her legs crossed, eating the peanut butter straight out of the jar with a spoon. She had added my Duke of Edinburgh hoodie to her Aztec look, and her long red hair was wound into a topknot.

"Well, she's not here, so . . ." Grace shrugged, as if Stella could only be with us or with Charlie. Maybe that was actually true. It did feel weird that Tilly and Grace were here and she wasn't.

"Of course she's with him," I said. "He got back from college last night. I've been with her every day since exams, but I haven't heard from her today."

"Well, I think it's a toxic relationship," Grace said.

I laughed. "A 'toxic relationship'? What do you think this is, *Dr. Phil?*"

"You know what I mean," Grace tsked. "He's really bad for her. Stella, of all people, could do way better."

"Yeah, I know," I said. "Shit, I'd better tell her about Freddie." I wrote Stella a text:

Where are you? Freddie is back from France and I think tonight is the night!

SAM
It all felt wrong. Totally, utterly, terribly wrong. What the hell were we doing? I decided to ask Robin.

"This feels wrong, man," I said. "What are we doing?"

He was kneeling on the wet grass beside the big steel bucket, pressing one final textbook into the mangled mass of textbooks already squashed inside.

"What are you on about?" he muttered, holding the books in place with one hand while he used the other to retrieve a cigarette lighter from his pocket. "I think it's pretty obvious what we're doing."

He sparked the lighter twice to check if it was working. It was.

"Yeah, what I mean is, it feels wrong to be doing this after what happened this morning," I said.

"We're celebrating, you idiot."

"That's my point!" I yelled as Robin stood up, swatting bits of damp soil off the front of his trousers. "There's nothing *to* celebrate. I already told you how badly I fucked up French. So if we're celebrating, then we're celebrating defeat. Who celebrates defeat? It's illogical."

Robin snorted. "We're not celebrating defeat *or* victory. We're celebrating *the fact that it's all over.* It doesn't matter how we did—it's the fact that we never have to think about those exams ever again."

He was way off, there. I'd thought more about that French exam since finishing it that morning than I had in the last six months. Which, to be fair, was probably why I screwed it up so badly. Fucking pluperfect tense. Who needs to go that far back into the past anyway?

Robin clicked the lighter again. "Right. Let's do this then, shall we?"

This had always been the plan. We'd agreed that the

day we finished our College Board exams we'd celebrate by incinerating all our textbooks. It was supposed to be a cleansing thing; a glorious cathartic bonfire that marked the end of childhood and the start of . . . well, not adulthood, exactly, but definitely a step in its general direction.

But, in reality, it was just the two of us standing over a mop bucket in Robin's backyard. If this was the road to adulthood, I was considering turning back.

Robin knelt back down and plunged his hand deep into the bucket to pull out my French textbook. He placed it carefully on top of the pile and held the lighter up to me.

"Here, come on, man. Show those French pricks what you're really made of."

I shook my head. "No. I don't feel like it."

He shrugged. "Suit yourself."

He sparked the lighter and held the flame against the corner of the book's cover.

"Why isn't it burning?" he demanded. "Nothing's happening."

"It's laminated, you dick."

The flame was just about managing to turn the plastic-coated corner a faint browny-black color. If we were going to use this method on every book, we'd be here all day.

"Why the fuck do they laminate them?" snapped Robin, letting go of the lighter.

"Probably to stop people like us burning them in buckets."

"Those bastards," he murmured. "They're always one step ahead. Maybe we could just burn the inside pages. They're not laminated."

"Then we'll be left with a bucket full of empty book covers. What are we going to do with all those?"

Robin chewed his bottom lip as he considered this. "We could cut them up into little pieces and bury them? Or put them in a box and throw them in the sea?"

"The sea? We live in London. The sea is at least an hour away."

"So? I could get my mum to drive us to Brighton when she gets back from work."

"This is beginning to sound like more hassle than it's worth, to be honest."

Robin groaned and stood up. "You need to perk the fuck up, Sam. If you're still like this tonight, then I'm ditching you as soon as we get through the door. End-of-exams parties are the best parties ever; that's common knowledge. I'm not having you ruining this one for me by whining all night. This might come as a surprise to you, given your lack of experience in the area, but girls don't exactly get turned on by constantly complaining about French exams, you know."

Maybe he was right. Maybe I could look at the French Fuck-up as a positive thing. The beginning of an entirely new and unplanned chapter in my life. No university, no job, no real conventional future: I could totally reinvent myself, starting this evening.

Robin only heard about the party tonight through his friend Ben, who knew about it via a friend of a friend. So there was a good chance we wouldn't know *anyone* there. I could become someone else. I could start introducing myself as "Samuel." That might make me sound deeper and more intelligent. I could be Samuel the mysterious drifter;

Samuel, who wears long coats and hand-rolls his own cigarettes and gazes off into the middle distance enigmatically during conversations. Rather than plain old Sam, who fails French exams and tries to burn plastic books.

The problem is, you have to have done something with your life before you can start going around calling yourself Samuel. You have to have *achieved* something. Samuel Beckett; Samuel L. Jackson; Dad's friend Samuel, who drives a Porsche and used to go out with Nigella Lawson: they've all earned the right to those extra letters. What have I ever done? Won an essay contest when I was fourteen and fingered Gemma Bailey in a gazebo. I'm hardly in line for a knighthood.

I'd always thought that getting into Cambridge would be my big achievement. But now that I'd screwed up French—and I definitely *had*—I was going to have to find something else instead. I just had no idea what.

You won't find many virgins called Samuel, that's for sure. You remain a Sam until you get past fingering, I reckon. Or at least past gazebos.

Robin picked up the bucket and stomped off toward the house.

"Right, let's just give the fuckers to Goodwill and be done with it," he muttered.

HANNAH

Stella and I were sitting at the bus stop where we had sat hundreds of times before. Except this time I was in extreme pain.

"I've been mutilated. I think I'm in medical shock," I said. "Have you got any sugar?"

Stella handed me a bag of mixed gummies. "It's just hair," she said. "You don't say you've been mutilated when you go to the hairdresser, do you?"

"Yeah, but what happened to me *in there* was not like what happens at the hairdresser."

Stella had booked me in to have my bikini line waxed as soon as she had found out Freddie was not only back but coming to her party.

"Hannah, honestly, it's just because it's your first time. Shit, all your first times are happening at once," she announced slightly too loudly.

The lady next to us shot a disapproving glance in our direction, and I winced.

Across from the bus stop is a gigantic H&M poster of a model in a neon-pink-and-white string bikini. She looks amazing, all impossibly long and brown and perfect. The poster has been there forever. Looking at it used to make me feel quietly excited. Because that was going to be me. I was going to go running and do my mum's Davina DVD and wake up having morphed into an H&M campaign version of myself. But obviously, none of that had happened, and I looked just the same as always.

"I'm going to buy that bikini for Kavos," Stella said.

We were going away to Greece together in a week, and I wasn't prepared at all.

"She's definitely had her bikini line waxed," I said, nodding at the poster, "and it *definitely* wasn't her first time."

Stella shrugged and got out her phone, probably to text Charlie. She wasn't intimidated by the model in the bikini because she is effortlessly cool. She's petite, olive-skinned, naturally sexy and mysterious, and boys always love her. She loves video games and movies like *Pulp Fiction* and *Scarface*. Her dark brown hair is dyed with random bits of lilac, and last summer she got a snowflake tattooed on her wrist. You can't see it in winter, but it appears when she tans. Out of all of us, she is the closest to the H&M girl.

Me, Tilly and Grace don't even come anywhere near. Tilly is tall and willowy with freckles. Her hair is her best feature. It's straight out of a Pre-Raphaelite painting, auburn and flowing with curls at the end. Grace used to be plain until her sixteenth birthday, but like my mum says, she has "really blossomed," especially since she stopped wearing huge shapeless sweaters as her everyday look.

I think it's really hard to see yourself how other people do. I have naturally blond hair, pale blue eyes to match my pale skin and a totally average body. On a good day people might call me pretty. On a really good day.

The bus came and Stella strode to the back while I waddled slowly behind her, trying to keep the burning pain around my lady parts to a minimum.

"You're walking like an old person," Stella said as we sat down.

"Well, it hurts."

She rolled her eyes.

I wanted to ask her about Charlie Allen, about *her* virginity and what was going on between them. She is a virgin *by choice*, which is a distinct category from just being a virgin. She has done everything *but* with Charlie. He is her fuck buddy without the actual fucking part. Or the blow job part because that totally grosses Stella out. He's hot, but behind her back we all say he's a prick who's using her. We know he deals drugs but we don't talk about it. She says she's happy with the way things are between them, but I don't think that's really true.

I can't ask her, though, because the whole her-and-Charlie thing is a no-go area. She'll never admit there's a problem, so we all have to pretend there isn't one. She can ask any of us anything, but we are not allowed to do the same back. Stella is just different like that; she's a closed book.

She is also the kind of person who just has house parties and is relaxed about it. Her parents have gone to France for the whole summer. You would think she would want to go with them, but she never does. This is the second summer they have let her stay home alone. They get her Marks & Spencer food delivered every week and send her allowance by Venmo.

"Are you still getting a bob?" Stella asked.

"I don't know. I don't know if I'm brave enough."

"You are way too uptight about hair."

"Yeah, well, I need to do a lot of things before college."

Stella got out her phone again. "Shall we consult the list?"

Last month, deep in study hell, we had made an action plan of all the things we had to do before college.

"'Hannah,'" Stella read out. "'Fall in love and lose virginity.' Well . . . one of those is getting ticked off pretty soon. . . . OK, next we've got, 'Get an amazing body. Get good at fake tanning. Get a new look. Get a bob. Practice having slow mannerisms to appear more enigmatic. Be less giggly and more intellectual.'"

I groaned. "Oh god, there's so much to do. Can you add 'Cope with failing history' to the list?"

"OK, you might need to prioritize. What about just getting a bob and sleeping with Freddie?"

I sighed and fished a gummy fried egg out of the bag. I don't know when everything got so complicated. Eighteen is supposed to be the age when you become an adult. When you are complete. How can anyone feel finished by now? I don't even feel started. I haven't done anything, I haven't been anywhere. Everyone around me seems to have figured it all out. It feels like suddenly it's the norm to be in a long-term relationship. To be having sex like it's no big deal, and have had your bikini line waxed to do it. It's like so much has changed since I was fourteen, but then at the same time nothing has. Sometimes I wish I could be that age again and just not worry about all this stuff. About what people think of me, and how I come across in social situations. When every weekend we used to sleep over at Stella's house and eat ice cream and drink cups of tea. I hate it that now people are constantly expecting me to have become something. And like I'm a failure because I just haven't. Everything seems like it was easier in *Pride and Prejudice*. My nan was married at eighteen. Married. I can't even operate an iron.

When we finally got to Stella's house, I went straight up to the bathroom to fully assess the horror beneath my underwear. As if it wasn't enough having pale red legs with veins showing through and weird albino blond hair and generally looking like a hobbit wife, I was now also deformed.

I didn't tell Mum where I was going because that would have been weird. I know for a fact there are some things she would never do. Like blow jobs and polyester clothing and KFC. I would bet a lot of money she has never had her bikini line waxed.

I can see why people become feminists now. All those years in health class learning about crabs and condoms and consent. Why didn't Miss Smart just get up and say, "As well as voting and learning to drive and being a good citizen and not getting pregnant out of wedlock, one day you will have to go into a room and put on a pair of underwear made of tissue paper and let a woman you have never met before pour hot wax on your cha-cha."

It looked like a raw, bloodied chicken with a Mohawk. And I was supposed to be losing my virginity *tonight*.

Underlined

We underline everything
you need to know about
the best YA books, the coolest
authors, and the latest trends.

WHEN YOU VISIT
Underlined
YOU GET:

- Personalized book recommendations, quizzes, lists, and videos
- Updates on trends, celebs, music, fashion, and more
- The chance to receive FIRST IN LINE perks such as early access to books, sweepstakes, events, and author content

---

Visit us at **GetUnderlined.com** and
follow **@GetUnderlined** on

Did you love this book? Use **#UnderlinedReviews** to tell us what you thought!